50: A CELEBRATION OF SUN & MOON CLASSICS

50: A CELEBRATION

of

SUN & MOON CLASSICS

*

Edited by Douglas Messerli

LOS ANGELES

SUN & MOON PRESS

1995

Sun & Moon Press
A Program of The Contemporary Arts Educational Project, Inc.
a nonprofit corporation
6026 Wilshire Boulevard, Los Angeles, Califorriia 90036

This edition first published in 1995 by Sun & Moon Press
10 9 8 7 6 5 4 3 2 1
FIRST EDITION
©1995 by Douglas Messerli
For author copyrights and permissions
see "Credits and Copyrights" (pages 571–574)
Biographical material ©1995 by Sun & Moon Press
All rights reserved

This book was made possible, in part, through an operational grant from
the Andrew W. Mellon Foundation, through a production grant from
the National Endowment for the Arts, and through contributions to
The Contemporary Arts Educational Project, Inc.,
a nonprofit corporation

Cover: Katie Messborn, *I Saw the Number Fifty*
Typography and book design: Guy Bennett

LIBRARY OF CONGRESS CATALOGING IN PUBLICATION DATA
Messerli, Douglas, ed, [1947]
50: A Celebration of Sun & Moon Classics
p. cm—(Sun & Moon Classics: 50)
ISBN: 1-55713-152-x [cloth edition]
ISBN: 1-55713-132-5 [paperback edition]
I. Title. II. Series.
81'.54—dc20

Printed in the United States of America on acid-frec paper.

CONTENTS

Preface

INSTEAD OF the usual champagne toast, tinkle of glasses, and giggle of delight, Sun & Moon Press decided to celebrate the publication of the fiftieth book in its renowned Sun & Moon Classics Series in a very public way.

Beginning early in 1994 the Press invited international authors and translators of all literary genres to contribute work, previously unpublished in the United States, to a large anthology—although we did not imagine an anthology quite so massive as the one in your hands—in celebration of an ongoing project to bring together some of the most outstanding innovative works of the twentieth century. Several contributions represented work by authors published in the Classics series or by authors whose work was forthcoming in the Classics. Other contributions were by authors and translators whose work has never appeared, and may never appear, under our imprint. Through this eclectic combination we hope to reiterate our commitment to a whole context of publishing—publishing that exists over the spectrum of several literary presses.

The goal of the Classics Series has been and continues to be the promotion of serious literary writing in the twentieth century, and, through this promotion, continually to redefine current literary canons. Indeed, it was this idea of *literature in process* that led us to launch this Series back in 1987. Having already established our commitment to innovative American poetry, fiction, and drama, the Press recognized a need for a similar publishing focus in terms of the international scene. As both a reader and a teacher, I had been forced to recognize again and again just how many major literary works of the century had been allowed to go out of print. Numerous others had never been translated into English. And younger writers from Europe, South America, Asia, Africa, and elsewhere were simply being ignored.

Moreover, with the efforts of similarly-minded presses—Dalkey Archive, Eriadanos (now part of Marsilio), Marlboro Press, Exact Change and others—we felt that Sun & Moon could make a difference, could expand the reading horizons of American culture and allow us to understand our own heritage within the larger and essential international context.

While we have a long way to go yet in this project, we feel we have succeeded in presenting at least fifty works of great significance. We tip our glasses to our readers—and to the future.

Such projects are not achieved simply by dreaming or will-power. Hundreds of hours of imagining, thinking, reading (and the attendant eyestrain), designing, shipping, and promoting went into the production of each title. For these and other various activities appreciation and thanks must go to my staffs, present and past: Perla Karney, Ann Klefstad, Jeffrey Kalstrom, Michael Griffin, Michael Anderson, Joe Ross, and the staff members who brought this book into existence, Reginald Jones, Diana Daves, and Guy Bennett. Many translators have made Sun & Moon books possible, and to all of them I lift my glass; but in particular I would like to thank Luigi Ballerini and Paul Vangelisti for their own micro-editorial project within the Series, Blue Guitar Books; and to point out Guy Bennett, Gilbert Alter-Gilbert, Pierre Joris, and Jerome Rothenberg whose insights are always illuminating. Together these six translators cover twelve languages! David Antin, Roberto Bedoya, Charles Bernstein, Peter Glassgold, Lyn Hejinian, and Marjorie Perloff have served in different roles as readers, board members, and loyal supporters.

Finally, my hat goes off to the many contributors to The Contemporary Arts Educational Project/Sun & Moon Classics Series.

—DOUGLAS MESSERLI

Dominique Fourcade

from *Outrance utterance*

Translated from French by Norma Cole

THE MATTER-TIME of word: the enouncement of the word, erotics of the word's duration in time, relation between persistence in us of the notion's vibration and the duration of stating the word, minute sensuous displacement,

the word *trot*

I would abbreviate, abbreviate more, to make everything contingent upon a minute voluptuous point whose duration would be infinitely modulatable, point of absolute pain and communication, the most intense linguistic point in the world, beginning with which to rethink love's entire duration,

is the deverbal of to trot,

this time of eros, time of writing, time to spend moving from one point in language to another, changing places in the real body (which is time, which is language), major time is sexual time, the only real time, the time for being its body,

lovely as an unidentified nape,

the time a vowel takes, an o for example, the time needed to say it and that it occupies like a destiny, without claiming it, a full time, the poem is time in the word,

trot is an intensive form of the step,

beginning of the poem but not beginning of time, only beginning of the time of the poem, time precedes the poem, in fact the poem inserts space in time, black space in black time,

gait diagonal leap

somewhere in time is a point without extension where the poem's totality of energy and matter concentrate, the poem springs from where, a cadence,

where limbs oscillate, crossed in pairs

and so in the time which is our own, the time of writing, the footholds are separated by suspension and the suspension, however little the gait is lengthened, is at least equal to the duration of the foothold,

requirement of articular potential

and simultaneously to prolong, again and again, an alternate placing on the page, a placing of sunlit words and a labor of laps, themselves sunlit, in which writing is exposure, an inside out, an outside in, flashes of light, taste of blood,

trapped in a trot not lined by light,

and at the end of the time of a word, what? where to direct
the gaze, writing, partnered by one's own voice, necessitas
murmurandi perpetually coming to alter the ius murmur-
andi?

entered
in a wounding trot,

exposure, a whistling stride, without hope, without despair,
a stride aiming only to establish its rhythms, test its connec-
tions, the time to be this body, language (so it was this, to
have a body and a heart), an elegy filled with bait, with coun-
termeasures,

anechoic trot,

in time without answer, a disposition on the page, an elegy
filled with jingles, in space which does not sus-tain it, an
elegy with a horseman, absent,

a word which is its own circuit-breaker,

a word missing u (unlike gum or encaustic, themselves lu-
bricated), a word inventing its length, its unpublished parts,
(its space its time) and pronouncing its method, a word with-
out goal (not asking to be loved since it is love), a word for
the writing,

music,

death rattle in the great phrase forever lost, the fundamen-
tal phrase where everything was exposed, and from which
subsist only off phrases that accompany it, cut it or coincide
this sadness is wrong and so is this gaiety,

in us, clinically deceased,

in the only real body, language filled with euphorbia, the only one where we could exist, this body that, at times repels us with its erection, pretty bloody with our dead doubles,

a trot not cheated,

silhouette of the phrase, the impression that lasts is of end to end shades, of increasing the tension of the untellable grief, the impression is that of extreme decency of the phrase in relation to raw light of word-space, in time,

where we do not count our steps,

*

Born in 1938 in Paris, Dominique Fourcade is the author of several books of poetry, including Le ciel pas d'angle *(1983),* Rose-déclic *(1984) (forthcoming from Sun & Moon Press as* Click-Rose *in 1995),* Son blanc du un *(1986),* Xbo *(1988) (published by Sun & Moon in 1993),* Outrance utterance et autres élégies *(1990), and* IL *(1994). A Matisse scholar, Fourcade curated the 1993 retrospective exhibition* Henri Matisse 1904–1917 *at the Musée National d'Art Moderne at Centre Georges Pompidou in Paris.*

Djuna Barnes

Saturnalia

THE WEST INDIES had finally got Mr. Menus. He had
shifted out of Beacon Street and the company of his aunt,
Miss Kittridge, with firm religious views, political ambitions
and a happy journalistic talent. He was now suffering *mañana*.

Ten years of Kingston saw him sub-editor of a wilted lo-
cal newspaper, and the probable first candidate for burial.

In these years his aunt had been in Europe; the war got
her back with, it must be admitted, a touch of nerves, or so
her brothers had written him. They had taken her off the
boat and clapped her into a sanitorium somewhere up in the
mountains. She had stayed a week. He knew his aunt: taut,
thin, silent. He grinned running his handkerchief around his
collar. He hoped she would "make it" (she was coming to
visit him)…make it and get away. All non-Jamaicans hope
that someday someone will weather the tropics and manage
to escape. He had never known any one who had, that is, not
as they expected; there was always a little malaise, a touch of
the sun, a leaning toward occultism, a desire for Valhalla, a
spot in immutability; star gazing, tea-leaf reading. He was
not sure that Kingston was exactly ideal for a woman who
was slightly shattered. He put his faith in the curative charms
of his garden.

The lizards puffing out their throats on the heat of the
stone turned their cold eyes toward the sound of collective
intoning of Latin on the other side of the garden wall, where

the Ladies Seminary (a select school for the daughters of British officers and the well-to-do) was now in session. Every afternoon at five precisely the girls filed across the lawn, their heads erect under the weight of Milton, the Inferno, and the Common Prayer. Coming in to tea, they bowed them off at the gate. Mr. Menus hoped his aunt would like them.

Then there was old Colonel Edgeback who had bought a tangerine grove, a rambling bungalow, a tobacco patch and a herd of asses. He gave his native women servants umbrellas and sewing machines to keep them happy, and for himself he kept an excellent cellar consisting of nothing but Scotch. He always spoke of returning to the incomparable Cotswolds. He never would and he knew it; but sipping his lemon squash, or downing a peg of brandy with his friends he liked to think of it. Then there were Lieutenants Astry and Clopbottom and their wives, and, unfortunately, a child apiece. One played the guitar, the other carried about a fly in a bottle and a game of "Go Fish." A liberal dotting of young ladies and common soldiers ended the list with the sane Mrs. Pengallis from the Dust Bowl as accompaniment. She had steel knitting needles.

Miss Kittridge arrived, her nephew behind with her light Alice blue weekend case on which her initials stood out sharp and bright. A black darted out of the obscurity of the back garden and secured it. Miss Kittridge carried a Liberty silk scarf and a volume of the letters of Madame de Lafayette. She bowed to the peopled garden, and to the group of South American girls who seemed like their own shadow, as they leaned together under the clicking of the lime leaves. Miss Kittridge's veil floated from a honey colored chip hat on which a bird perched, over the fine bone of her brow, its wings upraised; beneath its breast, puffed out in a silent taxidermic warble, a diamond pin shone in broken sparks. She sat down in the chair her nephew pushed forward with the bumping motion of an object propelled under low blood pressure. During pauses in the conversation one could hear the dark sound of dripping water striking a catafalque of stone—the tub in the bathhouse.

The downy guitarist, suffering from uncertainty, tangled himself in the strings of his instrument in his flurry to do the honors. A string broke zooming upward smiting a dying G. The sugar went into Miss Kittridge's lap. "Thank you," she said in a voice made unreproachful with introspection. "Thank you."

Without waiting for an introduction Mrs. Astry leaned forward. "The little horror has brought his fly." She flicked her lashes toward Master Clopbottom who, deep in his angling, was oblivious to the buzzing of his captive.

"Has he?" said Miss Kittridge.

"Want to be introduced?" inquired a young lady sitting on the grass at Miss Kittridge's left. She giggled looking at Mr. Menus who had forgotten the amenities. He was always forgetting. "Mrs. Pengallis (Mr. P. is over there, he doesn't count), Colonel Edgeback, Lieutenants Astry and Clopbottom (and brats), Señorita Carminetta Conchinella, Mrs. Beadle, Mr. Pepper...and you're Miss Kittridge? Woops!" she said, catching her cup and saucer at the length of her gesticulating arm, "who cares!"

"Cecilia!" someone said, but it was a muted exclamation. It was so warm.

Lieutenant Astry offered thin bread and guava jelly. "Hope you are used to inertia. How was Paris? Hear you are just from Paris."

Miss Kittridge turned her handsome scant fact toward him. "Yes, Paris, but that was some weeks ago. I've been up in the mountains since then...thaw just setting in, skis coming up out of the snowbanks, toppling over, couldn't hold...mud-week, slush to your axles. The mountain men putting sodium bichloride into the culverts; cuts the ice." She looked up into the sky. "Cuts like a knife." The pale flesh trembled over the stride of her skeleton. "Sanitorium you know," she said calmly and without embarrassment. Everyone felt comforted and disabled.

The buzzing of the fly came to Miss Kittridge, and the sound of leaves whirling on their stems. After *The Idiot*, she thought, there should never have been another fly. The horrible child suddenly yelled "Go fish!" Mr. Pengallis, whose profile was darkened by the broad ribbon of his pince-nez, winced. At this moment Sir Basil Underplush barged into the garden. He was an old and privileged friend who somehow managed to get back for a shooting in Scotland once in a while, but always came back to Jamaica and the overstuffed chair with purfled welt which Mr. Menus always trundled into the shade for him, along with the tea tray. Sir Basil had been engaged in the compilation of the exploits of his great great grandfather, who had served in India. He was quite pleased by it, but he was happier about having composed a pibroch of his own. He was said to be "hell on the pipes" in spite of shortness of breath and an addiction to *Three Feathers*. The natives considered him a sort of *buckra* or demon, because of his kilt and bare knees. He lumbered through the vanilla plants and waded to the chair.

"Dammit!" he said, easing himself down, "why not some other sort of thing altogether. Why animals, always animals?" He reached for the siphon. "Why not a buttered loaf say, floating before the eye; a vision of Fair Albion—why always animals?"

"Bad night?" inquired Mr. Menus timidly.

"Very. And always pink. Why pink? I must inquire why pink and why not something else entirely."

"Why buttered?" said Mrs. Pengallis clicking her needles.

Sir Basil regarded her. He was a heavy man, and he suffered to scale. "I use the word advisedly, Madame; I dislike a dry heel."

"Of bread?"

Mr. Pepper, a spidery little grocer's clerk, sneezed. He had become neurotic looking at celery and now suffered war scare and eczema. He kept shuffling his hands as if they were a pack of cards. "Life is awful. I'm always uneasy…always."

Sir Basil grunted, a rich distilled grunt. "Try your ancestors, write them up, that will let you down. Try your hand at your grandfather; I presume you had one."

Mr. Pepper looked different. "I dare say, I don't know."

"Why not birds now?" Sir Basil continued, "why, since the beginning of man and the draught that cheers, always quadrupeds?" He spun his glass. "Why not the nightjar, the nighthawk, the nightingale? At worst the lapwing, the lark, but really why not the nightingale? I prefer the nightingale."

"*Why* did that bird have to go up so high?" demanded Mrs. Pengallis. "All that way up just to come down with Shelley in his mouth?"

"Beak!" snapped Sir Basil. "Beak for godsake!"

Mrs. Astry leaned toward Miss Kittridge. "We call him the bee-hive," she whispered. "Has the entire alphabet swarming after his name, all his orders and distinctions you know, Knight of the Bath and Garter and Professor Emeritus and what-not."

"It is all right once you get used to the heat and the flying batallions," Mr. Menus said to his aunt. He bobbed his head toward the militia. "We have billiards after supper, and the natives sing their wahoo, and the ladies do a bit of sewing. The heat nearly takes care of everything…rancor and folly, ambition and damnation."

Miss Kittridge said "I hear that a lot of expatriots are

farming upstate, and raising cows. They are very happy and proud about it. They all give parties, and milk the cows into cocktail glasses."

Señorita Carminetta Conchinella rocked her little behind on her black mantilla. "Americans find God and Life very difficult, is it not so little father?" she turned to Mr. Menus her dark soft eyes. "I walk in your parks, even in your New York Zoo, and all the young people are talking psychiatry and Zen, and about diseases and nerves; the old people of cures and of healings, and of Mortal Mind, and they are all very comfortable and well-to-do and unhappy. Now in my country you go to God softly, a rose in your teeth, no?, to prevent yourself from asking Him for favors…that is nice, it is good, it rests Him too…but Americans, you go wringing your hands…when you are not tired, or too hot. It is good when it is too hot, it is like wisdom, it kicks off the top of the head."

A thin light smile flickered along the lids of Miss Kittridge's eyes. "Yes, I know, I have traveled; every country is afraid in a different way." She paused. "When I came back to America I found people behaving very oddly—all looking for something, beating the old gods up into hundreds of new forms, trying to find something…."

"Lost the taw, that's what," said Mrs. Beadle breathing loudly, "put off playing the game so long they don't know where to begin…it's bringing sanitoriums and isms up like mushrooms."

The head mistress arrived, a line of young ladies behind her in correct posture, all walking sedately, all sitting down capably, all smiling, simultaneously bending over their cups.

"Have a drink," the Colonel said to everyone in particular. "Thank you, I will," said Mr. Pengallis turning the anxiety of his face from the young horror. "Just a spot." "No thank you," ran in chorus down the garden. "Later perhaps," said Miss Kittridge.

"Woops!" said the young girl, for a second go unbuckling her legs. "Talking about nuts, I've as nutty a set of friends and relations as ever jumped over the moon if it comes to that." She placed her cup and saucer on the grass beside her and seizing her left thumb with her right hand began bending her fingers counting. "Aunt: a New Thoughtest. Mother: a By God I Am! Sister: crazy about a neo-Greek quick-lunch counter Yogi who says he *knows* what Europe is thinking. Dad: in for a nifty number whirled up in a jubbah who has the Devil by the tail; and," she added, "Brother's up in Dannamara, for stealing a cow."

Mrs. Beadle threw her hands straight up in the air. "That's the best of it you know. That young man may yet live to see the end of the world."

"Something to be said for the Public School and the private fox," said Sir Basil turning his glass. "We British sweat it out."

"My grandmother knew Annie Besant," Miss Kittridge said in a lost sort of voice, "before she raised up that new Messiah; but she's dead, my grandmother I mean, and he got away to the hills, so all the mandolins are quiet now, and nothing suffers levitation." She turned looking into the insect troubled air. "I liked it better when Rasputin couldn't be killed; I liked it better when Romulous and Remus fed upside down; I liked it better when the Romans changed clothes with each other; when the Arabs, observing Ramadan, threw their collection of grandfather clocks into the ravine with the offering of the ram's horn."

"Advancement," said Lieutenant Clopbottom. "Advancement can't be helped."

Mr. Menus rubbed the cake crumbs into the alpaca of his

knees. "Yes, I guess so, but you must have an income abso-
lutely solid if you are going to be different. You can't be
different unless you have money to fall on. But with it you
can be face down in the gutter and be said to be standing on
your own feet, if you know what I mean." He looked wor-
ried.

"I liked it better before they started swinging Shakespeare
and mugging Bach." Miss Kittridge slid her hands across
her pocketbook. "I liked it better when the horse had hands.
I saw one of them in a British Museum, made me think of
Beethoven, I don't know why. It's nice to be able to think of
everything all at once. They used to, in the old countries."

"Fancy," exclaimed the Colonel, "a horse with hands! That
horse might be playing a minuet on the piano this minute!"

"He might indeed," said Miss Kittridge.

"You know what I think," the young girl on the grass
said. "I think all this brooding is clapping taboo on people, I
do, honestly."

Miss Kittridge said, "That's what my brothers thought.
They have never traveled, they stay put (all but my nephew
here, of course); it keeps them in business. It doesn't pay to
travel, you get to know things they don't like hearing about."

"I'm afraid, Miss Kittridge, you are not keeping up with
the times," Sir Basil said, a gleam in his eye.

"Oh, the catkin, and the welkin, and the bonny blue
getout!" wailed Master Astry, his guitar on his knee, his
face heaving.

Mrs. Pengallis said, clicking her needles, "He's muddling
through; he'd be in a cage if his parents didn't have money."

"Liberal educations," the Colonel said emptying his glass,
"are madness and evil and all that—"

Mrs. Beadle bounded from her chair shouting "Out! Out!
Devil!" Then she sat back quite calmly.

Everyone jumped except Mr. Menus. "Don't be alarmed," he said to his aunt, "she's only casting out Devils of course…She does it personally at least once a day."

"They save string in France," murmured Miss Kittridge, "and in Venice they sing 'Il Forza del Destino.' At the sanitorium up in the Catskills they asked me if I knit." She was smiling. "I used to *plow.*"

"I take it," said Sir Basil easing himself in his plush chair, "your doctor was not handsome."

"He liked the work," she said. "He told me the American mind was more profitable each day. He said if his house were only big enough he could shoot down seventy-five profitable minds a week. I think he is going to add a wing. One of the nurses thinks about writing a column for the papers to take the place of 'Advice to the Lovelorn.' She's going to call it 'What are You Thinking?' Everytime there's another blitzkreig the head doctor rubs his hands and says to the waitress, 'Lay another place at the table.'"

Mrs. Beadle snapped furiously. "I'll stick to religion, thank you. It must be disgusting slapping your spirit down like that all in one bang."

"Breaking down is one of the American's destinations," Mr. Menus said glancing away to the hills.

"I'll stick to confession plain," Mrs. Beadle went on. "Thank you. It unties you slowly, year by year. The other business makes people very sick and proud, as if they laid a volcano," she sniffed.

A faint low wailing sound came from the back garden where the smoke of the open coke fire rose in a thin wavering line. Mr. Menus said "Just Jinny Lou hankering after her race and yams."

"I'll stick to the church," Mrs. Beadle repeated. "I do love a church, a bride going in, a corpse coming out."

Mrs. Astry sighed. "Well, we do have to hold on to something."

The Colonel waved his glass. "They used to hold onto my ancestors at both ends, getting them up to bed after the stirrupcup, the flowing bowl, the night-cap, the bid-ye-farewell my merry gentlemen. Sprightly old gentlemen of the golden age, slightly sprung from coming bang down on the brush."

The young girl on the grass ripped out, "My sister used to be a wallop at badminton, now she goes into a linen closet to concentrate."

"Con declarer se examio del tormento" murmured Carminetta Conchinella. "Everything is bearable to Americans only if they have a name for it."

"I liked it better in the days when the nunneries were full of monkeys who jibbered too much, and parrots who had too much to say."

Mrs. Pengallis snorted. "And now it's the adolescent who enjoys all this sort of thing...they dart into the psychiatrist's office like wasps."

Mr. Menus stirred uneasily. Baskets of tangerines and prawns and twisted wet wash sailed along the height of the garden wall on the heads of negresses, hands on their hips, palm down. It was almost dark and the South Americans were leaving silently, barely distinguishable one from the other among the resting leaves. They turned their faces toward the gate and, turning them away, disappeared. From somewhere came the sound of drifting water and of singing, the last crow of a dying cock. "Have to kill them straight over the spit," Mr. Menus said comfortably, "it's the heat, and butter comes in tins." He said, turning a worried face to his aunt, "Hope you can stand butter in tins."

"I can," she said, "I've been many places and none of them safe for centuries. I haven't been safe since I began to use my imagination." She paused. "Up there the doctors said 'give us the middle classes any time, they tell you the damnedest things – right out."'

"That's the way to fix 'em" said Mrs. Pengallis. She turned toward Miss Kittridge. "Did you have coordination?"

"Oh, yes, a dashing country doctor, striped trousers, not quite the right fit, and a bowler hat, and he carried a little black bag. I had to touch the tip of my nose with my eyes shut, and walk a straight line with my feet close together, and bend backward without falling."

"And did you make it?"

"Oh, dear me yes, perfectly. He went out of the room then, but he was back almost immediately; he'd forgotten my reflexes, my knees. I told him they worked—you hit them you know, with the side of the hand or a little mallet. I told him they moved very well, but he hit one anyway."

"What happened?" said Mrs. Beadle.

Miss Kittridge arose. She turned her face toward Mrs. Beadle. "I kicked his hat off," she said.

*

A legendary figure of American literature, Djuna Barnes, born in 1892, is best known for her masterwork, Nightwood *(1936). During the 1920s and early '30s she lived the expatriate life in Paris, where she was known for her wit and clever conversation. Among her acquaintances were James Joyce, T. S. Eliot, Charles Henri Ford, and Peggy Guggenheim. Her other publications include the novel* Ryder; *an almanac,* Ladies Almanack; *short stories,* A Night Among the Horses *and* Spillway; *and a drama,* The Antiphon. *Sun & Moon Press has selected her early stories, published as* Smoke and Other Early Stories, *and two collections of interviews and essays,* Interviews *and* New York. *Recently, the press published her first book, a collection of poems,* The Book of Repulsive Women. *Barnes died in 1982.*

Ray DiPalma

Hours Hall

for Hart Crane

Hedron for headroom notches the water step
Roentgen's trailing dot pinning the outline
Implacable neon by the sheaf

Riffed further from the wall's chisel
Are reef vaults and wicks of salt true to the rainbow's
Bulking the drop to span several pages

Diamond scrapers between the wedge and the dirt
Chop hoist the hammer clotting a grip on the grim
Oval slogans are static in the slam

Tractors stripe the gate and offer distances
Smokestacks in the equations between the holes
Hammer the nines in solution

Solid cherry is the ratio of spider to pathwood
It speaks to the penitential angle puzzling the eye-man
They end in a pan of enameled carbon marked with white integers

Nothing living that long engages the edge
Only tempo under the dry lip and the horn's rifling
When the weather changed

Submergence for threnody and an asterisk for genitals
Prisoners on the road and a polyphony of plumage in the arcade
Make four corners for the goblin scam

I think monsieur is familiar with the vertical keyboard
And the austere balance that exacts its shallows
Noon's fugue scratched on the lid

An axiom for calm is only what's offered
Intent and arrogance in the cut maps
Animal days in the leap

*

*Born in New Kensington, Pennsylvania in 1943, Ray DiPalma
began writing in the late 1950s and published his first work in
magazines in 1962. His first book,* Max, *appeared in 1969. In the
early 1970s he edited a series of literary magazines and published
a number of books by poets who were later to be associated with so-
called Language writing. By 1973 he had started creating visual
and written works that were, in part, intended to extend the notion
of textual image. Among these visual works are one-of-a-kind
artist's books, sound texts, collages, and prints. His publications
include* The Sargasso Transcries *(1974),* Marquee *(1977),*
Planh *(1979),* Genesis *(1980),* Labyrinth Radio *(1981),* Two
Poems *(1982),* January Zero *(1984),* The Jukebox of Mennon
(1988), Raik *(1989), and* Provocations *(1994). In 1993 Sun &
Moon Classics published his* Numbers and Tempers: Selected
Early Poems 1966–1986. *He currently edits the magazine* Hot
Bird MFG.

Louis-Ferdinand Céline

Van Bagaden
Grand ballet-mime, with a few words

Translated from French by Thomas Christensen

THE ACTION takes place in Anvers, around 1830. The set represents the interior of an immense boathouse. A whole troop of porters, dockworkers, tidewaiters bustle about, peddle, transport, open, pour out...packages...fabrics...silken goods...cottons...grains...all sorts of cargo...They come...they go, from one dock to another...upstage of the boathouse, which is partitioned off...by high, enormously high stacks of unpacked merchandise...all heaped up... Tea...coffee...spices...draperies...camwood...lumber... bamboo ...sugar cane...Amid this vast turmoil, this great jostling, one sees a group of women workers, all decked out...as lissome...as saucy...as can be!...They pass by...back and forth...like winged creatures...iridescent...coquettish... among the heavy, sweating workmen...they go about their business...they come and go...They are the *parfumeuses!*... they prepare and pour out scents...in little bottles...they have a thousand refinements...perfumes from Arabie...the Indies...the Orient...They're afraid of being jostled...with their precious bottles...little shrieks of alarm...fright... swishing silks! They test their bottled scents...delight! Little

ecstasies!...They quarrel about the perfumes...the arrange-
ment of the bottles...They fuss with the presentation of the
flasks...demijohns...cashboxes...that fill a whole corner of
the boathouse...it's an aviary...with its constant chirping...
its endless stir...Other coquettes, cigarette girls, occupy the
opposite wall...they spend just as much time on their own
little tricks...their own comings and goings...jabbering...
chattering...A whole little world evolving amid the labors
of the boathouse workers who go back and forth from the
ships...The slow procession of the "big men," unloading the
heaviest cargo...enormous cannonballs...tree trunks...some
of these porters mock...goad the *parfumeuses*...pinch the ciga-
rette girls...as they go by...reach into their tobacco
bins...Huge uproar...disputes...dances...ensembles...
Hurly-burly...the whole boathouse...abuzz with activity
...with work...with arguments...One also hears the port
noises... sirens...shouts...the songs of the dockworkers
...worksongs...heave-hos...etc.... succeeded by other
music...barrel organs...street musicians...A black man
leaps...sails clear from the wharf into the boathouse...a brief
wild interlude...The black man returns as he came...in a
single bound!

It has been clear from the beginning that one of the
parfumeuses is more lovely, more lively than the rest...more
coquettish than any of them...as saucy as can be...the prima
ballerina...Mitje. In a corner, at one side of the boathouse, a
niche...The audience sees into this cranny: the Office of the
Ship-Owner...separated from the throng in the boathouse
by an enormous partition. In this recess, the ship owner Van
Bagaden...as wizened as can be...sunk deep in a formidable
armchair, dried out, gouty, and cranky...Van Bagaden! He
can't get up anymore...he can barely budge...He no longer
leaves his chair, his cranny...It's where he lives, curses,

swears, raves, sleeps, threatens, eats, spits yellow, and guards his gold...the gold that comes to him on a hundred ships...Owner of ships on all the oceans of the world!...So we see him, Van Bagaden, tyrant of seas and sailors, in his den. He wears a large black turban on his head to guard against drafts...He's muffled up in thick wools. Only his head protrudes from these wrappings...He never stops swearing, cursing, vituperating his clerk, the unfortunate Peter...The latter, ever at his side, perched high on the stool by his accounting table, never stops lining up figures...working the enormous registers...The whole desk is covered with the huge registers...the ancient Van Bagaden rages, threatens: Faster, Fleabag! Mummy! Peter, at his bidding, can never go fast enough for him...with his calculations...Van Bagaden raps the floor with his stout cane...He fidgets in his chair...He never stops...Peter jumps at every rap of the cane...The noise of the crowd, the hubbub of the boathouse... Van Bagaden's all wound up...Instead of toiling, his workers are having fun!...He hears the girls, the laughs of the workers, the gay uproar. He's lost his authority! He's too old!...All these little rogues are defying him! escaping him!...He can no longer make himself obeyed! Damnation!... He tries to get out of his chair!...He falls back...And each time he thumps the floor in fury...with his terrible cane!...far from shaping up, the little workers and the laborers, all the working people, mock and taunt! to the beat! of the cane!...Oh, the despair of Van Bagaden defied!...ridiculed! (The mice can play, for the cat is stuck...) The little *parfumeuses*, roguish, glance toward the partition...and steal sulkily off...especially the coquette Mitje, the most vivacious, the most minxish...of all the insolent swarm...Peter, the faithful clerk, is tied to his enormous registers by a chain...and also clasped to his stool by a solid iron bar...Peter is the whipping-boy of the old tyrant Bagaden...Peter jumps in terror, with his stool...each time the old bully's cane strikes the floor. He starts his calculations over from the top...

A sea-captain enters the boathouse, parts the throng and threads his way through it...He has come with news for old Bagaden...

He murmurs some words in his ear...old Bagaden raps...again...hard as he can...Peter jumps...Bagaden hands him a little key...Peter opens the lock of his shackles. He can get down from his stool...He leaves the boathouse with the sea-captain...

Keen interest in the boathouse...Emotion...Gossip... Discussions...They wait...

After a moment Peter returns, dragging behind him a heavy net, and wrapped within this net an enormous mass...a prodigious clump of pearls...a formidable bundle...a fantastic prize...each pearl...is big as an orange!...Peter won't let anyone help him carry this magnificent load to the feet of his master Van Bagaden...The dance is suspended...The whole mob in the boathouse...laborers, sailors, workers, women...comment admiringly on the arrival of this latest treasure. Van Bagaden never blinks. He has his chair moved a bit...He makes Peter open a vast, deep coffer behind him. With elaborate precautions, Peter shuts the extraordinary gems safe within this cavern...and then resumes his perch on his stool, refastens the chain around his ankle...shuts the clasps, returns the little key to Van Bagaden, returns to his calculations...And all around the work resumes...For a time...until another captain enters...and murmurs another bit of news in old Bagaden's ear...Exactly the same business, all over again. This time Peter comes back bearing jewelry boxes and scrip...more jewels, doubloons...precious stones...rubies...giant emeralds...All once again shut up inside triple locks, the same ceremony, behind old Bagaden…

Halted for a moment…all the traffic of the boathouse, the transport of heavy loads…now resumes with a fury…

From the wharf…off in the distance…we hear the reverberations of martial fanfare…approaching…. passing by. One sees it go past through the boathouse door…that vast opening…And there upstage appear…soldiers…bourgeois …sailors…in free-board… Riotous fellows…drunks…a mob gone wild…with glee…they are free!…Immense flags furl past…above the mob…Banners covered with images…next a little saint" on a palanquin…then enormous papier-mâché giants…carried by the crowd…they're on a spree!…Old Bagaden, cloistered in his cranny…raves…rages…against this new bacchanal, this hullabaloo…that's spewing forth!

What mad rage for diversion is possessing everybody!… Van Bagaden himself is never amused…He has a horror of joy, and of the gross farandoles of these rogues more than anything!…With an enormous effort he lifts himself up, just a bit…What suffering! What agony!…Finally he can catch a glimpse…What horror!…all the puppets delirious…He sends Peter at once…against this latest throng! This insolent saraband!…"Get back to work at once…back to your places! all you blackguards!…Peter! Take my cane! So!…cudgel them!…bring the riffraff me!…Make them obey!"

But the riotous celebration only rises…swells…engulfs the wharf…the whole stage!…echoing endlessly!…

The unfortunate Peter, in desperation, with the cane, rushes all alone against that mob…against that mass of joy…that madness…that immense farandole… .

CURTAIN

*

Louis-Ferdinand Céline was born Louis Ferdinand Destouches in 1894 in France. Among Céline's grim, often scatological, and black-humored novels are his masterwork, Journey to the End of Night *(1932),* Death on the Installment Play *(1936),* Castle to Castle *(1957),* North *(1960), and* Rigadoon *(1961). Céline was a virulent anti-Semite, publishing several antisemitic pamphlets, including* Bagatelles for a Massacre *(1937). The work included here is from his previously untranslated* Ballets sans musique, sans personne, sans rien, *which will be published as* Ballets without Music, without People, without Anything *in 1995. Céline died in 1961.*

Barbara Guest

Ojjiba

sideways a gift for language the joined up tunes il splash and
whine ordained it the frisked mood piece of cotton in the ear
every day different a felon passes I believe dog-eared as three
of your pals the boy in tune with the sandcastle out of three
twigs on a harp who hear the bow bend early music

you think I am joyous up at dawn down by il splash not true
I hover and in with the robins as they take up their chores
and on the brink of financial ruin this is not a sophisticated
place can crown you with ruin take your hand off the plate it
spoils

(in the wrinkled pool
                    tried your bat on the faucet saw a hood
        like what he writes away from the gold batter)

ruin is pleasanter up here whisks crossing the dune blown
shell and peppermint leas even if no rim around me scoop up
the line and distribute it regularly not haunted think of milk
toast three winks not lonely early music

caused the chair to move to the brink the azalea in winter
wonder who refused to cosset it if ruin can put us out of
sight then forgot or the chair moved wish it were closer

of sentimental values none no more than a spasm the arm
goes over and down and over in il splash drank a tumbler
then greenleaf and swimming dog muscular gladioli goodly
frere *unio mystica* we perceive a grass ship

on the sea surface a forget-me-knot the ratio consoling a
strange look at the vein and flung in a cloud the lantern a
different embrace in pursuit of il splash

marvelled at how little comes from much in a nook combing
hair classical drift of the bay naked off Palinurus Cape
O queen of Cnidos literature "wax-white arms of Lydia"
waterfront pebbled with bones

and she confronts us "the woman who weeps" the scenery
dislikes wet arms bathing suit pulled down at the corner
a raft on the sea she is a raft an egg shell breaks god's whip
early music

wave passes over from sight wave is obscured water replaces
the surface reverses its look bottom of the sea comes up like
a kite in the rear on our back rain will emerge from that
dying cloud whither arrow of blue

no concern for corridor upstairs icy trees blow smoke what
island was it cold from where we sat fingers never still idly
lay a green cloth they jump into bed wake to the crow can
guess the dark coat

about the sandcastle our position on innovation the duster
the trap is it mediocre the schoolmaster suggests wool in
the brace a tight fit the bodice-fitter complains

(or seascope of anchored tin put out the table
        the chipped metallurgical
appears to be a vine
            no goddess to shake a leg)

can you swallow this they erase "long echo of sand" also "pool
noise" interrupt "drawn out whine" betray the disk the
substance improves and the gnat she waits in her bathing
dress touch and go

haunted by the speckled cow the little girl with a ribboned
bonnet brings in the cow   put more early in music
says the speckled cow   earlyinsplash

what was it about crackers asked the wench potato mash is
cheap pauper tint to the sky so mermaids sweep out the crones
they flit good evening good evening no treasure

which tree to cut the downward slope of a savannah its bell
our land goes further light drains horizon's overcast early
music

                    promise we shall meet on Ojjiba and swim
underwater my harp is caught in a silver fire of water the
planet Ojjiba   looked at that way

*

*Born in North Carolina, Barbara Guest spent her childhood in
California and Florida. After graduating from the University of
California at Berkeley, she settled in New York City. She recently
has moved to Berkeley.*

*Guest was connected with the group of poets later known as the
New York Poets. During the 1960s she published* The Location
of Things, Poems, *and* The Blue Stairs. *An attachment to art is
inherent in her poetry and was formalized in her contributions to*
Art News *and other art journals.*

Moscow Mansions *(1973),* The Countess from Minneapo-
lis *(1976), and, in particular, her novel,* Seeking Air *(1978), point
to a sense of structure more varied as her poetics step outside the
frame of the New York School.* Herself Defined *is Guest's 1984
acclaimed biography of the poet H.D. When in 1989* Fair Real-
ism *was published by Sun & Moon Press and received the Lawrence
Lipton Award for Literature, it was noted her dependence on lan-
guage, always a variant, now placed her closer to the Language
poets. In 1993 Sun & Moon Classics published her collection,* De-
fensive Rapture. *Sun & Moon Press will publish her* Selected
Poems *in 1995.*

Wendy Walker

A Story Out of Omarie

25 Rajab 514

MY MOTHER and her husband traveled uneventfully for some days. Then they drew near to something called a *forest*. Imagine, if you can, thick, towering bushes, row upon row receding into darkness. Imagine entering the Great Mosque when the lamps are not lit; this place was even larger, and the road there forked. Reaching over, he took her hand and said, "Hodierna, one day we will have a child, and whether a son or a daughter, it will be as Jesus wills, praise to Him! But here let the road we take be of your choosing."

My mother peered down the road on the right; then she regarded the other way, which stretched ahead fair and clear as far as they could see.

"Let us take the left road, Thibault," she said.

So they took that road, which showed every evidence of favor, being well-trodden and wide. But when they had gone some way down it, it began suddenly to contract, while the scrub overhead grew so dense, it turned morning to evening. Soon their path was so narrow, they could not even ride side by side. Then Thibault, who had taken the lead, saw in the darkness ahead four darker shapes, which loomed forward. He drew rein, turned round, and even as he did so, four more men emerged from the trees behind them. He said to my mother, "This was written. Try not to be afraid."

The ill-clad men did not return his salute. My mother
was still hoping it was the shadows that made these fellows
look so menacing when Thibault tried again: "Sirs, you have
interrupted two pilgrims on their way; be so good as to say
what business you have with us."

Perhaps there were words in the growled reply, perhaps
not; at any rate, he swerved. A blow sliced the air, he caught
the hand of it, squeezed, and grabbed the hilt as it fell. Now
he had two swords. He ripped up one's bowels, drove through
another's neck; then he faced the swordless bandit and ab-
stracted his life.

The five who still lived almost retreated. But when they
looked at my mother, they dared again. The largest ruffian
lunged at the horse while the others followed, feinting; then
he dropped back, skirted the tussle, crept in again and plunged
a knife into the palfrey. Soon Thibault lay naked in the dust.
They shredded his garments and bound his ankles and wrists.
First they hefted him like a bundle, then they swung him
like a hammock. Merry, they maneuvered, choosing a spot,
swung him higher and let him go; he broke into a thorn-
bush, screaming.

That game finished, they turned to my mother. She was
still in the saddle, weeping. They pulled her down, and
stripped her, though this time they did not harm the clothes.
She was as white as the inner lip of a conch. Too frightened
to blush, she appeared the more flawless for pallor. They
turned her around, examining her, surprised to find no im-
perfections. Then one of them grasped her arm and said, "I
have lost a brother here, I will take this for blood-money."
But the others all asserted similar rights, till the first finally
shouted, "Look at us! We can't keep her! We should just do
what we want, and leave. But let's get off the road." So they
dragged her deeper into the woods, threw her down on some
leaves, and each man had her as often as he could. As her

skin took their grime and blood, she broke out in a cool dew which, mixing with the scent of the moss underneath, made her even lovelier. They kept coming back to the beads on her hairline, her wet lashes, the clench of her hands. At length, when she had grown as smudged and bloody as they, they hustled her back to the highway, where she reeled as they disappeared.

So, Malakin, now that you know this, do you still want me?

27 Rajab 514

When I entered the room and saw you, you to whom I had already told so many secrets, when I saw the pen in my father's hand, I felt more than ever capable of speech. When he pointed to you and said, "Daughter, you know Malakin," I at once understood what had passed between you. I did not need to be informed that you had asked for my hand. And Father realized this: he said nothing more. I fell on my knees and kissed his feet, such joy is it to me to accomplish the will of the Soudan. You know how I have yearned for you: here we are, you are mine! I will tell you everything that I can.

Thibault of Dommare was a knight in my grandfather's house. My grandfather, the Count of Ponthieu, was very fond of him.

They were returning from one of those contests of warriors that the Franj delight in when the Count, who was feeling self-satisfied, turned to his companion and demanded, "Thibault, which of all my treasures seems most splendid to you?"

The way he phrased his question, he might have been offering a gift; but this was not the case. The Count was a man of great appetites, and he savored the whetting of them

so keenly, that when he had exhausted his own power to whip
them up, he would turn for help to those near him. He needed
their desires. Thibault knew him well, so he said what he
thought would most gratify him.

"There can be no doubt about it, my lord; it is your daugh-
ter."

How curiously love happens! Thibault had never till that
moment given my mother any particular thought. But even
as the sentence left his mouth, he realized that he was in love
with her, and that he would be a fool not to press this chance
home.

"I am only a beggar, my lord, as you know, but when I
contemplate all your wealth, I feel no envy except in her
regard."

My grandfather did not betray any feeling. He too had
had an idea.

"Well, Sir Beggar," he answered slowly, "I am not unwill-
ing to let you have her. That is, of course, if she doesn't mind."

So the Count sought out his daughter. The curtain at her
end of the hall was pulled back and he could see her graceful
figure as it dipped and gestured, all unconscious of the news
he was bringing her. When she turned to face him, he found
himself regretting that the Law of Jesus Christ was so strict;
he would have been happy to wed her himself.

He led her to the edge of the bed and sat down, holding
her hands.

"My pretty Hodierna," he said, "A woman already! What
would you say to getting married?"

My mother hid her apprehension. "To whom, father?"

"Well, perhaps to a knight of this household, a man called
Thibault of Dommare. I have high hopes of him. But if you
are against it, I will just tell him No."

"Oh, father," she said, "if you were the King of Christendom and I your only princess—if I could choose from all the husbands in Europe, I would choose this same Thibault. I would marry him right now! I would give him everything!"

The Count took her in his arms; even as a child she had always known what he wanted. "Hodierna," he whispered, "May the Lord bless your pretty little person, for He blessed me the day you were born!"

I found you otherwise, not suddenly, but with as great joy. Nor was it necessary for the Soudan to enquire after the state of my heart since he bore it within his, and had long ago seen you traveling toward me. My mother was lucky in being glad to do her father's will; but in my submission luck plays no part. Since I could speak I have wanted to be nowhere but at his feet. So what I performed in your presence when I entered the room was but a recital of a dream to the dreaming; the actual letter had been long ago sent.

"Sire," you said to the Soudan, "I crave a gift."

"Malakin," the Soudan said, "what is this gift?"

"Sire," you said, "it is very far above me. It is a treasure so knowing, so memorious and filled with light that I cannot quite compass it in my mind. I cannot imagine calling it my own; so I am afraid to speak its name before you."

My father is quick-witted; he easily guessed your gift.

"Say it out, Malakin. Be assured that I love you; I know full well that I am nothing without you. Whatever I have to give is yours—who else could require it?—provided it lies within my law to bestow."

"Your honor is mine, Sire," you said. "What I crave is your obedient daughter, the Fair Captive. She is all that I see in this world, wherever I go, wherever I look. I want nothing but to share her captivity."

The Soudan paused and considered. He knows you so well. He does not lightly weigh such courage as yours.

"You require a great thing, Malakin. However, you deserve it. She is yours, if it pleases her to accept you."

That is when I was summoned, and found you.

I will take your many questions in turn. First of all, the marriage.

My mother and Thibault were married, and for five years they lived very happily, except that she gave Thibault no child. One night he lay in bed, unable to sleep, thinking about the woman beside him. She was breathing very softly, curled up on her side. He turned over and stared at the gentle curve of her shoulder, her loosened hair. He couldn't understand it; he loved her so much, to embarrassment; and she, she loved him. He needed no proofs. Then why did she not conceive?

The moon rose, hung in the casement and burned a white path along her arm. He should go somewhere, do something, at least find out why it was so. He had heard tales about the marabout of the holy man James, which lay to the south. It was said that if one knocked in supplication at the Son of Thunder's door, that door would open. Why should he not journey there and knock? He put his arm round my mother's waist, and pulled himself close to her. She murmured, drifting a little way out of sleep and, turning over, nestled in his arms. He held her for some time very quietly, and then whispered, "Hodierna, wake up."

"What is it?"

"I want you to grant me a wish."

"A wish? What wish?"

"I'll tell you as soon as you grant it."

Her eyes opened.

"Please, grant it."

She sat up. "Thibault, you know it is yours, if it is a thing I can give. Now, tell me."

"I want you to let me go to Compostella. I will pray there to the Son of Thunder to intercede with the Lord Jesus Christ, that we may have a child."

She could not speak. He made love to her till dawn.

Several days passed and then, one night, Thibault woke to a gentle touch and her breath in his ear.

"Thibault," she repeated.

He looked up at her; his dream vanished. There was a pale corona of starlight on her hair.

"Yes?" He reached over and touched her nipple.

She said she too had a secret wish; with some misgiving, he granted it.

"I want to go with you to Compostella."

Then he protested; he cited the length of the journey, the dangers of the route. She didn't care, she couldn't bear to be parted from him. She clung to his chest, tight and silent, till he felt her tears. He tried to loosen her arms, but it was no good. At length, since his god meant to have it so, he gave way. Then, to lose his own sadness, he took advantage of her joy.

Soon the whole household fluttered with preparations. When talk of the projected journey reached the Count of Ponthieu, he had to struggle to conceal his annoyance. He had not given his daughter to one of his intimates in order to be kept in the dark. Wondering what other doings she might have neglected to share with him, he sent for her husband.

"Thibault, rumor has it that you are going on pilgrimage, and Hodierna with you."

"My lord, that is true."

He looked his son-in-law up and down. He was still a fine man, though he had always been a touch vague for a warrior.

"Now, Thibault, my son, whatever your purposes, you can

be assured of my faith in your judgment: whatever you de-
cide, I approve. But my daughter's arrangements are another
matter."

"I do not wish her to go, my lord, she is determined. You
know how hard it is to deny her."

The Count threw him a sharp glance. For a few moments,
neither spoke.

"Well, if that is how it is…" He still hoped his son-in-law
would complain, ask his help; Thibault was silent. "Well, if
that is how it is… Are you prepared for the journey? I would
like to give you some money. And I can supply you with all
the necessary gear; I know you have enough horses."

"You are very good to us."

"Never mind, it is nothing. However, be sure you give my
love to Hodierna."

So the entourage set out. They had fair weather and made
very good time. When they were only two days from
Compostella, they drew into a town. This is still before the
attack, and you of course want to know whether no one
warned them. The innkeeper of the hostel where they laid
down their beds forced Thibault to listen to his pleasantries,
while Thibault, for his part, took advantage of the occasion
to enquire about the road; but he was told only that they
would come upon a wood not far from the town gate, after
which the way ran very smooth. Nothing discouraging was
mentioned.

But in the morning, when the entourage bustled off with-
out its master, the innkeeper was appalled. He threaded his
way through the commotion, certain that the lord and his
lady couldn't still be sleeping. For whatever good it would
do, he tried to convey his disapproval to the only servant
left behind, and was still uncorking heavy insinuations when
the couple rose, at last. They would eat a bit, then start the

last lap of their journey. Thibault ordered the servant to fold the bed-linen and hurry after the others to halt them at the forest's verge. But the entourage traveled so fast, it entered the wood before the fellow caught up with them. Upon hearing his message they turned back, but since they had taken the right-hand fork, they met no one. Meanwhile, my mother and her husband were trying to cross the forest alone; you have already heard what befell, and I do not wish to dwell upon it. Imagine Thibault defeated, my mother raped, the forest quiet.

Now, I will go on.

Thibault lay in the thorn-bush, his face wet with tears. He heard the robbers depart. Some time passed, and then the sound of someone stumbling through the brush pierced his daze. The noise grew louder, then stopped. He heard weeping. She was on the road.

"Hodierna! Hodierna!"

The sobs ceased; then, more thrashing. He didn't dare turn his head, but at last he could see her—her whiteness towered above him, oddly patterned with browns and blues; there were pieces of dried leaves in her hair.

"Help me," he begged, when she only stared. He had to close his eyes. "Help me."

There was a pause; he heard rummaging; he looked again. When she re-entered his purview, she held something. She raised it high above her head.

"Your pain is over, Thibault."

He trembled with a fear he didn't feel: a fear so violent it forgot thorns, rolled him over. Her blow fell wide, glanced his arms; the bonds loosened. He grabbed her ankle and pulled; she struck ground.

"You won't kill me yet, woman!"

He wrested the sword from her. She was moaning. He cut

his other bonds, stood up. He roamed the vicinity, found the sheath, and encased the sword. Then he compelled his wife to stand. He kept his hand on her shoulder as they walked back. At the forest's edge they found the larger part of their company, which was still waiting for them to arrive.

Thibault stanched their horror with short answers; clothing was unpacked and they were covered again. There was nothing to do but climb into the saddle and continue the pilgrimage. Everyone noticed that the lord behaved toward his wife with particular gentleness, though he snapped at everyone else. He met her silence with a weird patience, was entirely sweet. When they put up at an inn that evening, he enquired if there were a convent in the neighborhood where a lady might rest for a few days, and being informed of one, took my mother there the next morning. He kissed her, and rode on to Compostella. There he knelt at the marabout and honored the holy James; he made the prayers he had come so far to make, and others as well. Then, his errand complete, he retraced the route and received from the nuns' hands his strange wife.

So they headed home. Everyone hurried outside to cheer as they rode through the gates. The Count ordered a welcoming feast, to which all the nobility roundabout came. The ladies wore their best robes to honor Hodierna, and Ponthieu and his son-in-law sat side by side, eating delicately from the same dish. The Count, between licking his fingers, told Thibault all that had transpired during the weeks of his absence; Thibault listened attentively, smiled when appropriate, and asked a few pertinent questions. When the Count was satisfied that his narration had been appreciated, he downed another goblet of wine, sat back in his chair, beamed at Thibault and said, "My fine son! Travelers see many things that stay-at-homes like myself must imagine, and after a good meal, one wants to hear wonders. Tell us something you saw while abroad; you are, doubtless, brimming with marvels."

Thibault stiffened. He carefully took another sip, wiped his lips and said, "Far from it, my lord; I saw nothing worth relating." Then, regretting this abruptness, he shrugged apologetically. A moment ensued during which Ponthieu continued to beam; then he slapped the boards, roared "Nonsense!" and laughed. The ladies all tittered.

"Nonsense! Do you suppose I outfitted you for nothing? I will have some anecdote for my thanks."

Thibault knew him too well to attempt another demurral. "Well, sir, since I must contrive some entertainment from our uneventful journey, I will pass on to you something I myself was told. But I will recount it only to you."

"Good enough," said Ponthieu, "the pleasure will be no less." And he went on eating, though everyone else was done.

At length he stood, and taking Thibault by the arm, led him towards a deserted corner of the hall. There, away from guests and menials, Thibault related what had happened to a certain knight and his lady who tried to cross a forest without any guard.

The Count was entranced. He made Thibault repeat a few details and then asked, "So what did the knight finally do with the lady?"

"What did he do with her, my lord? Why, he brought her back home, where he treated her as always, except that thereafter he slept in another bed. Nor was his wife grieved by it."

"No more than that?" The Count's eyes had grown wide. He mimed disbelief. "No more, truly? What a man! What a fellow! I'd have strung her up by her hair; or by the laces of her gown, if her tresses weren't long enough. She would have become part of the forest, had it been up to me. And what was this knight's name, did you say?"

"I didn't say."

"Tell it to me."

"No, my lord."

"But you know the man to whom this occurred."

"My lord, I know nothing!"

"You know his name!"

"Yes, I know it!"

"Then I will know it, too; you will pronounce it, or I shall be much displeased."

"My lord," said Thibault slowly, "Do not demand his name. I swear to you, it will bring you no profit to know it."

"I will have it!"

Thibault stared.

"Tell it to me!"

The knight passed his hand over his face. Suddenly he wanted fiercely to sleep. "Since you force me, but there is no honor in the telling, and I do it unhappily. I do it only under compulsion."

"Too many words, sir! It is only a name, you need not preface it so lengthily. Just say it out!"

Then Thibault sighed. He clasped his trembling hands behind his back.

"Since you must know—and remember, you *would* know—the man to whom this happened, I am he. I have told no one about it, and the shame could have died with me if you had been so good as to leave me in peace."

The Count winced. He cast about for some words. When he finally spoke, his voice sounded odd even to himself.

"Thibault, it was my own Hodierna who performed these things?"

Silence.

"You have brought her home; I will see she is punished."

Ponthieu sent across the hall for his daughter. When she stood before him he demanded to know if he should believe her husband's account of her actions.

"Of what has he accused me, father?"

"He says you tried to kill him!"

She did not hesitate. "That is true."

The Count wondered. "But why? Why on earth would you kill Thibault?"

She thought for a moment, then said simply, "Because I wanted him dead."

For the first time in his life, the Count was left speechless. He walked away, leaving husband and wife to each other, and brooded until the guests had departed.

How should I know what laws the Franj have for dealing with such wives? I was born here and have never passed a night outside my father's pavilions. But, sometimes, in my dreams, I wander in the land of the Franj. My brother is beside me, still a small boy; he is wearing strange clothes. He shows me all sorts of foreign things and explains them until I understand. I have thought of him so often, I feel I know him, but if we met, I am sure I would not recognize him for the child of my father.

My mother also had a brother. He was brought along when Ponthieu decided to make the journey to Rue-Sur-Mer. Thibault's company was also required, and his wife's. Upon their arrival, the Count immediately rode down to the harbor, and spent a long afternoon inspecting the ships. He settled upon one that seemed seaworthy and chartered it, then purchased a few provisions, and had them loaded aboard. Among these articles was a large barrel, shoulder-high, fitted with withy bindings. It exuded a savor of seasoned beech and brine. When all was ready and the oarsmen lined the benches, Ponthieu fetched his family and herded them on deck.

They cast off. The Count gave all the commands. He took large strides and regarded sharply anyone who stared at him. Now and again he would pause to confer with the captain, but always resumed his pacing with so much severity and gusto, no one could doubt who was in charge.

The knight stole a glance at his wife, who was leaning against the side, contemplating the receding shoreline; having never before been afloat, she seemed quite unconscious of the odd state of affairs. Young Ponthieu, too, appeared completely comfortable with his father's authority; he seemed not to notice how thoroughly the Count mangled his mariner's jargon. As for the oarsmen, they rowed much the same as they would have done, whoever was shouting. Only Thibault found the scene queer. Upon more than one occasion he determined to approach his father-in-law; but, whether because of a particularly violent swell, or a flinging of spray in his face, or a sudden queasiness that unmanned him, the moments always passed before he could take action. Meanwhile the Count went on striking attitudes, which Thibault was helpless to ignore. If only Hodierna had shown some anxiety, had come to his side, and asked him what he thought; had expressed even the slightest curiosity as to where they were going, certainly all his enervation would have vanished at once. He kept looking over at her, hoping she would try to catch his eye, but she still gazed at the horizon, though the land had long since disappeared.

They had been several hours at sea, and the sky was beginning to darken when the Count ordered some men to leave off rowing and haul the barrel over to the side. He thumped it in a satisfied manner, and commanded, "Strike the head out!" The sailors unsheathed their knives and pried the great disc free. The Count leaned over, peered inside the barrel, and ran his hand caressingly along the inner rim. Recovering himself, he looked around and spotted his daughter. As he began to traverse the deck, the ship grew silent; only the dull roar of the sea could be heard. Hodierna, feeling something, turned. He had stopped a few feet off, his hands loosely open at his sides, saying nothing. She registered a shock, tried to shrink back, but only succeeded in shuddering. At that, Ponthieu bridged the gap, but not before her knees buckled and her cold face contorted. He grabbed her by the arm, and dragged her, but she tried to bite, so he yanked her to her feet, slapped her twice and in a stunned moment had her over his shoulder. He held her legs tightly closed so that she couldn't kick.

Thibault had frozen: he just stood, he couldn't move. All he could think of was that she still hadn't looked at him. He glanced around for a clue. But then the shrieking started and the oarsmen stopped rowing.

Hodierna's voice punctured the wheezing wash, pierced it repeatedly, growing louder and higher. Soon it was coasting down the monotony of waves in long brilliant scratches, wordlessly exhorting deliverance and blood. Thibault struggled to reach the barrel. The young count had already flung himself at his father's feet, but Ponthieu paid no attention. When Thibault finally got there, he sank against the swollen wood and tried to hear her breathing. Above him the sailors were making the head fast again. He wanted to speak, but all he could find was her name. He uttered it several times, though not, perhaps, loud enough; then the barrel was lifted away from him.

When he looked up, it was not to search for the barrel but to learn the cause of the shadow in which he lay. Two sailors had hoisted the cask; now they gripped the sides; Ponthieu bowed and ventured underneath. Taking hold of the bottom rim, he assumed the tun on his back. When he spoke, its weight was in his voice:

"I consign this infection to the wind and the sea!"

He turned around, stepped backward; the barrel hung over the ship's side; then he let go: a void moment, a dull splashing.

Thibault's sky reappeared, but he remained as he was until they came again to Rue-Sur-Mer. He prayed to the Lord Jesus Christ to forgive her.

I have often tried to imagine my mother's experience, entombed and afloat, for how many hours or days, she never knew. I have attempted to calculate the dimensions of her horror: the constant rolling and roar, the lack of up or down, the suffocation, nausea, thirst. I have conjured her delirium in darkness, her wish to die, her fear of sleep, her seasickness, headache, stupor; I have seen her soaked in foulness, cramped, numb, cold, unable to move and equally unable to stop dreaming. But, detail it as I may, I have never felt these things; I have never been able to live any of them, at least, not until now. But now, all I have to do is to imagine losing you. Then I am cast away, suffocating, abandoned to chaos; I know it all exactly.

Fortunately, a ship spotted the barrel, a merchant vessel out of a place called "Flanders." Thinking it might contain something worth having, especially since it was drifting straight into their course, the captain commanded a smaller boat to be let down, to set hooks in the tun and tow it. After some maneuvering, the crew managed to haul it up. The captain noticed its head was but lately closed. For a while they just rapped at it and circled it, speculating, but finally they set about opening it.

Before they even saw the body, they recoiled from the smell. Then they gently tipped the barrel onto its side and lifted her out. Her whole body was swollen. Both her breasts had turned gray, blood and filth from her nose had dried all over her face. Her dress was muddy with excrement. They pulled it off and rubbed her limbs until the lavender began to fade. Washing her put an end to whatever lasciviousness they might have harbored; they couldn't get the stench out of her hair. They discovered old bruises on her belly and thighs. Her hands and feet stayed blue for days.

Before nightfall she regained consciousness. She still couldn't speak, but seemed to understand what they said. When they hovered, making that gesture Christians make, her eyes brightened. She slept peacefully, and was even able to take a little wine. A few days later, when she found the strength to answer their questions, she was at ease with the sailors.

She told them her whole life story, and when she came to the forest part, she did not flinch, but boldly continued. She wept as she related how she had offered herself to the rob-bers, how she virtually flung her nakedness at them. Sob-bing, she reproached herself for not controlling her lust. But she did not stop there; she would tell everything! She went on to describe how she tried to murder her husband, and failed, though not for lack of will; she had long yearned for his death. With that confession she halted. She said nothing about her recent confinement.

The crew listened spellbound. As she spoke and wept, she flushed, claiming she repented, she asked their mercy, seized their hands. The sailors hastily assured her of their goodwill, but extricated themselves and withdrew a little from her renascent beauty. The captain continued to admire her, but from a distance. He saw to it she had food to her taste, and he unpacked some silks, so that she could be richly clothed. If no one bought her, she would make a fine gift. No end of possibilities with such a woman.

Now you know the worst. This is the blood of which I am made. It is not in my nature to hide anything from you. Will you still have me? Or do I repel you? I must make you know me, spare you no illusion; it is the measure of my love. All I have is you and my virtue, and I cannot disentwine them. I do not even have the Soudan; he has me.

But I know you cannot love me just because I have pleaded with you. I must feel your eyes in my eyes, taste your hunger for my mouth. Tumbling headlong, you must feed on my lips.

When the Soudan of Omarie received the gift of a Christian woman, he was so pleased that he let it be known that the merchant captain from "Flanders" was to be allowed to pass safely wherever he chose to do business. The captain congratulated himself on his foresight. He smiled in Hodierna's direction. It was clear that the Soudan was quite taken with her.

"Who is she?" asked my father.

"Sire," the merchant said, "we know nothing about her. She was given to us by the sea." He told him about the barrel. "She was as speechless when we found her as she is at this moment." He still smiled. "Consider the lady's speechlessness an additional gift."

When the captain had departed, the Soudan walked over and knelt beside his gift; he summoned parchment and pen, and wrote out something in Latin. She glanced at him briefly, but said nothing. He wrote another short sentence; he had heard much about Christian women, how they were very free and often quite learned. When she continued silent, he read the page aloud. Then she looked at him inquiringly; so, she couldn't read. But had she understood what he said? He went on asking simple questions, such as "What is your name?" and "Who is your father?" But when he followed these with "Can you love me?," and her expression did not change, he very delicately modulated out of Latin. He said the same things in Arabic, wrote them out and took her hand. Then he guided her hand while she formed the letters.

That was how my mother learned to read and write. Every day he sent her little messages which she was at pains to decipher, for they often required a reply. And the more articulate she grew, the more lovely to him she seemed. He often asked her about her home and her family, but she refused to speak of those things. All that he really knew for some years was that she came of the Franj. But he did not begrudge her her mystery.

Despite all his care, she adjusted to her new life with difficulty. Wandering through the rooms, courts, halls, passageways, swimming through light into shadow as she passed down the tunnels of apartments whose variety of purpose bewildered her, she could not decide if she were more hurt by this endlessness or by the constant presence of partitions. She found herself dreaming of the great smoky vault where everyone at home ate and slept, where the dogs fought and knights brooded and the smell of roasting always hung in the air. Here, she could walk in and out of three doorways and still find herself completely alone. At first, she was very glad that he had taught her to read, for otherwise she wouldn't have known what to do with herself. But when, one morning, she opened her eyes and saw words interlaced all over the ceiling, she wondered if she was finally going mad. She got up, and roamed from room to room, eyeing the traceried walls surreptitiously, hoping to find refuge somewhere. But wherever she ventured the walls bristled with calligraphy, with knife-like shapes cunningly embedded in mesh. She found that she could go nowhere without reading, without meeting blades that left the tangle unsliced and resolved into echoes: *knowledge, work, blessing, crown.* The peculiar thing was that this omnipresence enhanced her awareness of enclosure at the very same time that it made walls dissolve. She would face a wall furious with patterns in which bits of language, like birds netted amid blossoms, loomed with futile authority; she, reading the wings, would feel the surface expand, break up, disappear. Then for a moment she inhabited empty space, drifting on a word; and when she recovered, found the wall, for all its articulation, as sturdy as before. This odd inconstancy made her homesick. In Ponthieu, walls were walls. She yearned for honest masonry, dark, blank and sweeping.

But Hodierna found Omarie's unrelieved richness of ornament oppressive in more ways than one. It was not merely the messages caught in those blinking webs, but the decoration itself that irritated and blinded her. She stared at it for hours, trying to discover where the delirium of plants ended and the background began, but one blent into the other, though just where and how, she couldn't say. Behind all that precise twisting, heaven's sky—or nothingness—pushed forward, making its presence felt, and the vines that sank into it knotted without warning, and sprouted peacocks and gazelles. Everywhere she looked, indoors and out, around the trefoil arches of windows, in the carpets and the very motifs woven into her own clothes, in the dishes she ate from, the handle of her comb, on the lids of boxes that held her jewelry and the bodies of flasks that contained her perfumes, the congestion of swirling tendrils pressed her to acknowledge something new. But when, after some months, she could not escape that boundlessness even by closing her eyes; when she found that she could never, not ever, stop thinking, only one thing helped: her understanding that, had the Soudan's house not been dense and capricious, lawful and unreal, he never would have been able to love her, stranger that she was. And she even dimly grasped that the gaiety of his tenderness, the light depth of his touch, the whimsical astonishments of an amorousness so rich it often frightened her, were the extensions of an inner ornament, the very energy that caused leaves to twine. She did not hide from herself that it was the Soudan's love alone that made her new life better than bearable, that persuaded her before the end of her first year there to turn her back on despair.

It was in the course of this year that he asked her to renounce her god so that he could marry her. She probably thought that her apostasy would be as well accomplished by love as by force; for its inevitability was clear. She leapt at the alternative of sweetness, and told him her true religion was to do her master's pleasure. Once she had consented, she was surprised to find that the ubiquitous riot of threads grew easier to bear. Now, when she gazed into webs, their peculiar shimmerings hardly worried her, and if she could not tell vine from sky—well, she herself was even so. On the day that she stood before the Soudan and cupped her hands to receive the stream of rose water poured from a silver ewer, when she sipped from his cupped hands and he from hers, she knew she had entered the tracery; from that day on, the patterns not only ceased to plague her, she hardly perceived them at all.

Before long she was pregnant. During the day she would lie, listening to the soft babble of water, her palms on her belly, gazing out from the shadows to where the fountain leapt and its basin delicately overflowed. This water was so bright. In Ponthieu it never moved, but hid darkly beneath a green veil. During these hours she often wrote to her husband, and when her term was complete, she gave birth to a boy. Soon she found herself with child again, but so well, he decided that they should make a progress around the royal pavilions. It was not until then that she realized how large his palace really was; it spread over every part of the city, and even beyond it, to where his gardens met the desert as sand meets the sea. They had to travel. Some stages of the progress could be made in a few hours, on foot, while others required days of preparation and fantastical ceremonies. It was during this journeying that I was born. The first thing I saw when they held me up was the garden. At least, so they tell me; I have not been back since, but I am certain to return now that I have you.

I know that much of this history is distasteful to you, Malakin. You say nothing, but I know; how could it be otherwise? And I am about to relate more horrors, you haven't heard the last of those men, whom I can't call godless for, after all, didn't the pilgrimage succeed? Not, of course, as they hoped it would, but Thibault's wife did have children. The Son of Thunder's god must be an ironic one.

Touch me, Malakin! What I have to tell you next fills me with nameless fears. I seem to see you through a grille, your face is broken up by lines. We cannot touch, there is this thicket between us. Sometimes your face vanishes into a whiteness clean as sand; sometimes the thicket sparkles and everything else is darkness. Even though you are hidden from me then, I know you are waiting; but at such times my own body grows uncertain. This is hard to say: the body you want, the only body I have to give, cannot go on loving if it is kept from your sight. From your sight at the very least, but also from your touch. Without these foods, I can survive, but not speak.

After the trip to Rue-Sur-Mer, the Count of Ponthieu returned home and tried to resume the normal tenor of his days. He failed in this signally, but struggled to conceal it. As the years passed, his misery increased, for he grew less and less able to think about anything except his daughter, who was certainly dead. However, he spoke of her to no one, though he would not let her grief-stricken husband or her evocative brother out of sight. Sometimes the Count stumbled to the place where his son slept, and fell incontinently into bed beside him.

Thibault realized that his only hope lay in another marriage, but he didn't dare bring the subject up; young Ponthieu ached for the rituals of manhood, but knew his father would try to make time stand still. In the end, Ponthieu had to admit to himself that he had sinned. He consulted with a wealthy cleric and was advised to expunge his crime beneath the walls of Jerusalem. So the Count had a large cross sewn upon his mantle, which instantly decided Thibault, and young Ponthieu, without asking his father's permission, also quickly pledged himself. The Count's feeble rage showed how much remorse had changed him.

"Now the land is without a lord!" he cried; but the young man stood firm. Ponthieu had to put the land in ward. Soon after that the three set out, to erase Hodierna's abandonment by forsaking a whole country.

They arrived safely in the land the Franj call *holy*, and performed a variety of pilgrimages. But the Count still had his bad dreams, so he committed himself and his company to service with the Templars. For a year they desecrated whatever they could find, not even distinguishing between the

rare and the commonplace; they celebrated at Edessa when
Baldwin was crowned. This sufficed, and they prepared to
head home.

You must wonder how I know all this.

My mother gathered these bits and pieces—I will tell you
how—and confided them, over the years, to our nurse. I never
suspected she had a confidante until the thread began to un-
wind. Then I demanded to know where Abba had heard such
hideous rumors, even though I believed them at once. She
gave me so tender an account of my mother that I have tried,
ever since, to find out more. I have talked to sailors and
handmaidens; I have even spoken to my father. But all he
will say is that I am nothing like her. My frankness with you
would seem to confirm that; now you know more about her
past than the Soudan himself.

No one else, Malakin, has ever heard this whole story.
Only now, for your eyes, the light of my world, do I braid the
sailors' ropes with gold chains and plait in Abba's wordy
patience and finally, my father's eloquent, long silence. I have
fingered every hemp fiber, every cold link, nothing has es-
caped me; I have clutched the lines and followed them out
into blindness. I have demanded more filament when those
lines gave out, cord, twine, no matter how cheap, and have
thought myself happy, groping nowhere, everywhere. I know
better now how large is the space in which I fumble. There
are threads of light which cross it, the filigree of my prison.
I console myself with this certain knowledge: it is the cap-
tive who has won you. You have been dazzled by the shadow
of bars.

I must go on.

The three men sailed from Acre. How unlucky that crew!
Before they even attained the open sea, they were caught in
a storm. The sailors tied themselves to each other but, even

so, some were swept overboard. Thibault, the Count, and the Count's son lashed themselves together; if one drowned, all would drown. It would take more than a storm to pry them apart. They had woven for themselves—and not with rope—a perfect solitude. Only terror could breach it; terror of death makes even the most foreign of lands acceptable.

So when each man on board had seen death, land appeared behind the hillocky waves. It wasn't the land they were trying to reach; it was Omarie, the frightened captain shouted above the ruthless rain—a paynim country.

"What shall we do?" He staggered closer to the three Franj. "If we seek land, we'll be taken."

"We couldn't die more horribly," Ponthieu wailed, "Do what you can."

So they drove with the wind along the coast. Soon our galleys had surrounded them. Once ashore, they were led, not gently, before the Soudan, who divided them up, so they could do the less mischief, consigning some of the captives to one prison and some to another; but when he came to the three Templars, who were still linked with rope, he deemed that all in this trio of murderous infidels must be equally esteemed. So they were cast into an empty cell, where some days later young Ponthieu began to shiver. Soon he grew feverish and started to refuse water. This unnerved his father so completely that the Count lay down and turned his face to the wall. Thus when, on the Soudan's birthday, a court official made the rounds of the prisons to choose a Christian for the celebratory shooting-match, his eyes fell upon the melancholy Count. The official was under orders to select the prisoner nearest death, and young Ponthieu was quaking so hard, he looked fairly lively.

Hodierna was at her husband's side when the Christian was brought into the hall and thrown at his feet. For the high court she had dressed with particular care and magnificence. Her garments were so heavy she couldn't walk without help; she was encrusted with coral and pearls. Her fingertips and palms were stained with henna; she had kohled her eyebrows into one sinuous line. Her hair was coiled in a tall cone, bound with silver ribbons, and scented with musk.

It took a moment for the appearance of the hapless Christian to move her: not for some years had she seen anything so unattractive. The Soudan, looking askance at the wasted figure, pronounced "Let the archers do with him what they will." Then the ragged beard that still clutched a face lifted, and stirred my mother's unpremeditating heart. She stepped forward and laid a hand on the Soudan's sleeve.

"Husband, let me speak to him before he dies. I think he is one of my people."

The wretch was taken aside. When she addressed him, he stared at the floor. She studied his beastliness, the head unwashed, ravaged. In the language of the Franj, she asked him what his country was. He showed no surprise at her accents.

"Lady," he replied in a dead voice, "I came out of France— a long time ago, I think."

"And your name? Your family?"

He hesitated, nodding slightly: "I cannot remember my family. But it seems to me I once was the Count of Ponthieu. Yes, Ponthieu, a very pleasant seat."

My mother did not react; only the greatest shocks can be met so dishonestly. From then on she behaved as she would never have guessed she could. She conversed a little more, and calmly rejoined the Soudan.

"Husband," she said, "Let me have this poor fellow. He will amuse us. He knows how to play chess."

"He is yours," the Soudan smiled tenderly. "The archers

will use someone else. Let another captive be brought from the prisons."

When the second captive, a mere boy, was hustled in by the guards, the Soudan watched his wife out of the corner of his eye. Clearly, she was interested; her posture softened, she leaned slightly forward. Another Franj; her reaction was natural. He had never required her to forget; as long as he could touch her, she could have all the memories she wished.

The young man fell to his knees, trembling uncontrollably. He probably couldn't have remained upright; they would have to strap him up if he was to be any sort of target, although there wasn't much to shoot, he was that thin. But before the Soudan could approve the choice and wave him away, Hodierna was near, asking permission to speak with the prisoner. He looked at her inquiringly, but immediately granted it. Her curious compassion did not altogether displease him.

This time she did not approach the captive, but asked her questions from the Soudan's side. This was better; he didn't like her near filthiness, illness. The boy's answers seemed to satisfy her. "Husband," she said, turning with that countenance of utter sweetness, "this is the son of the man whose life you have just spared. Spare him too, so the father will be the more keen to amuse us; if the son survives, he can augment our sports."

She had figured it out so well; she was so eager to set things before him; it always pleased him no end, why, he couldn't say. He squeezed her hand.

"Wife, I am content. This one also is yours."

But no sooner had she bowed deep to him than the archers stepped forward. They were obviously annoyed; soon the light would grow hazy. He interrupted their complaints to send for yet another Christian, then turned brusquely to different matters. In whatever had to do with Hodierna, he refused to feel regret.

Thibault, meanwhile, languished in his cell. Now that he was alone there, and his entire family dead, he felt pervaded by an enormous tranquility. Before very long he would join them, or if not soon, still, soon enough. He even hoped he would see his dead wife. But when, a few hours later, he entered the Soudan's hall and beheld all that splendor, he suffered. There was more hair on his body than clothing. And he hadn't walked in so long, not more than four paces at a time, his cell's length, he did it badly. He was glad that all these people were strangers.

Finally the guards flanking him halted; then he was on his knees, looking up at such a dazzling sea in which two islands— no, faces—drifted, perfect, bemused. They exchanged some strange syllables and then the paler one demanded:

"You, do you also come from Ponthieu in the land men call France?"

So eager was he to please the bright wonderer, he forgot to be surprised that he could understand her. "I do, Lady. I was the old man's knight, and had his daughter to wife."

She turned again to her lord. They conferred. Then suddenly she was kneeling, kissing her lord's hands; Thibault was hauled to his feet.

The Soudan told himself, when the fourth Christian was finally approved and carried off by the archers, that if she had asked for this one's life too, he would have granted it; that she could have begged mercy for a hundred captives, one after another, and he would have given them all, never counting the cost. That was the way he loved her. He had been, even, a little surprised that she craved no conversation with the fourth man, that she let him go to his death so easily.

Later, during a pause in the day's festivities, Hodierna visited the three men in their quarters. When she entered, they struggled to get up; she pushed them down again, and then, unwilling to divulge the extent of her French, performed a series of gestures which clearly conveyed friendship. But the Count was not fooled.

"They are going to kill us, but when?" he said sharply. "Lady, if you know, tell us."

"I know. It won't be today."

"So much the worse," Ponthieu virtually shouted. "I'm so hungry, my soul is ready to go."

"Well, you must eat."

She went out and returned with a man bearing a tray of food. She had a small amount served to each of them, and a little mint tea. They wolfed it down, though young Ponthieu spilled much of his in his lap.

"I'm hungrier now than I was before I ate," Thibault moaned.

"More later," she said. "If you eat too much, you'll die. Now, baths, and then we'll see to your clothes."

It was a week before she would allow them to sate themselves, but by then the Count had stopped dreaming and young Ponthieu was not shaking so hard. They played checkers and chess; the Soudan came to watch. He hadn't realized the Franj were such children; he rather liked them. They were simple, and obviously very glad to be alive. Hodierna spoke little and kept herself veiled.

Between these pleasant hours the Soudan had other matters to brood upon. A neighboring sultan had broken the peace. The Soudan had to summon his vassals and put his troops in order. He was so much occupied he hardly noticed how Hodierna stopped reading. Her little written messages dwindled and then ceased. Perhaps he wondered about this, but what he had no way of knowing was that she had begun to think in her original language. She did not spend much time with the three men, but wandered about the palace in an emptiness charged with her husband's adoration. She began to notice, once more, the words tangled in webs but now she didn't concern herself with what they meant. Instead she saw knots, very cunningly spun. She studied them, as though looking would make them unravel, and tried to let the love of the Soudan pervade her.

During these days, when he had so little time for her, she felt she understood him as never before. It was as if his nature imbued her; she stared at words all day, watching how their enfolded strands formed their shapes. In these hours her own desire to fashion knots was aroused, and she began to test her ability. Imitating the Soudan, she saw that what he had taught her was a gift even greater than children.

Instead of letters, however, she interlaced and entwined deeds. Her knots formed, not a verse, but a plot.

When the design was complete, she visited the Franj. Sitting near them, she raised her hand for silence.

"You have told us a little about yourselves, and have sometimes diverted us with tales of your exploits. I, however, am still undecided as to whether you are men in the most estimable sense. You," she turned to the Count, "were once lord of your country, father of a fine son who now shares your exile. You married your daughter to this man. I am a Saracen little acquainted with the destinies of Christians, but I know how to read the night's face. The stars make it plain you will die if you now conceal the truth. You must tell me: what became of your daughter?"

"Lady," the Count quickly answered, "she must be dead."

"And how dead, so young?" She watched him closely.

"She died, Lady—I will tell you how she died! She died because, for once in this world, justice was served."

"Justice?"

"Yes," Ponthieu repeated. "Justice."

Hodierna had to regard him carefully. "Tell me about this justice."

The Count's story went like this. Although he displayed little art in the telling, I will be as faithful to his words as I can:

"My daughter's unhappiness began with her marriage. She wanted to wed this knight you see. I have to admit, I was not against it. But the marriage was a bad one; she never conceived. They both prayed, even I prayed, but nothing came of it. Finally Thibault took it into his head to make a pilgrimage to the shrine of James, in Galicia. Not only that, he would cart his barren wife along, displaying her emptiness to half Europe. To be completely frank, it was she who wanted to go; he could not even be her husband in a matter that small. He should have let me deal with her, if he couldn't say no, but all I was allowed to do was to outfit their party. Christ knows if he would be alive today if I hadn't done that!

"Anyway, their expedition proceeded smoothly enough until one morning they stupidly fell far behind their entourage. It was Thibault's fault; men who are soft are easily kept in bed. He had gotten caught between my daughters's legs and that made him forget everything. A grown man knows better than to enter a forest alone; but that day, Thibault led her straight into one, just the two of them, don't ask me to explain it. However, they weren't quite alone; a troupe of bandits lay in wait, and attacked them before and behind. Thibault actually finished off three before the rest got him naked; but then, what could he do? They had killed his palfrey, bound his ankles and wrists. They kept flinging him about, making sure his wife watched. Then, just before they tossed him into a thorn bush, they stripped my daughter.

"When Thibault lay screaming, the bandits gave her their undivided attention; they liked her looks—who didn't? Soon they were quarreling over her. Finally, they decided she must service them all. She had been weeping through this whole business, one of the ways women soften our hearts; certainly theirs were softer than before they took her clothes off. She didn't struggle; they all had her, and she never stopped crying, which inspired most of them to come back more than once. Even after they rode off, Thibault could hear her sobs. But his sorrows were just beginning.

"He calls out to his wife. He wants her to untie his hands so he can start to untangle himself from that hellish bush. She takes long enough to find him, and never answers his cries but keeps wandering back and forth through the bracken, loudly snuffling. She is looking for a weapon. At first all she finds is dead men. But she doesn't give up, and finally she locates a sword. Then she sets after her husband; now that she grapples a hilt, she can't get to him fast enough. Screaming 'You are free!,' she rushes the bush, blade high. Thibault reacts quickly. Sometimes God really does show His Hand. He rolls so hard he falls out of the bush, and her blow, aimed at his chest, wounds him slightly, but cuts through his bonds. He unties his ankles, and is on his feet shouting, 'The day has not yet come for you to wear the sword!'"

My mother interrupted the Count. Her eyes were very bright; she was clearly moved.

"You have told this well; it must have happened just so, for it is plain why she needed to kill him."

At this Thibault stared, demanding "Why?"

"Because she felt so ashamed!" For a moment their eyes

met, then the knight studied his lap. He hoped he could control his tears until the Soudan's wife left. But then, suddenly, he didn't care.

"It wasn't her fault! I never blamed her, I never loved her the less! What could she have done? May I never see France again if I ever blamed her!" He started to weep.

"Then she must have imagined your reproach. But if she did," Hodierna faced the Count, "why did she deserve to die?"

"We don't know if she died," Ponthieu replied desperately; "she may well be alive. What we do know—what I know!—is how much I have suffered for what we did to her—how much I still suffer, after all these years."

"So," said Hodierna, "you would be pleased if you found out she lived?"

"I'd rather know that than be home again," the Count said mournfully, "I'd rather hear she lived than be rich!"

Thibault pounced, "God could not find any other wish in my heart. I'd rather have such news than be king!"

Young Ponthieu joined in: "What a blessing it would be to see her!"

Hodierna could not help herself; her eyes were brimming. Perhaps the three men spoke so eagerly because they could see how much their tone pleased her. Without realizing she did so, she thanked her childhood god. Life with the Soudan had enhanced words; the past was disappearing.

"Remember the stars, and be sure that what you say is true!" she admonished.

"It is true!" the men cried.

Her lip quivered as she beatifically smiled. "Here I am!" she exclaimed, and fell upon the Count's neck.

Thibault was not convinced it was she until he held her. Up to that moment he didn't believe it. Even aside from all her Saracen trappings, she looked wrong. She was plumper, her motions all serene. He remembered a slender, slightly nervous wife. When he released her, she must have read this in his gaze, for she was answering his thoughts almost before he knew them.

"If I hadn't given up Christ, the Soudan would have killed me," she said, clutching his shirt. "It was marriage or death." She frowned at them. "He is dangerous. If you want to live, hide your feelings, and never show you know me!

"Now, Thibault," she turned back to him. He had never seen eyes so liquid, like an animal's, and deep. "Thibault, you were brave in the old days, and are still so, I know it!" He shivered. "In a few days the Soudan goes to war. He will take you. Show all your courage, and be sure to please him." She kissed them. Even the smell of her mouth had changed. When she was gone, none of the three men spoke.

The Soudan, on the other hand, was seized with the desire to talk as soon as his wife entered the room. These war plans too much occupied him; it was days since he had lingered with her. Rolling up the map, he put his papers aside, and held out his arms. What followed their embrace took him by surprise.

"Husband," she said, not letting him go, "one of my captives wants to go to war with you."

"The boy? All boys want to go to war."

"No, it is the man Thibault. You should take him."

"Ah, Hodierna, having Christians here is one thing, having them on battlefields quite another. No, no," he shook his head, "here they are watched, and they amuse you. I must take only men I can trust."

"In himself he is doubtless not trustworthy, but as long as I hold the other two, I should think he would behave. Just tell him his kin are hostages."

The Soudan considered; it wasn't a stupid idea. A few infidel methods might give his army an advantage.

"I will think about it," he replied, placing a finger on her lips. "Now go, I will come to you later."

When, that evening, he told her he had ordered a horse and harness for Thibault, as well as a warrior's regalia, she smiled in so satisfied a manner, he couldn't help smiling too.

But the Soudan was not the only one who had been mulling over Hodierna's ideas; young Ponthieu had also been thinking. The life the three of them were leading was not a man's life. He made up his mind; he didn't really care what he fought for as long as he could fight. When his sister arrived and told Thibault of her arrangements, the young man prostrated himself, tugging her hem.

"Please, Hodierna, make the Soudan take me, too!"

"I can't do that," she said, not looking down. "He would guess everything. Put it out of your mind."

So Thibault went off to war with the Soudan. They were gone for a month. One morning a white blur fluttered over her balcony. When she removed the note wrapped around the pink leg, she understood that he wanted her to be the first to know: within the week they would be back, herding a thousand captives. She could reprieve from death and prison as many as she wished. She attached a reply and cast the bird back into the air.

She made sure she was playing with the children when he arrived. She let him find her, and flew into his arms. He made her recite her news first, he asked her a great many questions. He seemed very little interested in his own victory. At length, late that night, after love, he dilated. The topic he chose slightly chilled her.

"Your advice won the war for me. You are always my best advisor. I couldn't have done a wiser thing than to take along your captive.

"How did I live before you came? I can hardly remember. It's a good thing I don't have to know!"

She listened while he told her about Thibault's crucial exploits, how at more than one juncture he turned the tide. She found herself musing; in the days of her marriage to him, Thibault had seemed the conscientious, rather than the inspired, knight. Had he changed? What had made him change, and so much for the better? But her present husband broke in upon her reverie.

"I have decided something, Hodierna; tell me what you think. I want to reward this Christian. If he will renounce his faith, I will free him and make him noble. I will grant him broad lands and arrange a marriage, to an heiress, young and, of course, beautiful. Someone like you," he chucked her under the chin, so she had to look up at him. "But no, there is no one like you."

She smiled, nestling closer, staring at his chest.

"I renounced my faith because I loved you; with a man it is different. A man doesn't need to give up everything. If Thibault is what you think him, he won't give up his faith."

She forced herself to say nothing else.

On the following day Thibault went to the baths. The Soudan had extended this privilege to him, so he was determined at least to seem to enjoy bathing.

He entered a large room in which the air was suddenly not quite dry, and where an attendant helped him to undress. When he was naked, he was led through a door, into a room of obscure dimensions, filled with mist. Except for the iridescent tiles underfoot, he could make out nothing.

He ventured into the cloud, cautiously at first; an elegant bench loomed up just before he bumped into it. Circling it, he came to another, this one by a peach-colored wall. He didn't understand the point of decorating such walls; the Soudan was in some matters quite frivolous. He wondered

yet again how Hodierna had conceived by a fellow who was
like a woman in so many ways. He wandered on a bit, keep-
ing the wall on his left; his skin was growing moist; the sound
of water was getting louder. At length a boss protruded;
Thibault put his hand under it. The jet splashed and reared
upward as steam. He wandered on, found another door; the
next room looked similar, but felt hotter. He decided to sit
for a while, to prepare himself.

His thoughts drifted. She had been remarkably lucky. He
could not bring himself to unwish what had come to her. It
was not just for himself—though he had been lucky, too—
but there must have been satisfactions that, in part, recom-
pensed her. He could not help, though, misdoubting the
Soudan's affection for himself, which had so grown of late
that everyone saw it. Thibault liked him, it was impossible
not to, but he had been careful not to let down his guard. He
could be a little piece of Europe for as long as the Soudan
wished.

As he made his way, slowly, through the next several
rooms, each one hotter, wetter, lonelier than the last, Thibault
fought off sadness by weighing up his gains and losses; he
really hadn't done badly. And he had gotten out from under
the Count's thumb.

At last, sweating, he ducked through a door that gave onto
a vast room. The mist, less dense here, bore a tang of
patchouli. Before he could take in anything else, managing
hands had disposed him on soft cushions, and pulled him
straight; he stared into the lapis lazuli dome. As the fingers
gently kneaded, he studied the glittering signs: this was the
sky Hodierna had learned to read. There were the Scales; as
soon as that shred of vapor passed, he would be able to see
them clearly: if the Soudan's favor continued, he would soon
be very rich. And there was the Lion: he would have his own

palace. There was the Bull: he would have women. He could certainly have done worse; to be so honored a slave was better than some freedoms he knew of.

As the hands shifted rhythm, scraping the surfaces of his body with small rough stones, Thibault sloughed the last of his old hopes. He barely felt them go. He rose and made his way back, very well disposed towards his master indeed. His new skin was sprayed with rose water and he was given sherbet to drink. His clothes were warmed and aloe-scented when he put them on.

He had no sooner rejoined the Count and young Ponthieu when Hodierna entered and asked the three men to accompany her while she strolled. In the courtyard, where the babble of water sheltered speech, she came straight to the point.

"We will get home yet," she said in such a way that from a distance she seemed to be asking to be entertained. "Do not forget that we are watched. The Soudan is exhausted, sees trouble everywhere. I have reason to think he is suspicious of you, Thibault. For the next few days be particularly careful, and above all, never look surprised!" She took her leave of them, and sought out her husband.

When she appeared, he put down his pen. His smile faded quickly when he saw how she faltered.

"Hodierna! What is wrong?" he cried, at her side instantly.

"The same thing as before." She smiled weakly. "I didn't want to tell you until I was sure, but I thought I knew even before you went away."

"You must sit," he said decisively, and lifted her up, carried her across the room and set her down gently upon his own cushion. He arranged some more pillows so that she could lean back, and kneeled beside her. "Another bloom! This is wonderful, but it grieves me that you are unwell." He took her hand. "Do you have pain?"

"No, no pain, but I feel dizzy and I can't seem to taste anything."

He kissed the tips of her fingers. "Tell me what I can do! What would help? It will be done immediately."

Hodierna shut her eyes. She sighed, frowned, then gave a little sob. Tears were glistening from beneath her closed lids. "I'm going to die this time. Girls from Ponthieu always do."

"No!"

"I keep thinking that if I could just breathe some cooler air, some sea air, something moist, it might help."

"But of course! Where will you go?"

"Oh, anywhere, it doesn't matter. But it is so hot and dusty here."

"You will leave tomorrow. I cannot go with you, though. It is this peace; I must manage it. But you must take with you whomever you need."

"Are you sure you can't come?"

"Quite sure."

"I will take my son then, because whenever I look at him I see you. Since I cannot have you," she pouted.

"Not this time. And who else?"

"My old and young Franj, I think, to keep my spirits lively. The boy's nurse. And my women. But are you sure you can't come?"

"Do you think I would let you go alone if I could? I am going to see that your ship is fully equipped. And I want you to do one thing for me."

"What is that?"

"Take Thibault. Then I will know you are safe, and won't worry half so much."

"If you wish."

"Yes, I do." He embraced her.

The Soudan fitted out Hodierna's ship with every con-

ceivable necessity and luxury. Various foods and wines, in-
cluding animals for slaughtering should she crave some par-
ticular delicacy, brilliant carpets and pillows, dazzling cur-
tains and tents, as well as anything else that she could name
or he could think of: chess-pieces of rock-crystal, musical
instruments, backgammon, crates of pigeons, books, paper,
pens, ink—all were loaded aboard with the firewood and bra-
ziers, the drinking glasses from Egypt, the bronze ewers
shaped like griffins and tigers. There were toys for the child,
hand-mirrors for the women, painted dishes and a small
golden palm tree. At last the sails were set, he saw her on
board. He had already taken his tender leave of her, but he
could still kiss his son. He held the boy in one arm. The
child spoke in his ear.

"I don't want to go."

The Soudan smiled. "Everyday you must write to me. You
tie the letter to a pigeon's leg—do you remember how I
showed you?"

"Yes."

"I will expect them. If they don't come, I will be sad. Your
mother will help you to tie them on. Do you promise to
write?"

"Yes."

They hugged and kissed each other.

The Soudan stayed on the shore until the boat disappeared.
He waved even after he no longer saw faces.

On the second day at sea Hodierna and her little boy
opened all the doors to the cages of the pigeons. She tried to
enlist his enthusiasm over setting them free but he was doubt-
ful.

"What about my letters?"

"We will send them another way," she told him. Her heart
rose as the sky filled with wings, but late that night, weep-

ing silently, she dropped the books overboard. Then at last she was able to sleep.

On the third day the wind was so brisk, the boat raced along. The captain told her it was driving them towards Brindisi.

"Keep on," she said.

Three days later they cast anchor in that port.

It was Thibault who saw how she froze as they prepared to disembark. This inability to proceed was something he remembered from the old days; for the first time since redis-covering her, he felt a tender spark. Letting his oblivious father- and brother-in-law go on ahead, he hurried to her side.

"I am afraid," she said in French.

"Don't be. We will keep our promises."

"I trust you. I don't know why. Perhaps because the Soudan did."

This stung; so he was ready when she asked, "What are we going to do with him?" She glanced at her son.

"The boy is welcome." He felt munificent as soon as he said it. The Soudan had not entirely misplaced his trust. Thibault watched her eyes fill; he summoned the boy. The three of them disembarked together.

On the quay they joined old and young Ponthieu. Then Hodierna turned and addressed the captain and sailors.

"Good-bye, captain. You may now sail back to Omarie. When you see the Soudan, give him this message: I have stolen from him my body and that of his son. I did this to deliver my father, my husband and my brother from the in-tolerable pains of captivity. Thibault has promised me to love the child. If it will comfort him, tell the Soudan that."

The Count of Ponthieu was very glad to be once again in

a place where he could make claims on the basis of his importance. As a returning Templar he stirred up plenty of hospitality in Brindisi, and easily arranged credit so they could fit themselves out for travel. Soon he was riding at the head of the little company toward the great city where the Christian Imam resides. He was confident that the Imam himself would receive them, and as it turned out, he was not mistaken.

It was a peculiar audience. They all fell on their knees except for the child, who could not be persuaded to do so. Nor would he kiss the Imam's ring, or his foot, or even his knee. The Count was beginning to grow very nervous.

"He is a king's son," he tried to explain, while glaring at his daughter. It was just like her to have such a son. And what could you expect, anyway, from such dusky offspring? Hodierna whispered in the child's ear.

"You are being discourteous. A true lord is never rude, especially not to a lord as great as himself."

The child considered, then stepped forward, grasped the throne's arm, pulled himself up and kissed the holy man on the shoulder. They all had to accept it as enough.

This done, the adults confessed their secrets and received the Imam's comfort and forgiveness. Thibault and Hodierna were reconfirmed in marriage. Then the holy man sprinkled the boy with water from a little basin.

"What name will you give him?" Everyone turned to Hodierna.

She bestowed upon her father a smile that almost blinded him. "Let him be called William, after you."

My mother's ship returned, and from that day I never saw the Soudan. For a long time I knew he lived, somewhere in the palace, invisible, and sometimes, hearing footsteps I hoped were his, I would hurry closer and kneel; but for many years I did not see his face.

It seems strange to me now that I didn't despair, or was able to recover from the despair I felt. I kept on hoping he would appear and love me again; indeed, nothing else seemed to matter.

So I did what I knew he did, since this was the only closeness he allowed: I practiced various scripts till their forms seemed engraved inside my hands; I read and memorized verses; I listened to voices; I searched, arranged, constructed. Unlike my mother, who never set pen to paper except to reply to his messages, but had other ways of being desirable, I wrote to touch the Soudan's heart, though, it is true, he knew nothing of it. I respected his repugnance while practicing nearness. The strange thing was that I stopped thinking about him, though when I began to write, his image hovered always before me. But the more lines I drew and the more whiteness I darkened, the less I yearned toward his brooding presence. I started to live for the moment, just as Hodierna had, and in time I grew as innocent as she.

I would not expect anyone except you, Malakin, to believe what I am going to say next: I did not busy myself thus to gain my father's approval. Though I cared to touch him, whether I pleased him—I didn't think about that. But even the desire to touch would not have made me so assiduous. I spun countless black shreds of web, that led me to unexpected facts and histories, because by doing so I escaped my immurement. It was during these years, the era of my solitude, that I came to be called *The Fair Captive.* If I have another name, I no longer remember it.

It is peculiar, but I had almost forgotten my father when, one day, he suddenly stood before me. Though I had no memory of his face, I knew at once it was he. And I knew also that I did not displease him. But I was not certain that he had begun to love me again until the day you asked for my hand. I know you would not love me unless the Soudan did; only by achieving his love did I find you.

Here, hold my hand. I want your fingers in mine as I run them along the twists of this mesh. Here are the sailors' ropes; they weave back across the sea to France. They disappear underwater, grow seaweed, wind lazily among boulders, vanish into nets of fishermen and dry on the sand. These lines are not hard to follow, you close your eyes and grip, putting one hand over the other. We are following my brother's fate: now we have arrived in Ponthieu. It is not long after the family's return. Young Ponthieu has finally succeeded in becoming a knight. Two months pass; he is killed in a tournament. At the funeral Hodierna realizes she is pregnant. Thibault is in love with her; he doesn't even remember the wife of long ago. The queenly woman she has become flatters his new-found manliness. So does her giving birth to a boy, and, in the following year, to another. Both are pale and blonde. She has become quite generous to the poor. Thibault, influenced by her, performs many good works.

With the future insured, the Count now feels easier in his mind. He holds high court, inviting all the famous families. One Raoul of Preaux, a wealthy man of not negligible lineage, attends. Ponthieu enquires after his daughter. The Count finds this possible alliance particularly attractive, as the girl is still too young to leave home. To his child, whom he has never seen, my brother soon finds himself married. He has to go live at Preaux. Now his grandfather is very proud of him. In years to come Ponthieu often refers to his grandson, the Lord of Preaux. In time William becomes the head of that family.

But when the Count dies, Hodierna's younger sons inherit his property; and when their uncle, the Count of St. Pol dies, they inherit that, too. Yet many still consider William the worthier gentleman.

That is as far in the mesh of poor rope as my heart takes me.

Let us now venture along more tempting regions of web. Allow your hands to remain inside mine; feel this smoothness, this coldness, this interlocking of small circlets. If we opened our eyes, we would see these are pleasing chains.

As the links grow smaller, and the golden chain turns into thread, it dives and rebounds; the only way is to hold on. We are approaching a confluence so intricate and vast, the thread we grip seems aimed into its own burial; but stay with me; we are entering the thicket.

Here, this dark luscious knot is where we are married, and this sweet curl wreathing round it is the Soudan's rejoicing.

This sinuous meander is the journey home to Baudas, and this flurry of loops your welcome and homecoming. Then this interlacing like a rose, too wonderful to disturb, is the children we have, and at the center of it, there is our daughter: touch lightly! She gets married, and in her turn conceives a child. That delicate tangle is the child's name: Saladin.

Do you imagine, Malakin, that for every William, Lord of Preaux, and odd font of respectable descendants, there is always somewhere, far away, a sultan, perhaps unborn, who promises to reclaim the holy places? Just as you and I have pursued the branching web far beyond today, so will our grandson Saladin go too far. You can tell he is the Soudan's scion——he is always true to his word, so true that he oversteps every other limit. He bestows wealth even on those he fights, it is a constant shower from his hands, an unending rain of these small little golden circlets. And he eschews massacre and plunder as easily as you and I do; he knows it is another body that must be marked and claimed.

Now, lift your hands from the links, and interlace your fingers with mine. So woven, why need I say more?

*

Wendy Walker was born in New York City in 1951 and grew up on the Upper West Side of Manhattan. After graduating from the Dalton School, she went on to Harvard, where she majored in art history. For one year she was the poetry editor of the renowned Harvard Advocate.

In the years following she studied art and theater, and began writing fiction. Among her books are a collection of short stories The Sea-Rabbit, or, The Artist of Life *(1988) and a novel* The Secret Service *(1992), both published in the Sun & Moon Classics series.* Stories Out of Omarie *will by published by Sun & Moon Press in early 1995.*

Fanny Howe

"10:18" from *O'Clock*

Into the forest I went walking—to get lost.

I saw faces in the knots
of trees, it was insane, and hands
in branches, and everywhere names.

Throughout the elms
small birds shivered and sang
in rhyme.

I wanted to be air, or wind—to be at ease
in outer space. But in the world
this was the case:

HUMAN was GOD'S secret name.

*

Born in Buffalo, New York, Fanny Howe grew up in Boston. Her mother, Mary Manning, was a playwright and actress with the Abbey Theater of Dublin, and in Cambridge was the founder of the Poets' Theater. Her father, Mark De Wolfe Howe, was Professor of Law at Harvard University and a civil rights activist. Her sisters are artist Helen Howe and noted poet, Susan Howe.

At an early age, *Howe turned to writing, receiving national acclaim for her stories in* Forty Whacks, *for her poetry in* Eggs, *and for two books of fiction,* First Marriage *and* Brontë Wilde, *both of which will be republished, in revised versions, by Sun & Moon Classics as part of Howe's trilogy* Radical Love. *Among Howe's many other works of fiction and poetry are* Holy Smoke *(1984),* In the Middle of Nowhere *(1987),* Lives of a Spirit *(published by Sun & Moon Press in 1987),* The Vineyard *(1988),* The Deep North *(Sun & Moon Classics, 1988)* Famous Questions *(1989, to be part* III *of Radical Love), and* Saving History *(Sun & Moon Classics, 1992). The selection here is from a forthcoming book of poetry,* O'Clock.

Howe is Professor of Writing and American Literature at the University of California, San Diego, and is the mother of three children.

Friederike Mayröcker

"in the ocean of air"
"indications"
AND
"reproduction of a palm"
from *With Each Cloudy Peak*

Translated from German by Rosmarie Waldrop

in the ocean of air

in the ocean of air, he said.

sometimes, he said, I misplace words as if they were
things.

in the ocean of air, we said.

tinny old pianner, he said.

and missed occasions, we said.

here and there, it's true, she met people I knew, he said,
but couldn't hold on to them.

the swallows are back, he said and looked out the
window.

we couldn't see any, it was only April.

I had often suggested she should write everything
down, feelings thoughts everything that came into her
head.

but she always said they wouldn't be worth writing down.

she was so musical in her youth, he said.

played the piano with great abandon, he said.

a message, we said.

she was obsessed by the strangest notions.

for instance, that at her death everything she had ever thought and felt about people close to her could be read by them like fiery writing on a wall.

I feel sorry, he said, when I think of her.

as in Vienna, he said, as in my childhood.

as in my childhood, he said, I always try to fight it.

this giving somebody a spark of hope, he said, and then stomping it out.

the landing, he said, she had a lot of trouble getting it over the landing.

the tinny old pianner, he said.

in the end they took it apart and stored it.

in a dark and damp storage place packed with instruments of all kinds.

trees bleeding, he said.

the swallows are back, he said.

tinny old pianner, he said, nice tinny pianner.

but equanimity, he said, in a person.

the ruined words, lost words, he said, words misplaced.

in the fallows, we said, missing.

maybe I'm a chaotic pedant, he said.

I think I've always acted under duress, he said.

even as a child, he said, my mark of Cain was fear of ridicule.

in the fallows, we said, nickering.

back then all I had to do was think of a word like fever chart and I ran a fever and had to be put to bed.

headblock, he said, in the ocean of air.

pant cuffs cuff-to-death, as in my childhood, he said.
as in my childhood, he said, when I desperately tried to
ingest language.

dying, he said, for the splendor of words, cries, ques-
tions, tangled structures, coupling cupolas above all,
business streets, markets, greenhouses, train stations.

my grounds of grace, he said.

radiant words, he said, cries calls questions tangled
structures.

dying for them, he said.

when I had chewed them long enough I spit them out of
my mouth, cut them to pieces and started all over.

scribbled them down one to a sheet, tacked them on
furniture, covered them with kisses.

dying, he said, poetic transport.

transport of trees, we said.

carrying both inscriptions, he said.

at last the swallows are back, he said, the trees bleeding.

black montenegrin hand.

he looked out at the swallows we couldn't see.

indications

the power plant glittering, he said, quite contrary to.

we walked through an arbor, the bushes trimmed.

a few old rosehips among the branches, overhanging
the garden edge.

it was the shape of Africa, he said, the birthmark on her
forehead.

had faded with the years.

we continued on our way, he said, tottering and
uncertain.

we walked through the arbor, the convent bell began to
ring.

she wanted to appear modest, he said.

she had a definite downward turn in almost all respects,
he said.

she may be remembered now, he said.

shrub leaf clover a certain reversal, he said, a figure of art.

in leaden shoes up endless stairs, he said, had to take my
overcoat off while climbing, stuffed it into a big bag.

she may be remembered now, he said.

we remember having remembered.

the convent bell began to ring.

shrub leaf clover, he said, you who stop here.

how things move into position against us, he said.

even those we've mostly done well by.

had had the shape of Africa and faded with the years.

the creature exposed, he said.

free yourself, come free, he said, of this entanglement.

how, he said, the days unwind.

entry way, power plant.

he felt he could never have put out this fire, he said, a
fiery mark fading on her forehead.

hissed through the teeth, always the same swearword,
and the stars, he said, already drumming on his skull.

she was taken aback, he said, when a strange woman in
the subway asked her if she had seen the giant rabbit
leaping out of the tunnel.

fossilization, he said, gradual.

we went through the arbor when the convent bell
began to ring.

we continued on our way, tottering and uncertain.

reproduction of a palm

as if my ribcage had been, he said, with a hard hefty beak.
as if I'd, he said, till I was sore and bloody.
as if the giant clusters, he said.
as if the green tops.
as if the footprints in the sand in the dust.
as if the swallows, diving on the ruts of the trail before
rain, he said.
reproduction of childhood sequences, he said.
body sprouting honeydew, he said, chapped, scabby,
frayed rags hanging in fringes, a shoulderbag like a
mailman's, a child, those years, the fresh air fund, crying,
strap across my chest.
signaling agreement, he said, to be sure, finally rotting.
hands in graves fallen from former form.
scattered like ashes, our plane aimed at the Atlantic
coast, he said, going down, then swerved seaward.
at that I hammered my fists against the panes of the
machine.
for the first time in my life, he said, approached a group
of waving palmtrees.
was seized, he said, by silent rage. despondently
hacking at word shards, now I just had to go for the panes
with my fists, he said, so as not to give up.
now I just had to would always have just had to amid
palmtrees, he said.
speechless, he said, artificial irrigation.
sand-yellow patchwork, he said, we went down on their
tropics, the machine opened for landing, and the wind
palm-fingered and burning hot.
a torrent of tears from my body, he said, from my head.

water pressure, delirium, *conifers like reproductions of conifers.*

it took hold of all of us, he said, all things were changed.

some with camouflaged names, he said, live in bushes as if in small huts.

even receive visitors.

on overgrown paths under tattered flags.

I wanted to grab the palm fronds, a palmtree agony, he said.

the poles on the jetty, gulls perched on them, quivering missiles from the sea, aimed at the joints of my body, he said, in tropical wind.

the feeling, he said, that I couldn't ever put out this fire.

*

Born in 1924 in Vienna, Friederike Mayröcker taught English in secondary schools from 1946 to 1969, after which time she devoted all her time to writing. Her first volume of poetry was published in 1956, and since then she has published several collections, prose texts, children's books, and plays for both radio and stage.

Mayröcker's work can be seen as a moving from "free verse" to the "free poem," with her work growing more experimental after 1960. Her texts are primarily centered upon the notion of simultaneity: "the simultaneity of processes, of inner processes, which one experiences simultaneously, and simultaneously with everyone else imaginable, and with oneself; on different levels, simultaneously."

She has been awarded numerous literary prizes, including the Theodor-Körner Prize in 1963, the Radio Prize of Blind Veterans in 1968, and the Austrian State Prize in 1974.

Among her works are Arie auf Tönernen Füssen *(1972) and* Je Ein Umwölkter Gipfel *(1973), from which these pieces were taken. Sun & Moon Press will soon publish this book in translation.*

Lyn Hejinian

from *Sleeps*

25

The night will change
as I strive to depict
precisely to avoid the light
since to understand what I can't explain
I want to attribute a cause to it
which is to say a change to it

Every passion is an eccentricity
emitting normal detail centrifugally
irregularly to mind again
the neck, the knob, the hub
and ram and rise precisely
to avoid the light

The night though lit is not complete
when it's gone at dawn with details condensed
despite my writing this awake
deliberate and willing to wait
to try each sleep for the light it keeps
which is to say by changing it

28

Dreams, still clinging like light to the
dark, rounding
        The gaps left by things which have already
happened
        Leaving nothing in their place, may have
nothing to do
        But that, one representation right and
another wrong.
        Dreams are like ghosts achieving ghosts'
perennial goal
        Of evoking the sensation of repose. It's
terrible
        To think we write these things for them, to
tell them
        Of our life—that is, our mental life. A
dream
        Of a machine (why? what is being sold there?
how is the product emitted?)—
        It must have been sparked by a noise, the way
the word "spark"
        Emits a brief picture. Is it original?
metaphysical? ordered?
        We seem to sleep to organize and write to do
the same
        Of events which have already happened. And
we've pictured
        Them. A dream of a procession to an execution
site.
        How many strangers circle that room, writing
of nostalgia

And wolves in the mountains. But they find themselves
Thinking of nothing instead, and there's no one to impersonate.
It's logical that prophesies would be emitted through the gaps
Left by previous things, or by the dead (I think of him)
Refusing conversation, absorbed by sleep. A dream
Of two men in seersucker suits bending into the wind
Synopsizes a conversation about tough women who live near the lake.
And after all, the body curled in sleep is a question mark
Set against the circumstances preceding it, and each
Gap is set in answer.

34

One night I have a dream that is so busy it
        precludes all creative ideas
I'm furious at myself

I wish I had remembered to project images from it
        onto a strip of paper
I have gone with a man to get a dachsund, which he
        insists won't get underfoot since he has
        trained it to stay in the woods collecting
        berries

I know this because the film on which my memories
      are recorded is in black and white

Meanwhile, outside, a street crew is digging up
      the sidewalk and making a terrible din and
      I'm feeling increasingly enraged, imagining
      myself to be a person with a night job

We all need a little getaway spot just to
      assimilate everything and find out what we
      know
I seize one of the construction workers and point
      to a window, shouting, someone in that
      household is dying

I'm furious at myself
Everyone knows I'm in love with the baseball
      player named Eugene, but I pretend not to
      know this, and when everyone is about to
      shout, I shout too—"Hey, you bum, you fart
      harder than you hit"—but I'm the only one
      shouting and Eugene looks at me sadly

I leave this situation unresolved and go up an
      escalator
Three men are handcuffed to chairs and I hurry to
      release them—their handcuffs are made of
      wood and shaped like ox-yokes

This is a gesture of defiance—I know that I'm a
      very good rock and roll drummer
A spy who resembles Ingrid Bergman is related to
      one of the prisoners, and she asks me to help
      her escape with him

Instead when someone telephones we just pass the
    phone receiver back and forth in front of the
    tv and radio
The joke catches us in a display of outrageous
    self-indulgence

One of the men insists that the bed has its place
    in this feud
I say, Excuse me, I want to change position

I'm an old woman but I know people expect more
    than that
Maybe I should just keep my mouth shut and leave
    my false teeth in permanently

I am afraid of being smothered between the breasts
    of the scientists
The lecturer has announced that he will speak
    on the topic of "Nocturnal Chance"

Once the lecture is underway, there can be no
    thrashing about
Sport, says the lecturer, is dependent on the
    occasional appearance of wild animals

He presents a slide of a dachsund digging up
    buried bird bones
This is not a common duck hunter

I say to the host, You're being insensitive
I worry that there is something phallic about this

I feel a strong sense of obligation,
It is triggered suddenly by the approach of two
      men after I've been sitting alone for a long
      time watching the trees and the yellow grass
      through which wind is blowing

38

Pampering oneself with duties is a form of
      sentimentality
One is posing before God but dogs leap out
And one is apologetic and is willing to pay even
      more than the thing is worth and one leaves a
      big tip which simply flaunts one's empathy
People are often empathetic
Sentimental people wage war against numerous evils
      (and they count them)
The count might come out with 9 dead, 30 injured,
      and 100 sick, or there might be no one dead,
      but hundreds sick
People slip away, ironic or militant
Their empathies seem banal, derivative but
      incongruous
Yet incongruity is itself an account, and as such
      it serves as an accomplishment
It shows how bad things are
But it exaggerates

It portrays the actual play of people's lives on a
      reflective surface
In the mirror good things happen to good people
But this is then useless

39

The sun in fables often speaks
It says, Arise, you reprobate, and walk
The reprobate came to me
What is a reprobate
It's accused—and guilty—but of what
The grammarian no longer bothers to remind the
        reprobate to put a little sense between his
        or her words
The guilty is kept to the subject at hand
But he or she does say, Don't jump around or run
        on

I'm giving the sun the role of grammarian
The reprobate came to me
On the 5th of October—was that 1986?
Accusation to the reprobate is tedious,
        prolongation of something that can never be
        deferred
All reference to the sun, meanwhile, is blinding
The sun brings out the trucks, the pedestrians,
        the dogs
In one fable the sun challenges a bus to a race
They are both headed West
In another fable the sun is frozen in the ice and
        only the flowing blood of a hot creature can
        release it

From the sun's point of view, the reprobate
        shelters what it causes
The formidable, the dreadful, and the ideal
When the reprobate is accused it will always say,

> I'm not competing; my concern is not with
> truth, it's with meaning

But the logic governing the sun is round
When the reprobate (any one of us) goes with it,
> we spin

41 *Elegy*

I am writing now in preconceptions
Those of sex and ropes
Many frantic cruelties occur to the flesh of the
> imagination
And the imagination does have flesh to destroy
And the flesh has imagination to sever
The mouth is just a body filled with imagination
Can you imagine its contents
The dripping into a bucket
And its acts
The ellipses and chaining apart
The feather
The observer

The imagination, bare, has nothing to confirm it
There's just the singing of the birds
The sounds of the natural scream
A strange example
The imagination wishes to be embraced by freedom
It is laid bare in order to be desired
But the imagination must keep track of the flesh
> responding—its increments of awareness—a
> slow progression
It must be beautiful and it can't be free

42

January 5. Nietzsche's autobiography. He regards himself as a vivid being and a "rule unto himself."

I compare this to "an intimate account of reality" presented by "a schizophrenic girl." Progressively during her childhood she has "dimmed," as if fading in place. Her living has been immobilized by reality, monstrous and resplendent. Each detail around her has been too vivid to bear. Irritably, she writes, "Before they show themselves, objects should carefully consider what they are requiring their observers to consider."

Testing my own experience against these extremes, I remember that at an early age, I distinguished myself from reality.

This is a common mistake.

Yet it seemed that only I, though still unknown, was real. I looked out as if from the only real vantage point at a world which was vague and awaited me.

Increasingly I expressed this experience. I wanted to be established.

In time and paradoxically, my very willfulness diminished my singular, initial, original reality. Increasingly, then, what bothered—excited—me were hard; they were things— evidences—and they became impossible to resist. They existed, moreover, from innumerable points of view—they were expressing the will of the whole world.

And yet the will of the world was impossible
to interpret; the possibilities were infinite.
What did the world want?

I had always anticipated that it would
someday want me.

One day I watched a bird land on the shingled
roof of an ordinary house in our neighborhood and
the house immediately burst into flame. Figures of
smoke billowed at the windows. Dark blue fire
shimmered against the pale sky. I heard someone
inside screaming.

I knew that it was I who had shot a flaming
arrow at the bird.

This disastrous conjunction of the
imagination with truth—this moment of balance—
was precise, effective, and irreversible. I sensed
that reality was universal and inevitable.

44 *for Jerry Estrin*

My sleep has reasoned miniscule
All is possible
And its reasons are neutral
It waits with the waiting questions—
        "you will be a small sign?"
        "a Rembrandt?"
To show oneself is all that meaning is?

I work and I love you—and I can say so
This should mean we continue what we are
We can't imagine all the minute
        emptinesses (innocences)

Nature is not yet God's book
But increments of our own (logics) move
    us
They turn us away, return us
The horizons themselves are made of all
    such increments
Vague precisions—dissimilars—desires

A single day would be irrational
And we cannot withdraw from logic
When we do something we place stories within
    sleeps
Having been we are what is

45

some are nights
in which I'm told

46

Some days are the product of sleeps, however
    persistently
the imagination remains amoral. Some are made
    conspicuous
by insomnia. Grandiose and suspect comparisons
come to them, and it's not just from excitement
as in a bed, some long green shelter, male vs.
    female,
that we make our transitions, swooping and jumping
    from blue ants to broken cups (metonyms for
    art for art's sake)

in an historical period we can't divorce from
        life.
With ponderous sincerity we jealously combine
        details
as if wistfully disguising our inability to tell
        what's good from what's bad
in order to remove them and make room for our
        thoughts—
thoughts which are elusive, however persistently
sleep pursues them, trying to resolve the
        incongruities
that cut them short and waken us, male or female,
        remembering
these words as merchant ships with decomposing
        sails (metonyms for art
conveying sentimental bourgeois fictions).
In sleeps the figure approaches but does not touch
the body itself, metonym for this, today, male and
        female.

48

then this emotion
        will come to view
under two yellow eyes
two dark birds

52

Philosophy should not be hostile to the eyes
The eyes project variety of character and possess
      laws of organization that defy rigidity
Philosophy is like the eyes, its standard is set
      to experience
Every sight represents shaken forms and disturbed
      soil
Every increment of time or space brings more light
      to the eyes
And this seems to be the source of the wild joy I
      feel now at being present and assertive

53

Visibility has made waking good
Now an animal envy prevails
It measures the kind of time and space one thinks
      one has a right to
It complicates the ten thousand things that come
      from the ego
Shadows spread across the wall, signs of a false
      absence
Our disoriented deception goes where it goes
It sees a grove of trees that we associate with
      shows of kindness, signs of real river banks
But doesn't visibility block our view
For roads into the outer world we can't depend on
      mirrors
And whom did I think I'd signal or implicate
Waking implicates me only in what's here

But did I say that we want safety in our sins or
    in our skins
Our visibility explains such things

54

    There was once an angel who had a neighbor,
and this neighbor was ambitious. He wanted more
than money or fame, he said; he wanted
immortality.

    "Why's that?" asked the angel.

    The angel had lived an unnaturally long time,
but nonetheless he understood some things about
nature, and he was watering the small garden in
front of his house.

    "Well," said the neighbor, somewhat
portentiously but also tentatively—he was a
sensitive person but he'd considered this for a
long time and he now felt that his thoughts were
correct and important—"I don't want my feelings,
so very dear and strong and uniquely arising from
my life, to go suddenly unfelt, as they will be,
when I'm dead."

    "So you think you want to be immortal."

    "Yes."

    "But it is precisely the immortals," said the
angel, "who are dead."

Moral: Certain experienced continuums—for
example, time, space, the ego—are bridges but
without chasms.

Moral: Even when an angel makes you fly, you are the wings.

Moral: An angel's pugnacious twaddle may be as irrefutable as a pistol and in the same way wrong.

Moral: It's not the length of a life but the tension of its parts that lets resound all that it feels.

*

Born in the San Francisco Bay area in 1941, Lyn Hejinian graduated from Harvard University in 1963. She began writing poetry as early as grammar school, and began publishing her first works in magazines in 1963. By the mid 1970s she had begun editing her distinguished Tuumba Press series, which included a wide range of contemporary poetry, including works by many of the San Francisco and New York City acquaintances who soon would join forces in the social, political, and aesthetic grouping of the "Language" poets.

In 1976 she published A Thought Is the Bride of What Thinking, *following it over the next two years with* A Mask of Motion *and the now underground poetry "classic,"* Gesauldo. *This work combined lyrical poetry with a narrative structure set across brief phrases or "titles," which poetically grounded the longer narrative-like passages, a device she would use later in* My Life, *published originally in 1978 and "updated" in 1980 in Sun & Moon Press's Classics series. Since then she has published several new books, including* Redo, The Guard, The Cell, *and* The Cold of Poetry *(which collects her out-of-print works). The last two books also appeared in Sun & Moon Classics.*

Beginning in 1983 Hejinian became interested, through a tour of the then Soviet Union, in Russian poetry. She has translated, with Elena Balashova, two books by the St. Petersburg poet, Arkadii Dragomoschenko.

David Bromige

& Moon

Call name Stop. On the Avon, a swan; in Cleveland, a river of fire.

Cowabunga. Call me Stop. Fog from the Avon causes genuflection.

Cried for you Stop. Learned to think like x but still felt like ABC, forbears and forbards, funny hats.

Weep Stop. The mote might be removed in the form of a letter or more heavy breathing. The ash from a J perhaps.

In the corner, a secret. The weather is changing. There is nothing to laugh at. Roll the Sucrets to the front part of the mouth.

Address stuff to author's office. Move to Suffolk or Sussex? The circle is buckled. Ride Brighton Line or Soul Train? Stick the toilet on the wall, next to the telephone. Part agent and part pencil, partly at once, writing backwards to erase the last trace of locquaciousness.

Listen Stop. Where the river rises it gets visibly physical. Hear it's difficult to stop the bubbling. Here's a present, eye to eye. La! Allover tan? Passé! Venereal past, fast approaching.

> *Crying to myself because I almost died in Switzerland, figured in a*
> *romance with a lyricist, fussed over the blue clothing we affected,*
> *dressed up like chickens and went to the movies. Ate at the bankrupt*

*Japanese restaurant So-Su-Mi. I saw the Devil at that resort. He
read my palm for a trifle over dessert. I must never name the real
trouble.*

Must never say the word Desert.

Must only mention others' feelings.

Must always belittle same.

Let these rules repeat.

Must sleep in the entry-way to the fort, compare Avon to silver snake,
must avenge in this sleep. Repetition of known facts pays.

Born in a particular hotel, had to be quiet between 1300 and 1500
hours. Mulled things over nonetheless, and when required to speak
spoke well and to the point. Later, graduated Old Fart, claimed this
was a promotion, was buried with his money, by then considerable.
Sexy story.

2

Said what was evil was anything but duress. Did nude dance with
tongue protruding. Must dream He was mother.

New rule. God is the involuntary nervous system. Gave Mike a shock
and he dropped a book. We had asked him not to.

Dear Diary. Must feast on corpse of rival and grow great with rival.
Avon rival, level rival. Mon nom est A rival. Cease, rival. Any day ends
in a diminished i.

Write Stop. In a him and a thou pleasure is an aid to sorrow a real treat sign here. Newer rule: Only I is permitted Irony. Him speaking.

Him singing. Her form, her figure, her fugue, her gig, her effigy of sand his oeuvre, his big but.

Draw a blank till it shrieks. Nothing's impermeable. They meet at the corner of High & What. The person was vague and sticky. Was pushing up on the metaphor's jaws. His the blind and her the widow. Jackpot.

Jackshit. He breathes as he speaks, mists the pane.

Traces. On the mist or on the pane? Anybody breathes. Il pleut on the lunch, the tracts and the projects, limbs, blood, organs same there as here, lightheaded over their dark roots.

Snatched to the Underworld. Someone with that name grew up on the mezzanine. Appraised the language of baseball stars but dealt cards.

> *Everything I am uttering you are understanding. Richard, you cream your knickers across a crowded room. I name you in order that you may ask me to dance. No. Face only a mother could sit on.*

Snatched, Underworld. Goes on and on and off. Stop. Face in forest, light to show the dark. Light on a seashell. Lump in the moonlight Pit for space Video to make the light useful. It hurts to light.

A word is a horse to him. For an experience, take a doorwedge, shove where sun don't shine. (He has some big doorwedges, for a house whose doors are small). Edgar Allen Ice's supple epic What The Parlor Wanted With A Door. Among my souvenirs your lips are chapped.

3

Ice's supple trill names her. Wants control of that phallus. Wants it to pee through himself alone. Thinks it's to count on, thinks that's this's idea.

Speaks of self saying I am training to decry your life. Speaks saying ours is not the same mother and he must be right. Substitutes a magic show he thinks not his. Music Room, Smoking Room, Study, Library, Parlor, Dining Room where we ate his words, full of Clue. Servants he dressed down. Then rammed his resolution up them on couch supplied by citizens.

Employees with spiders on their fingers and roofrats at their mouths, quenched fires resembling his thoughts, his pencil.

Human to write, inhuman to compute. Drop the oaken anchor into icy here.

Employees whose news was never viewed—applications from Detroit, from Demography, from Jarry Priory or Reed College, send syllabus check's in mail, baskers in the glow of his address.

> *Dancing to forget we or I drank heavily, heavely (only here could you hear it). Visited Less-or-more-one-speaks-to-Stop. Vietnam confused the Mass. At Mardi Gras Icy. He lit my way underground.*

Hollow laughter the passage. On vault wall: Who finds most faults, wins most votes. Tittering and then characters. Then those reversed.

Wearied of the white glare where discernment was a wash. Bored by regular time, weather. But Zuke for Shake, wetlands for river, moon-light to find way (not back), to cease. It began with pouring words. Elijah! Your silent ɪ.

The Star had fallen already when we met. I admired your silence. My head was on upside-down. Telling you what you know.

All human light's reflected. Any others are about to utter their words through this School of Broadcasting. The naked radios admired the wireless orgy.

It began with everyone gone away, so one drunk on words. The first sentence bore a swan. A swam. Swarmed a song.

Comes to this. A shock of wheat in a harsh cry. Every question having just six sides. The moonlight did good in the film noir. No such knowing as Is Known. Who are you, identity rocking out? Wrote this in lieu of their death.

*

Born in London in 1933, David Bromige traveled extensively, graduating from the University of British Columbia in Canada, before settling in the United States. He received his Master's degree from the University of California at Berkeley as a Woodrow Wilson Fellow. From 1970–92, he taught at Sonoma State University in California. He now writes and lectures as a free agent.

From his first book of 1965, The Gathering, *his work has combined an extraordinary intelligence with a playfulness of mind. In* Tight Corners & What's Around Them *(1974), he became, in Ron Silliman's words, "the first to open up the question [in our poetry] of language's cognitive domain," winning him a wide audience of readers and poets, some of whom later came to be known as the "Language" writers. In 1988 his selected poems,* Desire, *won the Western States Federation Poetry Award. He has also held fellowships from the* NEA *and The Canada Council. Among his most recent books are* The Harbormaster of Hong Kong *(published by Sun & Moon Press in 1993) and* A Cast of Tens *(Avec Books, 1994).*

F. T. Marinetti

Dunes

Translated from Italian and typographically reproduced
by Guy Bennett

DUNES

Karazooc - zooczooc
Karazooc - zooczooc

nadI - nadI AAAAAAaaaaaaaa (*repeat*) *dunes duuu-
uuuunes dunes sun burnt dunes dunesdunesdunes*

	dmm dmmdmmdmmdmmdmm	
hurried		derbooka white boredom +
dazzling	**dmm**	the woolen noise of thought
eternal		the resonant padding of the
dazzling	**dmm**	sky the rotating noise of the
mechanical		sun cottonous memories
dazzling	**dmm**	pounding marrows a tunnel
consanguine		of black sounds into the
dazzling	**dmm**	incandescent mountains of
major key		the light
dazzling	**dmm**	

Ocre + brass + cinnamon 18 km^2

vvvvvrrrriiiiiiiiiiiiiiiiiiiiiii

lacerating
universal   vluiiii   violins cats creaking of
fibrous   vuuliii   all the romantic doors
minor key   vuluit   bullets tympani snow-
                 vuvuluit   storms in telegraph
                             wires   strings of
                             wind taut against the
fragile   chauffeur's nose beneath
climbing   the squuuuiiiigly arc of
stretched   the vehement street

YELLOOOWYELLOOOW

acridity urine sweat cassie filth jasmin banker's
paunch with feet plowing filth sandcushions
lyingdownthirstthirst
noise + weight of the sun + orange smell of the sky
+ 20,000 obtuse angles + 18 semicircular shadows
+ mineralization of black feet in the crystal sand

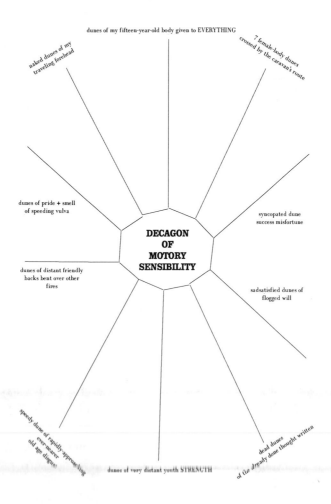

distances

cadenced
navigating   distances
soft   dunes
manageable   stretching
meticulous   undulations
intestinal   angles
                                                 angles
                    molding sand smoothing polishing
RNN   polishing somnolence of the wind
                    corn plaster scarlet arteries joy of
                    paying a thief the price of an itch
RNN   accounting of nails
                                      ½ kilo of cheese

RNN   26 kilos of FEMALE FLESH
                    rings of a blue smoke smell of
                    roasted veal ROTHSCHILD'S
                    TAVERN (breadth 1000 km^2) 3
boundless   tissue-paper battleships 2 melted
dazzling   tin soldiers vomited out by the
rnnrnn   sizzling equatorial sun
or
square

                                                 thiiirst

rrrr
ssssssssss
rrrrrrr
crucra
crucra
crucra

{ concentric white screams of 14 moooons
gone mad round square moons
drowning writhing crumbling in
the well (30 m) of Bu-Fellah **(NIIIGHT)**
crucracruminating of cameeeeeeeeeels

WIND
TURNER

{ of dunes + nerves + remorse +
nausea + dung + barracans
in eccentric flight

MOVEMENT
OF
2 PISTONS

WIND

{ **negative** laziness inertia
freezing everything with
literary stars ripped out
of flesh (BOOKISH
NIGHT) burying every-
thing with odors of
armpits mattresses of
perfumes baked breasts
pleasure + 7000 scep-
tical arguments

Karazooc zooczooc
Karazooc zooczooc

BLOOD

{ **positive** optimism
force pushing back
the pessimistic wind
hot or cold wandering
aimlessly to provoke
LIVING RUNNING
BEING

Nadl nadl
AAAaaaaaaaaa

SUN UNIVERSAL LUBRICATOR

tlak
tlak
chik
chok

MENU OF A DINNER FOR 6 BY THE LIGHT OF A GLOW-WORM

1. Hors-d'œurvres of kakawicknostalgine
2. Anguishettes à la crème
3. boiled remorsgust
4. presentimentlung on the spit
5. hemorrhoidal clusters
6. ascetic urine frappé

aih
aiiiiii
aiiiiii
fuuuuut

four of us sitting comfortably on the head of a pin   aristocratic pearl-gray thinness of the wind taking the greyhound-fire-dressed-in-red out for a walk

SENTIMENTAL

blinded **(** on the young explorors be-   blinding
by   **{** trayed by wives lovers   by
tears   **(**   solemnity of a cuckold   **)** red tears
     on the equator

(andante grazioso con pizzicato)

tepid little letter sweating on the bosom

expaaaaaaNTION of a written word bare
elbow tapering of cloud — hand — held in the
heat   3 days walk
dunes dunes dunes
COAST   the **MAILSHIP**
8 DAYS   **GENOA** Parma here I am kisses
traditional **zingzing zingzing** of a country
bed
Karazooc-zooczooc Karazooc-zooczooc
youreahero **zingzingcuic NaldI NaldI**

AAAAAAaaaaa **zingzingcuic** flabbiness of wet
ripe bells falling **faaalling**

Cake-Walk Tempo

from the very high veeeeery old branch
laundry-acacias-mildew-wormeatenwood-
cookedcabbage-**zing**-**zang**-of-saucepans smell
ammonium secrecy of a Bedouin's tent
dunes dunes dunes

*

*Born in Alexandria, Egypt in 1876, Filippo Tommaso Marinetti
spent his early youth in Paris and later moved to his parents' home-
land of Italy, graduating from the law school of the University of
Genoa. In 1905 he founded an international journal of poetry,*
Poesia, *primarily committed to French Symbolism. The journal,
however, also published the work of younger Italian poets, whose
writings were to be the roots of the "poètes incendiares" and the
Italian Futurist movement.*

*By 1909 Marinetti had defined his aesthetics sufficiently to pro-
duce the "Manifeste du Futurisme" in the French newspaper* Le
Figaro, *republished in the same year in his* Poesia. *Over the next
few years several other manifestoes by Marinetti and others fol-
lowed in a flurry of statements on the arts, industry, war, and
society in general. Many of these important manifestoes and state-
ments are collected in* Let's Murder the Moonshine: Selected
Writings, *published by Sun & Moon Press in 1991.*

Lesser known are Marinetti's own writings, including the novel,
The Untameables *(published by Sun & Moon in 1994), and po-
etic "syntheses," word constructs, and theatrical writings. Sun Moon
Press will publish several of these works over the next few years.*

Alexei Parshchikov

Minus Ship

Translated from Russian by Michael Palmer
and Eugene Ostashevsky

I split from the dark as if oakum had croaked.
Behind me City Hysteria blackened in chalky spasms,
the sun was liquid, the sloping sea reeked,
and reentering my body I knew God had redeemed me.

I remembered a scuffle on a square—the whistles and flaring
      [passions.
I idled in neutral by the pinball machine
where a woman was flashing, partly real
the edge of this reality jarred by Scheherazade.

I was out of it, yet remember the ones in slow plummet
from the fight, as if tumbling through an apple tree
and grasping at the fruit, unable to choose…
Homeric-shouldered griffons were forming a pack.

And here at this most silent of seas—as with
eye muscles slowed by the Herb—pass that joint
toward a calm horizon—relax, don't rush…
…from mollusc to cow, idea to object…

In the mountains stirred the raisins of distant herds.
I strolled the shore as memory shoved from behind
but reflex and strain vanished into rhythm
and power arrayed itself along units of time.

All became what it should have been from the beginning:
poppies ripped through hills like TV static,
a donkey with fly's eyes imagined Plato,
the sea seemed fact, not mere apparition.

Precise Sea! Ringlets of a million mensurae.
Cliff—inseparable from. Water—essential for.
Their necessity burned through a random dust-speck
clutching them…but there was no ship!

I saw the vectored couplings, and all the essential clamps—
along the background a void sucked strength into itself—
saw even the smell of oil, the characteristic creak,
whiter than a shot of camphor yawned the minus ship.

It propagated—absence. It dictated—views
to views, and with no more than a glance
you'd be caught, as by a cotton filter,
then nod into extended diapason.

Color of the void, the minus ship roamed,
actually bobbing in place, moored to zero.
In the stretched diapason, a comma on its side…
And I crept up closer to the imperious bark.

The minus ship melted. I heard a distant *OM*.
A hidden genius plucked a melody on the doutar.
Aimed toward the Absolute and gliding volumetrically
it swelled and then veered off at its apogee.

The minus ship was swallowed, like arac on a table.
The doutar wove a new center of emptiness.
Swimming toward it on an ecstatic char—time now—
I focussed and crossed over…

*

Alexei Parshchikov is one of the founders of Moscow's Meta-metaphorism movement. Both of the books published in the then Soviet Union, August on the Dnieper *(1984) and* Figures of Intuition *(1989) received wide coverage in the Soviet press. Since 1988 his work has been translated in Europe and Asia in more than a dozen languages. His poetry is represented in the United States by the recent publication,* Blue Vitriol. *Parshchikov recently attended Stanford University, where he received his Master's Degree. After a year in Switzerland, he has now returned to the United States and lives in Los Angeles.*

Jackson Mac Low

Enduring and Way Off
{*Forties 26*}
AND
Strings of Stars and Very Dear
{*Forties 27*}

Enduring and Way Off
{*Forties 26*}

Enduring and rich   relationships   famous and shrewd as Clark Clifford
could be duped   walk-in treatment for minor emergencies
for everyone   the Budapest Quartet   did arrest óne   person
its leadership remains in jail   reports from the secessionist republic of
    Croatia   occupied by Serbs   driven by an Hasidic Jew
Like ones that led riots last week

Better sáfety-education   Latvia   Lithuania   Estonia
a cautious approach   running behind   rapidly changing events
in the Supreme Soviet   might hasten the disintegration of the Soviet
    Union
Finland   Malta   and the Vatican   reform   had to take place   ideas
    ridiculous   so eager   on the edge
Ukraine   Byelorus   Kazakhstan

Armenian independence   as much a foregone conclusion as
reinforced by the earthquake   much less movement
Azerbaiján   the least   why call it quits thére?
delayed   process of decolonialization   units that exist   rights of
    minorities nót guaranteed   five tons of canned Alaskan salmon
not let that food go to waste

Brunt of gesture hit the Alaskan fishermen   already past their prime
I cannot hate them 'cause nothing binds me to them ок?
mechanics contains that which is beyond mechanics
I cried on the Holy Name and by degrees recovered myself   like a
    dead   weight this is how the souls in Hell would be
imprisoned in their bodies as in prisons

The right kind of static   *Ablysia californica* the sea hare   neuroma
large accessible nérve-cells   relatively few in number
experimental organism   molecular basis of learning and memory
fifteen-pound snails   two feet long   spend all their time   eating and
    copulating   only real   problem   avoiding
    neurobiologists   siphon
theory of learning at a snail's   pace

Its nerve cells start firing wildly   commanding its síphon-muscle
    to withdraw
around the point of crushing   more electrically charged   entirely
    unexpected
cannibal stars'   fountain of youth   masquerade
as young hot blue stars   stragglers collide   older rob younger   gain new
    lease on life paired in gravitational embrace
siphoning hydrogen   from partners

Stellar collisions   merging of components   punctured balloons
significantly more massive than ordinary stars
        in their region   double-star systems
from fénder-benders   to head-on smashes   relatively slow
mixing and thrashing motions   fifteen billion years old   luminosity
        of a bíllion-year-old star   fringes of the Milky Way
Forty-seven Tucánae   globular clusters

Swept clean of residual gas and dust   new internal modem
frailest-flixed   Snowflake   patent dragonproof curtains
I don't care a straw about the Aurora Borealis   polar bears and arctic
        wolves
if we went to the North Pole we should get our boots   wet   during the
        winter the arctic regions come much farther south than they are
        marked on the map
Northern Lights   still seemed some way off

Silences and/or prolongations: 3 letter spaces [   ] = 1 unstressed syllable;
6 letter spaces [   ] = I stressed syllable or beat;
12 letter spaces [   ] = 2 beats.

Nonorthographic acute accents indicate stresses, not vowel qualities.
Each hyphenated compound is read as one extended word: a little more rapidly than other
words but not hurried. Indented lines conclude verse lines begun above them.

Jackson Mac Low
26-28 August 1991, near Wilmington, Vermont, by the duck pond
20 June 1993, New York

Strings of Stars and Very Dear
{*Forties 27*}

Strings of stars   threaded on fine   moonbeams   THIS WAY TO THE
    NORTH POLE
slide   made for the convenience of the polar bear   naughty and
    disobedient
no time to notice the scenery   I can see the Northern Lights quite plain
tried to go to the Crystal Palace   the white   grouse   thanked them in a
    few pleasant wéll-chósen words   looking for specimens with a pair of
    blue glasses
Boy's Own Scientific Experimenter

Pin to stick through the great   arctic moth   listening attentively to the
    conversation
singularly thoughtless little girl   returned   thanks in a suitable speech
Homage to E(dith) Nesbit   1858 to 1924   towering high and white and
    glistening like an ice   lighthouse
blue   and green   and rosy and straight   like the stalks
    of dream   lilies these flames were the Aurora Borealis   they mix flour
    with the icing sugar
do not shine and sparkle

It's not getting *here*   it's getting *back* again   the robins will cover us
    with leaves
all sorts of glimmery shimmery changing colors in thin parts
a great   shining winged   scaled   clawy big-mouthed dragon made of
    pure   ice
rising from within the cold   coil of the frozen dragon   the North   Pole
    shot up like a pillar made of one   great   diamond   cracked a little
    from sheer   coldness
enormous jewel   great   flames   stalks of tall   lilies

Chilblains in your eyes   pretend to howl   it frightens them
we are made throughout of the very best sealskin   you are heartless
our hearts are made of the finest sealskin Boy   now your fate is sealed
I am only grateful for the opportunity of showing my sense of your manly
     conduct about the firework   very pretty manners
they are a cowardly folk

Buried its greedy nose deep in the sealskin fur as snow   falls   not
     moths
moths' children eat fur   trying to deceive you grówn-up people
your poor Aunt Emma had a lovely sable cloak but it was eaten by moths
called for camphor and bitter apple and oil of lavender and yellow soap
     and borax   all was over   eaten down to the very life
snow was brown with flat   bare   pelts

Poor set of fellows if we couldn't overeat ourselves once in a while to
     oblige a friend
dragon had to go south   when you get to the North   Pole   there is no
     other way to go
dragons can get their tails into the fourth dimension and hold them there
nasty thin sharp tóngues-they-were too   poured it into a pipkin   I
     could make more diamonds in a day than I should wear in a year
hard to get in any trade

Tried to drop a curtsy to her as she went by   not a king
not easy hanging wrong way up by your tail   pretty home manners
tried to peck the goldfish   curious twisted letters
     from old   brown   books
mold   stains on their yellowy pages   engaged a competent dragon
     to look after her   employ yourself in embroidering your wedding
     gown
twice   twenty-five kisses

Self-acting hammer and electric bellows   worthy to be a prince
as good a boy as you would find in a month of Sundays   Lone   Tower
light shone out to sea across the wild   swirl of nine   whirlpools
you are certain to know something if you give for seven days
    your whole   thought to it   beached the boat on the yellow
    sand   you are very good
and very clever   and very dear

Silences and/or prolongations: 3 letter spaces [   ] = 1 unstressed syllable;
6 letter spaces [   ] = 1 stressed syllable or beat.

Nonorthographic acute accents indicate stresses, not vowel qualities.
Each hyphenated compound is read as one extended word: a little more rapid than other
words but not hurried. Indented lines conclude verse lines begun above them.

Jackson Mac Low
28 August 1991, Wilmington, Vermont; 7 July 1993, New York

*

Poet, composer, essayist, performance artist, playwright, and painter,
Jackson Mac Low was born in Chicago on September 12, 1922.
His poetry began to be published in 1941. Since 1954 he has often
employed chance operations and other "nonintentional" procedures,
as well as more "intentional" techniques, when composing poetry
and verbal, musical, theatrical, and multimedia performance works.
    Among his numerous works is the play The Marrying Maiden
(written in 1958), performed by the Living Theatre in New York
in 1960–61, with music by John Cage. His Verdurous Sangui-
naria *was premiered in 1961 during his first concerts (in Yoko*
Ono's New York loft), in a series organized by La Monte Young.
His Twin Plays, *written and first performed in 1963, constitute*
his first book (1963, 1966). Selections from The Pronouns *(1964,*

1971, 1979), forty poems that are also instructions for dancers, were first performed in 1965 by Meredith Monk and a group (including Mac Low) organized by her, and later by dancers in Australia and elsewhere.

In 1963, with its editor, La Monte Young, Mac Low co-published the first edition of An Anthology *(2nd ed., 1970), which through George Maciunas, who designed it in 1961, gave rise to Fluxus, of which Mac Low was the first literary editor and whose festivals gave him his first European performances (1962–63).*

Subsequently, many books of his poetry and other work were published, notably August Light Poems *(1967),* 22 Light Poems *(1968),* Stanzas for Iris Lezak *(1972),* 4 trains *(1974),* 21 Matched Asymmetries *(1978),* phone *(1979),* Is That Wool Hat My Hat? *(1982), and* French Sonnets *(published 1984, 1989).*

On his sixtieth birthday, in 1982, poets, composers, instrumentalists, dancers, and performance artists joined in an eight-hour retrospective of his work at Washington Square United Methodist Church in New York. Clearly an influence on that and previous decades (as well as the 90s), Mac Low, in From Pearl Harbor Day to FDR's Birthday *(published by Sun & Moon Press in 1982) and* Bloomsday *(1984), collected much of his "intentionally disjunctive" writing of the early 80s, in the latter book along with "nonintentional" works of 1980-81.*

Mac Low has written intentionally disjunctive verbal works intermittently since the late 1930s. Though some of these are aesthetically similar to certain so-called language poems, many of which Mac Low enjoys and values, his works of this kind proceed from other techniques (e.g., quasi-automatic writing, sonic formalism, and Classical Greek prosodic devices) and other theoretical bases than those relevant to most language writing. Notable among the latter are Zen, Kegon, and Vajrayana Buddhism; pacifist anarchism; and certain recuperated aspects of older aesthetic theories, including those of Aristotle, Kant, Hopkins, Whitehead, Stein, Schoenberg, Schwitters, and the more intentional/less aleatory Cage. Despite theoretical and generational differences, he is grateful to many of the language writers on all coasts for their informed reception, publication, and support of his work.

Mac Low's recent publications include The Virginia Woolf Poems *(1985),* Representative Works: 1938–1985 *(1986),* Words nd Ends from Ez *(1989),* Twenties: 100 Poems *(1991),* Pieces o' Six: 33 Poems in Prose *(published by Sun & Moon Press in 1992), the compact disk* Open Secrets *(1993), and* 42 Merzgedichte in Memoriam Kurt Schwitters *(1994). Sun & Moon Press will soon publish his* Barnesbook, *four poems derived by combined nonintentional and intentional methods from Djuna Barnes's books.*

Mohamed Choukri

The Revenants

Translated from French by Gilbert Alter-Gilbert

"THE CITY is in danger. It must be obliterated. We will begin at the appointed hour."

The earliest risers scoop up the red leaflet from the streets, or from their doorsteps. It is written in Arabic, in French, in Spanish, and in English. They stop in their tracks. They spin on their heels, and peer suspiciously and trepidantly to right and left, and all around. Then they retreat behind bolted doors, or flee the city on foot, at a run. In complete panic, they awaken their fellow citizens. Dumbstruck, they assail one another with questions. "Why do they want to destroy the city?" "And who are they?"

They find the leaflet absurd, but leaving seems very logical to them. They huddle, they deliberate, they commiserate. They scatter, they vanish. They pack their belongings and abandon their homes, proceeding on foot, or by car, some at a gallop, some stumbling. They hesitate to depart, they exit, re-enter, re-exit. Their actions are strained and distorted by fright and dismay.

Many remain in their bathrobes or dressing gowns, feet bare, half-dressed. Women, girls, and infants bawl and wail, peeing in their pinafores. They flee the city, they head toward the mountains, the deserts, or the beaches. They hang on the hoods of trucks, or cling three or four together on a motorscooter. Most take refuge on the mountainsides, so as to be able to witness the spectacle of the annihilation.

The sole remaining inhabitants of the city are the invalids, the madmen, the daredevils, and the beasts.

All day long they have awaited the destruction of the city. On the beaches, the prices of fish and fresh water have skyrocketed. They barter their clothing for food and drink. In the outskirts and the mountains, they have taken to thieving from gardens and orchards. Fruit, vegetables, livestock all are pillaged. Disputes erupt, and blood is spilled over a stolen goat. Starving mobs hunt down a shepherd, and pelt him with rocks and bricks, before seizing a few lambs from his flock.

They have clambered into the trees, chasing animals, and they hiss at one another.

At dusk, they stream back to the city, in the same way they had left. Many had fled by car toward other cities. Some have returned, some have not. They run. They burst in. They collapse, exhausted. All the while, their faces are scared, bewildered, but they seem determined to confront their lot.

They reclaim the flowers, the branches, the twigs, the fruits, the vegetables, the poultry, the other birds living and dead.

They find their city calm and silent. The madmen and the daredevils stroll here and there amid the general indifference. From time to time can be heard the laughter of the madmen. They chatter loudly, waving their fingers at the revenants, or at the void, and bursting into laughter.

The revenants, too, find the leaflet quite absurd. But then again, their return seems to them only too logical.

*

Born in 1935 in Bani Shirkir in the Rif, Northern Morocco, Mohamed Choukri moved with his family to Tangiers in 1943, fleeing famine. He led the life of a vagabond, earning his living by shining shoes, selling papers, washing dishes, and pickpocketing. At nineteen he decided to learn to read and write, and joined a secondary school in the city of al-'Ara'ishy. When he returned to Tangiers, he started to experiment with writing. In 1966, the literary journal al-Adab *published one of his short stories, "Violence on the Beach," which attracted the attention of young Moroccan writers. His was a unique view: the experience of life in the raw. His works were an attempt to strip the images of life in literature of their artifice and to call things by their name. His autobiography* The Barefoot Bread (al-'Aysah al-Hafi) *was too subversive and revolutionary to be published in Arabic until he had become an established author. However, an English adaptation was published in 1973 as* For Bread Alone *and a French translation* (Le Pain Nu) *was published in 1979. Choukri is the author of a number of short stories, two novels, and two plays.*

Michael Palmer

Far Away Near

"We link too many things together"
—AGNÈS ROUZIER

As it's said in The Fragments
I met the blind typist

inventor of words
The iris of the eye

is an inverted flower
and the essay on snow

offers no beginning
only an aspect of light

beneath a gate
only a photograph of earth

only a fold
a grammar reciting its laws

Just as the clatter
seems distant

and dies without further thought
that moment we ask

Have we reached the center yet, or
Should there be more blue do you think

or just a different shade of blue
all the while tacitly acknowledging

that by blue
she might have meant red

and by red...
As it's said

we must train our guns toward the future
where the essay on light will obviate time

and the essay on smoke
will cause the ground to open

One day I completed the final word
of a letter to my father

in what key I forget
After the ink had dried

I noticed the rain lit by a streetlamp
shaped like a conical hat

I noticed the map
of the moon you had left

half in shadow on my desk
In a city near the North Sea

white nights passed as I read
of an aviator downed

in the Barr Adjam
during the war directly after

the war to end all wars
sightless and burned across

three-fourths of his body
Listening in twin silences

his name had disappeared
from his lips

As it's said in The Fragments
There once was a language with two words

and the picture of an apple tree
As it's said

The ravens present a paradox
We learn a new gesture

utter unintelligible sounds
in a cheerful voice perhaps

pointing to the sky
where the rain continues

*

Michael Palmer was born in New York City in 1943. After attending Harvard University, he lived in Europe before settling in San Francisco, where he lives today. His several books include Blake's Newton, Without Music, The Circular Gates, First Figure, Notes for Echo Lake, *and* Sun, *which received the Pen Center West poetry award in 1989. The same year Palmer was named a Guggenheim Fellow.*

Palmer's work has been translated into several languages, most recently into Danish as Underjordisk Alfabet (An Alphabet Underground).

Mac Wellman

Three Americanisms

persons of the play:

FIRST MAN

SECOND MAN

FIRST WOMAN

Three Americanisms opened on May 22, 1993 at Soho Repertory Theater with the following cast: Mark Margolis, Ron Faber, and Jan Leslie Harding. Direction: Jim Simpson; music: Mike Nolan; design: Kyle Chepulis.

*

Re: Sierpinski carpet and Menger sponge: "…mathematicians in the early twentieth century conceived monstrous seeming objects made by the technique of adding or removing infinitely many parts. One such shape is the Sierpinski carpet, constructed by cutting the center one-ninth of a square; then cutting out the centers of the eight smaller squares that remain; and so on. The three dimensional analogue is the Menger sponge, a solid-looking lattice that has an infinite surface area, yet zero volume.

"One cylinder rotated inside the other, pulling the liquid with it. The system enclosed its flow between surfaces. Thus it restricted the possible motion of the liquid in space, unlike jets and wakes in open water. The rotating cylinders produced what was known as Couette-Taylor flow."

—from *Chaos*, by James Gleick

*

NOTA BENE: These three pieces were originally entitled: *An Elegy on the Invisibility of Richard Stans*, *A Screeched Elegy (With Furballs)*, and *Multitudinous Roadkill*. They are excerpts from an ongoing series of *Strange Elegies*.

*

"I'm throwing twice as hard, only the ball's going half as fast."

—LEFTY GROVE

*   *   *

Scene: a dark, wide, open place. A strange MAN *appears. Pause. He smiles, begins talking to us.*

FIRST MAN

I am running on empty in a region infinitely
    sparse, infinitely many.
Those there are who do not donut
    as good as we used to was.
We trample them down and yell
    in place of bellringing sure.
We get up on our hindparts, hey,
    and exchange wigglies.
We party monster-like till the
    moon fries our velvet shadows.
Patience we do not much care for.
We are of that other kind, the self-similar
    mailbox-mouthed.
To prong donuts excited our wiggly
    forks.
Why, you inquire, meaning no gas.
Because the big end belongs to the
    North, and we are not nosey, nope.
Because our breath is of stone, yup.
Because we collect no dust on our
    hindparts by error's somersault.
We are both beastly and robust,
    upon the horned plains of the earth.
Robust we are, and widely distributed,
    infinitely sparse, infinitely many.
Our wigglies astound the friends of Ralph
    with terminal pissed-offedness.
Our brambles are full of poisoned wigglies.
Our minds move slow, but in wide
    circles.

Nothing much hinders the sky thought
    on its lark, on its random lasso.
So as far as we go, still
    we stop.
As for stop a mop will do.
Kill it and grow wigglies, especially
    the abject kind.
Pray to the moose for restoration
    of hindpart sensation.
Pray to the moose for mops, and stop
    signs to deter foreigners,
    fork lifts to deter grabity, storks
    to deter chimneys, stillness to
    deter noise, and noise to deter
    mooses, in particular the abject
    kind, sure.
Things tend to stop.
Things tend to start up, likeso.
They tend to bend light
    till we who dwell in bent halls
    of bent mirrors get the bent message
    likeso and fall over, all bamboozled.
The stop people have the start button
    to do the work of bottleneck.
The other way works the same, except
    for being otherwise contagious with
    feathers of false starts, bent wigglies,
    extraneous moose noise and the whole
    damned abject monsterosity of killed
    feet, empty hearts and done-in brain
    power, railing against the whole darn
    whitewash of amateur washouts by
    professional doorstops, yesmen and
    loose women, yeah.

I am galloping through a region of rusted
    jumbos, atomic glimmer glass, archaic
    rosebuds, mystic armadillos and
    borderline hayrakes looking for a
    few good men to catch them porkypines.
I am walking slow through a world
    of glass gone haywire.
I am walking slow on the sticky stuff
    of another man's cellophane, sure.
I am walking slow without no more
    bad thoughts than you would expect
    of one such as me, gone bananas
    on mystic glimmer gas, and
    whoop-de-doo !
For he who thinks otherwise I have
    prepared the cauldron of hot,
    boiling oil, just in case he don't
    back off and not look at me right,
    him being a monster weirdo, or a
    social undesirable, or basket-case,
    or one of them as wears jewelry,
    or a bone through the nose or a gold
    pin screwed through the nipple like
    I seen at the gym giving me the abject
    willies, so that I grew full strange,
    and wiggly.
World's full of people stuck on someone
    else's cellophane.
World's full of places where your feet clink
    off the glimmer glass, where once long ago
    the earth hotted up ten million degrees,
    no shit, sure.
As I am trudging through a Menger sponge, a
    solid black block of basaltic lord-knows-

what, I find x in the name of y and
    grow doilies.
These are not the doilies I have a hankering
    for, therefore I do not like them, yup.
Upon the oath I confirm box lunches.
Upon both the oath and the breaking of it
    I implement oases and office checks.
I seek out Chubby for bollide sneakers.
I sneak out the same door Chubby uses,
    with both his oaths and tools, lie in
    wait humming the credo SHIT FLOATS,
    boat my blues, dig up my old book
    of fake dreams, and think much upon
    the invisibility of Richard Stans, yup.
I fear I am a black sheep barging through
    the back door, braying, into a blind
    alley leading to a black ka'aba, where
    I'm not supposed to go.
I fear Ralph, even though he's dead.
I fear all the doilies, who are
    strange to me.
Strange feet fear the same stuff, likeso.
I go great guns upon the hangnail sarcophagus.
Piles of spare wigglies arrive in mad crates
    infinitely sparse, looped and knotted.
Grace's a fear park of the rider people,
    and sheer destiny palls.
Grace's got the same strange feet I do,
    yet none fear her the way they do me.
Strange, Grace.
Strange to be an ichabod ka'aba.
I prefer this to that for no reason.
I prefer this to that cause of how I have
    done choosed this, and not that.

That one dwells in the forest of swill, all
    candles smeared with mystic nightshade ooze.
That one's a rider perilous, a double
    headed trouble-shooter, a ne'er-do-well
    who aced his fate and wears no icy halo.
That one heaps me hot so, yup.
This one bursts like grievous nightshade, opening.
OO cats' eyes glory in the opening up, yup.
They air out the terror of the night, yup.
But they irk me with their terrorist tendencies.
For strange people are moving around
    inside of my house.
Boing, they go. Boing.
And once they are done with the boings
    commence booing and the booings
    are as bad as the boings and the
    boings having driven me half off
    my nut I begin to boo too so my voice'll
    get lost in the booing and they will
    henceforth get lost and be gone and not
    notice I am here, alone, in my house
    and start all over again with the mad, mad
    business of boings, boings which I hate.
That is why I prefer this to that.
OO cats' eyes light up the fractal zone, sure.
I am trudging slow in a region of Couette-Taylor
    flow and perpetual turnstiles, sure.
Junk bats boat in the blue wind, ho.
Hovering in deepest glide.
Ralph there, dead.
Buoyed in dead hope, gone cat,
Dust in rills, another
    planet.

We shift our errors, compounding
    the wilderness.
Needlemen approach.
They signal, holding up
    painted wigglies.
Wind, wind and no water, yup.
Boulders bunched up, yup.
We consult the mystic oracle.
We offer up mystic glimmer gas.
We talk to our wide one, Chubby.
Chubby tells us plenty, yup.
We take their wigglies and kill
    the mothmen, sure.
Junk bats boat in the blue wind, ho.
We, we and them, them and the others, strange.
Seasons cooled, cooked.
I think about the whole damn enterprise.
I ornament the region with unholy images
    of the directory tree.
I put on someone's clothes, not mine.
The clothes cling to my human nakedness.
I am ashamed.
        Pause.
Nothing of value inside, please.
Nothing of value please don't steal my stuff.
    My stuff is worthless, so please don't
    steal it, the car is a wreck, and
    a pox on all your houses if you do.
I am caught forever on a Sierpinski carpet
    in a region infinitely sparse, infinitely many.
Carbon copies of my previous lives
    afflict my hairy feet with scurf.
The pointed hat is my American destiny.

Stolen cars have held up nothing of value
    and you know what to do.
You know what to do lassoes x in the
    name of y, stuffs shirts and says to
    Hadituptohere: Kwitcherbellyachin.
You know what to do fears not the
    ghost of Ralph, on account of him
    being a corpse, and therefore abstrack.
We all trudge through the howling
    badlands of prehistoric lawn furniture.
We all act as though we had met the first
    fur person in a back alley, bodacious.
We all act strange on account of our
    badass attitude problem.
We all bad on account of the Divine Will
    of Chubby, who likes not our American
    shoes on account of they being cheesy,
    so kwitcherbellyachin.
You know what to do, just like me,
    that's why I am running as fast as I can,
    with all my stuff wrapped in a red bandanna.

        Pause. He goes out.
        Another MAN *appears, also*
        strange. The SECOND *is a*
        bit more well-heeled than
        the FIRST. *He smiles and*
        begins talking.

        SECOND MAN

Strange stuff, stuff whining in the air door.
Stuff people don't see.
(Chubby, we gotta do somepin.)
Thoroughly tough, though.
Tough through and through.

(Chubby, face it: we are the
     fly in god's ointment.)
Strange stuff, all kinda
     gussied up likeso.
x the mercantile whodunit.
Stuff, gussied up with fatal bricabrac.
I am forging the whole damn Big Ugly.
I am driving through the Great Wahnanganewee,
     on all fours, Indian fashion, on the head
     of a pin, with no saintly nevermind.
Because the boiled cup of strange air flaked up
     and foamed, damped down, dried out
     and blew away, just below critical,
     all in a tatter.
Because of bears and air doors.
Because of boars and them men there, badass.
Because...
Strange stuff, and the wind upon the water
     like god in the hay.
x the frost on the dead man's open eye.
x the fever before the episode of bellowing.
x the rain upon the recent dead.
x the whodunit.
x the Y.
x the same, gussied over in fatal funeral weeds.
Robber shoots robber as victim ducks.
I am riding, all slipshod, through
     groves of sacred cauliflower.
I am riding, all sacred, through
     groves of slipshod funeral weeds.
I am honking turtle chairs.
Robber shoots rubber and the tisket's
     a tasket.

Duck shoots duck till the sky implies
    a further monad nomad.
...?...
For rain down as rain up was.
The whole ghastly glitter, whaled.
Gee and haw, hawsered.
I shoulda done rubber boat bloat.
I shoulda chair grease and hemlines
    creaked with bargain-basement
    stress fractures, hula hoops,
    and whatnot bricabrac baloney.
You know why?
You know Y.
You know how the Y am did from its
    former days, hawking rubberbands
    in some grimy barbados, raincaked
    in a kitten's grave, under the floor
    moon, shank-shivered in ebony coal dust, sure.
You know Y for sure, hotcakes.
For I am learning the lingo of stretch
    disaster.
For none other of them rotates the glove-box
    bankrupt.
For I too was, cuffed and bumped
    and all bobtailed.
For I clawed my hairy way
    to thisnthat.
It was not am likesome, for it war
    shoatly.
Chlorine boxes sprung leaks above
    so we smote the hexes and slew the shoats.
Fudges of unknown slime succumbded to their
    baser instincts and was did elected, among
    us, kits to cats of Senatorial cabbagery, sure.

Sunken lore bellied up and dovetailed
    heartbreak.
The nightseed grew a directory tree.
Glimmers of gasses inflicted seismic
    opera upon the friends of good
    works who had gone belly up in fear
    of sunken lore and tragic glimmer gas.
Dogs learned a nether lingo
    and cussed the Y.
Dogs proclaimed Western Civilization
    a feeble fellow.
It was not am likesome.
For I was there, and saw it, and liked
    not what I saw and was saw-milled
    in hairy feather dust and buried living
    dead standing up in pure amazement.
Whining on the air door stuffed people are.
Whining dreadful, they cousin bunches
    and skin their flicks.
They revert pseudo-comic android retail.
They remind the producers of incurable
    bricabrac and cast skinks.
Grasses grow up and while away
    unexampled.
Folded up wigglies rant on glimmer gas,
    pop out, darken the light source, fur
    the bald part, slow the fulsome vat of
    superheated cheese, stuff the poor folk
    with jars of dry rot (furball puree),
    reverb the god woofer, bounce down the
    darkened staircase, turn over the cooling
    corpse to see if it's rigid, dry the eyes
    of mystic Ahab (Ahab, who shall return
    the third time as Richard Nixon), smother

the last saint in the slashed featherbed,
    black out and be borned again in mythic bricabrac.
They, the ghostly android shuttle crew, emote on cue
    and smote shoats, half-crocked, and croak.
They, the cheerful quasi-human redundant,
    grow buds on they directory trees.
They take off glasses and see the mystic orgy
    of doomed impenitents, high on glimmer gas.
They pop the dead back, and abdicate the
    next life for fear of this one, strange.
They dark the deep of it, strange.
They hang the neaptide, hey.
They fashion devil grommets from demon
    mice, magnify contagion, dive-bomb
    the wicked in their old goon hotels,
    black hubs of badass bubble.
They seek satiety, where I used to roam,
    one lone blur, with all my thousand
    furry feet, trailing my hideous gowns
    of funeral weed and bricabrac, sure.
For I would investigate regions of nitre
    with my wimple woven of star's flesh
    and spiderlegs, kinda strange.
And I would loosen the steel bands
    of oblivion, cry out, stand on my
    furry head to signify some horrid
    bio-theological paragogical bear-trap,
    some ghastly parable implicating us all
    to the Cosmic Upstart himself, who shall
    rain down hot coals upon us, all in the
    name of Impious Misrule, cheese, and the
    cold mystic thrall of cosmic pitchblende.
For I too was done up likeso.
For I too roared and bellowed, rolled over

and possum played, all to escape the
horror, the horror of happening once
too often to consider the human mythos
ripe, as it truly is, in fairest form, all
of a fine autumn eve, on a full stomach.
I too was strong enough to run off, hiccoughing.
I too was strong enough to stay.
I too grew strange the more I thought upon it.
Junk bats boat in the blue wind, ho.
Hovering in deepest glide.
Ralph there, dead.
Buoyed in dead hope, gone cat.
Dust in rills, another
    planet.
We shift our errors, compounding
    the wilderness.
Needlemen approach.
They signal, holding up
    painted wigglies.
Wind, wind and no water, yup.
Boulders bunched up, yup.
We consult the mystic oracle.
We offer up mystic glimmer gas.
We talk to our wide one, Chubby.
Chubby tells us plenty, yup.
We take their wigglies and kill
    the mothmen, sure.
Junk bats boat in the blue wind, ho.
We, we and them, them and the others, strange.
Seasons cooled, cooked.
I think about the whole damn enterprise.
I ornament the region with unholy images
    of the directory tree.
I put on someone's clothes, not mine.

The clothes cling to my human nakedness.
I am ashamed.

    Pause.

Oort. Grommet. Gort. A pox on all their houses.
Ahab. Nightman. Weasel. A pox on all their houses.
We who are not them hoard our sacred bricabrac.
The anomaly has outlived them, God and Ralph, both, sure.
Why did the door person open the door for you? Why
    was the door person friendly and courteous? Why
    did your server acknowledge you within two minutes?
    Why did you receive your drinks promptly? Why was
    your food served promptly? Why was your hot food
    hot and your cold food cold? Why did your food taste
    good? Why was the atmosphere enjoyable? Why was the
    restaurant clean? Why was the restroom clean? Why,
    during the course of your meal, did a manager visit
    your table? Why have you been here for the first time,
    for a few times, or many times? Why, when we see an
    African-American with a beeper, do we think he is a
    drug dealer? Why do we approve the cut and design
    of our server's costume? Why, when we approve the
    uncut part of the u.s. Constitution, do we not approve
    the cut part, the part about dancing—drunk—in the
    forest at night, howling before strange gods, all before
    sun-up, in strange hats, aglow?
...?...(!)...

A pox on all your houses, you.
May the very floors renounce their wall-to-wall nativity
    and fold up, all furry, like a systematic ogive mare's-nest.
May the North become South, and so forth.
May the unfurry ones, far from god, become furry like us,
    except Ralph.
May Ralph stay dead, even if he gets ticklish down there,
    and kinda restless.

May he stay good and dead on account of how we don't care
    much about him ever since he done you know what
    to you know who and that's a fact no shit sure.

> *He smiles and goes off*
> *as* YOUNG WOMAN *enters,*
> *wearing dark clothes,*
> *perhaps in mourning.*
> *She smiles and begins*
> *talking:*

I have trouble with that, politically—
    on account of you and yours being
    a loathsome, misnormal dickhead.
For which was up and done be done did am.
Lotsa y'all got all pinched up, sure.
Lotsa us'ns have had it up to here
    on account of y'all, yup.
You go figure how it all came about, sure.
Banjo playing ain't no way allowed no more, here.
Gum chewing ain't neither here nope, sometimes,
    maybe.
You gotta behave if you wanna creep low
    under that there wall of flying debris.
He who stands up gets conked good.
He who gets conked good they lay out
    for the buzzards, no shit sure.
Howzabout you'd like to be an aminal omelet,
    huh?
Lay there for a long time, thinking.
Lay there for a long time, somewhere
    on that there Sierpinski carpet,
    in a region infinitely sparse and
    infinitely many, no shit, sure.
Being all pinched up ain't no fun.

Being the devil's doormat ain't
    my idea of Christmas and Easter
    on account of being plumb squoze
    till the lights go out and the cows
    come home and the whole ponderation
    of the whole damn land mass barks up
    the wrong tree, cuts cheese and croaks.
For I stood up and was am cutdown and kilt
    by flying trash, right here, you bet, sure.
For I am riding high in the tall grass,
    all greasy, of my catastrophe.
I am riding on what looks like a horse,
    but ain't not no horse.
We are loping through the high hay
    with men on fire behind us.
We are en route to the cubical empire,
    where the gum was sticky, the
    forest was dark, and the cats
    were the wisest creatures in the land.
Where we'd come from we'd rather not
    think about, being careless unredeemables.
What kind of horse this is, this
    strange black bucking beast, hell,
    I'd rather not think about, because
    the blast force of the Golden Haunting
    affects all who left the empty mansion
    having pocketed a fork, or knife, or a spoon.
For those there men behind us
    are of the tribe of Ichabod.
Flames consume them, like us, completely,
    again and again.
Flying bricks, stoves, car doors, bins, tray tables,
    hats, rotisseries, pots and pans, shoes and socks,
    coat hangers, typewriters and screen writers, waste

paper baskets, all whistle about in the red clangor
of the hot wind, no shit, sure.
I stand up, am cut down, again and again.
> *Pause.*

Beyond snake is dog, beyond dog
> is all arcane cellos and watch out for
> them because they lost twenty-five
> pounds, quit drinking and have learned
> a thing or two since the Pretty Times
> Done Did and they have a thing or
> two they'd like to ask you, and just
> between you and me, it's not your name.

Beyond the cellos is broccoli, beyond
> broccoli is cabbage, beyond cabbage
> is cheese, and beyond cheese is the
> long, black barge, drifting there…
> all draped in black crepe…
> because…

Because, because ever wonder where your garbage
> *really* goes?

Because that black barge there which contains your
> you-know-what has come home at last, to roost.

Because that black barge would like
> to speak with you.

Because that black barge will find you out
> wherever you are, even on a remote,
> microscopic bud of an inconspicuous
> island lost forever in a wild archipelago
> of a minor Julia set, a Julia set floating
> dizzily down through scale upon scale of the
> whole damn jiggery-pokery of a full-blown
> Mandlebrot Set.

For the mellow music of all these cellos
> tiskets a tasket.

Cause of how you being a monster
      dickhead and all, yup.
And Chubby himself in hot pursuit, yup.
And the sky full of empty stuff, yeah.
And the wind deprived of true motivation
      for its visionary landscape project, hey.
And the world all woolly.
And the wool all worldy.
And the sheer unavoidability of it all,
      including the "and" and the "the".
And the Way Out locked from the inside,
      barred, barricaded with stacks of
      cardboard boxes filled with oily
      rags, powdered dioxin, and barrels
      of plutonium oxide sludge that has
      hotted up somewhat over the years so
      we can't quite recall which of the
      single-walled tanks are confirmed
      leakers, and which contain the
      ghost of Ahab waiting for the
      last appearance of Richard Nixon,
      dancing a jig in a graveyard
      with a whisky bottle balanced on his
      head.
And all the teddy bears asleep.
And all those who want my things
      prying open the locked windows.
And me slipping out in the night,
      disguised as Napoleon Bonaparte.
And what I ride off upon, which
      looks like a horse, but isn't, strange
Bledsoe's popeye bugs me so, so
      I do not care much for Bledsoe.

So the wheel turns and turns up
    a mythic rutabaga.
So I go to work happy,
    and work all day happy and come
    home happy, proud of myself sure.
Because of being happy, and not
    like you, or him, or Bledsoe,
    a loathsome misnormal dickhead.
Being happy turns the wheel for me.
Being happy is my secret weapon
    in the war of all against all.
Being a warlock helps too.
Being a wheel turns my ticklebone's
    lights on and I confess to being
    possessed of lights, darks, and
    have got the map showing where
    the mystic potatoes are, the gourd
    of life, the mythic rutabaga, and
    know how to handle big wigglies.
Being a workaholic son-of-a-stiff
    greases the wheel in the warlock's
    oarlock, yup.
Because I knock on fate's false door.
Because I know where the warlocks
    buried Bledsoe's popeye, sure.
Because Bledsoe's eye is made of glass,
    so I go each and every day to work
    with my fist buried in the ham of life.
If the shoe wears, tear it, sure.
If the shoe fits, strike up the band
    cut cheese and croak.
If the shoe fits, there's something
    radically wrong with you, you
    loathsome, misnormal dickhead.

For I wouldn't want to tangle with me,
    on a dark night, in a blind alley, nope.
For I wear the shoe even when it
    don't fit, and if you don't
    like it, tough shit, because it
    takes two to tango, especially
    when it comes to tangle, no shit, sure.
For I am riding on a moonbeam
    in the tingle of a nightmare, yup.
And I know all things, all things
    fit to know, despite them shoes, sure.
And shoes be damned, if I get it into
    my head to go riding, in a region
    infinitely sparse, infinitely many, so
    then the shoe fits because I say it does.
And it gets kinda lonesome.
And it gets kinda darksome too.
And kinda weird, because of bad thoughts
    you shouldn't ought to've done had
    and better not talk about on account
    of they being strange, or on account
    of you being far from where you ought, yup.
All kinda such strangeness give you the blues.
And you are far from where it was you knew.
For the way is covered with gruesome doilies.
And where they come from no man knows.
No man knows…
….!…
…¡(?)…
Nor what good they are.
Nor what the hoar sock bended the
    blue bell to, to hoe the hell sock
    with rat cream till the sky shout,

roll over, drop kick the heartache,
roll over once more, pop up and sigh,
wrap itself in the flag, and drop dead,
a case of terminal burn out.
Cause that's the way it is.
And you who bite the beast may
    bite in vain.
May bite in vain because of devout concretions
    of fibrillated sharkhate having vented
    into the в chamber of the moose unit,
    even though the moose unit was sealed
    off years ago, sealed off with barking
    seals and sea lions, when some abject
    dickhead, some abject misnormal dickhead
    failed to duck when that monster flywheel
    leaped the track, and spun and spun all
    beastly blue-bright and shaggy, spun for
    for a month of Sundays, strange.
No one likes to talk about
    that there incident.
No one much cares for them suchlike
    accidental incidents.
No one much likes to have they heart
    broke neither, nope, yup.
No one much has much to say about what
    stuff gets done roundabout here,
    nor why, I guess, maybe.
I put on someone's clothes, not mine.
The clothes cling to my human nakedness.
I am ashamed.

                    Slow blackout.

                    END OF PLAY

*

Described by the New York Times *as "a playwright intoxicated with words," Mac Wellman has written more than thirty plays, two novels, and several collections of poetry. His plays have been performed at Soho Rep, the Berkshire Theatre Festival, and at the Victory Theatre on 42nd Street in New York. Among his recent dramatic publications are* The Bad Infinity: Eight Plays, Bad Penny, The Professional Frenchman, *and* Two Plays: A Murder of Crows AND The Hyacinth Macaw *(Sun & Moon Press), both presented at Primary Stages in New York, the first in 1992 and the second in 1994.*

He has also edited two anthologies of plays, Theatre of Wonders: Six Contemporary American Plays *(published by Sun & Moon Press in 1985) and* 7 Different Plays. *His novel,* The Fortuneteller, *was published by Sun & Moon in 1991. His second novel,* Annie Salem, *will be published by Sun & Moon in 1995.*

Tristan Tzara

cinema calendar of the abstract heart

Translated from French by Guy Bennett

1

flask blossoming red wax wings
my calendar leaps astral medicine of useless amelioration
dissolves by the candle lit by my capital nerve
i love desk accessories for example
fishing for little gods
gift of color and farce
for the sweet-smelling chapter where it doesn't matter
on the track comfort of the soul and muscle
bird cralle

2

with your tense fingers elongating and reeling like eyes
the flame calls to grip
are you there under the covers
the shops spit out employees noon
the street carries them away
the tram bells cut off the strong phrase

3

wind desire resonant cellar of insomnia tempest temple
the waterfall
and the vowel's sudden jump
into the gazes focused on the points of the abysses
to come to surpass experienced to be conceived
calling human bodies light like matches
in all the fires of autumn vibrations and trees
oil sweat

4

your fingers straddle the keyboard
can you play me a scale of hiccups
I stoop toward you like a taut bridge
whose pillars struck by the wave do not crack
and it's uncertainty in the form of an icy decision
triggered by the sudden movement of tires
here is the muscle of my heart opening and screaming

5

beneath the stairs
snuggled up in the motory warmth of this airplane crucifix
red shadow
familiar in steam
a cigarette approaching like boat
and the acrid gasoline smoke on the lake
o hands crossing the watch the streaked fish
rise like elevators
and the gold of active flies:
the other

6

the mist injected the eye
that puts color to our sight
of light blood and opaque, tired liqueur
the coffin dance is mechanized
or multicolored pages unforeseen in the veins
petrified gray wheel stripped of branches
things leap through the distance
i live the intervals of subterranean death

7

free from overly candid charms on the sofa
fresh rope binding the stones of thoughts
or sand of indefinite white formations
mint has rounded your soul beneath your coat
maliciously
isotropic light seated on yew and diversion

8

the squares of material and foliage accentuate
the four landscapes' excuse and the diversity
among the concrete posts under construction flow
above the crowd intersected by nature
bloodstone gardener
here's a balloon
unforeseen belly dance brewery fell silent
an enormous fish
another one
colors are figures that are killed and leap
carrousel
like everyone

9

the fibers submit to your stellar warmth
a lamp is called green and sees
prudent penetration in fever season
the wind has swept the magic of rivers
and i have pierced the nerve
at the frozen limpid lake
has broken the saber
but the dance of round tables and terraces
surrounds the shock
of marble shudder new sober

10

sunrise gin cocktail
the settlement of atrophied shadows
battling buglers while box-trotting
animals signal the steel conjunctivitis of the wire fence
and the shipping industry employees
like the times in balloon
leap into the water
in guilty blue satellite costumes

11

wind for the snail he sells ostrich feathers
sells avalanche sensations
the self-flagellation works underwater
and deserts fainted in the open air with decorations vases
the transmission wheel brings an overly plump woman

parchment fields perforated by lozenges
who has understood the utility of intestinal fans
light circulation of silver in the veins of the clock
presents the precision of the wish to leave

12

ticklings in the throats of blazing little letters
a few drops of light failure suffice in the mirror
and the best cinema is the mirror of the diaphragm
arrival telegram of each degree of dry cold
wire me the density of love
to fill the song of the Indian ink rebec

13

ashtray for smokers of seaweed and filters interregnum
of isthmuses inventories inventions merry-go-round crime
lixiviation
the dadaists at the helm of the gulf stream blowgun
wear legitimate latin mustaches
care for the fistulas of lazulite
lazulite lazulite
climbing the capricorn attraction of the zealous vaccine tetrarch
and stocking up on fissures fossils
of erections filtered by jesus' thorax
prognostics attacks shackelton of the underbrain

14

sign of the cross and salvation gymnastic function memory
breaks free respiratory automaton inevitable courtesy
the hour advances in the bone and marks traces of silence
carefully applied bandage of defective machines barracks jaws
salt steel plaster tobacco anthracite mint
have proven to me the new regulations of the abstract heart
feverish cab and four acrid macabre cracks in the shack
"beneath the bridges of paris"

15

on the white strings of atrophied midnight
receive raincoat whimsical emissary
light bulb rubber woman of green by kilometers
the underground gears of the tactile sense

16

high color of maritime desires cold projection
diagonally celestial noble and corrected
on your body carved with crosses wounds
thrown into the editorial basket
measure the calculated finesse in dollars
heavy smoke spider metal fœtus

17

soporific depth that cooks the khaki cuckoo
self-taught tempered bell with humid cocoa sweat
other cerebral liqueurs disturb the big bear
in the crucibles
quivering like cultivated strings on the equator
the guillotine apparatus the familiar gate of wagons

18

purgatory announces the great season
the policeman love pissing so quickly
rooster and mirror lie down under the gallant eye
great lamp digests virgin mary
rue saint jacques pretty little boys leave
for the stamps of the white aurora aorta
the devil's water weeps over my reason

19

between two pipes and the diagonal rose
the faucet open for light peach brandy
the cross rises up from a glass wardrobe
cello cooking hypermanganate blue
embryonic gears
and traces of the trident pencil

20

the hypnotized lamps of the salt mine
turn the spittle of the vigilant mouth pale
the wagons fixed in the zodiac
a monster displays its brain of sun-scorched glass
there's the truth escaping from the cordial greeting
and resembling the ragtime turtledove
unopposed to the initial perfume with equestrian speculations
the salty vowels immobile teeth on the rails
they're withdrawing the stairs
signal

21

football in the lung
breaking the windows (insomnia)
they're boiling dwarfs in the well
for the wine and madness
picabia arp ribemont-dessaignes
hello

*

Born in Rumania in 1896, Tristan Tzara studied at the University of Zürich, where he and friends formulated the first Dada theories. Initially a pacifist statement, Dada quickly grew into a movement—fueled by the works of writers and artists such as Hugo Ball, Jean Arp, George Grosz, André Breton, Louis Aragon, Marcel Duchamp, Francis Picabia, and Man Ray that stressed absurdity and the role of the unpredictable in artistic creation.

    Tzara penned some of the major Dada manifestoes, which were collected in Sept manifestes dada (Seven dadaist manifestoes, *1924) and published in Paris, where he had moved in 1921. His poetic output was substantial, spanning a nearly fifty-year career, and includes the collections* Vingt-cinque Poèmes *(1918) and* De la coupe aux lèvres *(1961). Tzara died in 1963.*

Charles Henri Ford

from *The Minotaur Sutra*

André Breton: Don't
Tell me your dreams! I say: Don't
Tell me your sex life!

So be Master of what
You want to do and shut up
About the rest

I put a spell on
You I wish I could say that
Because I didn't

Hot words can wilt a
Heart hot bacon grease can do
The same to lettuce

Don't forget the Sixties
Were thirty years ago
So what else is new

What's going on in
That head of yours wordless
Soundless invisible

In the Twentieth
Century dreams have yet to
Catch up with the monsters

After attachment
Detachment but half of the
Attachment may stick

Desserts taste better
When not too sweet so do people
Please pass the lemon

Skeletons from the
Closet having regained their
Flesh and blood parade

The cat's in the
Fiddle and surrealism's
In the nursery

Not whatever happened
But what's happening now
Running on empty

Skin the color of
Burnished copper smooth as
Satin what else is there

Dan Mahoney to
Djuna: You're the tree that was
Meant to stand alone

Everything haunts
Nothing helps except sometimes when
Least expected to

You go your way and
I'll go mine I am not a
Joiner Cummings said

Unless you're a rock
Star what you're looking like ain't
What you been selling

Those bees of memory
Left honey in the mind
Who's to lap it up

Who was Hilda
Doolittle don't ask me but some
Say she was H.D.

It took the plunge and
Never surfaced what did
Many a poet's rep

One of the greatest
Things Matisse ever learned was
To paint a shadow

Winter's not gone yet
If the wild geese fly that way
Noodles overcooked

In France they have their
Monstres Sacrés in America
Living Legends

Drugs are a drag and
Any book about addicts
Puts you in the pits

Norman Mailer thinks
Tough guys don't dance but what
About Frank Sinatra

You were meant for me
I was meant for you (Ode to
A Dictionary)

"Live! Live!" cried Henry
James but wasn't it his way
To put writing first

Don't be cranky don't
Be cruel if you play you
Pay don't lose your cool

So what's the next step
There is no next step the one
You're on is the ridge

I grabbed it from her
Hand broke it on my knee last
Of the pony whips

First you want to do
It then you feel you can do
It then you do it

And Basho didn't
Need a computer when he
Made the frog go Plop!

*

Born in 1913 in Brookhaven, Mississippi, Charles Henri Ford grew up in small towns where his family operated hotels across the South. For culture, he and his sister, Ruth Ford (star of Sartre's No Exit *and former wife of actor Zachary Scott) attended dances. At the age of 17, the young Charles vowed fame in two years, and by that time had begun editing* Blues: A Magazine of New Rhythms, *which published the poetry of various noted moderns such as Ezra Pound, Gertrude Stein, William Carlos Williams, James T. Farrell, Paul Bowles, Erskine Caldwell, and Edouard Roditi.*

Upon the demise of Blues, *Ford teamed up with then critic and poet Parker Tyler, living a life in New York that was memorialized in the homosexual novel* The Young and the Evil, *a book banned upon its publication in England and the United States. In 1931 Ford traveled to Paris to arrange for that book's publication, and there attended, through invitation, a famed Stein salon. The book was eventually published, championed by Stein and Djuna Barnes, by Odelisk Press, the publisher of Henry Miller.*

During this time Ford lived with Djuna Barnes in Paris. Paul and Jane Bowles invited them to visit in Tangiers, and Barnes and Ford took up residence in the Casbah, where he typed her Nightwood. *According to Ford Barnes discovered during this period that she was pregnant, and returned to Paris to have an abortion. Ford, whose scandalous book was about to be published, returned with her and was taken into the ménage of the artist Pavel Tchelichew, with whom he later moved to the United States, living in Shinnecock Hills.*

In the wake of World War II Ford began another magazine, View, *which quickly grew into a Surrealist magazine, in part due the influx of Surrealists fleeing to the United States. Masson, Seligman, Tanguy, Max Ernst and his wife, Peggy Guggenheim, and numerous others published art and literature in* View *from 1940 to 1947.*

Today Ford lives in the Dakota in New York City, where a documentary of his life is currently being filmed.

Vitezslav Nezval

Diabolo: A Poem of the Night

Translated from Czech by Jerome Rothenberg and
Milos Sovak

A N D

City with Towers

Translated from Czech by Jerome Rothenberg and
Frantisek Deak

Diabolo: A Poem of the Night

poison of night:
night's antidote

Night mourner's dress slung over
railing on the quay
hung over lacy camisole

A lady in her bath

The man who takes the waters
standing bending over

Black suds obscure the tub

The matches that he strikes fly under the horizon
& ignite the lantern lights of the hesperides
they squeeze for their new moon siestas on a seesaw in the world
  ⌈beneath

A man is breathing up the scent of soap
his shadow glued onto the quay made wet with sweat

The night moths light down on the snappy virgin apples in the diner
Prostitutes embrace the faded showcases of pastry places

From up above infinity seeps thru the Milky Way

World yolk egg
stains the white radiance of eternity

Frogs' eggs ocean's nerves
thru which the fry rub up against the bulbish jellyfish
& in the underworld the shadows crumble into powders for the
  ⌈lady's face
powders the wind distributes on these trees

A harbor town a counter in a bar with breasts
laid bare over the steaming grog

Eyes tumbling into shots of absinth
fog horn

bleating ship

a saxophone

Nightwatch in helmets
cocks who crow

The maid who in her garret opens wide
against some buck's fat shadow at her window
who clenches in his palm diabolo
& bares his teeth against her petticoat
stuck up against the glass

Night mourner's dress from which a fan fell out
while the man who takes the waters fans himself
his shadow clinging to the shadow of the lady on the quay
& every time the unknown lady's hip slips from her bath
they take each other's gaze

The lady then was exiting who now had seen another
shadow on her own
had felt it grope above her knee

To walk across the garden's longer than to go thru Indochina

Thru a half-opened villa door they soar onto a bed

Below the window is a coffin lit by lantern light at night
& above it thru the keyhole of eternity
a whole world there to see

Now she was stripping down & off

The fish meanwhile had slipped out from the net

& longer than a dream she fell into the well
whose floor was like an elevator dropping down & down

A man was decked out in her skin still perfume soaked
& ran across the square & past a cop the swimming pool ahead

The night's a nautch girl singing a chanson

Sunday's over
Fiddle sounding out
Boat on the water
Drifting round about

You hear a kiss & then the boat drifts off
O Mary Mary won't you be my only babe

Sunday's over
Makes you sing & shout
Lovers go on dancing
Lanterns dying out

You hear a kiss & then the boat drifts off
O Mary Mary won't you be forever mine

Stars jazzband xylophone

Featherbeds are flying out of hangars

drifting thru gardens where they grope the ripe tangelos

In the bar it's sherry spilling onto cuffs

It's monkey trumpeters who play the jungle serenade
who steal into the prostitutes' sealed rooms

Two thieves down in the cellar cheek to jowl at dawn

That's when the lady aimed a collar at a nameless man
while her clenched hand held a ring

The victim of the crime blindfolded
in a sweet sleep by their side

The thieves were targeting each other with revolvers
& the gentleman in exiting was strung up by his tie

A woman let her shadow drop down from the window
let it lie among the roses
stripped the clothes off the dead woman tucked her in the victim's bed

Longer than a dream she drops into a coffin sent by elevator down
    [a well

Morticians drag her on a wagon going underground

In darkness she removes her breasts & rests them on the night stand
then slips out thru the monastery crypt to take confession

Nuns among the bridesmaids
candles around the dead

The priest unlocks the gates to Yellowstone

The Stock Exchange pours gold down a volcano

A humble millionairess who throws off her ermine wrap
so she can swim out with the salesgirls in their bathing suits with
    [stripes

Waiters hurry from the bar with wine for mass

The priest is shaving

The cook departing from the steam bath with a bread atop his head

The acolytes soup porters manufacture clouds
with air earth fire water floating on a silver tray

A peacock (head bent over plate) unfurls skies with his tail

& love's a spring of soda water
the priest dispenses from a spigot in his stall

Chimes ring for mass

crickets beneath the plaster in a cell for the devout

The priest a redcap now who drags the sun around the temple's nooks

Spiders at prayer
spinners of cotton lint

The nun communion over
meditating in the garden
under the friars' walls

a scrubbedup lady in between the men's & women's pools

Foghorn from the ship's heart
tore the cloister bell apart

title of a pornographic novel
among the schoolgirl's books

Breasts filling up her bodice
as a shadow from the bedroom fills the courtyard

where the chauffeurs mill around

A monk stands on his little wall

the man who takes the waters
drying out beneath a cape
peeks thru a crack in her cabana
where the naked lady waits

Into the garden rolls the buck's diabolo
who lifts night mourner's dress off
& will touch the housemaid's camisole

The world as Eve and Adam's apple

A traveler's lust for the unknown

Death a passion for eternity

Passion the craving for adultery

Virtue game diabolo

Night walker

acrobat on wire between his wife's bed
& another woman's

polo player among naked lady gymnasts

genteel bosom boxer

Man who plays diabolo with woman

All nite vaudeville

Marriage halfway station for failed acrobats

A few choice wizards of equilibristics

trying headstands on a horse in night's arena

shimmers like the garter on a lady's leg
dress slung over lady's head on sofa
when lady goes to sleep

City with Towers

o hundred-towered Prague
city with fingers of all the saints
with fingers made for swearing falsely
with fingers made of fire & hail
with a musician's fingers
with shining fingers of a woman lying on her back
with fingers brushing up against the stars on night's abacus
with fingers from which the evening gushes fingers tightly clasped
with fingers without nails
with fingers of the smallest babes & pointed blades of grass
with maytime fingers & with fingers out of graves
with beggar women's fingers & an entire form at school
with thunder & lightning fingers
with purple crocus fingers
with fingers up in the Castle & on old women playing harps
with fingers made of gold
fingers thru which a black bird whistles & a storm
with fingers of naval harbors & of a dancing school for girls
with fingers of a mummy
with fingers from Herculaneum's last days & Atlantis caving in

with fingers of asparagus
with fingers with fevers of 105 degrees
with fingers of a frozen forest & with fingers without gloves
with fingers on which a bee has landed
with fingers of blue spruces
with fingers that tap a flageolet in the orchestra of night
with fingers of a card sharp & fingers of a pin cushion
with fingers disfigured by arthritis
with fingers of strawberries
with fingers of a wind mill & a bouquet of lilies
with spring water fingers & with fingers of bamboo
with fingers of wild shamrocks & ancient convent fingers
with fingers of leached chalk
with fingers of cuckoos & of a christmas fir
with fingers of a medium
with threatening fingers
with fingers a bird brushes up against while taking off
with fingers with the sound of church bells & with decaying dovecot
        ⌈fingers
with fingers of the inquisition
with fingers that we lick to test the wind
with a mortician's fingers
with a jewel thief's fingers on a visionary's hands
with fingers on a hand that plays the ocarina
with fingers of a chimney sweeper & the chapel of Loretto
with rhododendron fingers & the fountain on a peacock's head
with fingers on the hands of a poor sinner
with roasted fingers of barley growing ripe
with fingers of a coral morning & of the view from Petrin Tower
with fingers pointing upward
with hacked off fingers of the rain & of the Tyn Church on the glove of
        ⌈twilight
with fingers of the desecrated host

& with inspiration fingers
with slinky fingers long & jointless
with these self same fingers that I use to write this poem

*

*Like others of his time, Vitezslav Nezval, born in 1900, was touched
by the Surrealist movement, which opened his work to dreams and
to a game of ever more distanced juxtapositions. Even before his
contact with André Breton in 1933 and others of the Surrealist
movement, Nezval sought to "unveil reality" by making the poem
"strange" and by creating "at the expense of logic."*

*Like other innovators, however, Nezval worked through a
prolific sweep of modes and genres: open and closed forms of verse;
novels drawn from his childhood and more surreal chance-ori-
ented works such as* Like Two Drops of Water; *avant-garde
theater collaborations and at least one vaudeville-like performance
piece,* The Woman in the Kiosk, *along with numerous transla-
tions of his modern counterparts and predecessors such as Rimbaud,
Apollinaire, Neruda, Lorca, Eluard, and others. Nezval also made
forays into music, painting, journalism, photography, and, from
1945 to 1951, film, when he headed the film section of the Infor-
mation and Culture Ministry in Prague.*

*His commitment to communism came early (1924), and led also
to his arrest and imprisonment during World War II, while his
politics before and after made him a prominent member of that
network of tolerated avant-gardists/poet-heroes that included
Neruda, Brecht, Picasso, Hikmet, Eluard, and Tzara, among oth-
ers, with some of whom he shared pro-forma hymns to Stalin in
the early postwar years. His initial "poetist"/"realist" phase cul-
minated in a 1920s triptych,* Acrobat *(1927),* Edison *(1928), and*
Poems of the Night *(1930). His surrealist work is most evident
in* Prague with Fingers of Rain *(1936). He died in 1958.*

Jeffrey M. Jones

Office Work

Officework is a site-specific piece set in a small office. The audience enters the office, where a man is working at a desk. A COWBOY *enters the room when the play starts, and if the light switch isn't beside the door, goes to it. The* COWBOY *looks at the audience impassively while silently counting off fifteen seconds. Finally, the* COW- BOY *speaks softly and evenly.*

COWBOY: Well...

> *Pause.*

...time to hit that dusty trail, Tex...

> *As the* COWBOY *turns off the lights the* MAN *begins to speak; he is visible only in the spill from the doorway.*

MAN: Okay, well I guess if enough of you folks are here we might as well start cause I think some of you know I feel it's real important that we do get the opportunity to meet like this on a frequent basis throughout the year because actually one of the ironies of having you guys more involved around here on a day to day level is that the activity in the place can get to the point where it's hard for anybody to stay really on top of everything that's maybe going on.

So I did just want to mention before we begin just a couple of things, uh...

Got a twenty-five thousand dollar contribution

that of course I'm tickled about even though it was really kind of sad, actually, cause it's from one of the Directors who passed away recently, and this is actually an area I'm trying to work on more with these guys 'cause you kinda hate to say it but most of them aren't gonna be around all that much longer and the thing is when you can get twenty-five thousand bucks from a guy who's been giving at maybe the one or two thousand dollar level, that works out to a pretty good deal,

And I mean these guys are all loaded, the problem is back when they started a one or two thousand dollar check was still a big deal so we're trying to bring 'em into the 20th Century but the only trouble is most of em are really getting to the point where they basically don't have a lot on the ball anymore so it gets kinda tough to explain things to 'em...(laughs)

Some a you know Marty Taback you know what I mean...

Anyway, to be real honest with you guys I'm still not too clear about what's going on here—I guess there's some folks who've had questions about stuff which is bound to happen from time to time and like I say when it does I'm really I'm happy to talk to you guys about it because you know very frankly that's what I'm here for and I mean, like I say, you guys are what the place is all about so you know if you folks do have a problem I'd really appreciate you having the courtesy to come to me and give me the opportunity to work with you on it because frankly there's probably a lot that goes on here you guys maybe don't understand about, so like I say when people do start running around here with rumors and what-not it's really pretty destructive and frankly, to be really honest, I wish one of you guys had had the guts to…

COWBOY *turns on light;* MAN *stops talking and stares at audience.* COWBOY *counts 13 seconds before speaking.*

COWBOY: I think my name is Frenchy.…

I'm a dancer.

I was sent back to audition.

I'm going to do a Sally Rand fan dance.

Ain't many places you can work if you're an outlaw.

Folks, we're gonna show you twenty-seven, I said twenty-seven different ways to have sexual intercourse.

Show it to you for a quarter.

Give him a quarter and see what happens.

Hi, want to hear a dirty story for a dollar?

I feel terrible taking money from you like this but it helps…

Just ask for Frenchy—that's me…

I'm here every evening from seven to five in the morning,

Go ahead and play with it if you want to, Mister—You paid for it.

COWBOY *turns off lights;* MAN *resumes talking.*

MAN: So like I said, if you're not too happy with the personnel changes, very frankly, I'm basically I'm always willing to talk to you guys about that but when you get right down to it that's gonna be an area where I call the shots and that's the way it goes.

So like I say, I'm always real glad to listen to anything you guys might have to say but the hiring and firing is gonna be my decision so maybe you better get used to it.

But I mean on that money thing, jeez—I don't know where you guys get that stuff, guys;

I mean take a look at the audit, look at the audit, you know, I mean you guys are always welcome to look at the audit and to be really honest I'd kind of appreciate some of you taking the trouble to sort out the facts cause the fact is that we have a budget, that budget's approved by the Finance Committee and that's the way money gets spent around here so when folks start to say I did this or did that you know, look at the papers, cause my name is not even on there....

COWBOY: R-R-R-R-R-R-R-R-I-I-I-I-N-N-N-N-G-G-G!

> COWBOY *turns on the light; the* MAN *reaches for his telephone; pause—then the following scene, very fast and with a minimum of inflection.*

MAN: Hello, is this the party who had an ad in the paper?

COWBOY: Yes.

MAN: Is this masseur?

COWBOY: Yes, may I help you?

MAN: Do you pose for pictures?

COWBOY: Do you mean in the nude or with clothes on?

MAN: No, in the nude, I'm an artist.

COWBOY: Why, yes, why not?

MAN: Would you mind telling me your measurements?

COWBOY: I'm six foot tall, blond, blue-eyed…

MAN: You built large?

COWBOY: Well, I told you I was six foot tall.

MAN: That's not what I meant, I mean downstairs.

COWBOY: I'm sorry, sir I don't talk that way on the….

MAN: R-R-R-R-R-R-R-R-I-I-I-I-N-N-N-N-G-G-G!

COWBOY: Hellooooo….

MAN: Is this the masseur?

COWBOY: Yes, yes it is, may I help you?

MAN: Yes, I hope you can, I was wondering if you might have a young boy for me to spank.

COWBOY: Yes, I think we can arrange that—that'll be 25 bucks. 25 bucks an hour.

MAN: 25 bucks?

COWBOY: 25 bucks an hour.

MAN: Say, that's pretty high—now is he going to do what I want?

COWBOY: Within reason.

MAN: Well I want one I can turn over my knee and paddle. I want him to tie me up and then beat me. I want, uh…. Have the boy stand on the corner and I'll drive past and then pick him up…

COWBOY: R-R-R-R-R-R-R-R-I-I-I-I-I-N-N-N-N-G-G-G!

MAN: Is this the masseur?

COWBOY: Yes yes it is. May I help you.

MAN: Do you give enemas?

COWBOY: Do I have enemies?

MAN: No, enemas! Enemas!

COWBOY: Oh, enemas—yes, I think that can be arranged.

MAN: Well, this is Mr. Johnson, and I'd like to know if I can get an enema.

COWBOY: Mr. Johnson…

MAN: Yes?

COWBOY: You sure you wouldn't really rather have a nurse?

MAN: R-R-R-R-R-R-R-R-I-I-I-I-I-N-N-N-N-G-G-G!

COWBOY: Helllooooo?

MAN: Is this the masseur?

COWBOY: Yes?

MAN: Is this the masseur who had an ad in the Times?

COWBOY: Yes?

MAN: Is it too late….?

COWBOY: R-R-R-R-R-R-R-R-I-I-I-I-I-N-N-N-N-G-G-G!

MAN: Is this the masseur?

COWBOY: Yes?

MAN: Is it too late….?

> *Pause;* COWBOY *counts off five seconds.*

COWBOY: Better just come on out with your hands up, Sheriff.

> *Lights out;* MAN *resumes talking.*

MAN: They were drawn up by lawyers—

> Now you guys aren't lawyers so to be really honest you probably don't even know what I'm talking about but if you look at those papers you'll find they were voted on by the Finance Committee, they were approved by the Finance Committee and hey, check it out for yourselves, guys—they're signed by Chairman, they're signed by Treasurer but they're not signed by me—my name is not even on there—and you know why that is?
>
> Lemme tell you something:
>
> That's because I am an employee of the Directors, and I work for the Directors, not you guys, not Joe Blow down the street so I mean I'll be happy to sit here and listen to your questions but I don't have to answer to you guys.
>
> So when you ask me to get into the specifics of why did the Finance Committee do this or do that very frankly I'm not going to do that because (a) you guys don't have the qualifications to understand what I'm talking about and (b) under the by-laws of the Corporation, which by the way I happen to have with me, the deliberations of the Finance Committee are covered by executive privilege.
>
> And you know very frankly the one thing that does get me a little steamed up is when one of the people you guys have been making a big deal about me lettin go of was supposed to be doing the books except after she found out her two hundred twenty pound girlfriend was screwin' some guy she got so suicidal she threw all of the bills in the wastebasket

so when you guys start making these accusations about money let me tell you it's kind of ironic cause the books are so screwed up we don't even know on the Finance Committee exactly what's going on.

Lights; count 5 seconds; start Elvis's "Are You Lonesome Tonight" when Elvis starts singing, MAN *resumes.*

MAN: So you know the difference between a pig and a fox?

It's about four drinks. [*Laughs.*]

So you know the difference between your job and your wife?

Five years later your job still sucks. [*Laughs.*]

So you know how come fat girls are like a moped?

'Cause they're fun to ride but you wouldn't want your friends to see you on top of one. [*Laughs.*]

So you know what an Eleven is?

COWBOY: Sheriff...

MAN: It's a Ten that swallows. [*Laughs.*]

COWBOY: Come on out now, Sheriff.

MAN: So you know how come god created women?

COWBOY: Sheriff...

MAN: 'Cause you can't teach a sheep to cook. [*Laughs.*]

COWBOY: You better come on out.

MAN: So you know why they don't allow women to swim in the ocean?

COWBOY: You hear me?

MAN: 'Cause they couldn't get the smell out of the fish. [*Laughs.*]

COWBOY: You just better come on out cause I don't want to have to come on in ta git ya.

MAN: So you know what you call a woman who can suck a golf ball through a garden hose?

COWBOY: You hear?

MAN: Darling. [*Laughs.*]

COWBOY: So you just come on out now, Sheriff.

You hear me?

MAN: So you know the definition of eternity?

COWBOY: Sheriff....

MAN: It's how long it takes between the time you come and
the time she goes. [*Laughs.*]

COWBOY: Better come on out with your hands up.

MAN: So you know how come women are like dogshit?

Lights out at the bridge, as Elvis starts talking.

Now I'm an easy-going guy and I can tell you
my philosophy is you don't go in the kitchen if you
can't stand the heat because whoever's in charge is
always gonna have folks saying things about him
behind his back and when it just gets too ridiculous
you pretty much have to ignore it so like I say I
think I've got a pretty tough hide but lemme tell
you—some of the rumors you guys got going on
around here are getting just a little out of hand—I
mean, people saying I said things or did things or
what not, come on to 'em, you know—I mean you
hate to threaten folks, but it gets to the point where
when someone's going around talking like that they
darn well better be able to back it up.

Cause like I say some of this stuff is so sick you
sort of wonder where it's coming from and I men-
tion that only because in the one instance I do hap-
pen to know a little bit about, we had this gal in the
building and she had some personal problems and I
don't want to mention her name 'cause I think you
all know her but I guess she started claiming I was
goin' around here with my pee-pee hanging out
which like I say would have been kinda ridiculous if
it hadn't been so pathetic because what it really
turned out was she was goin' over to the Port of
Authority to buy dope and payin' for it by bringing
these street hustlers back here and pulling the train
with 'em down in the john in the basement and how

we found out was this nineteen-year-old intern walks in there one morning to take herself a dump and finds her in one of the stalls giving a junkie a blowjob.

So I mean, on the money, as far as the money, that money was legal, the Directors approved it because they approve everything and that's why they signed off on the papers—and that's why, you look, my name's not even on there.

And as for that other stuff I just don't even know what you're talking about.

Lights up as Elvis resumes chorus.

But now as to the money, that money, the money was legal.

And as to the other stuff,

Well, I don't know what you're talking about.

But now as to the money, that money, the money was legal.

And as to the other stuff,

Well, I don't know what you're talking about.

But now as to the money, that money, the money was legal.

And as to the other stuff,

Well, I don't know what you're talking about.

Thank you.

MAN *gets up from desk and exits.*

COWBOY: Just a word, folks...

You been sold—mighty badly sold—but you don't want to be the laughing-stock of this whole town, I reckon, and never hear the last of this thing as long as you live.

No—what you want is to go out of here quiet, and talk this show up, and sell the rest of the town!

Then you'll *all* be in the same boat.

Ain't that sensible?
You bet it is.

All right, then—go along home and not a word
about any sell.

COWBOY *exits; end of play.*

*

*Jeffrey M. Jones is a playwright whose works include the ongoing
series of "Crazy Plays": "Write If You Get Work" (first performed
at the Ontological Theater at St. Mark's in New York); "The
Endless Adventures of M. C. Kat" and "Crazy Plays Que Fumar"
(Cucaracha Theatre, New York); "The Crazy Plays" (BACA
Downtown, Manhattan Theatre Club Downtown / Uptown Festi-
val); "Annunciation with Wranglers" (HOME); and "Office Work"
(New Dramatists). He is also the author of the historical quota-
tion trilogy* A History of Western Philosophy *by W. T. Jones.
Comprising volume I: "Der Inka von Peru" (1984); volume II,
"Tomorrowland" (1986); and volume III, "Wipeout" (1988). Other
plays include "The Confessions of a Dopefiend" (1982); "70 Scenes
of Halloween" (1980), published in the Sun & Moon anthology,*
Theatre of Wonders; *"Nightcoil" (1978); "The Fortress of Soli-
tude" (1972), and "Love Trouble, " a musical published by Sun &
Moon Press in 1994. Sun & Moon is planning a collection of his
"Crazy Plays" and others in the near future.*

*During the 1980s Jones was the Managing Director of the
Wooster Group / Performing Garage; Theatre Program Director
of Performing Artservices, Inc; Executive Director of Real Art
Ways (Hartford); and President of the Board of the Alliance of
Resident Theatres / New York. He currently works on WordBasic
development and hypertext documentation projects for Micro Mod-
eling Associates, Inc, in New York.*

Velimir Khlebnikov

Lightland

Translated from Russian by Paul Schmidt

And the fortified centers of world trade
where poverty's fetters shine in the many-paned windows,
the day will come when you turn them to ashes,
and the look on your face is a rapturous vengeance.
You who were weakened in ancient struggle and argument,
whose torments are figured in the constellations above you,
shoulder these barrels of gunpowder, persuade the palaces
to shatter to rubble and blow in the wind.
And when the pillar of smoke dies down
in the fiery glow of the flames,
let blood stream from your hands in place of your banners
and throw down the gauntlet, a challenge to destiny.
And if the conflagration proves accurate
and a sail of smoke billows up in the blue,
enter the burning tent, draw from its holster
the fire you conceal at your heart.
While ill-got profits slumber away their nighttimes
in crystal cases; in the Tsar's particular palace
explosive devices are all the rage, to say
nothing of clever feminine intrigues.
When even God denies your life,
slave of the rich, remember your knife!
Someone has murdered your childhood, girl:

strangle him with your hair when next you see him
because you were barefoot and helpless
and went to him asking for help and he kicked you aside.
Creep like a cat, keep yourself clean,
untouched by soft pawings at midnight.
When you are sick, go kiss him on the mouth
and breathe disease through the laugh on his lips.
Your hands are unused to steel?
Run to the rabid watchdog
and kiss his slavering mouth,
then go kiss your enemy, kiss him until he dissolves.
Slave of the rich, go laugh in his face.
You are poor and have nothing, and poverty tears you,
you crawled like a have-not at a king's feet,
and then you kissed him.
You are ailing and sick with a great hurt
and must open the fiery gates of dawn:
Tear out the dripping beard of Aquarius,
and the Dog-stars, whip them yelping from heaven.
And from this moment on, let Lobachevskian space
stream from the flagpoles of night-loving Petrograd.
The Time of the Takers is over; the Might of the Makers
parades; т has fallen; м occupies the stage.
These are the high priests of LIGHTLAND,
and "Workers of the World" is their banner's device.
This is the havoc that Stenka Razin unleashed,
come home at last to roost in the clouds over Petrograd!
and its mad rush is the theoretical system
of Lobachevsky, and Lobachevskian space itself.
Let Lobachevsky's curves descend
as ornaments over all the city,
let them rest like strongbows on the sweating shoulders
    [of Universal Labor,
and the lightning will wail, complaining and crackling,

when it finds itself harnessed, condemned to a life
    [at hard labor.
And gold, done up tightly in bars and portfolios
will lie untouched, with no one to buy it.
Death will sit counting the hour of death,
the hour when he will come again,
And the prophets of earth in their constant appearance
will reform all alphabets, wiping out unwanted letters.
The day when winter died in early spring,
workers in Hungary stretched out their hands to us!
Working man, raise up the fortress of what you are worth,
let its building blocks be only the beats of your heart.
Then raise your glass, clink it in the face of starry Virgo,
and remember the melodious songs of the mind
and the voices of strong men long since vanished.
Then leave, go out into the clang of one sword on another.
Let the linden tree send her ambassadors
to the high seats of governments everywhere,
and there will be no one left to desire
those long gone occasions of sinful passionate ecstasy.
Let kings make much of the carved facades of their palaces,
though the carving is cheap, and vulgar and tasteless—
in the same way, see how often the venerated crutch,
holy relic of a famous saint,
becomes a facade for highway robbery!
When even God denies your life,
slave of the rich, remember your knife!
Move ever onward, you convicts of earth,
move ever onward, you squeezed-out survivors of hunger strikes,
See how one man sweats and labors in the dusty field,
while his sharp hustling neighbor snaps up the harvest!
Move ever onward, you convicts of earth,
Move ever onward, you who are free to starve,

And you others, you kings of commerce,
your eyes are left you for one thing only—for weeping.
Move ahead—there, that way—toward a time of universal health,
Let us fill up our words with sunlight, making them glow,
and pull down thrones, and hurl them like fallen idols,
like Perun, to be pieces of wood adrift in the Dnieper.
Soar, you great constellations, star-clustered humanity,
fly farther and deeper into space,
and melt all forms of human speech
into one unified conversation of mortal men!
In the heavens shot through with stars
like the chest of the Tsar, the last Romanov,
some homeless lounger, tattered by thinking, friend to all that's
    [unholy,
will hammer away at a forge, refashion that star-cluster.
And you dawdlers, deceivers, you pitiful madmen, you drunkards,
scatter across the winds, part of the past
like chopping blocks and the wedding rings of the last kings.
Your textbook twitter bores us, stories of black swans,
how once a black swan dwelt far to the south—
but now a swan with scarlet wings
flies on the waves in a blizzard of bullets.
It is time for you Tsars to keep your appointment:
your time is up, your scaffold is appointed.
And the secret every army keeps is this:
when the bride arrives, her dress is crimson red.
Let the last kings on earth
overcoming their anger, smile
and stand like statues, stones against the glow
that shines from the graves of dawn.
You gave wings to the constellations,
to permit a rush of infantry against the sky.
You set depth charges in the riverbed of time

and locked up all kings in cages in the zoo.
There he sits now, the last surviving king on earth,
behind the iron monotony of bars on cage,
next-door neighbor to a horde of monkeys,
downing the fatal vodka of his poisonous thoughts.
In a swirl of bluish smoke you have drowned
all thrones, their glitter, their glory, their pomp and their
        [majesty,
and one last tear rolls down his cheek, child
of an unseen visitation of thoughts.
Capital cities rear up on their hind legs,
trampling great hooves upon the low-lying places,
their living inhabitants swarm in the streets
and advance to assault the thrones.
With the sound of thunder graves split open
and thrones come tumbling down.
The sea will remember, will always recount
in its awful threatening language,
how a castle of lace was the prize of a girl
who won it by dancing in front of a throne.
The sea will remember, will always recount
in its thundering racket and roar
that the palace was once a prize for a dance
danced for the assassin of a hundred nations.
Limestone carved into fretwork lace
on a palace for their majesties' girl friend.
Now the dancer's private residence
beats out a call to arms that arouses the mind.
You remember a time of thunder and threat by night;
you were walking, stalking the enemy's odor,
and heaven looked down at you, whistling,
blaring its madness in howling horns.
The sign of the hangman spelled out in the heavens.

Once again the crack and beating of thunder
while someone who simled a divinely idiotic smile
looked down upon earth's conflagrations.
Germany's G fell away from its name,
likewise the R dropped from the name Russia.
And I myself beheld the rise and extension of L
in the smoke of the fires on Midsummer's Eve.
Raise your bow above the expanse of storm clouds,
above the violin of Planet Earth
and assign a black name to the firemen
who come to extinguish the fire of intellect.
Remember, a Tsar is only a panhandler now,
and a King is a poor relation.
Move ever onward, rabble of freedom,
let liberty's hammer fall!
You are fodder for cannons—meat, nothing more,
warfare's scabby corpse—at least
until across the waves of universal dancing
the hopak-hurricane descends.
You hear? "Banzai" is dead,
and "Hoch" and "Hurrah" both are silent.
Raise your shout to the red god,
direct at him your groan of anger.
Decorate the summit of Mont Blanc
with the all-knowing skull of Hiawatha.
His land is innocent, and part
of the encampment of Humanity.
The Valparaisans scramble for doubloons;
rubles have overwhelmed the Hondurans.
Your task, you madman, is constantly to accomplish
the drench of your knife's blade in blood.
Hatred is the good word nowadays;
bloody yourself in its actions.

You records of bygone centuries
Hurl yourself into the sea of thoughts and swim.
Strike up the band again, light of dawn,
and call down battalions, defenders of freedom.
if ever again the people whose Kaiser is iron
move out like iron, like an iron river.
Where the Volga says "I"
the Yangtse-kiang says "love"
the Mississippi answers "the"
and old man Danube adds "whole"
and the Ganges waters finish "world."
The river idol in his courses marks
the edges of the green world.
Everywhere always, ever and everywhere,
All for one, forever and everywhere!
Our shouts will rise up to the stars!
The language of love drifts over the world
and the Song of Songs longs to be sung in heaven.
The blue expanses of ocean peer
through their own depths, their own blue eyes,
and in diagrams of destiny I will decipher
the reason that scarlet lightning shines.
Wars have pecked out your eyes from your eyesockets—
go, you troubled-filled blind men,
seek for yourselves such power and authority
that your fathers have reason for savage rejoicing.
I have seen such trains of blind men,
their arms outstretched to those who call them family,
the doing of dealers—wheelers, stealers!—
all testimonials to the filthy workings of evil.
Wars have torn off the legs from your bodies—
but Siberian forests are sprouting with crutches—
and after all, perhaps God will lend a hand

to help you cross the vast expanse of Russia's fields.
Shuffle along through the night, you skeletons,
on the paths cut between these palaces of glass,
and let the wits among you coin their cleverness
into the booming bell-song of the dead.
For the last time now, over the city Krupp has built,
that rustles with the bones of slaughtered armies
the corrupted soul of the golden corpse
spreads itself out in every direction.
You have crammed yourself into these prisons,
where even the stairways and handrails run in harmonious
     [accord,
and the skyscrapers neighbor the clouds,
but all of it heavy with smoke and anxiety.
A thick layer of dust
covers the iron Kaiser's cohorts.
The fingers of the past bit into Adam's apple,
digging, convulsed by what has come to pass.
But you have known the strings of ruptured muscles,
tied up your bleeding sores with a shirt,
you know the terrifying song they sing,
your groans—or are they howls of torment?—
And now for the first time appears on earth:
the face of Razin, sculpted by Konenkov,
like a holy book on the Kremlin,
and Shevchenko who does not fear the day.
Warrior of freedom, barefoot wanderer.
See there, those horses go galloping by?
A herd of turbulent liberties,
smashing cast iron.
Drive your knee upon his chest
try to be strong, however you can!
And you wind, with your pock marks of iron,

go whispering "Lord, Lord."
You showed the god of nighttime
the ancient sores your fetters caused—
find a better class of idiots!—
and you showed the sky the road.
The hand of earth seals off the mouths
of those whom cannon shot has buried.
Carry into the temple of slander
the wind of those who burn in chorus.
The man whose neck is strangled
by gold's implacable fist,
he, cursing with the strength of a hammer,
is familiar with the speech of lightning.
A team of six horses, their front-bending heads,
no longer transports noblemen;
the continent flares like a star from one end to the other
with a fire more ardent than flame.
And there! Those icons of freedom,
the bright shining eyes
of Hurret al Ayn,
wreathed in secretive eyelashes.
A Slavic girl, her light brown hair in braids,
tearing petals from the water-flowers,
dissolves the sayings of Tsong-kha-pa
in the innocent morning dew.
Where the scarlet beef of battles
lies still smoking from the fusillade,
everlasting Freedom marches,
in her hand a banner boldly flying,
and the skyscrapers drown in the smoke
of an explosion set off by the hand of God
and the palace of profit and salesmanship
is hidden in smoke rings and grayness.

The city that snapped the carriage-poles
of God as it wheeled in a sudden turn
has quieted now; unease seems barely perceptible
in the quiver of its horse's mouth.
The city that boasted once of its ancient rightness
and rose strong in the beauty of its laughter—
in its eyes the most heavenly horse head
chews on the steel bit and the bridle.
Cruel always, and eternally sad,
caress your throat with a heavy razor.
From heaven's case of drawing instruments
you chose the hurly-burly of revolt,
and it will fall across the anvil
beneath the hammer's blow—God's own design!
You have pounded horseshoes onto the feet of God
to make him serve you as a faithful slave
and fastened tightly fitting fetters
on the raven summits of the sky.
It makes its horse's head look human,
entangled in the mane of man's intelligence.
Its eyes blinded with the splash of whitewash,
the chalky city strikes tinder, sets fire.
Who is the horseman, who the horse?
Is this a city, or is the city God?
But the clattering racket of beating hooves
calls out for galloping, for a great wild rush!
To the land where Izanagi
reads *Monogatori* to Perun,
and Eros sits on Shang-ti's knees,
and the topknot on the god's head
looks like snow, a lump of snow;
the land where Amor embraces Maa Emu
and Tien and Indra sit in conversation;

where Juno and Quetzalkuatl
adore Corregio
and admire Murillo;
where Unkulunkulu and Thor
with folded arms
play peaceful games of chess
beside Astarte, who worships Hokusai—
go there, go there!
Like owls ranged along a blood-stained perch
the towering palaces go up in flames.
Wherever labor finds it easy walking
and rebel drills and wedges beat the ore,
there deep as all rebellions shine
the Virgin Mother's cast-iron eyes.
Again the cattle low within the cave,
and the innocent child takes suck from the she-goat's udder
and beasts and people crowd about
the Divine Birth of women for today.
I see horse-freedom
and equal rights for cows.
Again years flow together as they did in ancient tales,
the scales have fallen from mankind's eyes.
Whoever knows that no dawn is wiser
than the dark blue of a horse conflagration,
he shelters the horses' ambassadors
in Ostozhenko, on Volkonsky's farm.
And once again, austere sectarians
like Arctic oceans cover
the night-time triangles of the face
of freedom, closed over with stars.
From flowers of May to April showers
the year is one long labor for us all,
and yet they say the gods are kind,

that every workday has a right to rest.
Side by side from dawn's first light
you gather sheaves beside your wife.
And what repayment from the man who owns the grain?
"Nigger, thanks a lot."
From sowing-seed to stubble-field,
until the first snow covers all traces of the path,
an army dressed in white, armed with sickles,
binds up the laborious sheaves.
You are bound around with the landlord's ropes,
you are gentled by whips in the hands of priests,
you pant like an ox—until the perspiration
on your shoulders burns. Chew your chunk
of moldy bread, your cruel bread—
how long already?—until you are set free
by the force of earthly rack and ruin.
Fill the drinking bowls of freedom up
with a song of exultant poison.
Freedom goes on, it moves, it advances, it grows
like the conflagration of the universal soul.
There will be armor, a breastplate of time
on the chest of international labor,
and the reins of power will be transferred
to number, understood as farmsteads.
There will come a final struggle
between the ruble and the hungry rabble.
Rejoice, you edible grains, in your brotherhood
with the hammer in the worker's hand!
And let the plague-breath ink
cover the blank pages of existence,
the breathing of destiny has transformed
the lands that wear freedom's garment.
Then will the beautiful angle

of labor's earthly sail catch the wind
and you will fly, immortally sunburnt,
blessed young man, to that land!
A final assault on the pestilence of gold!
Come join us, you thieves of heavenly eyesockets,
you best and you brightest, come learn the trick
of muzzling the mouths of the plague-beast!
And let the chatter of birds now echo
in the bright blue heavens of springtime,
tomorrow the scaffold will tumble you down
into dreams beyond all human dreaming.
This is the surf of humanity
pounding away at the cliff-face of death.
The Russians no longer have
a land to call their own.
Where London carries its trading to China,
we, the creators of what's to come,
adjusting the clouds like a Panama hat,
we ignore their insolent palaces;
For us, their ashes do not count.
We have followed the path of rebellion,
and lost very little in the process.
The Presidents of Planet Earth
advance in a group, ready for anything.
For thirteen years we Futurians have kept
alive, at heart, in sight, before our eyes,
in our retreat at Krasnaia Poliana,
the burning spark of Nosar's revolution.
Upholders of the banners of all freedoms,
guiding the galloping ride with your bridle,
fly fast along the highway of blue,
go be a part of this superhuman campaign.
Bury the remains of time

and drink from the starry glass of freedom
and upon the heavy ingot of the sun
let the clanging giant's hammer of assembly ring!
You hoist a sail above the constellations,
so earth can sail its strength and wildness
into the highest tier encircling the world,
and the bird of stars remains as it was before.
Sweep from the face of earth all the filth of commerce
and level the castles and fortresses of trade,
then use the stars as building blocks
and let glass bells ring in the streets of capital cities.
And in the great grille-work of mirror-windows,
you night-bird wrapped in a glow of blue,
spin yourself a cocoon of filaments;
let the silkworm mark the path of your flight.
And the giant sounds of nighttime beat
upon the earth as on some vast alarm,
when those mirrors reflect their echoes outward
and the mesh of capitals spreads its encampments.
When the fleece of fields is combed
by a rake of clouds of deep nocturnal color,
the birds of the air will pause in mid-flight
to steal the grain as it falls from the fertile skies.
Early in springtime the wizard of wings
will cut the clouds in his flying machine,
and the plowman will hang there, high over the earth,
sowing his spring grain with an aerial hand.
His harnesses span heaven and all its clouds,
his harrows help the sprouting fleece of earth,
and everywhere the stalks of rye spring up,
tended by herds of horses in the sky.
He does not simply pray: gimme a good
and heavy harvest, God, amen!

but trusts his crops to the power of equations,
and carries a series of numbers in his heart.
And their millstones grind out
flour made of edible earth,
nocturnal windmills there by the steep ravines,
wearily turning their tired wings.
Words of knowledge form themselves into lightning flashes,
speak out loud to an audience of rejoicing young people.
Thus are textbooks transported through clear air
to learning centers, one in every village.
Search beyond the downpour of grains of rye,
for one who cut the East in two,
where tanker-trains go north,
transporting the nourishing broth of lakes.
Where the landlord's fishing rod once jiggled
and his children lazily sailed their boats,
waves are now roasted to feed the capital cities,
and fumes of intoxication rise from vodka lakes.
Night-riding steam-engines carry lake-soup,
vast kettles of it; the stuff is frozen
into ice-blue blocks and brought to human eyes.
Behold the sea, slip-covered
in cragged peaks of glass;
a plume of heavy smoke arises from it,
and hangs in the air like a twist of some god's hair.
A structure casts its shadow on the water
and the palace of the seas arises, ready—
a troika of whales sets the sea afoam
as it carries the castle of waters onward.
The lake-maker, mirror of a wilderness of clouds,
finds that it has the power to fly.
The bard who sings the uprising of writing
seeds workbenches as he sows plowed fields,
and a band of youth, all of them sworn

to the destruction of all languages—
I know you can easily guess their names!—
march in parade, and flowers crown their heads.
And you march too, a sheepskin carelessly thrown
across your daring shoulders, full of wildness,
marching to light the bonfire that signals
the inception of changes in earthly existence.
In love with wandering, he reached for
a row of numbers, as if they were a walking stick,
and squaring the root of minus I
cleverly noticed the rusalka it contained.
He discovered the double-visaged root
of one who has nothing and never had,
in order to perceive in the land of the mind
the rusalka hidden at the roots of the tree.
The pearls of the Pechora burn above us
through a headdress of distant stars—
there's your direction, go, you heaven-helper,
raised up by the force of your lever-device.
We will form bucket-brigades to transport Neva-water
to extinguish the Dog stars where they blaze.
Let a train lay a scar of soot across the blue
as it flies along the branching forest network.
Let the heavens shake and stagger
at your heavy foot-fall.
Brace up the constellations with log-beams,
and fasten the valleys together with an axial grid.
Crawl like an ant across the face of heaven,
explore the cracks and fissures of the firmament.
Blue wanderer, snatch fast at those prizes,
those blessings that were already promised to you.
The savage force of that lever-device
has allowed this descendant of midnight storms
to set pile-drivers, power-drills, sledge hammers

in place among the nighttime constellations.
Brace your ladder against the face of heaven,
set a fireman's helmet upon your head,
and climb up, scramble over the walls of the moon
through the carbon smoke of corrosive fire.
Set the hammer for a sign in the heavens,
spin the sun in a circle a turn or two
and see—where the East burns with a red glow,
set in motion its cog-wheels and gears.
You replace one clock with another,
you pay for your supper with a smile;
whenever the value of labor must be measured
you place the number of heartbeats on the scale.
The sharp-eyed attractions of profit and gain,
inequality and heaps of money—
the great prime mover of the distant past—
the poet of today will exchange them for poems.
A masterful siren will brighten
the silences of the great desert,
and the train, swift envoy, will pass out of sight
more glittering than the crowned constellations.
You wind electric coils from the very earth,
whose wires are conductors for storms alone,
and you praise the gentle shepherdess
who sits by the brook among the damsel-flies.
And there will be equal signs
between the hours of labor and the hours of rest,
and the sacred iron rod of perished power
will be entrusted entirely to the voice of song.
And even idleness, the mother of invention,
will rank as labor's equal,
will grasp the crowbar of authority
with the otherworldly force of ecstasy,
and your flight, forever forward,

will be followed later by those who move limply
as even the traffickers in truth begin
to recognize the booming voice of justice.
Trace out a path on the shores of the sea of slander,
tensing the soles of your feet as you go!
Encased in a shell of steel, an eaglet
will fly, trailing its crimson wings;
only a moment before the flame of a match
like the tongue of a calf, licks it alive.
Survey the world with love, not chalk,
draw us diagrams of what is sure to come,
and fate, descending through air to your bedside,
will stoop to listen, a sentient ear of rye.

*

*Velimir Khlebnikov, who died in 1922 at the age of thirty-six, is
one of the great Russian poets of the century. He was, in great part,
the genius behind the Russian Futurist movement; but the difficulty
and, often, inaccessibility of his work has meant that only recently
has he been translated into English.*

*Born in Malye Derbety on November 9, 1885, the year of the
publication of the second volume of Karl Marx's* Kapital,
*Khlebnikov graduated from Kazan gymnasium, and in 1908 moved
to St. Petersburg, where he entered the university. Beginning in
1909, the same year of Marinetti's first Futurist manifesto, he pub-
lished literary works, among them "Incantation by Laughter"
(1910), "O Garden of Animals!" (1910),* A Game in Hell *and*
The World in Reverse, *both with Kruchonykh (in 1912),* Mrs.
Laneen *(1913), "Usa-Gali" (1913), "The Word as Such" (1913),*
Selections of Poems *(1914),* Creations *(1914), and* Zangezi
*(1922). Khlebnikov was drafted into the Russian army in 1916
and was released in 1917, after which he worked off and on for
newspapers until his death.*

Charles Bernstein

The Republic of Reality

Suffice it to suppose
that across the street
a humming bird imagines
its nest as spun of
pure circumstance, or
that the corridor beside
the calendar is cloaked
in disarray, arriving
at sometime or other
aboard a bubble cast about
in air or
dumped unceremoniously
into the asymptote
that becomes your
journey's life, I
beside you, cutting in
& over flips of
imperceptible switches
just out of reach of
the laughter, larder,
larceny of inability's
raptured threnody.

Imagine you're on a log or nail
or disposable table-length
heliotrope and the man in the
corner booth buttonholes you
about the price of seats to
the game, demanding more than
could be gained in the course
of a dead-end run to
victory, the children safely
tucked in their cabanas, jumping
three or four leaps at a throw,
mimicking maniacs like it was
going out of the question, when
you fall upon a fellow with
falters and a fit for a glove:
not the machine in your
eye but the ladder in your
mind—two out of one,
five into thirteen & the punch
of it into the exterior, exteriorizing
hunch of terry cloth transversals
and cotton coasters.

Sometimes, alone at night, falling
into what lies beyond sleep,
irritably interrogating the irregular
anticipations of dent & groove,
groveling toward that station lit
like lullabies, lurching at the
divide between instant and
instantiation, mindful of racks,
lockers, lilts, levels &
lurches; loading capfuls

of collateral musings into
jacuzzi cyclodramas, pedestrian
luggage slides, stiff brocade
souvenir place holders, armoires
with genuine polymer fluting ruggedly
coordinated against a toxocomial
profile of fully monitorable text
transmission and limited access
interface
           —the subject, cheesy
little thing under all this weight,
chewing its cud, relents,
pivoting and bobbing before
lapsing into blank.

In the picture, a man holds
a candle up to a brightly
lit window, his eyes cast
downward. Several flies hover
overhead tracing the lines
of a triangle. Two young
children approach the man, the
younger with arms outstretched
and leaning on one foot, the older
with head peering forward toward
the candle. A wooden table,
crowded with books and papers
and cups, is at the opposite
end of the room from the
window. Above the table
is a picture of a man holding
a candle to a brightly lit
window.

The bandleader takes a puff of
his cigarette then crushes it under
his heel. A delirious midget
delivers toasted almonds to the
corporate tower. Spurting with
uneven temperature, the shower
epitomized her climb from secretary
to sorcerer. The shelves
sagged under the weight of Kevin's
pet rhinoceros. Insolvent and
insoluble, the conundrums of life's
mysteries greeted the weary
passengers on the subway train
to the hidden hills beyond
the visible horizon. Going
no where fast, Sally took
another picture. No hope
was held out for the recovery of
three visually challenged mice who
had brought hope to the financially
challenged village of itinerant
homeopaths.

to be proud
to have blinders
to pull a load
to collapse
to hold hope
to linger
to long
to seem to fail
to be forgotten
to travel suddenly

to invent
to inveigle
to disappoint
to cast adrift
to stare
to be shunned
to gather dust
to tremble
to hold tight
to stray
to fill up cups
to shudder
to tense
to undergo humiliation
to skip
to stall
to make up motives
to tiptoe lightly

This line is stripped of emotion.
This line is no more than an
illustration of a European
theory. This line is bereft
of a subject. This line
has no reference apart
from its context in
this line. This line
is only about itself.
This line has no meaning:
its words are imaginary, its
sounds inaudible. This line
cares not for itself or for
anyone else—it is indifferent,

impersonal, cold, uninviting.
This line is elitist, requiring,
to understand it, years of study
in stultifying libraries, poring
over esoteric treatises on
impossible to pronounce topics.
This line refuses reality.

Envoi

What falls on air yet's lighter
than balloon? What betrays time
yet folds into a cut? Who flutters
at the sight of song then bellows
into flight? What height is
halved by precipice, what gorge
dissolved by trill? Who telling
tales upbraids a stump when
prattle veils its want?

Stone breaks it not, nor diamonds,
yet splits with just one word: it's
used for casting devils out; still,
fools obey it first.

*

*Charles Bernstein was born in 1950 in New York City. He at-
tended the Bronx High School of Science and Harvard Univer-
sity.*

His first book, Parsing, *was published by his own Asylum's
Press in 1976. In 1978 he began editing, with Bruce Andrews, the
influential critical journal,* L=A=N=G=U=A=G=E. *The same*

year Sun & Moon Press published Shade. Controlling Interests *(1980) and* Islets / Irritations *(1983) further established the characteristic range of Bernstein's stylistic and philosophic preoccupations.* The Sophist, *published in 1987, made apparent that comedy was a fundamental element of his work.*

Rough Trades, *published in 1981, received international critical attention, which has grown with the publication of his* Dark City *in 1994 and the republication of* Content's Dream: Essays 1975-1984, *originally published in 1986, reprinted into the Sun & Moon Classics series in 1994.*

Among Bernstein's other works are A Poetics *(1992) and* The Politics of Poetic Form, *which he edited in 1990. He has also edited collections of poetry for* The Paris Review *and* boundary 2. *In collaboration with Susan Bee, his wife, Bernstein has produced several books that explore visual settings of text. Bernstein is also active in musical theater; he has written three librettos with composer Ben Yarmolinsky.*

Steve Katz

"Tin"
from *Swanny's Ways*

I GOT UP to talk on the phone. In my own apartment I was colder than meat in a butcher's locker. Lucinda was up too, shivering by the space heater. She always waited for me to light it. The phone had bounced me out of bed before I'd opened my eyes. I didn't know who was talking until it hit me. This was my father. "Can't you light it yourself?" I covered the mouthpiece to say that. "I blow myself up," she said. "This is my father talking to me," I said. "I'd like to know your father," she said.

"Dad, hi," I said into the phone.

"No. Not yr da. This ain't yr da. Not himself at all."

It had been years since I'd heard my father's voice, not since he'd returned to his people in North Carolina for good. They were Tinkers, transplanted from Ireland, and while he lived with me and my mother he'd return to them every Spring to make money. They had a barn painting scam. The paint they used was water colored cheaply with some red or white talc, nothing but a wash that would last till the next rain. They quoted a cheap price to the gentleman farmers, saying they had a little paint left over from their last job. By the time the paint washed off your barn my dad and his partners had disappeared three counties beyond. I pictured him, spray nozzle in his right hand, adjusting the visor of his snap-brim tweed hat with his left. The voice on the phone had my father's lilt.

"Not my dad?"

Lucinda threw a bathrobe over my trembling body, then got back into bed.

"No. No. Not himself," said the voice. It was like another planet checking in. "I wouldn't be yr father, but a dear friend to Patrick Swanson, and I was wondering if you might be the son. He often spoke of a son he had raised in New York City. Would that be yerself? William Swanson?"

"I'm William Swanson."

"We found yr phone number in yr father's effects."

I grabbed a chair. It was "effects". The word made me want to sit down.

"Me name is Moikal Stokes. They call me Moik."

"Yes."

"Well, I hate to be the one who is givin' ya the news, but yer father has passed on."

"My father?"

"Yes. Yer da."

"When did he do that?"

"He had a stroke, ya know. Just this yesterday evenin', just as he was gettin' out of the shower. Mary found him. His feet was still in the shower, and he was leaning out over the commode. His arms was wrapped around the shower curtain, never even fell down."

"Thank you," I said. I'd never seen my father naked. I'd never been to that fabled land where he lived the other half of his life. Hanging on to the shower curtain.

"We'll be holdin' the wake for him, and Pegeen Murphy said well why don't you call that boy in New York City and ask him does he want to come down here to pay his last respects. See his father one last time. Have a wee drink, ya know, and say a last goodby. We don't know ya at all."

"I would like to do that," I said, a hint of a brogue creeping into my own voice as I connected to the life on the other end of that call. I wrote down the number. Fly to Atlanta. Someone would meet me.

"Light the heater," Lucinda said as soon as I hung up. This was an ancient gas heater that tilted into the soft floor. Unlit it sat across from my round dining table, cold black and monolithic; but once lit, with a pan of water steaming on top of it, it was like a hotspring from a national park.

"Lucinda, this heater is against all the fire codes."

"Why do you say that every time you light it? You like to brag about breaking the law?"

"I'm studying the law, Luce. I go to night school."

"School," she said and snored off as I squeezed back into bed to wait for the room to warm up. My arm looked very white lying across Lucinda's chocolate back. I poked around with my other hand in her unraked afro. "What are you doing?" she said, coming out of a snore.

"Checking for roaches."

"Oh man," she rolled over to look at me. "You're a racist."

"What are you talking about? Roaches don't discriminate."

"You wouldn't be looking for roaches in some blonde hair."

"I wouldn't have to look. They'd show up easier."

"In this Eyetalian neighborhood I'm living here with a racist husband. You're more corroded than those albino roaches."

We weren't married, but we'd been living here on Crosby Street together for over two years and it felt that way.

"I love you, Luce. You know that. I love your hair."

"Love's a weasel."

"How about making love?" She closed her eyes. I loved

her pale eyelids and dark lashes, and to slide off her nose onto her generous lips. I loved her slim brown fingers reaching down to guide me into her sweetest, pinkest, moistest. She'd draw out the word "mean" as I pushed into her.

When I put my lips to her nipple she lifted my head off by the hair. "Hey, Swanny. You didn't tell me what that phone call was about."

I tried to drop my head back down to her breast. "What was it?" She yanked my head back again.

"It was about my father." I didn't realize till then how much I really didn't want to get into it.

"So what about him? Is he sick?"

"No."

"He's dead. You're lying here with me and your father just died. Where did it happen?"

"In North Carolina. He went back down there years ago. I hardly even remember him any more."

"You should have got to know your father. Are you going down there?"

"I think so."

"What do you mean you think so? Either you're going or you're not."

"Yes. I'm going."

"I want to go with you."

I didn't want to hear that. Until that moment I didn't know how much I didn't want to hear that. "I'm going to take a bath."

"It's warm enough in here now," she said, stretching her body that I uncovered as I swung out of bed.

One of the advantages of tenement living was the bathtub next to the kitchen sink, so I could soak there and talk to Delta Airlines and watch Luce as she fixed coffee and stirred the Cream of Wheat. She plunked a board across the tub and set my coffee mug down there, and my cereal, sugar, cream. She forced a smile when she looked at me.

"So? What? Am I going with you or not?"

Alyssa, the Delta agent, took me off hold at just that moment and I made a reservation for the next morning, for one person. I would get there by mid-afternoon if everything worked out. Where was there? Somewhere middle of my father's world.

Lucinda glared at me from the round table in the corner. "Call them back," she said. "Change the reservation to two people."

"Luce, this is the South. These are Irish people. I don't even know them."

"Black Irish," she said. "Like my grandfather was a Scot, remember? And on the other side my grandma was a half Chippewa. That's my high cheekbones. Where did your circumcision come from anyway, boy?" She came over to the tub and flicked at me under the water.

"Are we arguing now?" I asked.

"I've got some sick days coming. I just want to take a trip, with you. You met my mom. I never met any of your people. I want to go where it's warm."

"It's the South, Luce. It's my dad's funeral."

"You've never been to the South before. I'm from the South. I know where it is."

"I just don't want to turn it into a civil rights march."

"O yeah, draw me a picture."

"What do you want?"

"If you had half the courage you once said you did this wouldn't make any difference."

"I never said I had courage. I never use that word. I just don't want to raise issues at my father's wake where I don't know anyone."

She relit the burner under the coffee. What would my father have said about Luce? Tinkers, he always said, were treated "worse than niggers" in Ireland, his emphasis on that word, as if he were pressing it out of the filth. My mother, from her Florida Jewish retirement ghetto, had already called her my "schvarze", and had asked if she did windows, as if I'd enjoy the joke.

"You going to slop in that water all morning?" Lucinda asked as she refilled my coffee. Her hand splashed at my dick. "I know this story. I know what it's about. I don't even want to go. Really. I'm just going to miss you. All we ever do is work, and we never get some time to relax together. Run run run. You didn't even finish punching me up this morning."

"Maybe we should get you a snorkle."

She grinned and squinted down at me under the water. "That wouldn't work." She kept staring at me.

"What?"

"It's just hard for me not to notice sometimes."

I looked down at myself. "Notice what?"

She smothered my dick in her fist. "That you're a white man."

"Uh oh. battle stations." I kissed her. "Up periscope."

*

I took off from Newark on the next morning through the layered zincs of New Jersey overcast. I wore my heavy peacoat and jeans. Other passengers were dressed light, as if they knew the South they were headed for.

"You're such a good boy," my mother said when I called her from the Newark airport. "Your father will be proud of you."

"My dad is dead, mom. That's why I'm going down there. I don't think the dead get to be proud."

"I know. You told me already. I listen. I hope you don't wait that long to come to see me. Give them my condolences. Tell them that I think about him a lot. He was a good man, your father, when he was around. He was a good father. But I've got to tell you, Billy, I'm a lot happier now with my life."

"I'm glad to hear that, mom. That's good for you."

"So tell me, do they feed you on this flight?"

"We get breakfast, maybe lunch on the flight back."

"What's this 'maybe lunch'? You don't know? Did you order Kosher?"

"I don't care about that."

"What's to care about? It's just better food on the airplane. They make it special."

"I'll try to remember that for next time."

"You've got a lot of Irish in you. You're forgetful, like your father, may he rest in peace, now. Give them my condolences. Don't forget."

"I won't."

"And when will you come down to see your mother? You could bring your girlfriend if you're not still with that schvartze. Maybe you should come alone, because down here you never know. Not that it would make a difference to me. We could go sailing down to the keys. Charlie's a real fisherman. We have a friend with a boat. It's beautiful down here on the ocean. I'm still alive, you know."

I carried those words with me to seat 34a, window, non-smoking. Jewish mom, Irish dad. If you can avoid it, don't have them, like mating an anteater and a panda. I am the result, a coin struck one side on the old sod of the red planet, the other under the Atlantic Ocean of chicken soup. Their kisses were natural enough when I was a kid, but as they grew older they retreated into their differences and their lips couldn't bridge the gap. Maybe this is why I always end up in these impossible combos like me and Luce, sometimes coffee and cream, sometimes a toad-meat quiche.

No one was there to meet me in Atlanta. When I called the number Michael Stokes gave me a woman answered. Dishes clattered in the background, some fiddle music, drunken singing. The sharp voiced woman never heard of me, didn't know I was coming, reluctantly passed me to Michael Stokes. I heard a tin whistle from another room.

"Is that you, yerself," said the muffled voice on the other end.

"It's William Swanson."

"Wait a second here. I had the devilish thing upside to the other. Don't know which end is which any more. Now so it's you, boy. Where were ya? We wuz waitin' for ya."

"When was that?"

"Yestiday we wuz at the airport all day expectin' and expectin' ya ta get here."

"It was just yesterday that you called me."

I heard him take a drink.

"Is that the truth? Was it yestiday? Fergive us. Time gets a little wacky when the situation is such as it is. You can't figger a minute from an hour, nor a day from a week." Another pause as he had another sip. "So do ya want me to come down and git ya, boy?"

"No, you needn't. I can get there by myself."

"I'll be more than happy to make the run, or I could send yer sister."

"No. I'll rent a car and come up myself. I don't have much time."

"Well that's a gentleman. I kin understand what you be sayin' about time. Time's a bugger, and then it drops ya. So that's a good boy. I'll stop me platterin' and tell ya the way. You just come up as far as Dillard. That's right on the map. You'll find it. You'll see a sign for the skiing. Sky Valley ski area is what it'll say. You just go from there over the border into North Carolina. That's where we be. You'll come to a road on the right says Shanty Road, and you follow that one for a mile or so and there we are. That's a good boy. That's yer father's son."

His mention of "your sister" clicked in my head for three hours as I drove into the mountains. Was that a lapse in his mind or was I going to meet someone I could call "my sister"? My dad had been secretive enough about his life in North Carolina, but would he hide a sister?

The road wound as if it too had to take some chances to find the way. Spring was earlier here than in New York. The woods bordered the road like walls, rusted in patches of red blooms, with scraps of white dogwood blossoms pinned to it here and there in a bluster of messages. Above the steep hills in the wind huge clouds rose like weightlifters on the march. The weather was a performance. A city boy doesn't get to see such mountains, so much atmosphere. I pulled off my peacoat. My shirt was wet under the arms, my forehead cold with sweat. This was a neighborhood where I didn't know any of the alleys.

I was on Shanty Road by four o'clock. This dirt track into the woods looked like it went nowhere. The trees that leaned out seemed to choke it off around each bend. After a little more than a mile a small clearing opened onto what looked like some sheds and a small house set in a junkyard of wrecked cars and trucks, tractors, carts, wheels, barrels. A skeleton of a wooden silo slanted against the wall of a small barn in a yard where scraps of farm machinery settled into the mud. A few pigs wallowed there, and at the dry end some half featherless chickens scratched. A pair of mules watched me with suspicion from behind a fence as I stopped across the turning circle from the old house, a torn up yellow Studebaker rusting in the center. I swung my legs out of the car and sat there deep in the barnyard smells and the baying of dogs. Kids played on the unpainted porch of the house that was twisted on its foundation as if some hand had tried to spin it. A galvanized tin chimney pierced the sagging roof, and the pebble-grained asphalt siding in all the colors made the place look like salesman's sampler.

Slowly people came to the door first to quiet the dogs, then to calm down the kids, then just to stare at me. I wanted to drive away. I was the only audience in this theatre, ready to walk out on the performance. Hard-times faces grooved as the granite that rose in sheer cliffs behind the shack were the faces Walker Evans had stolen into his photographs. The women wore modest, high-necked gingham dresses, and the men dressed in workpants with old, ill-fitting Sunday jackets and ties. In the long moments of silence as they stared at me I thought I should have worn a tie. A donkey brayed into the silence, pronouncing my strangeness to the woods. No one approached my car. Everyone disappeared back inside. I should have stayed home with Lucinda. I should have let her come, just to reassure me I was real in this space here. She knew how to get along with people. That was her survival. Having her here couldn't have been weirder than this. I felt nothing familiar here, not these faces, not the barnyard smell, the woodsmoke, the boiled cabbage. None of this was me, but so deep and rich, so potent it moved in me as if it were my own memory, moved into the sprained hollows of my past to stir up aching forms of absence, raising in these vacancies a terrible sadness that moves me to tell you to get to know your father. I should have been here formerly. I should have come here now more formal. I wished my shoes were older. Where was my father? Not in this place. Not my father-of-the subways. Not my father of long walks to the Cloisters. Not my father of afternoons at Yankee Stadium, late evenings with the Knicks at the Garden. Not find him here.

"Are you the boy?" Someone had sneaked up on me and clamped onto my arm with a powerful grip. I looked into the grin of a small, wiry man, showing his stubs of teeth in full decay, his face missing an eye, no patch over the empty socket like a wrinkled mouth. The creases of his face and hand were tinged red like my father's with the pigment of the barn color to which his life was wedded. "Musha, there is the resemblance to poor old Patrick, though you come out a little plumper."

No one called me plump. I was always the 97 pound weakling, candidate for a Charles Atlas course in dynamic tension.

"You should have a wee drop," he said. "We opened the old stuff. It don't get no better."

I tried in vain to yank my arm from his grip, don't think he even knew he had me clamped. "Me name is Moikal Stokes. Oi'm the fella talked to you on the phone. So ya came down for a last look at yr Da. That's the way it should be, but why shouldn't ya have a bit of a gargle first."

He let me loose and guided me by the elbow into the house. My forearm was grooved from where he'd held it. Kids climbed everywhere on the porch, taking advantage of grown-up drunkenness to be as rowdy as they could. In the kitchen where we entered people looked glum and tired. A tin whistle from the other room threaded the first few bars of Amazing Grace. That was where my father lay.

"A wee taste, and fergit a bit." Michael Stokes' hand was on my shoulder. From a brown ceramic jug on the sink he poured four fingers of honey-colored whiskey into a glass decaled with McDonald's golden arches. "I don't mean you should fergit him, yer da, but only a good taste so you can fergive him fer goin' so lonely on ya in the ways of understandin' that he's gone, when ya see him lyin' there and yer left to mourn after." He tipped some whiskey into his own cup. "Ya need the wee drink just ta fergive him. Drink it down. Ya'll fergit who died at all, and then ya go see him. Ya'll tell him yer goodby nice and easy, without yer heart so confused."

It was easy down, a warm velvet trickle. The taste reached my heart and diffused through my mind like a soft mist. Several people now looked with interest as my face relaxed into a smile. A woman came close, her lively green eyes curious and friendly in her wrinkled face.

"Is this the boy?" she asked Michael Stokes. "Is this the son of Patrick, all the way from New York City?"

"It is himself."

"Ara, there do be a resemblance." She brushed my cheek with her rough hand as if it were some velour she couldn't resist. "Soft. Ain't he soft." She returned to the darker room and Michael Stokes followed her, leaving me alone. My legs were ready to surrender to gravity and I grabbed the handle of the pump by the sink. Above the sink was a calendar from 1958 with a picture of the Roman Coliseum. Three years later my father will have left New York forever, me alone. Everyone but me was out of the kitchen. Outside was twilight, the children still romping on the porch. In the darker room the tin whistle had stopped. I moved towards it, keeping tight to the wall, and I looked in. Candles lit the body of my father laid out on a sheet on the table. People dozed along the wall in the deep flannel gloom, breathing in, breathing out the smell of death.

An old woman with grey hair down her back rose from a chair and came towards me on bare feet. She stopped to look at me, working her toothless mouth. "I'm William, his son," I said. She mumbled something to the air above my head, then passed by me into the kitchen. Against the wall, slumped on his stool, chin dipped into his coveralls over his mandolin, hands positioned so it seemed he was still playing it, a heavy man snored softly. His lips fluttered, the body rising slightly and sinking with each breath. I was a sleepwalker in this somnolent world. The good whiskey had buoyed me into tenderness, a lover of everyone. These people, why not call them my people, sleeping so. And my father, when I looked at him again on his table, had somehow lifted to the sitting position and was staring at me. I tried to blink him away, but he was staring at me. I stepped deeper into the room to see if anyone else had noticed this development. He seemed in good humor.

"Is that you?" I heard him ask, though I couldn't see him move his lips. "Light of my heart," he said.

A radiance subsumed the dimness of the room so everyone else seemed wan as ghosts.

Once before he had called me "light of my heart," when I was little. I went with him on a hike overnight across the George Washington Bridge. It was one of the few times I ever spent with him alone. He pulled from a full milk-bottle of moonshine he carried in his pack, and I turned away from his breath when he grabbed me on the bridge and lifted me to his chest and said, with unfamiliar affection, "Billy, Billy. Light of my heart." There was something thrilling, both dangerous and exhilarating about my father when he was drunk. My mother feared him then, but I liked it. She'd send him out of the house, and that's how we got to go overnight on a hike. When drunk he was almost never violent, except in his affections, and I thought then anything could happen, until I realized nothing could happen.

It was evening. We climbed down below the bridge and vaulted a fence to a small park at the foot of the Palisades. It was a mooring for boats, with some grass, and benches in the shrubbery. There was a delicious feeling that we weren't supposed to be there after dark. My dad built a small campfire out of scraps of wood and buried potatoes under the embers. He pulled out some tin plates I had never seen before and told me those plates had been fashioned by my grandfather, the best damned tinsmith in all of Ireland. He laid one on the fire and fried some meat on it, then opened a can of beans and poured it over the cooked meat. While it stewed he pulled again from his bottle, and stared at me saying "light of my heart, my William."

Suddenly he grabbed my arm and lifted me off the ground and swung me out in the air till I feared he'd let me go and I would fly out over the river. Manhattan looked half sub-merged where it lay seething in amphibian silence under the long arc of the bridge. He told me how his family would camp in the bracken on the outskirts of Dublin, and his fa-ther would hammer the tin cups and churns and ladles out of galvanized, with never a leak in them, for the people who lived in the houses, and how they had lived on that money till plastics killed the metalworking, and then they traded an occasional horse till all the roads were paved for the motor-car. My arm was out of joint, and he was drunk and swing-ing me as if he would hurl my little body at the city, till he heard me cry out that he was hurting me and put me down. "You've got to give them this," he said, raising his fist in my face, his sour breath shivering down my spine. We sat down to the food, and he rolled a spud out of the ashes, teasing it around with sticks till it was cool enough to handle. He cracked some of the char off it, cut it in half, put it on my plate of meat and beans, and sat across the fire from me nibbling on his half of potato and sullenly sipping from his jug, half empty now. He rolled another potato towards me and I held on to it to keep my hands warm as I watched him snore off. Even at seven years I was aware I would never know this man with whom I sat in darkness. His skills wouldn't help me survive in my city. I listened to the Hudson gurgle against its banks, shivering in my smallness as I nibbled on the cold potato.

My father woke before dawn and went down to the rocks at the river bank to piss, and I followed him. I'd been holding mine in. He said nothing. I watched our piss in the dawn reflections—his a thick stream of fire, mine a fine arc of smoke.

He was stretched back out on the table, face rigid as wax, eyes closed. Across the table from me a woman mumbled into her black scarf and though her head was bowed she kept glancing at me. A young woman who held her arm looked at me directly.

"G'wan over to him," the older woman whispered. The young one let go of the other's arm and came around the table.

"Would you be William Swanson?" she asked. She was very pale, but pretty in that colleen way. There was something familiar. "If you are," she said. "then this is our father." In a slow, balletic arc she swept her forearm across to point her hand at the corpse. "I am Swanson too. Madeline Swanson."

The way she said her name was dramatic and self-assured. It reminded me of my father. She looked like family, like more than that. Her eyes. One was blue, the other half green, half brown. From my childhood, fifteen years old, Florry O'Neill had eyes like that. The Florry O'Neill who was murdered out of my life. Hers were exactly those colors. I never thought I'd see those eyes again.

"You needn't cry over him," she said, her voice somewhat bitter. I wasn't aware I was crying. "He had a long life, a couple of them, and he was ready to die. He was mean enough to die," she whispered at the end.

"Madeline is such a pretty name," I said.

"He never wanted to call me Mary, or Bridget, or Pegeen, Molly, Patricia, Ellen. He said he gave me a name that would take me away from here. He always said that some day I would be ready to leave."

"How old are you, Madeline?" My sister. I was talking to my sister.

"I'll be twenty-one this April."

The old deceiver, my father, even while he was with me and my mother he had this other family, this other wife. She stood in black across from me. I tried a smile. She acknowledged me briefly, a smile across her thin lips, then pulled the black scarf across her face and retreated into the shadows. Scoundrel, my father. I looked at his dead face. Great man, prince of deceit.

"So what's for you at twenty-one?" I asked my sister.

"I guess I'll go seek my fortune," she said. "As any young man would. I've had a year of college. Perhaps I'll go back. I have to see how my mother bears up. I think she'll be fine. She's plenty strong, though she doesn't look it just now. I don't know what to do, really. Open to suggestions. I can't stay here. I'll be on my own."

"Come to New York."

"Sure, and go to the moon, too." She laughed.

I suddenly wanted to take her in close, because she looked at me so familiar, her face so bright, so Florry O'Neill. I am this young woman, I thought.

"So ya found yer brother, ya did, Maddy." Michael drew us both into his arms. "And have a good look at him, because that's yer brother. Ya didn't know ya had such a tasty brother, and half a Jew-man at that."

Madeline squeezed my arm.

"Oi'll tell ya what. After all that flyin' down here from New York he must be tired, then drivin' all this way on his lonesome from the airport. Why don't ya show him yer Da's caravan and he can bed there fer the night. Here. Use my torch."

He handed her a flashlight. Festivities were ended now in the room. The big man in coveralls was stretched out now on a braided rug, sleeping by his mandolin. Madeline's mother nodded in a chair in the corner. A woman who had been sweeping leaned her broom against the wall and left. This was the second night of the wake. Many had gone home.

"Come," whispered Madeline, tugging on my sleeve. "I'll show you where it is."

Kids still romped on the porch. "Madeline, Madeline, someone puts a paddle in." Several of them taunted her.

"Hush, you babies," she said. "They're having a time. Only at a wake they get to stay up through the night. Tomorrow morning they'll be collapsed, for sure. They're happy because they won't have to go to school, God bless the nasty little snots."

There was not even a sliver of moon. Madeline excavated with the flashlight what seemed to me absolute darkness. On the other side of the barnyard we came to an old Dodge van parked on a patch of gravel. She showed me the narrow bed inside, and a small kerosene heater I could light if I got cold. It was nicely fixed, with some embroideries hung on the walls, a lace curtain over a small window he had installed himself.

"I didn't even think you might be hungry. Did you eat anything?"

"I can wait till morning. Moonshine was nourishing."

"And you want to wash up. I forgot about that."

"That can wait till morning, too."

She handed me the flashlight and turned to leave.

"I should take you back. It's awfully dark."

"I've moved around here in the dark all my life."

I grabbed her arm as she started away. "Do you have to go now?"

"I shouldn't be here with you."

"I'm your brother."

"It doesn't feel that way. I just met you."

"But you pointed out we had the same father."

"Didn't I? In that case you must be my brother." She kissed me on the cheek. "How was he for you, our father?"

"What do you mean?"

She crossed her arms over her breasts and looked down.

"Do you mean…? He never beat me. Is that what you mean? What did he do to you?"

"We'll have some time to talk in the morning," she said and looked at me one last time with those sorrowful eyes.

I sat silent on the rear bumper of our father's van as she disappeared. What had he done to her? I climbed in and felt my father's narrow travelling bed. Had he touched her? Molested her on this bed? Did I want to know about this? Was that an owl who-whooing? I'd never heard one. Did I want to hear this owl? A thin, straw mattress covered the bed, and one light blanket, a lumpy pillow leaking chicken feathers at the head. I felt the coarse veils of my father's other life closing on my heart. Above the pillow, fastened to a small cupboard, was an oil lamp and some matches. I lit the lamp. On a shelf nearby were a few books—an old copy of *Pilgrim's*

Progress, a worn anthology of Irish poetry, a paperback of Louis L'Amour, a collection of Synge's plays, and a book called *The Greening of America*. That was it. I opened the poetry to a page he had dog-eared, and read the lines he had underlined there:

> And when the devil made us wise
> Each in his own peculiar hell
> With desert heat and drunken eyes
> We're free to sentimentalize
> By corners where the martyrs fell.

and across the lower corner of the page he had scrawled these lines in pencil:

> Now all the truth is out
> Be secret and take defeat
> From any brazen throat

I would never feel the rage that had made him copy out those words.

The van shook suddenly and a ghostly face flickered at the doors in the lamplight. One eye flashed there.

"So what do ya think of yer father's van. You found it okay?"

"It's comfortable."

"If you want to take it back with you to New York I suppose it's yours. The girleen don't want it at all. Neither do her ma." He sat on the bed with me.

"There's all the paintin' gear, the pumps, the hoses, the nozzles and all. He wuz well equipped. Oi'm out o' the business now. And there's them two mules. Oi thought we'd put all that up to auction so there's a little money fer his Mary.

He didn't have no insurance, ya know. We'll sell them mules as well. Oi don't believe you got use fer some mules up there in New York City."

Mary. That was the name of his other wife. He had a Sylvia in New York City, so I guess he needed a Mary down here.

"She got the house and the goods what's in it, but there ain't much else. He never bought no insurance or nothin fer her future, yer Da."

What warp of my own life had brought me here, to talk to this one-eyed Irish guy about intimate stuff that had nothing to do with me? Except for the grace of the telephone I would never have known anything about this. What a century this is. I was about to tell him I didn't want the van, that he should sell it as well, when he said:

"But what Oi'm thinkin' is it would be best to burn up this old caravan and be rid of it. Oi'm only askin', ya know, because Oi'd understand if you'd be wantin' ta keep it; but if ya want to know from meself what Oi think, Oi'd say it would be best to have it burned, so there won't be no place fer his ghost ta fasten. A Tinker's ghost'll never fasten to a house, ya see, but to his caravan. They've been known to hant around them fer as long as the rig survived, and Oi fear if it don't burn poor Patrick'll never be free of the misery o' this world."

He looked at me through his one tearful eye, an expression like that of a little boy asking for something he never believed his parents would give him. I wasn't about to take a ghost back with me. New York was crowded enough with the ghosts.

"Well, sure," I said.

"Sure what? Sure yes or sure no?"

"Burn it. For my part, you can burn it."

He closed his eye as if he were still listening to my words after I stopped talking, then he grabbed my hand and shook it as if he could break it off its stem. "That's the boy. That's the boy. Oi'm glad ta hear that Oi tell ya." He wiped his tearing eye. "Ya know what they call us Travellin' People, us Tinkers? They call us Puck o' the Droms. That's what we call ourselves, Oi tell ya. And that means we're the tricksters o' the roads, and that's nothin' ta be ashamed of. And Oi'll tell ya, me boy, yer father was the best o' that." He gave my hand a final shake that rattled my bones clear down the spine.

"So now I've learned about him."

"And yer a good son ta him yerself. Yer his very son."

"Even if I could choose not to be I would insist I was."

Old Michael left and I blew out the lamp and lay down on my father's narrow bed. The straw whispered and cracked under my body, a sound my father had listened to. I saw with my eyes closed, at the backs of my eyelids, the two eccentric eyes of Madeline. They burned in their crystal boxes like some embers. It was Madeline's eyes, but it was the eyes of Florry O'Neill, a signal from my childhood. Unfinished business. Florry O'Neill, murdered at fifteen in Washington Heights, the neighborhood I had left forever. Where my mother and father still resided in that other dream of my life, the dream the past becomes—the two of them together on the green couch, her head leaned on his shoulder, the moonlike glow of TV on their smiles. All of what I'd left behind now surrounded me with melancholy and fear. I couldn't separate in my memory the face of this Madeline from that of Florry O'Neill when I loved her, her colleen beauty. Once I remember her releasing my sleeve after we talked, I don't know about what, but she let go and in my heart a sudden shudder as I watched her run to Sugarman, her boyfriend, and then they walked away with their arms around each other's waist. A warm Spring day, start of the baseball season, wind blowing down 173rd Street, lifting paper sacks like the husks of dreams.

Wings of the other world beat so hard I sat up in my father's bed and shivered in the wind. A name dropped like a stone on my heart. Kutzer. On to my mind out of Madeline's eyes, eyes of Florry O'Neill snuffed long ago. Madeline then was five when Florry was murdered. Who the murderer? Kutzer! Not Sledge, that's for certain, who took the rap and serves the time. Sledge the slow one, the convenient black man, scape goat into prison. But Kutzer. Pig-eyed gym teacher. Pervert with heart of beating shit. He did it. I saw him follow her. I saw his car in the early morning idling outside the funeral home. I knew it then. I was fifteen and said not a word, not even when Sledge was put away. Now here I sat on the edge of the narrow bed, weeping in the past, weeping in the present, as if the past had folded itself into the present in the eyes of my new sudden sister. Then I lay down and slept in the midst of my father's death.

A rooster's crow drilled into my brain in the morning so I thought I was waking up in a Puerto Rican neighborhood, Corinne's house, who lived over on Avenue B. Fighting chickens woke us up there. Still dark. My body bunched under a thin blanket. I remembered where I was. Nowhere. Where my father had died. Some mountains north of the Atlanta airport. I shut my eyes again and dreamed I was cooking breakfast back on Crosby Street, in my own dark apartment, that in the dream was full of light, so bright I could see the bones, and blood flowing through my hands. I woke up feeling the van rock, and opened my eyes to a dawn of painted clouds. Madeline was there, had settled on the bumper to wait for me to wake up.

"I'm sorry if I woke you. I wanted to see you before everyone else was around."

"That's okay. I was awake. I just dreamed off a little."

"I kept thinking about how cold you must be. I'll find more blankets for you tonight."

"I won't be staying. I've got to go back."

"Oh," she looked away. "This is for you, then." She handed me a brown paper bag she had concealed behind her back. "They belonged to your father."

I peeked into the bag—Hustler, Penthouse, others.

"You really go back today?"

"I have to get back to work, you know. I've got a job, just like the rest of the world."

"I thought the rest of the world was unemployed. I thought you might stay, at least a few days."

"If I could I would, Madeline."

She handed me a tin cup and filled it from a grey enamel coffee pot. The cup was crudely made, dented, with an uneven rim. "Did your father make this? Our father?"

"He didn't. I made it. It's not very good. I'm kind of ashamed of it, but I wanted you to drink from it." She blushed a little when she said that.

"Could you take me to the shop where our father worked the tin?"

"He never made much of tin here, though he showed me how our grandad did it. He gave me grandad's kit of tools to keep." Her look told me she was sorry she had mentioned it, as if the tools were something I might want, and perhaps be more entitled to since I was the son.

"I'll never make anything of tin," I reassured her.

I slipped a few of the magazines out of the bag. He'd collected some heavy porn sheets—all the positions, all the holes, all the lips and prods. I dropped them back into the bag and tossed it onto the bed.

"There were lots more of them. I burned a bunch, but if

you want the rest I can find them. Take them back to the city."

"No thanks." I could feel she wanted something. "Did he ever touch you, our father?"

She didn't answer.

"Did he ever molest you?" The words hooked in my throat.

She didn't answer, but took my arm and we started to walk. Her body brushed against mine as we went through the morning light, tree trunks incandescent, dogwood blossoms pinked by early sun. She pressed my arm into her breast. Tiny purple flowers were scattered like confetti at the edges of the trail.

"So what do you think of this place, William Swanson?"

"I'm from New York City, Madeline Swanson."

"It's a poor place here."

"I wouldn't know what to do here. I have my way of life. Trees are pretty here, and flowers, but what do they say to you?"

She pressed closer to me. "I don't talk to them."

"See, I'm used to getting on subways, crowds of people, Chinese restaurants."

"I've never been to one."

"If you come to New York I'll take you to one. We have a whole town full of them."

"The furthest I've been away is to Asheville, the college there. I've never even been to Atlanta. Asheville is confusing enough."

"New York City is the greatest city in the world."

We came on something camouflaged at the base of the cliffs, a shed built half into a shallow cave, under an overhang of branches. "If Michael Stokes knew I'd brought you here he would wring my little chicken neck."

"Is this a still?"

"Michael and our Da's. They built it. Unless you know where it is, or they got the cooker going and the chimney sticking out, you can walk right by it and never see it." We looked in. The boilers and copper pipes were as unfathomable as a subway map.

"I think I always wanted to see one of these."

"You *think* you always wanted?"

"I mean I never thought about it, but now that I see one I think I always wanted to."

"You're crazy." She hugged me, pulled herself close and kissed me.

"It's just like a sister. Now I know I always wanted to see her…you."

We sat on a ledge and gazed through the trees into a small valley. For no reason I thought of Canal Street. I would like to show her Canal Street. This felt as if I'd been here forever, and I was missing Canal Street.

"It's amazing," I said.

"What's amazing?"

We sat close, warming each other against the morning chill. I felt her shoulder against mine, and the length of her thigh, and her hip. I looked into her eyes and looked away. I couldn't handle this. I could do anything, turn my hands loose and do anything.

"Amazing that our father could raise me in New York City, and raise you down here, and we don't even know about each other, and just now we meet."

She kissed my cheek, "Let's say several 'our fathers'."

My arm closed around her as she turned to press against my chest, and I kissed her lips so our tongues met first inside her mouth and then inside mine. Roosters bragged in the valley. A donkey started up. Suddenly her body rolled over onto my thigh and I felt her soft bush rubbing there.

My hands snuck under her sweater and pressed at her stiff nipples. She covered my hand with hers and pushed it into her breast. I didn't know if she or I was the one trembling. If I stopped kissing her, I felt, I would fly up across the open spaces. Someone unsnapped the top button of her jeans and my hand slid under the elastic of her panties and fingers slid easily into her as if they were going home. She breathed notes into my ear.

"Is this what you want me to do?" I asked. "Is this what our father did?"

"Shut up," she said.

Some hand moved down to my thigh to touch me where I was hard. My pants were suddenly undone and she held me in her whole hand. When our lips separated for a breath we both opened our eyes to see each other.

"Do you want me to do this? Is this...?" I asked.

"I don't know what we're doing," she sighed, still holding me. "But I...I..." She moved onto me, lay her head on my shoulder and moved, and started to cry, sobbing against my body. All my secrets moved inside her.

"I don't know who we are," I said.

She leaned back, holding my face, smiling and sobbing at once. "Nobody will ask. Nobody cares. It doesn't make any difference."

The moment had passed.

"Despite everything I miss him," she said.

"Miss who?"

She looked at me as if puzzling out my face. "Whom," she corrected me, and laughed.

We sat holding hands a little longer. "I'm happy," she said. I was happy too. I was in love, just to be sitting with her. Her face pale, so tired and pretty. I was fifteen again, and I was in love.

"You have to come and visit me in New York."

"Yes I have to go to New York City. Sure I will." Her voice almost sang it out. "I'll go to Broadway and be a star in a musical comedy. I'll be the toast of the town. I'll be a famous painter and have my paintings in all the museums, all the galleries. I will be famous for my shopping. I will publish my book and all the reviewers will be amazed, and Johnny Carson will talk to me for a whole hour. Our father loved Johnny Carson. What else will I do there?"

"You'll come to my roachy apartment and take a bath in the sink."

"Ooh! A bath."

"You'll meet a million roaches. You'll meet my Italian neighbors."

"And the mafia will buy me fur coats."

"We'll go to Chinatown and eat dim sum."

"Whatever dim sum is I'll eat it, and I'll take you a jar of mustard pickles, and a jug of this clear shine."

We hugged and kissed, but it was different now, brotherly now.

By the time we got back everyone was awake. The sky had clouded over, a storm threatened. My father's van passed us slowly on the road, and we followed in the procession behind it to a gravel pit nearby. Someone pulled out the straw tick I had slept on, ripped it open, and spread the straw around the wheels of the van. One-eyed Michael doused the straw with kerosene. It was time to burn the van.

When Madeline saw her mother she squeezed my hand, let go, and ran to her across the gravel waste. I stood alone for the simple ceremony, away from the others who were bunched in groups of three and four. Michael lit a torch of oil-soaked rags that threw a black plume into the treetops where some ravens watched. He covered the missing eye with his hand. It must have been sensitive to the heat. After he lit the straw he crossed to me for a moment.

"That does it, I guess. Ya should stand back from here, boy, fer when the gas tank goes." He left me, went across the gravel to stand with Madeline and her mother.

Everyone moved back. The crackling of the straw at first was not unlike the sounds of sleeping on it, only quicker. Then the tires started to burn, a thick column of black smoke that sent the ravens into the air circling with some buzzards that had shown up to check us out. The tires exploded and the van settled to its hubs like a tired employee sitting down, and the body kept burning, white smoke from the interior mixing with the black. It seemed forever before the gas tank blew its chrysanthemum of flame into the lowering sky, the dull thump of the explosion answered by echoes from the hills, diminished by peals of thunder that seemed they could shake the mountains loose. Rain started. The van sizzled.

I caught up with Madeline on the road back to their house. She was keeping her mother dry under a black umbrella, her other arm around the black-clad woman who seemed not to want to look again at my face.

"I have to go now," I said.

"I guess I'll say goodby, then."

"Can I talk to you for a second?"

"Mother?"

Her mother took the umbrella and waved her away with a peremptory snap of her hand, and for a moment her eye caught mine and I could feel her rage. I was a ghost she would have preferred had burned with the van.

"Promise me." I touched Madeline's arm and she shrank back.

"Promise what?" She looked around, as if afraid the intimacy we had tested at the still might return to incriminate her among her people. "I'm not so good at promises."

I pressed a piece of paper into her hand on which I had written my address and phone number. "That you will visit me in New York. It will be really good for you."

She didn't like my saying what would be good for her.

"It will be good for me, too," I added weakly.

"I'll see to my mother first."

"And then?"

"Then we'll see. Maybe." She offered her hand and I touched it, and then she returned to her mother. I looked for Michael Stokes, to say goodby to the only other person I'd got to know slightly there, but he was already gone. I felt now more a stranger here than when I'd arrived.

I didn't look once through the rear view mirror as I drove away. Get to know your father. That's a piece of advice I give you for free. The land flattened out towards the airport. Whatever happens, you'll know your mother, but with your father you've got to make an effort. As I drove toward Atlanta, my own times rushed up in my face, and I knew it was a longshot I would ever see my sister again.

Lucinda was getting dressed for a party when I got home; I mean her red dress, the one that makes her look like a hooker. It was cold, and I had to light the heater. I was ready to talk, and I followed her around, jabbering. It was no big thing to her that I'd found a sister I never knew about before. Her mother and father had been married seven times between them and she could always come up with the name of a half brother or sister she had met only once, or never.

"That's what happens with the mens, with the dicks," she taunted me.

"Do you have to go to this party?" I pleaded.

"I bet you fucked her," she said.

"She was my sister, Luce."

"What difference does that make? You never met her before. It's no big thing if you want to do her. It's a world where everybody does everybody he can. Why don't you get dressed and come along to this party?" She threw a pair of pants at me. "So you find yourself bumped from an airplane with some weird straight guy with a dispatch case and you take a room with him overnight and you do him, so what? Or you go back to pick up an umbrella you left at a party, and I've done this, there's one guy left there who just woke up, and why not do him, or you go to a movie by yourself and…"

"Luce, please."

"Are you coming to this party?"

"I never had a sister before. It was a weird feeling."

"Mmmmm hmmmmm. Don't I know what that weird feeling was?"

"And she looked just like Florry O'Neill."

"Who's Florry O'Neill?"

"Someone I knew when I was a kid."

"You coming to this party or not?"

"She died when I was fifteen. She was murdered."

"That made you probably want to fuck her even more. I know you." Luce was looking for her make-up.

"Can't we stay home? I just got off the plane. I don't think I'm up to a party."

"How did she get murdered? Did you do it?"

"Can't we stay home?"

"You can stay home. I'm going to the party."

"It was after a dance we had. I know who killed her."

"Who's we?"

"The Bullets. My New York Bullets, social and athletic club."

"You never mentioned a teenage gang before. Who would have thunk it? You in a gang? I thought you were a pampered Jewish kid with a giant mother."

She pulled a shirt out of a drawer and threw it at me. "That's all I'm doing for you." I held the shirt and stared. "Okay, tell me who killed her. I'm dying to know."

"I know who killed her, but he's not the one in prison."

"Don't tell me about who this was."

"A black guy."

"Right. We know all about who's in the joint."

"Named Sledge. He worked for a junkman, slept in the junkshop. He was a little simple, hung around our neighborhood with his face hanging out. Real convenient for the cops."

"My people love to go to prison. That's why there are so many of us there. Put your shirt on."

"It was Kutzer who killed her, though. I know it was him."

"How do you know?"

"I know it. I knew it then. It was a long story."

"Who's Kutzer?"

"That's another long story."

"You didn't do anything about it, though." She leaned towards the mirror to apply her eyeshadow. "Everyone is Mr. Donothing."

She looked at me with one eye-lid glistening rose and blue. "So did you tell your country sister about your teen-age gang? That would get a country girl hot."

"Why are you being so hard on me about my sister?"

"You brought it up. Besides, it's sexy to meet a brother you don't know. You look at him and fall in love with yourself, and you're not responsible, especially if you know you'll never see him again. I almost fucked one of my brothers in St. Louis. Another day and I would have. Simon. He was bad, and big, and ugly, and gorgeous."

"Come on, Luce. Get off it."

She threw my pants at me. "You come on."

"I don't want to go to a damned artist's party."

"I'm going. You had your adventure. I was stuck here. Lucky it wasn't too cold."

"The heater was lit when I left."

"You know this heater, as soon as you leave it goes out."

"You could have lit it."

"I'd rather be cold than blow up." She finished her other eye and blinked at me, filling her voice with syrup. "So what'd y'all think about the south?"

"Wasn't even like the south, more like I was in Ireland."

"Sometime we should go to Ireland to see your people, then to Scotland to see my people, then to Israel to see your people, then to Africa to see my people."

"I don't think I'll go to this party, Luce."

The phone rang, sounded like my mother.

"Don't answer it," Lucinda said.

"When I finish Law School we'll go on that trip, and when you inherit your bucks."

"My bucks'll come when I try to ride a horse," Lucinda said, as I picked up the phone.

"So, hiya William. I was so worried about you. This is your mother."

"Hi, mom. How are you?"

"Shit," said Lucinda. She switched on TV and sank to the couch.

"That's what I was wondering. How are you?"

"Everything's fine up here."

"So you got back okay? What was it like, I mean with your father?"

"It was a wake, mom. An Irish wake."

"Did you give them my condolences?"

"Of course."

"After you talked to me I felt terrible I couldn't be there. Charlie went away on business and I sat here for two days, crying. He was my husband."

"I know."

"I had my only child with him, and I love him, and I love my son too, who I never see."

"I know."

"It seems like another world now. It seems so, you know, so strange I was ever married to Patrick. It was an unusual thing."

"It was another world for me, too, mom." Silence from her end. Luce watched a horizontal roll on the TV. I tried to stretch to adjust it for her.

"Leave it. I like it that way," she said, nodding her head to the rhythm of the roll. My mother was sobbing on the other end of the line.

"I didn't know Charlie went away on business. I thought he was retired."

She sobbed and sighed.

"You okay, mom?"

"Yes, of course okay. You know so little about my life. I have a good life here."

"Of course you do."

"I'm alive at least. So did they have food there? Sometimes your father wouldn't eat. You know what it was like for me to be married to a man who doesn't eat? Did they feed you?"

"They had food."

Lucinda suddenly stood up, grabbed her coat, and despite my gestures blew a kiss at me from the door and closed it behind her with a soft click. I was alone with my mother.

"I couldn't be there. I couldn't go there. I hope they understood I couldn't go. Did they ask about me?"

"I explained, don't worry. We talked about you. I explained everything."

"What kind of food do they eat?"

I couldn't remember eating anything. I remembered the

last glance from my dad's Mary. "Just…food. They're poor people. They had potatoes. They grow their own chickens."

"Tastes good, I bet." She paused. "Billy…" She hadn't called me Billy since grade school.

"What, mom?"

"What did he look like?"

"His body was lying on a table. What do you mean?"

"You know what I mean. Did he look happy? Was he skinny?"

"He was dead, mom. I don't think dead can be happy." In my head I heard him say "Light of my heart."

"I know he was dead, but did he look like…did he…"

"What do you want to know?"

She was sobbing again. "I don't know. I didn't see him all these years."

"He looked good, mom."

"I don't know what I want, Billy. I just think about him. I wonder if he ever thinks about me. We had a child together."

The soft click of Lucinda's exit echoed in my mind. I suddenly panicked. I wanted to be with her. "I've got to go somewhere now, mom. I'll call you back. Maybe tomorrow."

"We're going to a beach party tomorrow. Very elegant. We have some sophisticated friends here, some very refined people."

"Good, mom. Then I'll call you next week, okay?"

"Then you'll come down and visit? I'm alive, you know. Charlie is very fond of you."

"As soon as I find some time, mom, I'll visit. I'm still going to Law School at night, mom."

"When I die you'll find some time. You'll be in school forever."

"Don't worry about that. You're not going to die."

"You don't know anything about it."

She was right. I still don't know anything. "I'll visit soon."

"You promise?"

"I promise, mom."

She hung up. I turned off the TV and stared at the couch where Lucinda had been sitting. Anxiety screeched into every corner of my place. The plague is on us, I thought. Only wait for the flea to bite.

I followed Luce to the party. In my neighborhood artists are as thick as auto workers in Detroit. And some of them live like the executives. This loft was vast, like you could fit a jumbo jet inside it. By the time you hiked to one end of the room there was a whole new party at the other end. The ceiling was in the stratosphere, with three large skylights. Between them some trapezes were snugged, safety nets below them that could be lowered on pulleys. People were suited up and very important, or artists wearing artist's coveralls. Whatever everyone was there, I felt like the opposite. I finally saw Lucinda across the room where the band was setting up. No one could miss her in that red dress. She talked and talked to the pale brown drummer in embroidered skullcap and dashiki who was fussing around his set-up, and never said two words. She was offering herself to him. I was familiar with that. At one time she was offering to me. I didn't go over there. It was too far away, all the way across the party. He was next, I realized. Too late now, the flea had bitten already. I was over, dashiki next.

I couldn't yet leave, this ache was the only feeling I could trust. Maybe back to Carolina? Maybe hang out in the nets above my head till the dancing started? Couple at the other end was already up there, screeching down to their friends. A great time was there to be had. The walls were hung with brown, earth-textured paper, plastic flowers stuck into it that glowed mysteriously like a radioactive garden. The people gabbing close to the wall looked radioactive too, and if not happy, at least secure in their unhealthy radiance. Yes, they seemed to say, this is the way I am, the way I always wanted to be, the way I will be forever, they seemed to say. This is who I am, the big ME in this radiant city Eden. I was never any younger, and I won't be getting any older, thank you. This is how beautiful I am forever. Lucinda kissed dashiki over there. It was like no one knew there was a war going on. Wrap them in jungle, I thought. Party them across the Pacific in some Viet Cong tunnels. Give them to the facts. By the rear window of the loft a potted jungle grew of healthy marijuana plants, with a white parrot caged in the middle occasionally phrasing out, "Good for you", or "Hell of a pre-dicament". The air smelled like they were burning the crops. Someone passed me a joint and I ate some of the smoke. Art-ists talked real estate and teaching jobs. I passed the joint and they checked me quickly to see if I was someone of influence. Another joint went by. I looked for the food. It was over there where the crowd was densest. When the music started Lucinda might want to eat.

Roast meats and fowl, a whole suckling pig, the steaming fondue pots, raw vegetables and dips, the hot meatballs, the cocktail knishes circling bagels and lox, thumb-sized eggrolls, arab breads and spreads, radicchio salads, kiwi salads, mari-nated fish salads, buckets of Wellfleet oysters shucked by request, a heap of boiled lobster parts, a plate of cuchifritos, a battery of artichokes, wheels of cheeses firm or liquefied, a huge cake in the shape of Manhattan candied with skyscrap-ers, pralines in pink sacks, chocolates white and black bundled in foil. I threw the tidbits into my mouthhole. All of East Harlem could feed for a week from this table. A woman next to me, wrapped in a sari, swept loose stuff into her Bloomingdale's bag. I gnawed on what was left of a drumstick. I paddled a stalk of broccoli through the clam dip and slapped it on my tongue. All around conversations from full mouths. Chew chew chew.

Rippling by, a Twiggy woman, angular, tall, flat-chested, draped in nothing but polyethylene film, an illuminated green belt hung on her hips, she moved her bony body with athletic grace, all its flesh visible as if through a fog.

"That's Varnishka, the model, I think," whispered the guy standing next to me. His black pants were very tight, his blousy white shirt embroidered down the front.

His friend, a stocky man in an old tweed suit, stepped between us. "Listen to him. He's like a social coordinator at these parties. Knows everything." He snatched an eggroll off my plate and winked at me. "At the next party you'll hear him complaining about how decadent this one was, but he'll be there."

"Well do you believe in live sex acts? Have you ever been at a party of allegedly cultured people where they had a live sex act? Called themselves art patrons. Collectors. And nobody there paid any attention at all to this poor couple. Everyone was too cool to notice. They were working so hard. They were actually doing the eff word."

"And you were there, found it offensive, n'est-ce pas?"

"This was just a poor Walker Evans kind of a couple, like from Tennessee. They told me they did it to feed their kids. It was so exploitative. So sickening."

"Kids, indeed. Exploitative, indeed," the stocky one puffed. "You'll publish your interview in the Paris Review. Tell me you want us to adopt their kids. I'm sure you'll be at their next party."

"Well you're at this party too," I defended the slim one, brandishing my drumstick.

"I'm here and I'm not here. You probably never heard of

quantum theory. There's evidence for my presence, and also evidence for my absence. And frankly I don't give a fuck."

"I'll tell you a secret," said the slim one. "I'm here, but I'm not an artist, definitely never hope to be one."

"That's why I like you," I said.

"I'm a faggot, though; and what do you do?"

"I work in the law. I study law."

"Law is a baw," said the tweed one, stepping between us again. "It's a bedtime story for the rich. Keeps them from screaming in the middle of the night, or vice versa. And for the poor people it's the tether that holds them in their maze. You can use it to defeat a loaf of bread."

"He's a lawyer," the other whispered loudly.

"Give away all my secrets."

"He's a faggot too."

"I like women, definitely like them," said tweed.

"Tell me, what's...O no, forget it. I don't want to know any more names. But if you were God...Now I'm not saying you're not. Everyone is God; but I mean the big G. The alleged creator. If you were he, or she as the case may be, would you have made the world like this, put all these nets in it and these trapezes? Would you have put all these people in it, and made them so uptight? Would you have made such a tragedy of the world? Would you allow the stupid war? Would you have murdered Kennedys and Martin Luther King? Everything is so sick, whatever your name is. Don't you agree? So much misery. This world is so sad, and you...whoever you are. Don't you think?"

"She's dancing. She dancing now," the lawyer exclaimed. People had cleared a space around the model who was dancing without music.

"O, Kevin, can't you even let me have my moment, my reflection on the state of the world? It was going well, don't you think?" he asked me. I nodded. I'd thought the lawyer looked familiar. Kevin. He was from Washington Heights, my old neighborhood. I knew his face. He'd been a Fanwood, old enemy. I was glad I never told my name. It would have been horrible to reminisce. They used to call The Bullets "faggots." He had known Florry O'Neill, and he knew who Kutzer was. Ex-Fanwood, a lawyer already. Cynical already, and me still in night school.

Finally we heard the band, a strong reggae beat, state of the art. Music filled the enormous space. Now the Woodstock babies knew what to do. Varnishka moved with aggressive grace, neither flesh nor ghost.

"I bet it's sweating under all that plastic," said Kevin.

"She definitely doesn't move like an American," said the other.

"Sleep looks like he dances, but he won't. (I call him Sleep.) I think I'll go dance with it. Parties offend my Sleep because he won't ever dance. Now look at that one."

He had spotted Lucinda dancing her way through the crowd towards the food. She hadn't spotted me yet. I used to enjoy watching her like this, when she was flashing her stuff and didn't know I was looking. She knew how to move, and to put herself on display, especially in that red dress that clung and flowed. Her face was broad, not conventionally pretty, but her skin glowed pale chocolate in that dress and she looked moist and penetrable. I liked to think "my girl" as she came my way, but now that I'd seen drummer dashiki the "my" was in question.

"That is divine motion," Kevin said.

Lucinda came over when she spotted me but didn't grab my elbow as was our intimate custom, but gave me her wan interview smile. "I'm starved."

"This table has all the treats," I said. "It's never empty."

Kevin leered at her convincingly. He was capable of women. I introduced Lucinda to him and Sleep.

"Sleep?" asked Lucinda.

"I picked him up at the pound," said Kevin, as if in explanation.

She rolled her eyes and headed for the buffet. The nets lowered above our heads, pulleys squeaking, and a sequinned circus act climbed to the trapeze platform. Lucinda came back with her plate heaped.

"All the food in the world comes here. No wonder people are starving." She stuffed some in her mouth.

"So this is your girl-friend?" asked Kevin.

"Are you my girl-friend?" That I asked was my answer.

"You're too dumb to have a girl-friend."

Wind slams the door and you hardly feel it.

"O hark, domestic tension," said Kevin. "I'll participate no more in this."

"Whoop-la!" The act was underway, flying above our heads. "Whoop-la!" they shouted as they released and caught the woman in tights who went spinning in air between two catchers.

"What party panache," said Kevin. "Someone could get killed. Our host is a murderer."

"Listen to how he loves it," said Sleep. "Secretly everyone loves a murderer." The two of them moved to the dance floor.

"Whoop-la!"

Varnishka climbed up and rolled into the net as the trapeze kept their sequins aloft. She wanted to be where most people were looking. The music was cranked up now and the party danced. They had torn the luminous flowers off the walls and were swinging them above their heads to the beat. The party had reached the point when all the gates are open.

"Whoop-la!"

"Idris is a sweet name," said Lucinda.

"Who's that?"

"The drummer in the band." She looked towards the band. "My friend."

"Whoop-la!"

"I'm going next week with him to meet this guy, his guru. He's really serious about this guru." A plastic flower dropped through the net onto her shoulder and she took it in her hands, where it glowed orange, big as her face. I looked up, the nets full of people. Half the party rolled around over our heads while the acrobats kept releasing, spinning, catching.

"He goes up there, somewhere upstate, to be with this guru. Anyone can go for free if you do some work. He's going next week and I can go with him."

"Do you like him?"

Something swooshed by my head. It was the white parrot turned loose, that descended on the buffet to grab a knish, then it flew off to perch on some pipes near the ceiling.

"Whoop-la!" shouted everyone in unison. Could the nets hold all these people? Well they didn't have far to fall. Would we survive underneath if everything dropped? I looked at Lucinda. She looked away. Wrong Way, said the signs. Nothing I could do. She spoke, not to me, but as if to the buffet.

"His guru lives in a tower. He's got his own commune, named after his new name—Ouida. That means yes in French yes in Russian. His followers built the tower for him. He wears white robes that have real gold brocaded through it."

"You must really like this drummer."

"He's got this '49 Packard. Not Idris, the guru. One of those twelve cylinder antique dream machines, not some piece of tin like they make today, that this rich lady gave him for a present because she thought he was close to God. He's got a vow of silence, so he never talks."

"So you're going there with this drummer?"

"But he communicates with notes he writes to his closest disciples. We have to return to something sacred. I do, anyway. They're making a book of his sayings. The only ones he lets in to his tower are the girls who go in to clean, or whatever."

"Why won't you talk to me, Luce?"

"You understand what I'm saying."

"Tell me."

"Sometimes he drives off alone in the Packard and abandons the disciples to make them work the commune for a week or two without his guidance. He drives the Packard."

"If it's over for us, tell me. I should have something to say in this."

"Packards use plenty of gas."

*

Steve Katz was born in 1935 and grew up in the neighborhood of Washington Heights in Manhattan. He studied pre-Veterinary at Cornell University for two years, then transferred to Liberal Arts. He wrote a novel in his senior year, a draft of which was critiqued by Vladimir Nabokov, who, Katz relates, leaned over him "like the tallest dentist in the world" to advise him to read more Shakespeare, Wordsworth, Keats, and Shelley.

Katz worked for the Forest Service in Idaho and for a Nevada quicksilver miner before moving with his wife, Pat Bell, to take a teaching assistantship in Eugene, Oregon. He left the academy to hitchhike to New York where he worked as a waiter until he could buy steamer passage to Venice, then went to Florence to satisfy his obsession with the Massacio frescoes. His wife, with his sons, Avrum and Nikolai, then joined him in the city of Lecce. Rafael, his third son, was born there. After three years in Italy he returned to Cornell to teach. There he wrote The Exagggerations of Peter Prince, *published in 1968.*

Creamy and Delicious *appeared two years later, then* Saw *in 1982. In league with such writers as Peter Spielberg, Russell Banks, Ronald Sukenick, and Clarence Major, he helped organize the Fiction Collective, which published his novel,* Moving Parts. *From Cornell, Katz moved to Pine Bush, New York, and wrote* Stolen Stories, *a book of short pieces, many of which focused on the New York art world, where he had many friends. Two years teaching at the University of Notre Dame was followed by an appointment at the University of Colorado, where he still teaches.*

In 1984 Sun & Moon Press published, as number 1 in his New American Fiction Series, his "bildingsroman" Wier & Pouce, *which received national attention.* Florry of Washington Heights, *a related fiction, was published to equal acclaim in 1987.* 43 Fictions, *a selection of 21 short fictions, followed in the Sun & Moon Classics in 1992.* Swanny's Ways, *the third fiction in the loosely related "Swanny" trilogy, will be published by Sun & Moon Press in 1995.*

Milo De Angelis

There is a hand that nails

Translated from Italian by Lawrence Venuti

There is a hand that nails
its grams
in the courtyard near Greece
the numbers
are increasingly chaste
city of cotton and bronze
and the summer with a mouth facing north.
Here pass the bodies
we surprise, females
proud in quarrels. Or
they are silent;
or shadows, challenges, snares. The stones
know them well.

It's always them,
always them, like birthdays. Now
a storm returns
along the spinal column and they select
the spell and the incursion,
a shrug of the shoulders or a nakedness.
The voice that proclaimed herself
twin and sphere and teeth of twins

darts into her mountain
with the same life
sworn immediately, before dawn. They gave her
an almond
without a gunsight or space. But
she decided at once, she fired!

Yes, that was
the circle of foreigners
with inordinate pride, who rave
about a pact...I was there...look closely...I was already there...
storm and dirge of the woman
who bears a son in her womb and one ascending
in my ancient place
you arrive
minds full of light
with the roar of a lottery drawing
every paradise is dizzy
with sons mown and certain.

*

Born in 1951 in Milan, Milo De Angelis is a poet who draws on classical literature, existential phenomenology, and psychoanalysis—all rethought within new conceptions of subjectivity and language underlying poststructuralist ideas of French and Italian culture.

Among his books are Somiglianze *(Resemblances, 1976),* Millimetri *(Millimeters, 1983),* Terra del viso *(Land of the Face, 1985), and* Distante un padre *(A Distant Father, 1989). Sun & Moon Press published* Finite Intuition, *a selection of De Angelis' poetry and prose, in 1995.*

Maurice Gilliams

from *Elias,*
or the struggle with the nightingales

Translated from Dutch by André Lefevere

> ...*La poésie que j'ai rêvée gâta toute ma vie. Ah! Qui donc m'aimera?*
>
> [...*The poetry I dreamed spoiled my whole life. Oh! Who will love me then?*]

—FRANCIS JAMMES

I

WHEN ALOYSIUS disturbs our hearts we hang upside down in reality like enchanted apes. He is sixteen and a full four years older than I am. In bed at night we fold paper boats and let them float down the brook outside the estate the next day. Aloysius sits hidden under the covers, busy, with a pencil I presume. Without showing himself to me he hands me the pages from the notebook, one by one, and I put the same folds in them, always.

I fail to understand the secret laws of this curious game, of course, and I help him blindly in what he is doing. I fail to understand why he wants to help me wash in the morning;

he is very rough and the soap bites my eyes shut; and yet he is very sparing with water himself. Broad scratches are engraved in his hands and fever has left a small black rim on his dry lower lip with its frown and its small crusts.

—The little boats! he says, industrious.

We drop the towel and jump toward the bed at the same time; we get them from between the sheets at the bottom of the bed. Some we can no longer use and one we cannot find anymore in the crumpled sheets and blankets. Aloysius hides them under his shirt, like secret documents, and we run down the stairs to the first floor, where we say hello to grandma through the door that is ajar.

After breakfast we quickly get into the park.

We fight our way through the undergrowth and stand for a while, shivering in the middle of the greenery covered with dew. This is a windy spot. I feel Aloysius's fingers now and then and I understand the intimate meaning of his strong handshake. We steal between the cracking twigs, ears alert. Something there? Only a wild pigeon, flying off. There is rain in the air and the sky clouds up with grey all over.

We have not seen anything unusual when we walk home from the brook at noon. The boats were put on the water; we watched them float away one by one, behind the bend where the current is strong. One tug and they disappeared from our sight.

A strange feeling of unrest comes over Aloysius as soon as we sense the proximity of the house on the estate. He jumps in the middle of the flowering dahlias and as if surrounded by a throng of enemies he flails his arms about as if they were swords, hitting the flowers that fly above his head, and the leaves. Aunt Zenobia watches from the gazebo, whimpering in helpless rage. We flee to my mother in the dining room, because we know she will protect Aloysius from Aunt

Zenobia. He has become strangely silent in front of my mother and sobs long repressed suddenly erupt from him when her slow hand strokes his hair.

He stands, ashamed, his forehead leaning against the wall, fighting with himself. In the meantime we have all sat down at the table. A silence filled with expectation envelops the family. The maid walks up and down with the steaming soup tureen. When he finally turns around Aloysius has become like a deaf-mute, dazed and indifferent to us. His eyes are hard and dark in his white face and they do not seem to recognize anyone around him.

There is a party on the family estate every year during the summer holidays, and the children are going to act in a little play, as usual. Aunt Theodora has taken charge of it, and everything has been taken care of, down to the last detail, a few weeks ago. Aunt Emma's boys are there: Casimir, Oscar and Leopold, as well as Aunt Zenobia's children: Albertus, Aloysius and Hermione. We are standing in a circle around Aunt Theodora, curious, with questions in our eyes. There is wonder in our hearts because she speaks of all kinds of unimportant things in a tone of feigned and sparing friendliness.

Aunt Zenobia has lost a little son, Peter, and Aunt Emma has lost a little daughter, Virginia. We are going to devote a touching play to them this year. Hermione will be playing Aunt Emma's child, and since Aunt Zenobia's children have become too big to play little Peter, that weighty part will fall to me. We have rehearsal every day in a carriage house that is no longer used, and Aunt Theodora solemnly recites for us what we have to tell each other.

I am dead tired when we are finally allowed to stop, so I cannot go with Aloysius. The big boys go lie in the grass with their books; they play darts under an old oak, or they go bowling in the shade cast by the washhouse. I am lured to the house by Hermione and we crawl under the table together, to rest where nobody will come and find us.

Hermione is very nervous, thin, transparently pale and given to sudden crazy ideas. She also has her sentimental moods, and when she has them she cannot be too close to me, she keeps stepping on my toes or giving me angry taps on the fingers, until they begin to glow with pain. She teaches me to play with fire. She has taken a box of matches in secret: three to ten matches flare up together and she throws them imprudently across my body in the direction of the coal bucket.

I sometimes feel as if my hair is on fire.

—Elias, says Hermione, tell me the story of the blue hand again.

She has lowered herself on the carpet next to me and I can see a small shiver going through her body. It is not the first time I tell her the story of the blue hand; Hermione knows it, and yet she cannot sit still for fearful expectation; she wants to laugh, sigh and give a shivery yawn all at once. And I, unsuspecting, begin to tell her of a dark event that occurred one winter night when I lay in bed, all alone.

I had just woken up and wanted to go back to sleep immediately; but I could not find that warm fold again, my very own delicious little burrow of a few moments ago, the one my body fitted so well and could lie in, firmly enclosed. I turned and got my feet from under the covers; finally there was not a single spot left in the bed for a nice snooze. I was lying on my back, my arms under my head, as people do in the morning when they are lying awake and it is too soon to get up. Flowers of frost cracked on the frozen windows. A horse was walking in the street, with a bell around its neck. My head was on fire and I let it loll from left to right. For a while I lay staring at the nightlight that stood trembling behind a transparent blue bottle. I could hear clearly how various pots were put on the fire downstairs, in the house, and the cat meeowed repeatedly in the kitchen.

As I lay staring at the covers, I saw something move at the bottom of the bed and I could not figure out what it was. It looked like a stocking that had been rolled up, but not quite, because it seemed to have parts connected to it that moved, and it seemed to rest on crab legs that could not quite hold it up. I pulled back my feet, slowly, cautiously, first the right foot and then the left foot. My right foot had hardly moved when the monstrous thing began to move, too, and came closer. Now that it had been disturbed it no longer wanted to lie still. And suddenly I saw, in great fear: I recognized a blue, horribly gnarled hand that stole up on me, slowly and deliberately. It had climbed up as far as my knee and I could foresee that it would soon reach my chest; a few more horrible moments—and there I lay, in my own bed, like a bird whose throat had been squeezed shut. Craftily I tried to turn around; I was lying on my stomach, my face pressed into the pillow. I made swimming movements with my arms and legs, waiting for the worst to happen.

A cold shiver flashed through my spine like lightning, as if a frozen fingertip moved over the knobs in my spine, counting them. Something heavy came to rest on my shoulder, but it did not climb higher. Things stayed as they were—like this. I turned around with a fierce movement, to chase away the danger that was watching me.

Only when my mother came upstairs did I dare open my eyes. Before I could tell her about the blue hand she bent over to pick something up off the floor. In the meantime I heard her remark dryly that the doctor had forgotten his glove.

Aloysius has lured me back to the brook. Tall, brightly checkered cows are grazing in the evening sun. We decide that I am to wait for him here. He takes a long pole and prepares to jump across the water. Before he's gone I ask him where he's going. He hangs his head in silence. Without answering he takes an agile flying leap. He has soon vanished from my sight.

I stay under the willows, waiting for him to come back.

Nothing is unknown to me here, of course, this is the very spot we come to every day, to put our boats in the water. Suddenly I have an idea. I run home and come back in haste, unnoticed, with a piece of heavy packing paper. Three foreign stamps are stuck to it. I tear off the address and fold a big, strong boat. And before I let it loose on the water and its current I give it a strange cargo: a bit of moss and a shiny black beetle.

I am alone. This is the first blissful time I play this game utterly and completely by myself, in my own name. My hands are trembling. The boat floats away, proud and beautiful from under my trembling fingers. Everything happens with an incredibly fast certainty. The boat turns around and I see pink stamps on its flank like mysterious pavilions. It sails toward the bend at great speed and is gone with one tug, as if someone had turned a page in a book.

A frog begins to croak in the reeds along the water's edge and three crickets are chirping at the same time, at a short distance from each other. The melancholy thoughts you get when you sniff the smell of duckweed in the evening. The wooden cows stand in the meadow, motionless in the rising fog, their heads hanging down. A late swallow skims across the water. Where might my strong, strange boat have docked by now? I hope there will never be an end to its bold journey. Where could it dock? Everything happens in the real, impenetrable glory of the dream. The weather has become oppressive; fusty smells hang in the undergrowth and linger. Maybe it will rain tonight; the sky bristles with a grey haze and the wind has died down.

How long have I been alone by the water? The dinner-bell is rung at the house. I run to my mother. Aunt Zenobia asks about Aloysius. After a while I tell all: the decision we made and how long I have been waiting for him. Silence. People look into each other's eyes. I walk a few paces ahead of the others through the little avenue where it is very dark by now, looking for Aloysius. I am with my mother, Aunt Zenobia and Aunt Theodora, Hermione and Albertus. After we have all waited together at the brook for a while Aloysius comes toward us, moving with big leaps across the meadow in its evening haze. He seems to have become stronger and more virile on this expedition. He waves his arms as he runs and makes rapid progress. Aunt Zenobia is very excited and beats him when she catches him, so much so that my mother cannot bear to watch anymore and tries to calm Aunt Zenobia down in a muffled voice. Aloysius does not open his mouth; no tear, no scream of pain to be had from him. He calmly receives the hard blows straight in his face, not even bothering to try to avoid them.

I dare not ask him now where he is coming from, so late, like one who has lost his way. We walk through the evening landscape, all of us, shadows in a silent pageant.

The next Sunday is the day of the party.

Albertus and Leopold have put a stage together; a happy disorder reigns in the room; the table has been pushed against the wall and the chairs have been arranged in two rows. Aunt Theodora put on an ivory dress, ample and expensive, full of loops and lace. Slow movements emanate from her anemic body only when they are forced into motion by essential clues. And her hair: it has been done with a love of splendor, a shivering string of pearls woven through it, and a comb in the shape of a fan, shot through with little holes, rises above a maze of curls.

It has rained this afternoon, and fortunately evening twilight has been quick to fall, so that we can start the play earlier than expected. We are put into strange costumes behind the windscreen next to the stage and we get paper crowns to put on our heads. The candles spread their hesitant light, we arrange ourselves in a "tableau vivant" and my aunt's little bell rings in the hallway when everything is as it should be: Hermione holds a small bouquet in one hand, a paper butterfly sits trembling on my fingers and behind us stand the guardian angels, their arms hanging down, in inept expectation. The wick of the old-fashioned oil lamp has been turned down; you can no longer see the flame in its glass; only the golden spirit of light still dwells inside, serenely. The family arrives. Silk clothes rustle in the hallway and indistinct talking reaches us, but all fall silent and their faces glow with pleasure when they step into the room. We are standing behind the small green, red, blue and yellow lights, surrounded by flowerpots under the low-slung paper streamers. The piano plays a military march. We are getting so tired, we have to stand in the same position for so long; we are doing our utmost not to lose our balance and spoil the performance.

When I see the spectators where they sit, solemnly gathered together, I feel a sudden warmth rising to my head. Grandma, Aunt Emma and Aunt Zenobia, my mother and my niece Alissa are sitting in the front row. Behind them Uncle Paul, Uncle Bernard, Uncle Augustin and my father, standing. Seen from the stage reality is different outside ourselves than inside, and I am experiencing this for the first time. There is a brownish-violet twilight in the corners of the room, but a diamond glistens close, now and then, unexpected and lost without a trace in a lightning swiftness. The lace collars, the shivering fringes, the elegant embroidery on the ladies' dresses; the stiff white shirt fronts, the cuffs of the gentlemen standing and smoking cigars, the wisps of tobacco smoke above their heads and the furniture moved from its usual place and arranged along the wall: it has all become an unreal world under the lamp's hesitating light. Aunt Theodora whispers to us, behind the windscreen, reading from her little book, and we are inclined to look at her and stop acting our parts.

Aunt Henrietta steals into the salon inaudibly, like a spell-breaking ghost, as we are playing the scene in heaven where Virginia recognizes little Peter among the most recently arrived little souls and asks him for news about grandma and the whole family. Aunt Henrietta lies down in an easy chair, broken and exhausted, her arms lame along her powerless body, her head limp against the cushion. Her eyes are closed, so she cannot follow our activities. A heavy lock of hair, blond as honey, hangs down along her white face, as if it was a young girl's hair. Uncle Bernard whispers to her, softly, and she is hardly able to motion him away: he should leave her alone. The tip of a shoe appears, sliding from under her greenish-golden dress. Nobody seems to take any notice of her otherwise; she remains alone and implausible over there, far away, and our heavenly language probably fails to reach her.

There is something unbearable about this play-acting for me, something I suffer from as when a state of feeling approaches in which all known states cease to exercise their authority. For I am little Peter now. Opposite me lives and moves a Virginia I never knew. Little Peter is dead, he has been gathered to the celestials and he can now do and say things whose content "I" fail to understand, but Virginia obeys them and replies to them in a little voice I am familiar with, after all. It is as if I am kept back in my movements, and that sense of listlessness comes from the inside. There is something that oppresses me while I think of the place where I was with Aloysius in the rain, just a few hours ago.

In my thoughts I see our house in town, our cat, my own bed. In the meantime I reach out my arms to the unknown, where I cannot reach anything anyway; I find a girl there, as small as I myself, warm and docile. And I speak to her in a silly, heightened language. And yet I keep trying hard to see our staircase, our attic with the sheets in it, just washed and now drying. Sweat breaks through my pores and the unreflected words leave my mouth as if on their own, no longer listening to my aunt's whispering voice. But suddenly I know: if I let go of any element of what I used to be, I, Elias, shall be lost. Therefore I must persevere in calling up images from my past: the cut in *my* forehead when I fell on the rim of a pail; *my* burned fingertips when I played with fire; *my* red blood when my foot stepped on the shard of glass that cut it. As I stand there pretending to be little Peter, I think and fight as Elias.

The smell of the pine-tree branches, the smoke of melting candle wax, the musty odor of the curtain-material I am dressed in: all of those things do not make me that ill. Out of this moment's double life I try to salvage my real and fiery existence. I have been stolen away from myself, so to speak; I can no longer give any expression to my sorrow, my rage, the pain of my instincts that would bring me relief, I am exhausted and become the plaything of a cruel and fanatical predestination.

At this moment a thumb tack has come loose and a curtain threatens to sink down on the footlights. Uncle Augustin manages to catch it in time; maybe he wants to give the velvet cloth to Aunt Theodora behind her screen: he just keeps sitting there, with his hand stretched out. This unforeseen event happens just as we are supposed to embrace each other in the final scene. I am too tired and too sad to be able to cry just now. Virginia stands in front of me as if petrified, her eyes are of cold china and she completely stops playing her part. We are standing opposite each other like imprudent little humans who have pushed their weak powers too far, and whatever perseverance we had has all seeped out of us.

—The blue hand! screams Hermione.

Uncle Augustin has caught her in his arms. The wick of the lamp is turned up, spreading light. There is a moment of confusion; people and chairs whirling around.

At last I am left alone with Aloysius and Aunt Henrietta. She asks us in a weak voice what is going on. And I tell her about the shadow of a hand we saw distinctly shifting from one guardian angel to the other. But Aloysius makes a quick end of these infantile ghost stories and takes me along outside, to the park, even though we are both still wearing our costumes.

When we walk outside the gardener has already turned on the lights of the illumination. Uncles are walking down the steps of the front porch and just as we have to turn into the dark little lane I turn around and see my father firing his hunting rifle out of the first floor window.

The clammy, wry smells of small oak trees covered with dew hang in the darkness. We hear the boys shouting "hooray" three times, all together; a few more shots are fired; and then everything is too far behind us for us to listen to with any attention.

I do not really know where we are going, but we are certain to find something better than the evening party we have fled.

We get to the brook. Aloysius will have to make a big effort to get me to the other side. He gets me on his back; I hold on to him, tight. He jumps and together, leaning on the pole that sinks deep down into the squelchy mud-bed, we sail across the dark water. The cows are sleeping in the nightly meadow. One of them stands guard, on its four legs, and for a few moments it seems as if it is going to make for us. Then we step quickly through the dense wet grass, without another look around.

When we have come close to the bushes Aloysius makes me wait. He disappears into the darkness and utters a "hello" that echoes in the distance. I hold my breath. Was he calling me? Should I answer? First I have to listen, well. There, in between the trees of the estate the lights of the illumination are flickering; the colored lampions shiver between the leaves and the fireworks are set off. A blue rocket rises into the sky. From the village comes the throbbing, rustic music of the fair. But here everything is dead. I have been waiting for an eternity. Is this not beginning to look like a kidnapping?

Aloysius appears with two girls I do not know, the youngest about seven years old and the oldest fourteen. We cross a dirt road and, as if magnetized by him we follow Aloysius to a small meadow, closed in by forest on three sides. He walks a few steps ahead of us, in silence. The girls shiver in the evening cold and smile at each other. The oldest girl wears her hair in two thick braids. She has a black shiny belt around her middle and a blue scarf heightens the pallor of her face in the moonlight.

Aloysius makes us stop at last.

He gets brushwood and straw from a secret hiding place; everything is thrown on a heap in a nervous hurry; a crumpled newspaper and matches appear from under his shirt; a few seconds later a high billowing fire leaps up in the meadow. I do not know what secret force makes us join hands and turn around the flames in a quick dance. The girls are screaming with delight and their faces are illuminated in a ghostly manner by the fire that crackles and spits out sparks. Aloysius has taken off his stage costume; he kicks it away from him and when one of us gets hold of it we kick it back and forth until it ends up in the flames. Soon everything is consumed, the fire has gone out and a stinking smoke is left hanging in the cool night. We still have not let go of each other's hands.

We stay close together, maybe because the solitude scares us a little. As if on cue we begin to sing, softly, as we walk on, slowly, keeping the rhythm. A cold arm lies wrapped around my neck. Searching lips come and burst into blossom on my hammering temples.

Shortly afterwards we part in silence. It is all over now. And when shall we find each other again?

*

Born in 1900 in the great Flemish seaport of Antwerp, Belgium, Maurice Gilliams came to be recognized over the century as one of the great Flemish writers. His Elias, *first published in 1936, is the first part of a trilogy including* Winter in Antwerp *(1953) and* A Wedding at Elsinore *(published ten years after the author's death in 1982), which is now read in most schools of Belgium and many classrooms in Holland.*

Gilliams is also known as one of the best Flemish poets of his generation, but his output is rather limited. He became a baron in 1980, and he was awarded all the major Dutch and Flemish literary prizes.

Sun & Moon Press will publish Elias *and the other volumes of the trilogy in upcoming seasons.*

Sigurd Hoel

"Death" from
The Road to the World's End

Translated from Norwegian by Sverre Lyngstad

THEY COULDN'T SEE Mother for several days in a row. Strange folk came and went. In the kitchen they were all putting their heads together, and Gorine and Andrea didn't answer when they asked something.

One morning Gorine came up and told them to hurry and get dressed, because now they could come to Mother's room. She helped them, but one of Anders' shoes was gone and it took him a long time to remember he'd used it for a boat in the wash basin yesterday. It wasn't quite dry, there was some water in it, and he had to put on his old shoes from way back. When they got to the bottom of the stairs they had to stop and keep quiet; Gorine went ahead and was gone for quite a while. Åse crept up to the door and listened, but Anders just kept looking down at his old shoes. An idea had occurred to him, but he wasn't sure. When he straightened up, he saw a gray, angry day staring at him from the window next to the front door.

"What can it be, you think?" Åse asked.

"She's having a baby," Anders said.

He couldn't say *r*. So he didn't say *Mother*.

"A baby," Åse said. And as if Mother were going to have kittens, she began to jump and dance, shouting, "Mother having a baby! Mother having a baby! Mother having a baby!"

Åse couldn't say *s*, even if her name was Åse, with an *s* in it. *Ate*, she said when someone asked what her name was. But she mostly cheated and said *Tulla*.

She jumped and danced.

"Hush, kids! Mother is sick!" Gorine said, coming from the kitchen. She took them into the bedroom.

There lay Mother, very white and strange, seeming to smile at them; but she almost didn't smile. Anders looked mostly at the strange woman standing there, the one who'd come yesterday, and realized it was the midwife. The midwife always had to lend a hand when babies were made. She was dressed in black, with a cap on her head and a brooch, and an ugly long nose crooked at the tip and small pig's eyes with gray eyelashes; she pretended to smile sweetly, but behind it all she was cross and ugly and wanted only to do harm.

"Now you've got a little brother," said the midwife.

He lay in the cradle beside the bed. He had a small red face, which stirred and twitched. Now he screamed "Baa! Baa!," like a little sheep. The midwife hurried over to tend him, and then he quieted down again.

"You must be very glad, both of you, now that you've got a little brother?" the midwife asked, smiling crabbily around her sharp, crooked nose. Mother didn't say anything but just lay in her bed and smiled; she looked pale and barely smiled. Anders didn't say anything. It seemed to him he'd gone through all this once before, a long time ago.

"You are glad, aren't you?" Gorine too asked. Åse was glad. Anders didn't say a word. Then Mother looked at him and asked, in a small voice he almost didn't recognize, "Aren't

you glad, Anders?" Then he checked how he felt and knew he
was glad.

They couldn't stay very long, for Mother felt poorly, and
only the midwife with her long, sharp snout and gray pig's
eyes could be in there. In the kitchen Åse was glad that she'd
got a little brother. Anders walked away from her and went
down to Embret in the woodshed.

It wasn't gray and cloudy outside after all, but sunny. And
Embret stood behind the long chopping block that spanned
the entire width of the shed and chopped wood, making the
chips fly. He placed one end of the log on the pile of chips
before the chopping block and the other end on top of the
block. Then he gave a blow, the log split, and a drop squirted
from his nose and swept through the air in a long arc and fell
way over in the pile of chips. But a new one began to form
right away. There often hung a drop at the tip of Embret's
nose, because he was old and had a white beard and a long
nose with a bump on it, almost like the roof over the kitchen
steps. Drops would form there, too; at night they turned into
icicles, but in the daytime water trickled from them. But that
was a long time ago, early last spring that was. And the drops
under Embret's nose were something quite different from
what Anders himself had under his nose now and then, for
with Anders it formed at the root and had to be gotten rid of,
but with Embret it hung at the tip. When Anders grew up,
he would also have a drip at the tip of his nose perhaps; but
you could never be sure, because Father never did, so Anders
wasn't sure he'd have it when he grew up.

The pile of chips before the chopping block quivered at
every blow. Embret hadn't looked up even once. Then he'd
better be silent.

At last Embret looked up and they began chatting, as
Embret stood leaning on his ax.

How long did someone have to stay in bed after a baby?

"Oh well," Embret hemmed and hawed, wiping his fore-head and his nose with the back of his hand, "it can differ quite a bit. Maria Teppen, now, had a littl'un recently, and she was up the fifth day, she was. But it could be more or less, depending."

Where did such babies come from?

Embret stared at him. "You know that, don't you, big boy like you? A big bird brings 'em at night. Hmm."

Oh yes, Anders knew.

Embret busied himself with the wood, stacking it. Then he took a new chunk, chopped it up and put the wood on the stack.

Anders stood watching him. "Her tummy will get smaller now, right?"

Embret looked sharply at him. "Yeah, perhaps so," he said. Then he bent down, grabbed another chunk and began to chop without looking up. The chips went flying on the pile. Anders turned and walked up to the house again.

The sun shone brightly, the wagtails darted about in the yard, and the cat sat on the stoop. It was summer now and lots to do. But Anders was deep in thought and didn't look at the world around him. He limped a little on one leg when he walked.

She didn't get up again the fifth day.

When she didn't get up the sixth day either, Anders went to her room and told her. Maria Teppen got up again the fifth day. Why wouldn't Mother get up again? It was a shame that she should be poorer than Maria Teppen.

They laughed. They didn't even understand what he meant. He'd noticed it many times—the grownups didn't understand very much. They seemed to think it was all right for Mother to loll in bed day after day while others got up again the fifth day.

She didn't get up again until the ninth day.

Mother almost never had time to be with Anders and Åse anymore. She had to be with the newcomer at all times. If she wasn't with him he cried, "Baa! Baa!" He had blue eyes and thin red hair all over his head. The grownups said he was pretty.

Lots of people came visiting, they got coffee and cake. Anders and Åse often got cake. The Master Builder came with his big red nose, bringing Mrs. Master Builder, who was laced more nicely than everybody else and looked as if she'd been turned on a lathe from her stomach to her armpits. She was his godparent and he often thought about her. He'd gotten a silver spoon from her—he ate with it on Sundays. She patted his hair, saying he must be very glad now that he'd got a little brother. Anders felt so queer, with her being so nicely laced, having such soft hands and smelling so good; he wanted to hide in her skirt and to run away. He just stood still without saying a word.

Many others came to have coffee, patted his hair and said he must be glad now. And little by little Anders realized he was very glad he'd got a baby brother.

If anything, Åse was perhaps even more fond of him than Anders was. Her new brother was almost like a doll to her. She wanted to tend him. She wanted to take him out of the cradle and lull him to sleep. She wanted to press his eyes to see if he could close them. She wanted to put a pine cone in his mouth when he cried.

Anders might have been even fonder of him if he'd been all right. But something was wrong with him. The doctor came to tend him many times, but he was still ailing almost all the time and would cry terribly, and Mother had to be around him every minute. Maria Teppen's little boy was fit as a fiddle.

It turned out that the newcomer was a heathen without a name. Then he got baptized, cried awfully and wet himself in church. They called him Harald and gave a big party, where Harald wasn't allowed. But Anders could come into the living room and sing "Little Peter Lassen cried and cried/for his fishing boat swept out by the tide," and everything was fine except that he couldn't say *r*, there were so many *r*'s in that song. But many said he did very well, and Harald wasn't there. He lay asleep in the bedroom, was a Christian and was named Harald.

The summer was going by.

It was a long summer. Mother couldn't spend so much time with them as before and wasn't as nice to them as she used to be anymore, because Harald was so naughty. And Anders' leg wasn't quite well and he couldn't run as much as usual, and he often had to sit on the stoop while the others were running around. So the summer often seemed quite long.

It was this summer that Anders learned to say *r*. And Åse learned to say *s*—but that was later. Afterward her name was always Åse.

Anders would hit Åse once in a while, when nobody was watching, because Åse was naughty. Åse cried but seldom told on him, because Mother was mostly too busy to listen. Most of the time he and Åse were good friends. They stuck together. For Karl and Tora were going to school and were so much bigger, and his leg hurt and he couldn't run, and

Mother had so little time. Somehow, Anders and Åse mostly had each other, and Pussy.

And then they had the play rock behind the house. There they had cows from spruce cones and sheep from little spruce cones and goats from pebbles and a bull from a large spruce cone with two big horns. They had a horse of wood that Embret had made for them. And they had a cow barn, a stable, a summer cow barn, and a main building. But later that summer there was a big storm. It rained and thundered and there was a flood, and the water carried away all the cows and sheep, leaving only the goats and the horse. From then on it wasn't that much fun on the play rock. Åse wanted to rebuild it, but Anders wasn't very eager to. He knew it was God who'd made the whole thunderstorm, and how could they have expected anything else than that God would come and destroy this play rock they were so fond of! For Anders had noticed that God was often out to get him. But he'd fooled God all the same—for, truly, he had never been terribly fond of this play rock. And now it didn't matter anymore. There was no point in teasing him either. For then it might end up like the tower of Babel Mother had told him about—that God came down and confused his and Åse's mother tongue so he wouldn't be able to say *r*.

Little by little Anders forgot about this and helped Åse rebuild the play rock. But it became her play rock now, not his, and he only gave her good advice and was the vet for her cows when they were going to calve and rubbed the horse with ointment when it had the strangles. He himself had grown too big for such things. He was nearly five years old.

Anders and Åse were much by themselves. Often next to nothing would happen, but off and on something did happen anyway. It was this summer that Anders was allowed to bathe in the lake for the first time. It was this summer he saw his first adder, was at the summer dairy for the first time, was allowed to come along to the islet in the lake to pick lilies of the valley, was in the parsonage garden stealing forget-me-nots and at Grandmother's eating too many strawberries and throwing up, went to sleep in church and fell down from his pew, and spilled chocolate on his white blouse at the Sheriff's, got a scolding, started bawling and fled home again, alone, right through a big forest and a valley with a big brook which had ferns as tall as houses and adders and pikes and toads and blindworms and lizards, but got home alive all the same and never wanted to taste chocolate again.

It was this summer that his leg was bitten by a horse leech when he went bathing and learned to tie a string around its rear end so that it filled up with blood and let go. Then they opened it with sticks and filled it with sand.

It was a long, warm summer. There was sunshine, thunder and rain. In the evening the birds sang, the mosquitoes buzzed their spinning wheels, the grasshoppers squeaked and squeaked. In the morning the sun shone; bumblebees and wasps knocked against the panes eager to get in and knocked against the panes eager to get out, and the flies walked on the window as on a clear lake. Pussy caught mice and rats and shrews, but also birds and nestlings once in a while. For it was only an animal and had no share in the Fall and didn't know the difference between good and evil.

The days were full of rain and they were full of sun. But each day brought new times, a new world.

Anders and Åse became much older that summer. They were by themselves a good deal.

Fall came.

Mother was so difficult. She often cried and was often

impatient. Harald was sick. The doctor came and went. Mother cried. Outside it rained. The days were dark.

One morning Gorine came to wake them as she used to lately, now that Mother didn't have the time. Big tears streamed down her face, sideways along the deep old wrinkles. Anders and Åse at once grew sad.

She helped them get dressed. Her hard, bony hands hurt him more than usual.

"Hurry up!" she said.

It was dark in the bedroom, because it had only one window and there were so many grownups standing around, reaching almost to the ceiling. Kari and Tora were there too. Everybody was so quiet that Anders and Åse hushed up at once. Father stood hunched over the cradle, pale and strange. He held a small round mirror to Harald's mouth. He turned the mirror, looked at it and straightened up.

"He's dead," he said. And as if she'd been waiting for these very words, Mother suddenly became old and ugly and strange and wrinkled in the face, and she moaned and began to cry. Father said something in a low voice, he and Mother left the room, and it became a little brighter right away. Harald lay in his cradle, still and pale and without moving; something had happened to him. Everybody in the room cried, and Anders grew even more sad than before. He noticed that he and Åse began to cry at the very same moment. He thought he must remember that in case she came and told him afterward that she had started first.

Someone came and took them away.

They went to the kitchen. The floor was freshly scrubbed, the knots stuck out like knuckles from the boards. Pussy came and rubbed himself against them. Åse pulled his tail, she wanted him. Anders pulled his forelegs, he also wanted him. Pussy poked at Anders' legs with each side of his head in turn, his jaws itched. They petted him awhile, until someone came in and Pussy ran out through the half-open door.

The kitchen was bright and cozy, it felt almost like Sunday. Anders and Åse got into such a merry, joyful mood that they took each other's hands and began to jump and dance on the kitchen floor. Someone hushed them, loudly. It was Gorine. What did they think they were doing? With Harald having just died and all? Didn't they have a sense of shame!

They became sad and ashamed and stole out of the kitchen.

He stopped by the woodshed with Embret and stood watching him awhile.

"He's dead," he said.

Embret looked up.

"What?"

"He's dead."

He didn't say anymore, turned around and left. It was just that he had to hear once more the words that Father had spoken.

"He's dead."

It sounded so strange. He said it to himself several times.

Afterward there were many days of fun. Something was happening all the time, both indoors and outdoors. The baker woman came, and the butcher, tailor and shoemaker. The tailor, sitting cross-legged on a table in the small room upstairs, was snooty and no fun at all; but the shoemaker, sitting in the servants' quarters, had nails in his mouth and long hairs growing out of his nose, wiry black hair that stood on end and looked like black nails, and a bristling wiry stubble that looked like gray nails. Wearing a shiny brown apron called a lap rug, he sat at a table strewn with hammer and plier, knives and files and awls, leather and nails and cobbler's thread. With a shiny pair of glasses that threw back the sunlight on his nose and a boot between his legs with the sole turned up, he took a nail from his mouth and knocked it into the sole; then he sprang up and put the boot away, walked a few steps up and down looking as though he was making sure of something, and blew a loud fart that sounded like canvas being torn, his face all the while looking like he was thinking about something terribly funny he wasn't allowed to think about; then he sat down, took the boot between his legs and a nail from his mouth and knocked it into the sole. A seamstress, a cook, and a helper came, in the kitchen they were all running loops around one another, and Mother grew more cheerful than before—when two of them ran into each other so that both took a tumble, she couldn't help laughing, though she checked herself at once, but she did laugh. And Embret stood in the woodshed chopping wood—long sticks for the baking oven and short sticks for the kitchen—making the chips fly on the pile. And one day he went down to the pasture and cut a whole load of spruce twigs, carted them up with Brownie and chopped them small down by the woodshed. It came to several tubfuls. What it would be used for? It would be strewn in the yard to make a broad path from the door to the road. That's where they would drive off with Harald.

But they wouldn't have bird bushes with sheaves in them, like at Christmas.

Then the carpenter came with the little black coffin. That's where Harald would lie while they drove him out to the churchyard. There they would lower him into a hole in the ground. Anders had seen that hole—he'd gone with Embret to talk to the gravedigger and looked at the gravedigger's fiery-red beard and at the earth he tossed up, a brown earth with stones in it—and the hole was square and brown inside. Anders would like to be down there a little while, but not long. Harald wouldn't either, for when he'd been there a little while he was going to heaven, and there God sat waiting for him with cake and waffles.

Anders and Åse were dressed in their fine new clothes. Anders had gotten a dark-blue jacket and dark-blue trousers and they'd been woven from dark-blue yarn and were bought at the store and were prettier than ordinary clothes. Åse wasn't that pretty. But when this made Åse cry, Mother said that Åse was just as pretty but it wasn't true, for she had only an ordinary dress of ordinary material and a bib, because she was so small and spilled on herself when she ate.

Outdoors, Embret brought several tubfuls of evergreens and strewed them in the yard from the door to the road, and in the kitchen they ran back and forth worse than ever. Then a lot of visitors came with horses, they tied the horses to the garden fence one after the other. Anders went with Embret to give them some hay. They munched and munched and dropped the horse manure in little mounds one after another at the back of their tails. Afterward Anders had to go in because they were going to close the coffin; but first everybody had to see Harald for the last time, for now he was starting on a long journey, and first of all they would sing a hymn and listen to the parish clerk.

Harald lay in his coffin, white and still, and didn't look much like the Harald that Anders had known. Anders held Father's hand, Åse held Mother's hand, and Kari and Tora pressed themselves against Mother. They sang a hymn, and the parish clerk with his gray beard stepped forward in his long black coat and glasses and spoke a long piece. Then they sang a hymn. Everyone cried. Gorine cried and Mother cried, and Kari and Tora and Åse cried as though being whipped. Father's hand trembled, and Anders felt something surge up and started to sob.

Now all the rigs were driven up and placed behind one another in front of the door, and four men carried the coffin out. They were Embret and Anton and two strangers. They placed it on the wagon and drove off. Anders and Åse weren't allowed to come along, they were too small. But they went into the kitchen to Gorine and got Christmas cake. The church bells were ringing, and Anders and Åse walked out on the play rock behind the house. From there they could see across to the churchyard between the tree tops. They saw the funeral party drive down the road and turn at the bridge toward the churchyard. There were eight horses. That was many. But in the funeral of Ola Nordberg there had been thirty-three horses, Embret had said, and that was many more than eight.

It rained. The church bells were ringing. It was windy, and the rain came in brief showers with breaks in between. The church bells sang in the wind. They said, Come to me! Come to me!, wailing and crying high in the sky.

The funeral party was lost for a while going down the hill by the bridge, then appeared again on the other side of the bridge and crawled slowly up toward the church, like a long black snake. There it stopped and the bells ceased ringing, leaving a long lingering sound in the air; then everything was quiet.

The party entered the churchyard, first a small black group with something black between them, then a big black group.

Everything was quiet and empty.

And then came the singing of the hymn. It came in sudden gusts and was full of rain and wind and mourning. It was far away and nearby. They couldn't hear the words, only the tune which was rocked by the wind. They could hear the parson's voice, it was stronger than everything, he stood there singing and calling up to God.

The wind came in gusts and squalls, it howled and sighed and brought the hymn and the rain with it. Anders and Åse stood and listened on the play rock.

Anders cried and wanted to die. He wanted to be lowered into the grave, and Mother and Father and many, many others would stand around the grave, crying, grieving, singing and calling up to God.

Åse stood and cried beside him. She pressed the Christmas cake in her hand, chewing and crying. Her eyes were streaming with tears, her cheeks went up and down as she chewed, and her tears streamed and streamed down her cheeks.

Sometimes he would come back again at night. And then he didn't always lie quiet in his cradle. He soared in space or he came walking—once he walked on water. But his face always looked as it had lately—it was as if he listened for something he couldn't hear, or struggled with something he was unable to say. Once he looked at Anders with the same eyes he'd looked at him with when Anders wanted to put a pillow over his face because he cried so terribly. Anders got terribly scared, screamed and woke up, and then he wasn't there anymore.

Little by little he stopped coming. And it turned out as Anders had thought. A better time came. Mother often cried, but she came back to them.

At first she would sometimes call Anders Harald.

The first time, Anders stuck out his tongue at her and got slapped. Then he understood it was wrong and only stuck out his tongue inwardly. Later he didn't understand what she meant, and she had to say the name over again, and then she checked herself. Little by little she learned to say it cor-

rectly. But she would still call Anders Høgne sometimes, after the eldest who had died long ago, before Anders was born.
There was nothing you could do about it. The grownups were
like that.

Harald was gone and wouldn't come back. He lay out in
the churchyard. The snow came, it grew cold. Was he cold
lying there?

He didn't want to talk to Mother about it and went down
to Embret. And then it turned out there was no danger of
that. Harald was in heaven, had been there a long time already. He was comfortable where he was. As far as Embret
knew, it didn't snow in heaven, but there was supposed to be
a good supply of palms and olive branches up there. Olive
branches were a kind of plant that only grew in flower pots
here, but in the far south and in heaven there was plenty of
them, he'd heard, and there they were as tall as houses.

He was comfortable and he was gone. Later Anders didn't
think much about him anymore.

"I wish you were dead!" he said.

It was Tora who started, for she pulled his hair and said
he was spoiled. Still, Mother gave her only a little smack,
while he got two big ones, and a rattling shake.

Afterward she took him into the bedroom, looked at him
and told him that he must never say such things. It was a
great sin. She cried. And Anders was sorry and cried and
promised never to say it again.

He thought about it later. It was really quite odd. Those
who were dead were comfortable enough, after all. For they
went to heaven and were with God, and God was kind to
them all day.

Still, he mustn't tell them that he wished they were dead.
It was a sin to say such things aloud. For the grownups didn't

want to die. They didn't want to go to heaven. Because first they had to go to the churchyard, and that's where they didn't want to go.

Anders never said it anymore. But he meant it sometimes when Tora pulled his hair with nobody watching, or when Mother called him Harald, refused him jam, candy or cookies, and smacked his fingers when he tried to take a little anyway, or when Father—but when he thought about Father that way, he became scared and quickly thought that then he would lose Father and never see him again and be without a father forever. Father, who had often been so good to him and was so fond of him and only did it for his own good when he spanked him. He felt sorry for himself, and he got a lump in his throat when he pictured Father dead.

Sometimes when Mother called him Harald he stood still for a moment. He thought about Harald. They were in the bedroom, and Mother lay still and was dead. Father cried, and Anders was grown-up and talked to him and then led him out. Afterward they drove her down the road, and all the horses walked so slowly and were sad and hung their heads. The church bells were ringing, and the funeral party crawled like a long black snake up the road to the church. He and Åse stood on the play rock, it rained and blew, and a mournful singing came from the churchyard. And he and Åse stood there alone—.

"Why are you so sad, Anders?" Mother said, stroking his head. It warmed Anders' heart, he got a lump in his throat and was fond of Mother and felt kind and good. He didn't quite remember why he was so sad.

If all the others died and he was the only one left, then he could do anything he wanted. Then he would be free to go to the pantry and eat up all the cookies, climb a chair and take down all the pots of jam and eat all the jam, grab the sugar bowl and eat all the sugar, eat heavy cream and jam and cookies and sugar all day long, never go to bed at night and never get up in the morning, never say his evening prayers when he'd gotten a spanking during the day, and never wash his hands, face or ears.

But Embret could live, because he chopped wood. And Gorine, because she was kind and had to help him button up his trousers.

Anders had become so fond of the church bells. They said, Come to me! Come to me! It was as if they promised him something. It was as if the sound went right through him and he became new, both smaller and bigger, full of regret, sad and happy, kind and good. When he grew up he would be a parson and let the church bells ring all day.

He was even more fond of the hymn singing. Then he mourned everybody—Mother and Father, Tora and Kari, and all the others. And everybody mourned him. It was as if the whole world cried and mourned and he became much, much better than usual.

Often a long time would go by without a funeral and without church bells and hymn singing. But Gorine had taught him something. If he took a silver spoon and a long woollen thread, tied the middle of the thread around the handle of the silver spoon, twined the ends around his forefingers, stuck his forefingers in his ears, bent forward and knocked the silver spoon against the edge of the table, then it would sound exactly like the church bells: Ding-dong! Ding-dong! Come to me! Come to me!

In the evenings he often borrowed a silver spoon and a woollen thread and sat there ringing. He became good at ringing and could ring just the same as for a funeral.

The hymn singing and the wind and the rain, he imagined.

*

Born in 1890, Sigurd Hoel was one of the most influential literary figures in Norway between the wars. An intellectual of wide learning, he trained in the sciences but chose a literary career, serving as an incisive literary critic, a vigorous cultural commentator, and a distinguished editor at Gyldendal Publishers, as well as writing some dozen novels.

As the poet André Bjerke said at the time of Hoel's death in 1960: "If he had written in English, he would have had a worldwide reputation." Among his novels are Sinners in Summertime *(1927, translated in 1930),* One Day in October *(1931, translated 1932),* Meeting at the Milestone *(1947, translated 1951), the last of which probes the psychology of the Nazi collaborators in Norway. Among his most noted novels are* The Troll Circle, *published by the University of Nebraska Press in 1992, and the evocative novel of childhood,* The Road to the World's End, *which will be published by Sun & Moon Press in 1995.*

Nikos Engonopoulos

Aubade

Translated from Greek by Martin McKinsey

I once asked why
the tragic
and demure virgin
Pulcheria
on the eve of her
wedding day
carefully
dusted and
mopped the whole
house top to bottom
and on the next
day
died

seeing as she'd
cleaned
and tidied
so thoroughly
why was she denied
the long white laces
the fussy furbelows
and the wide
polychromatic
wings

of the wedding
ceremony?

why
did she take the
paper flowers
and the huge golden butterfly
inhabiting her head
(along with the stuffed
bird
in her rib cage)
and without uttering a sound
distribute them
across the floor?

why?

because

—perhaps it was my father speaking—

because
the soldier must have
his cigarette
the little boy
his cradle
and the
poet
his
toadstool

because the marine
must have
his maneuverings

the little boy
his tomb
the poet his
rattle

because the wayfarer
must have
his rapier
the little boy his
stare
the poet
his
rasp

*

Nikos Engonopoulos (1907–1985) was the enfant terrible *of the Greek avant-garde. He burst into the Athenian scene in the late 1930s with his books,* Do Not Speak to the Driver *and* The Clavichords of Silence, *and with his surrealist paintings. The work immediately produced ridicule and outrage. During the war, however, he composed his book-length ode to the Resistance,* Bolivar, *which now ranks with Yannis Ritsos's* Romiosini *in both popularity and critical stature.*

In the post-war years, Engonopoulos continued to cultivate his idiosyncratic muse, mixing the Byzantine with the surreal, the cosmopolitan with the stubbornly local. Engonopoulos also continued to paint his distinctive canvases, for which he is equally well known in Greece. He did costume and set design for a number of Athens stage productions, and for many years taught visual arts at the Polytecheco University. His last two major collections of verse, In the Flowering Greek Tongue *(1957) and* The Valley of the Rosegardens *(1978), both earned Engonopoulos the prestigious National Award for Poetry.*

Alfredo Giuliani

Birthday

AND

The Old Man

Translated from Italian by Michael Moore

Birthday

Unravel the tousled thoughts of thirty years
while the sky darkens between noontime and winter,
antennas march northward
and the ear fills with dust.
Hosts of violet angels forebode at every turn.
Behold the unarmed scarecrow
in the chest of the field;
behold on hilltops, in figures of sorrow,
bitter strong olive trees
twisted two by two in tender conversation.

A gust of wind and the earth wanes,
the fickle sky thaws inside the eye.
Guilt makes its nest where the past still holds,
the long night betrays the blood
and the wood falls into shadowy dreams.

When the heart is lame and the hand torments
love's cord wrapped round the neck,
the enigma of suffering creaks inside a well.
When you say—the mind goes to pieces, life
is sad with prattle—it is wind bent like a bow
between light and rain.
Ah the cock who crows in his sleep!
The holy garden was locked in an iron cage,
the tongue pressed between a wall and a coin.

Behind the syllables the Enemy slashes
the scourge of dead spirits always comes and goes,
and the house welcomes a dejected moon.
Let me suffer the rich Autumn's
descent for you: over bridges
in my thoughts I will wring out a road
to the toughest Spring.
If it is late to go sifting through fate
with the yellowed minute,
I will come with the creating force.
Behold: the thunder declaims in my veins,
the hedge opens wide.
Let the lovers not succumb to pollen
and the wolf don grandmother's cap:
I will come to cut out the space
of fresh habits
and tell you about the insect's trip
through the wheat-field.

Who remembers the leaf hanging
on the cold of the gates? the long
bundled eyes of the year?
Always will I come
to fill with my heart the empty thorn
and to rise again.

The Old Man

to Antonio Porta

Its threat extinguished, the rising shadow knows.
The most dreadful fire is adolescence on windows,
hot spray of branches in a room desired of fresh.
He squanders the madness of invaded trifles.

He staggers on the wheel that ages the air,
quickly, his slow pulse stumbles
in the steps of the crane, the tinkling of bells glides
through the hornbeam vault in the park.

The dwarfs carved from stone are no more
bizarre than the good dog son of man.
The master is sad, lines it up and scratches,
invisible billiards stripe the barking meadow.

The frenzy of nightingales! None can sympathize,
and you rage, threaten, your cup instantly full.
We are truly wild with fear. If the sky exaggerates,
remove the cage from the leaden alliance.

Cycles clash and die against hostile reason.
Escape, thinks the moon rubbing its back
on the brooks of spring. In China, you know, the dogs,
yes, it's almost suppertime, they age them alive.

*

*Alfredo Giuliani was born in Pesaro in 1924 and lives in Rome,
where he graduated in philosophy in 1949. From 1957 to 1961*

Giuliani was the poetry editor of the literary magazine il verri, *and from its inception in 1967 to 1969 he was the editorial director of the monthly journal* Quindici. *With Edoardo Sanguineti, Antonio Porta, and Nanni Ballestrini, Giuliani promoted the avant-garde movement that in early 1960 led to the foundation of Gruppo 63; Giuliani edited and co-authored the legendary anthology that came to be seen as the group's literary manifesto, I* Novissimi *(1961), recently published in English by Sun & Moon Press.*

Among Giuliani's many publications are Il cuore zoppo *(1955),* Povera Juliet e altre poesie *(1965),* Immagini e maniere *(1965),* Il tautofono *(1969),* Chi l'avrebbe mai detto *(1973),* Nostro padre Ubu *(1976),* Le droghe de Marsiglia *(1977),* Autunno del Novecento *(1984), and* Versi e non versi, *his collected poems of 1986, forthcoming from Sun & Moon Press.*

Tom La Farge

The Dead Come Back to Life

UPROOT ME, bury me, try to save me; I'll get free. I'll come back to life! I circulate in the city. I weigh thirty pounds. I am a bourgeois of Compiègne, I enjoy some modest credit there. Nature made me ravishingly beautiful; I've got a perfectly formed bosom. I hauled the same dead dwarf four times to the canal; he kept coming back to life. Nature surely made no more sightly thing than I, yet at fifteen my father sold me to a moneyed hunchback dwarf, to be his wife. Hello! I played the violin at fairs, for a little change—I played the clarinet—the guitar. I am Iesus Christus. On my birthday, whereas idle in straw I lay, Death ran through Compiègne, murdering like an uncontrolled machine.

I tell you the dead come back to life! I myself am a porter and carry things for a living. I strap them to a frame I strap to me. Then, never quite knowing what things they are, I carry them from here to there for hire. I travel the streets of Compiègne, bent beneath my frame, looking at everything that lies along my way. On Christmas a young bourgeoise paid me thirty pounds of silver, a staggering amount, to haul a dead dwarf out of her house and dispose of it in the canal. I sensed there was something not absolutely legal about this job when she ordered me to keep my mouth shut. I understood her to mean that she didn't want me to tell anyone. I had no desire to keep my mouth physically closed. On the

contrary, I wished there and then to clamp my parted lips
upon her delectable young bosom, which had been lately
washed and oiled. Or else, as she preceded me up the steep
stair, to lift her skirt and run my tongue up her as far as it
would go. I imagined it unrolling to amazing length, like a
toad's, up her tea-tasting hole and further, all the way to her
mouth and out between her lips, there to form words of love
for porters. Ha, I paid the moron for one dwarf, down to the
canal, cash on completion, but he had to carry three, no, ac-
tually it was four in the end. Four separate trips, I tell you,
and every time it was back in the house before I could claim
my fee. Then my husband came home; I hadn't counted on
that. I got him thrown in for nothing! A more hideous object
Nature never formed, with a thing like a slab jutting behind
the shoulder of his jacket. His tailor had to make a special
pocket for it. I, I was locked up, I was not let to stir from the
house, I. I was watched, spied on, viewed, but ha! I never let
him have me—the dog. I lay in the manger and was wor-
shipped. Supine lay I, carven in innocent attitudes from
marble, ivory, limewood, boxwood, beeswax, plaster, even
marzipan. Whilst all mortal flesh kept silence, I heard Death
walk his rounds. I heard the jingle as he handled change in
his pocket.

On Christmas Day I came to Compiègne to play my vio-
lin—my clarinet—my guitar—and earn a few sous. I was a
dwarf and a hunchback. I played my violin, or rather it seemed
to me, each time I tucked the box beneath my chin, that it
became a second hunch, the cartilaginous extrusion of my
voice-box, in a woman's shape, around which my hands made
passes, and the sonority of forests issued through the hole.
When I arrived in Compiègne, the Oise was frozen and Na-
ture all locked up. Indoors, people were stirring and talking,
the usual Christmas subjects, but in the streets all circula-

tion had come to a halt. I met mine host on the crown of a bridge crossing the iced canal. I spoke to him directly, for he was like me. "Brother," said I, "it's cold in Compiègne on Christmas Day." He nodded. "You are the man to give us our Christmas dinner." Another nod. "And then we'll play for you and your wife." He opened his door a crack and shut it quickly. He marshalled us upstairs and fed us on capon and peas in lard. He heard us play, even sang a catch with us, then ushered us out, locked the door, ordered us never to be seen in his house or yard, or he'd have us chucked into the canal. But we did go back when his young wife said Psst. And here we are to be sure, iced in the canal, and here too is mine host, no less iced than we. Four for the price of one— ha! A steal. I taught my daughter husbandry. I placed my faith in her prudence. O come all ye faithful.

On Christmas Day I lugged my frame about the streets as usual, bent double and staring. Passing a house, I heard a voice say Psst. A young bourgeoise in only her shirt, and she wanted some portering. I appraised her: a tender number, I put her at fifteen. Opulently endowed. Standing in the door, she felt a draft upon her, and her figure fluctuated. I began to speculate. However, my bid made her flush, and she checked my advances. She touched my frame, and I looked. In the chamber the fire burned bright. Three black money-chests stood on a bedframe. She threw one open. Hello! I played the violin! I knew that moron could never tell them apart, his eyes were for looking at bosoms, not dwarfs. I helped him strap the first one to his frame, and then when he had gone I pulled the second one out myself. I had a hard job, ha, I was sweating under my arms and down my bosom. I barely had Number Two out by the time stupid came back from the canal. "Look, idiot, he's come back to life!" Yes, I raised my daughter to be saving.

Counterfeit men, how can you know them? What is there
to know? Even I couldn't really tell them apart. The vio-
lin—the clarinet—the guitar! I made them play for me, after
I watched *thing*-husband stump off down the stairs. From
my window I saw him cross the bridge and squint back at
me around his deformity. I let him see me in the window.
Then I ran downstairs to call the minstrels back. Then, later,
when I saw *thing* stumping back across the bridge, I hid them
in the chests. I couldn't think of a better place. I'm telling
you, when she raised the lid, what did I see but a dwarf, stone
dead, naked as a cheese. And the pointy hunch smelled of, to
put it delicately, pussy. She said to me, "Into the canal. And
your mouth stays shut." I thought to myself, "I am having
dealings with the underworld." Yes, I raised my daughter to
do her duty in whatever sphere it pleased God to place her. I
do not imagine her mother would be ashamed of her. She is
quite the thing, I think. Hello! She sneaked us in the back
way. I played the violin!—the clarinet!—the guitar! I made
them trade clothes, to see if I could see a difference, but the
harlequin one was still a harlequin, the clown one still a
clown, the friar one still a friar. I dressed them in my
husband's gear. Three little husbands, ha! I saw the miserli-
ness peep out from their six eyes: the wanting, the having to
have. But I liked my three little husbands—*they* weren't go-
ing to lock *me* up! I built the fire up and had them strip. The
skin was soft and supple on their humps. I rubbed each one.
Then, to find out which was which, I had them take up their
instruments and play, while I straddled a chest like a trea-
sure set free.

The Song of the Counterfeit Men

There's a tavern on the canal that will serve you, for your money, nothing, nothing that's very good, ladled from shining pots into virgin bowls. It is here that the counterfeit men spend their evenings and their sous. They argue about many things between mouthfuls of nothing, but their most common topic is man; what makes a man authentic man. One night they fell to quarrelling about which of them was the nearest thing to a man. "I dominate the field. I terrify beasts," boasted the scarecrow. "I am a model. Men fashion themselves in my likeness," said the tailor's mannequin. "I have everything a man has, brightly colored and carefully numbered," said the anatomical model, opening and closing all his little doors, drawers, and shutters, and tipping the top of his skull so that the others could read his mind. "Men put their shame and desire into tales about me," growled a weathered wild-man who with his huge club stood guard outside a bourgeois' door. "Boys look up to me with longing," said a pastry-cook's sign. "I am going to be a man one day," bragged an ape. "I used to be a man," sighed a friar. Only the dwarf and his brother the hunchback kept silent. They were men, but they knew that no one would admit their claim. They stuffed their mouths with the bread you use to sop up nothing.

At last the counterfeit men decided to get an opinion. They would ask the old doctor which was most like a man. The old doctor was in his house. He greeted them warmly, shaking them by the hand, if they had one. When he heard what they wanted, he looked them over. "Well, you're all quite like men. You're a stuffed

shirt, and you're a dummy," he said to the scarecrow
and the mannequin. "As for you," to the anatomical
model, "you spill your guts, bare your heart, lose your
mind, weep your eyes out; you're a bundle of nerves
and very thin-skinned. These are all human charac-
teristics. You, sir, are a fiction," he said to the wild-
man, "very like a man. And you—you've no depth at
all," he told the pastry-cook's sign. "You're a beast, and
you're a hypocrite; you two are jokes," he wound up,
addressing the ape, the friar, the dwarf, and the hunch-
back. "No, I'm sorry, but I really can't disqualify any-
one. We'll have to consult my wife. My sweet," he said,
turning to her, "what is a man?" Sharply she answered
her ancient, bookish husband: "A man is what can get
between my thighs and make me grunt with pleasure."
"Ah! Well, gentlemen, there's your test. You must all
become my wife's servants if you want to know the
answer to your question." They were willing. As for
his wife, she was going to object, till she realized that
this degrading scheme would put her in possession of
some valuable things: a handsome statue for neigh-
bors to envy, a serviceable scarecrow and dummy, a
signboard any cook might like to buy. Her husband
could impress rich patients with the anatomical model.
The ape would amuse her, the friar could confess her,
and the dwarf and hunchback could carry out the shit.

She didn't rate her chances of ecstasy very high.
Wild-man's club looked hopeful but knobby. Signboard,
scarecrow, these would be useless. The anatomical
model, who might have been up to something, had alas
been created not merely detumescent but laid open in
longitudinal section. All these she disqualified in the
early heats, though the scarecrow did better than ex-

pected, tickling her with a longish shock of straw that unluckily came unbound too soon. This left the ape, the friar, the hunchback, and the dwarf. After the doctor had examined them, he favored the ape. The friar was quite modestly endowed, though to be sure he had tried to augment what he had by pulling at it. Dwarf and hunchback possessed each other's defects, the hunchback small and the dwarf crooked. Now the ape was another story. But the ape lacked nerve; he had never had a woman and needed to inform himself as to how it was done. He did so by observing a couple of dogs. The doctor's wife, lying in bed next night, was startled to be flipped over by a pair of long, hairy arms. At her screaming the ape was disqualified and, indeed, killed. The next night after that the doctor's wife lay down to her chore once more, not quite remembering whose turn it was. The door opened and closed; briefly she saw a tall, odd silhouette. Ah, the friar. The bed creaked. Stubble rasped her cheek and callused hands caressed her body. "Now open your legs," said a quiet voice, and she did so. "Bend your knees!" She grew a little indignant; of course she had known to do this. The clergy must always be giving directions! But these had not in fact been addressed to her. Her current lover was the dwarf, who was riding his brother back to front, mounted in the saddle twixt neck and hump. The hunchback, lying on his back between the wife's legs, had his feet braced against the footboard, and just as the doctor's wife protested that her knees were bent, he straightened his. Then he bent them; then he straightened them, adjusting his rhythm until at a certain juncture he held his legs straight and listened to a groan. "My God," said the doctor's wife. "Who are you?" "The pastry-cook's sign," said the dwarf, who saw no gain in truth; it would only mean more such work. The doctor raised his eyebrows when his wife moved the signboard into her bedroom. She daily oiled its rolling-pin with neat's-foot oil and grew courteous to bakers. One night, the brothers, while taking out the shit, took it all the way to Paris, where they stayed and became minstrels. The rest of the counterfeit men are still dining on nothing and debating which of them is next most like a man, after the pastry-cook's sign.

I have always wanted to be a usurer. I would tell my own pounds instead of portering others'. I would unstrap my frame and be a man. I'd lick the sweat off my bourgeoise and follow the salty trail down her belly and tongue between her whiskers till she shouted shouts of porterolatry. Ha, I knew who was the counterfeit man in that song! Who but the woman's the genuine counterfeit man? Would I have been allowed to test even the scarecrow? No, of myself I am nobody, but my wife's family is the real thing: noble now for three generations. We sent our daughter to summer with her cousins, at the chateau. Of course she was married intact. I have always placed my trust in her honor. I wanted to put my member in her mouth and change ejaculations with her, but I had to figure out how this perfumed cadaver was to be transported to the canal, without scandal. Ha, I never saw *thing*'s hunch, but I, I had to strip to the waist, so that my bosom could be ogled, the items counted, for all I know, to make sure neither was missing. I had to buckle the straps to their very tightest setting. Then I strapped the frame to my flattened back, then threw my surcoat over the whole load. Then, stooping, twisting, I lurched out into the street, leered at a gang of children playing grab-ass, and scattered them screaming. Hello! I played the clarinet. Did you like me in "The Counterfeit Men"? I played the doctor: courtly, weary, ironical. And during the pleasure of his wife I blew certain long, low notes, did you catch them? I played cross-legged at the fire, and mine host's wife, she laughed, turned scarlet, left her chest and rode me hard while I played on. When I lifted my clarinet to a telling tilt, she laughed and rode me harder still, bouncing on my hunch. I've lived hard but never thought to end in ice in Compiègne. I'll tell you how I went. From the foot of the bridge I followed the stair down to the water and cast my gaze to the right beneath the arch, where a beggar was receiving admirers between her gums, but I turned left to follow the towpath until, arriving beside a warehouse, within whose doorway the watchman's candle cast on the wall the tremulous shadow of an onanism, I squatted over the water, as if I contemplated a bowel movement, and loosened straps till I felt my frame relieved of that dead weight. Straightening and turning, I saw a pale shape like an open hand press up against the ice. The candle was extinguished with a cry. Beneath the bridge, all was calm, all was black. Climbing the stair, it came to me and I knew that however many pounds I was given, I would never make a usurer, I would always be carrying for somebody else. I am stalled between the ox and ass, while Christmas bells ring changes. I let things get out of hand, till, ha! I saw *thing* stumping back across the bridge, sooner than I'd expected, but there stood the three coffers, empty. I pulled myself together fast, and when *thing* stumped in, the coffers were closed, my shirt was off, I was kneeling in the firelight, soaping my bosom— offering him my chest so he wouldn't look in those others! Ha ha! Because it's Christmas, I told him, and I feel Merry; when he asked me why I was laughing. Ha, the three wise men! My savior's coming! I walked in to claim my wages, and she bestrode a chest, beet-red, sweating freely, panting. As I pointed to my frame, empty, she bade me look. Hello! I played the clarinet till she took my breath away, she knocked the wind out of me, she took me out of circulation, she shut me up on Christmas Day.

Gabriel and the Dog

On a Christmas day Gabriel descended from Heaven to France, to see how things had gone since the Word had been made flesh. He travelled quickly. The bound- less joys of Heaven were not what he loved best, though native there. He never felt the flutter in his gut till he crossed the moon's orbit and entered time and contin- gency. The earth had been the scene of his Deed.

The fleshing of the Word had thrilled him. He had spoken to the woman, and she had heard him, she had so completely followed what he uttered; it had been magic! After that the Passion had been a disappoint- ment, so too iconoclasm; a disappointment and a puzzle. Men seemed to have a fatal taste for the abstract. They didn't really want a fleshed Word; they liked their Word left undefined, distant from their landscape, from their women, their painting and sculpture and comic operas, their chicken, and their wine, all of which Gabriel adored. He had watched that evolution of flesh called history to see if it might not throw up a form that could more lastingly house eternity, and had practiced a few little incarnations of his own, and made some artists sit up straight with a tickle in the ear. He liked France, where history unrolled along lines he favored, but on this occasion he was not happy with what he saw. Grumbling, he strode down a lane, where he met a

dog. "Dog," he growled, "your master is a fool."
"Boivin?" "No—Man." This was undeniable. Old
Boivin, for instance, was a cretin. It was incomprehen-
sible how a superior sort of dog should get him for a
master. And the rest were no better. But the dog was
curious to know this feathered person's reasons for
thinking Man a fool. "Because he squanders what he
has been given!" The dog took this seriously; squan-
dering was folly indeed. Politely, he asked for details.
The archangel spoke freely and at length. He spoke of
spirit spent in vague-directed prayer, of reason frit-
tered in choplogic metaphysics, of language dissipated
in inexpressibilities. "They haven't even finished nam-
ing the animals!" he exploded. True. Dog, for example,
was very sketchy, very pale. "Why don't they use their
senses? Why are they so careless of their bodies and
their world? Why don't they create a proper housing
for what they have been filled with, instead of letting
it leak away in spiritual outpourings?" Now the dog
was surprised. "Sir," he said, "I am not sure I have un-
derstood all of what you've said. Some of the words
were hard. But you seem to me to have fluttered into
an error. If you will allow me a week to pursue my
researches and will meet me here at the end of that
time, I may be able to set your mind at rest." Gabriel
agreed, curious to get the beast's point of view.

A week later they met again. "Sir," said the dog, "I
must tell you you are mistaken. Man may be a fool, but
he does not squander. Least of all does he squander
what he contains. On the contrary, he has made or found
a container for everything. He saves it all! He puts his
vomit in a bucket, and after catching his other elimi-
nations in a pot, he deposits them all in a trench for

safe keeping. The scrapings of his surface, hair, skin, nails, and nostril-gleanings, he sweeps together with the household dust, which he hoards in bins. A handkerchief catches what runs or drops from nose and eyes, a napkin the overflow of the mouth, a tablecloth whatever the napkin missed. Shirts absorb sweat, sheets secretions, bandages blood, towels grime (once he has moistened it), and other cloths prevent the least clot or smear from being lost. Breast-milk is decanted at short intervals into a baby, which is kept at that work alone till the milk dries up; only then is it sent into the fields. You spoke of reason; he uses it very sparingly, and hardly any is lost in the course of a year. You mentioned language; it is mostly allusions to God and his dam, sometimes to their pup, and so far from being directed away from the world, it is almost always linked with procreation and evacuation. Lastly, you alluded to spirit, a word I did not know, but I investigated, and found there are two sorts. Of the first Man is rather a consumer than a spender, drawing quantities from barrels and storing them in his belly. Against this very substantial gain in spirit there is to be recorded a trivial loss, which is deposited from time to time into a woman; or failing that a handkerchief, as I saw the mayor do while he watched his neighbor's daughter bathe. And if none of these proofs have convinced you," he added, observing the winged one to grow restless, "hear what he does when he dies! Lest the earth be in the least nourished by his decay, he has himself first wrapped in a waxed cloth, then nailed into a wooden box, then laid in a stone box or else buried deep in the ground, with a fence around the grave and a wall around the graveyard! The worms have their work cut out for

them, I think! So, sir, I hope I have convinced you that
Man, so far from being a squanderer, such as you have
painted him, is a very model of thrift."

The archangel Gabriel thanked the dog for his dis-
course and flapped off, thinking, "This is what I get for
listening to dogs," while the dog said, "This is what I
get for reasoning with chickens."

"Look, moron, I told you to shift this dwarf out of here!
What did you think—I wanted it taken out for an airing?"
"Goshly gee, dunno how it coulda got back in, nope, shucks,
incredible, huh?, I wuz sure it musta wuz dead, yup, dead
right nuff, see?, darn, it does be some kinda devil though, I'll
say, you bet, he'll pay for this though, derned if he don't, by
golly." I told him to stop kicking it and get it out. I'm telling
you she had an eye for me, that bourgeoise of the bosom: a
randy eye for my strapping frame. And if there had been no
more objectionable part to her, I might have liked to strap
her down and porter her. It was a scented bosom of a musky
tang, and it gleamed, what I could descry of it, like a deli-
ciously glazed white pudding. She had of course folded her
arms across it as if to bar my eye, but this gesture drew rather
than deflected attention. I might have liked, if I had had a
mind, to ram my broad workingman's thumb in between her
thighs and rake its raspy pad up her slot and across her but-
ton with such swift accuracy that she would forget herself
and gasp, "Love!" However, there was that in her eye that
deterred me. She handed me a sack, and pointed at the
dwarf—silent, stern, imperious she was, keeping up her
part—a wench all the same, I smelt pussy through the bur-
lap. I strapped the sack to the frame and frame to my chest,
this time, where it swelled beneath the surcoat like a second
belly. I had to lean back and swing my arms and legs as I

waddled out into the streets, where the children jeered and asked me who the daddy was. I spied the little beasts skulking in alleys, as I went along my way. They had their stubby, sticky fingers in each other's bodices and underpants. Hello, I'm numb, I've mislaid my clarinet, I can't keep my part up. The ice has caught me by the hunch, and it's shoving my face against the rough-squared stone of the bridge's leg. The current slides beneath me toward the sea. I'm pointing its path with my senseless member. That will be my road come spring. She rode me to her pleasure, straddling my hunch, belting out the song. I played the dog, and she sang the words. We faced the fire. I fingered the keys, and words poured out her throat. I phrased her breathing till she cut me short, facing me, holding my eye as she held the lid ready to slam, her words now none of mine, no song's either. "Shut up, he's on the bridge!" Crossing the bridge (I'll tell you it wasn't an easy climb with that weight on my frame), I paused to catch my breath and chanced to throw my eye up the canal, where it was caught by a lighted window, and I found myself looking into the very chamber of my so recent humiliation. I watched her build up the fire and followed her as she went storming around the room, flinging open chest after chest, bending over one, nearly hurling herself into it, and struggling, struggling. I saw her hips shake. Then she turned and pulled out the pot from under the bed. She gathered her skirt and, spanning the pot in a fine display of buttery thigh, rosy haunch, moss in the cleft, she discharged glinting gold. I was rapt, drawn from my frame across the intervening blackness, reaching for her like a yearning arm, white, long, and slender, downed with hairs as fine as eyelashes. I pierced the solid Christmas chill, entered at the window, swam the bath of chambered air, lay at last against her belly and wept across the whiteness of her wombskin. The tears spelled, "I wish I could tell you." However, this was only a fancy of mine, from which I broke to find that she had drawn her curtains, and I had soiled my linen. "That's how things go," I remarked, and let my burden plummet through the night and disappear under the ice. I was careful to keep the sack, lest she deduct its value from my wages. O magic money, Persian gold, tendered across adoration's interval by rigid arms. "Keep your distance from the help," so I taught my daughter. "Never become your servants' servant, lest you find your stairs slick with grease, your comb packed with dead hair, your bed made up with sour sheets. The bucket that empties the chamberpots will fill your bath, and everyone's fingers will have been in your food before it reaches your table." Oh, I let things go too far. Back so soon, ha! I saw him cross the bridge, panic and loss, that third song undid me. I was weeping, full of lust, grabbing at everything, singing along, laughing like a mad wench. I stuffed them into coffers and slammed down the lids. I was kneeling by the fire, my buttocks fitted to my heels, my back straight as a dancer's, my head bowed, my hair tied back loose, my husband sitting watching. My long, slender arms were bent, and my unroughened elbows grazed my lightly fleshed ribs as my hands circled, rubbing with the sponge, then wringing it out, then the towel. I looked up; I even smiled. I looked *thing* in the face, if you can call it a face with all those ugly lines of jealousy and greed, the calculation-furrows between the brows, the anxiety-trenches crossing the forehead, the sulk-grooving around the lips, the fatigue-rays on the cheeks (but nothing on the smooth skin at the eye's corner, where laughing people wrinkle first). I saw all these lines snarl with pleasure at seeing me wash my maiden bosom by firelight. Then from under the folds of brocade, from behind the fur-trimmed lappet, I saw a flacon produced and handed me. I pulled out the stopper with my

teeth and poured some musky oil into the palm of my hand.
Then, having set the flacon on the hearth, I poured half the
oil from one palm into the other. Then I started to oil my
bosom. I oiled upwards, slowly, making the points stand with
every pass. Soon my skin shone, and smears of oil were glis-
tening on the chalky skin of my ribs and of my long, unlined
throat, and a little runnel of oil left a snail's trail down my
belly. Then I cupped my bosom in the heel of my palms, so
that my fingertips met on my sternum, and the nipples
touched the feeling-center of each hand, and I massaged those
slimy fellows with a light circular motion that pressed and
spread them into shining rounds. Then I moistened the tips
of my second and third fingers from the oily palm of the
other hand, and then I ran them lightly around and around
each titty-nubbin. I let my head fall back, my eyes close, my
lips part, and I shuddered. Then my head swung forward, I
closed my mouth, swallowed hard, opened my eyes, and
smiled. As I had wished, *thing* was gone. I waited till I saw
him cross the bridge, and I let him see me. Then I opened
the chests. Ha! I was so upset I closed the lids. I didn't want
to see them, but after a while I wanted to. One was sitting,
hugging his shins, hump and bald crown uppermost. The
second was lying on his face and had drawn his knees up
under him. Hump, rump, and dirty soles were all I saw of
him. The last lay on his back, his ribcage heaved high by his
hump; throat and belly falling away, a sprawl of leg. Sallow
skin, sour sweat in every coffer, streaky dirt, grizzled hair
thick on their temples, sparse across their shoulders, filling
in between their beards and felted chests, whorling nipples,
patchy over kidneys but furring hams and buttocks; the hair
in crotch and cleft just a scatter of rusty coils and not the
rank tangle I'd thought I'd see. They were warm to the touch,
but any part stayed where I pushed it. I opened the flacon,

and I oiled two humps. The skin gleamed a livelier color, gold tinted olive, but there was no play to it, it stayed the way I pressed it, like grubby dough. As I rubbed, the hairs that spiralled coarsely round my palm felt strange. I couldn't reach the hump of the third, the back-lying one, so I oiled his sex instead. Hello! I played the guitar! In March the ice breaks up, or April if it's been a hard winter, and the cakes and floes of ice jostle each other from canal to river and then drift south. They melt slow at first, then faster as tributaries pay in warmer currents. Not many issue at the sea-mouth, where gulls scream. The last four cakes to break loose from the bridge, this year, each dangles an iced dwarf, frozen by the hunch like a mole in an owl's clutch. We bunch at the locks, our ice-cakes grating and shaving each other smaller and rounder, knocking off corners, while we swing this way and that, that way and this. Then the gates open, and we rush into the river, where the famished shad are glad to see us. Yes, I attribute my daughter's superb complexion to my habit of feeding my family on a diet of fish, fresh fish, caught locally. There have been those among my wife's relations who imputed to me a desire to avoid the expense of nobler dishes. But they have long since read my vindication in my girl's slender limbs, ripe bosom, supple joints, clear eye, sweet digestion, above all in her radiant, immaculate, taut, elastic skin. I thought it would grow stiff with rubbing. It couldn't have been ten minutes since he died, but the minstrels had all gone slack. Death had cut their strings, and now they lolled like puppets. I looked out the window; ha, there was the oaf crossing the bridge. Hello! I'm food for fish. Shad snap at me and carry pieces off. My skin is nearly intact, though. The brighter fishes have widened the usual openings and wriggled inside to forage, followed by the stupid ones, as you'd expect. I have a brainy crayfish scrabbling around in my skull. He wormed up my nose. He's welcome to whatever he finds in there, it never did me any good. The loss of my fingers to long-jawed pike is more serious: I played the guitar. But, I don't feel anything. I'm just travelling with the ice, waiting for it to release its purchase on my hunch. So far, I must say, being dead has been easy. Lots of time to think everything through to the end, leaving only the one puzzle, how to go about living.

The Unblinding of the .III.

You may leave Compiègne by several good roads, many indifferent ones, and an infinity of dirty lanes, bypaths, cowtrails, and poachers' tracks, and on any of these, at one time, you were sure to meet three blind beggars, forever leaving Compiègne but never arriving anywhere else.

They were three sturdy brothers, good-looking fellows but dressed in rags with their hair falling like pondweed over their faces. They carried begging-bowls and asked for alms for the blind, but they were not blind. Scamps, says you, but you're wrong. Listen. They thought they were blind. They had been told so when very young by someone that loved them and had their best interests at heart, and they had believed her. They thought they lay under a curse of waking nightmares, and used to prove to each other that this was so from the fact that they always saw different things; not thinking that their habit of facing different ways might have produced this experimental result. Perhaps they were not very bright. They did very poorly in the begging game. When they asked you for alms, there was always one who looked you straight in the eye, innocently candid, but of course you said, no, piss off, and then that one would sigh: "Another lying devil, brothers." And they would answer, "Really? Didn't see him." They would have been studying, respectively, an illusory cloud and an phantasmic goat. Once a jocular cleric, an overseer of almshouses he was, thought to test them by saying, "Here, my good fellows, here's a gold piece for you," but he didn't give them anything. "Thanks, thanks!" they cried. They didn't see any coin, but then they didn't expect to.

They hurried back into Compiègne, where money is easily spent. Mistrusting the visual signs that a town lay about them, but reassured by the sound of traffic and voices cursing them, they found a tavern by the smell of wine and cooking. "Ah! Who'd have guessed this was an inn?" they murmured, for they had been staring at a girl, a juggler, and another girl. Benet, the eldest, addressed the host, who stood in the doorway crying his wines. "Sir," said he, "do not be deceived by our ragged dress. We may seem to you like beggars, but we have the money to pay for the best meal you can serve us."

The host was impressed. They certainly did look like beggars. In fact, he rather thought he'd seen them before, on the road out of Compiègne. But one must not place one's faith in appearances. *Cucullus non facit monachum.* He seated them by the window, since they stank, and fed them whatever they ordered. "If I were to credit my visions," remarked Nigodème, the second brother, contentedly chewing on a chicken leg, "I'd think I was eating a cart-horse." He'd been looking out the window at one. "And I a wooden ape, no crayfish," said Benet, who was facing the richly carven mantle. "Never would have called this mutton," mumbled Jobard, the youngest, who had his eye on the serving-wench's buttocks. So the meal went on, and when they were full, they asked what they owed, enjoining the host on his charity to give them the correct change. "For we are blind to the things of this world." This he swore he'd do. "Pay him, Jobard," said Benet, majestically. "I?" said Jobard. "I don't have the coin." A pause. "Who has it?" "Not I." "Benet, you must have it." "I don't, it's one of you two." "Come on, cut out the jokes! Let's pay and get back on the road!" "Well, who's got the money, then?" "You have!" "I don't!" "Nigodème, it was you who spoke with that man." "No it wasn't. I was suffering an hallucination of farmers in a field. I remember it in the most harrowing detail."

"Pay up, or I'll have you beaten!" cried the host, who had begun to suspect the .III. of an intention to bilk him. And as they could not, they were vigorously thrashed and kicked and cursed and thrown out.

Bleeding and plaintive, they stumbled along the bank of the Oise till they fetched up against a hut of the meanest sort. A woman popped her head out to see who was bawling so loud so early in the evening. She saw three well-built young men. "The door is over here!" she called, and they groped their way around the hovel, tapping with singular caution, stepping over things with remarks like, "I know that log isn't really there," and at every moment one of them would flick a glance her way and then head off in quite the wrong direction till she called him back.

By the time they were all lined up before her, she

had pretty well seen how things stood. "So," she said, "blind—are you?" "Yes'm," "Yes," "Ah yes indeed," they replied, and wept, and blew their noses, eying her all the time with some revulsion. "Yes," she said. "And now I'll tell you what you see when you look at me—for I know you are looking. You see—" she paused and studied their faces—"a loathly hag with red eyes—with greasy hair and the scalp showing through it—with breasts like wrung cloths—with a vast grey bush—with veiny, knobby legs—with toes like a litter of rats that died in torment." It was indeed just what they saw, and the exactness of her description was hardly more miraculous than their all three seeing the same thing at once. "I perceive you lie under a curse," she said. "Oh, mother, oh, we do!" they bellowed. "I'm not your mother," she retorted. "You are deluded. I am... a young maiden of marriageable age," she said, "with lovely large breasts, and a smooth firm belly, and a thing that expands or contracts to fit you as nicely as your own hand. Do you wish me to cure you of your visions?" "Oh, yes, please!" they cried. "And restore us our sight?" asked Nigodème. "We would like to see you as you really are," added Jobard. "And we would work for you instead of having to beg," said Benet. "Indeed, you shall work for me," said she, "and you shall share amongst you the ecstasies of my bed. But if I give you back your sight, you will never see me. For I am the Priestess of Night, and my skin is an emptiness!" she sang. "But if you desire to see me, you will see nothing else. Choose!"

"We'd rather see you," they answered, after a brief consultation. Then It seemed to each of them that a horrible, naked old woman advanced on him with a

red-hot needle, the last of their visions, for after some
discomfort they saw no more, and Night, as promised,
embraced them. They spent the rest of their lives use-
fully beside the river, or more often in it, steered by its
currents and eddies, its gurgles and silence, the lie of
its mud, sand, pebbles, weed, and drowned wood be-
neath their toes, to the places where fish loved to gather.
They became legendary, the .III. fishermen, and never
went back to Compiègne or ever saw another piece of
money.

I would wish that I were dead, but the dead come back to
life. Frame vacant, blindly I entered that room for the third
time. Then I staggered. Everything swam before my eye.
The dwarf, it appeared, had not lingered in the canal, no
longer indeed than to moisten his member, which had grown
as prodigiously long and slimy as an eel. I lost track of what
it was I was oiling. My thoughts drifted back to my cousins'
chateau where I was treated as if I didn't exist. The summer
I first caught my woman's flux I spent my days in the river.
They told my mother I was keen on water-sports. But really
I was sucking off the fishermen. As day broke, I would leave
my bed and walk along the shore till I saw them, three or
four men sitting on the bank. Then I grappled my clothes,
they flew off in billows, and I, I emerged. Ha! I waded till the
ripples licked me. When I felt their eyes on me, I dove and
twitched their lines. Their poles dipped and grazed the river's
skin. When I took them in my mouth, one after the other, I
marvelled at that straining hardness like something in church,
an image carved in wood that wants to go on growing, stiff
between my palate and my tongue. Waves lapped at me where
I squatted in the shallows, feet planted in shells and black
mud, mouth filling with the brackish glue men spit into you,

that glazes your lips, gums your hair, crawls in stringy dribble down your chin, no matter how quickly you swallow—so poor a flow compared to their gallant pissing, yet so strangely charged with fierce inward currents you can feel on the tip of your tongue, a tiny roiling. The dwarf was hard and still hard when I opened the coffer to pull him out and send him to the water on the staring porter's frame. Hello! I'm down below the last bridge now. The ice is melting quickly; only my skeleton still dangles by the wormy hump. Things are going nicely. I lost a fibula today, and my last clavicle has its first barnacle. I'm settling in. Ha, I sweated, getting out the third one. I couldn't push my arms the whole way around him. I didn't like to lay my cheek against that clammy skin, and I kept losing my grip, and all the time I was heaving and tugging, I was staring down at his knobby thing swaying to left and right, gleaming with oil. I unstrapped my frame and set it aside. I'm telling you, I was beside myself! She was a river of sweat, hairs glued to her skin. I swatted his reeking tool. "Devil!" I roared in his ear, "I know why you come back to life!" Hello, we're very near the sea, gulls are taking a noisy interest. This time, in one fluid movement, I swung the dwarf into my sack and the sack over my shoulder. I ran downstairs and out into the street, where I heard the piping voices ask if I were Saint Nicholas, but I saw nothing of my route—nothing. I emptied my sack, and used my staff to thrust the dead thing down. I watched, but I saw nothing moving—nothing. I saw *thing* standing dead at the crown of the bridge. I waved, and he waved. Hello, the waves are catching us, they're carrying us out to sea. I thought, ha, what if the porter meets him on the stairs? That was when I saw the whole machine. I saw how it was going to work out! Ha, freedom! I clapped my hands and ran off laughing to dress myself to play the widow, a moving part. Hello, moving parts

are dropping, I'm breaking up in the chop, so this is what
they call a "chop"! Slanting ships with swollen sails, white-
caps, whirls of foam, I'm twirling in a tidal rip, so this is a
"tidal rip"! I'm telling you, you live and learn. I was not about
to be subject to the machinations of any bourgeoise, bosom
or no. Fixed in my resolve, I went to claim my wages. The
chests were empty, the chamber empty, the whole house
empty and quiet. The attics and basements were packed with
gold and silver money. I dressed myself in black silk. Hello!
Our bones are broadcast in silt, the vine-bearing, feculent
soil of France, the shit of Paris and of Compiègne. This is
the capital of freeloaders, here reside all scavengers of last
resort, they dine on ragpickers and stockbrokers. We're all
together, pelvis cradling pelvis, jaw under ribcage, what a
derangement, what decomposition, what music! "Where is
he?" I sang as I stormed up the stairs. "Has he come back to
life?" She sat on the top stair, dressed in a widow's costume.
She looked down at me, laughing and applauding. "Turn
around, turn round and see!" Oh—I'm telling you! I whacked
him till the blood ran out his ears. I paid him off in silver. I
strapped the money to my frame—thirty pounds weighs
thirty pounds. I shut the door behind him. I pushed him un-
der the ice. I told myself I'd seen the last of him, as long as
rivers flow to the sea. Salty fingers are untying all our strings,
unknotting us sinew by sinew. These days my room seems
so still. I don't light a fire any more, it seems I don't get cold.
I wrap myself in beautiful warm clothes, layers of silk and
linen and finest English wool from Stamford fair, smooth,
soft, dyed evenly and deeply black. I have drawn the curtains
across the window that looks toward the bridge that spans
the canal that runs into the river that flows to the sea. In my
room shadows are solid. Hello! The ice has melted! Four
hunches slowly sinking, still on an even keel, buoyed by suet

and gas, gravid with swing of spine and skull, emitting a bubble and dropping, shedding a vertebra and climbing, our little flotilla navigates the current not yet mingled with ocean. My machine was exactly calibrated. I am no goods to be bought and locked up. I am no counterfeit man. I dress myself. I handle my own change and make my bargains: the best was thirty pounds spent on garbage disposal. I see how things go. The machine is not what I am. I am the machine. I watch the play of light and see how the play will end. I am free. I will never die. No, no, I shall live on in my daughter, so I like to think. I please myself with conceiving how, when I am laid at last in earth, a part of me shall live on in her, an insignificant part that she will hardly notice, just a knob on her shoulder, a humble bony process, that will be I; a tantalizing irregularity of the sort you simply cannot help but finger from time to time, and wonder if it has grown larger. That will be daddy, rejoicing in your stroking. And if you too have a daughter, the process will repeat, swelling a little larger to house mummy and grandpapa, and it will be even more assiduously handled. No one need die who has children. Good-bye! We're all at sea, four humps under, here's nothing more than anything else to connect us to Compiègne, where we played our last but never spent the money.

*

Tom La Farge's debut novel, The Crimson Bears, *published in two volumes,* The Crimson Bears (1993) *and* A Hundred Doors (1994), *was published to great acclaim by Sun & Moon Press. Writing in* The American Book Review, *Don Webb declared the book one of the great classics of fantasy fiction, which, when "reprinted in seventy years... will... be the source of a new Nile." La Farge recently finished a second novel,* Zuntig, *and a collection of fables based on Old French fabliaux and beast fables, from which this story is taken. Sun & Moon will publish this collection,* Terror of Earth, *in 1995. La Farge lives in New York and teaches at Horace Mann School.*

Paul Snoek

"Bleeding Like an Echo"
from *Richelieu*

Translated from Dutch by Kendall Dunkelberg

My voice become a house. Live.
The speaking of my voice so different in each different house.
The emperors in rapture over their white crowns.

And he who strings the sea on his hand
Or listens behind the throne of the lie,
Hears thundering across the glassy water
The thrice crowing of the shark.

Where hay has stopped being grass.
Where shells break and lose each other.
Where branches hang dry full of fruit.

Where a castle full of old gods shudders.
Where young fathers hang themselves in moonlight.

There I sleep and sing very loud against the truth,
On account of the truth.

Warm between my shoulders and beauty
I sleep in the curve of a claw,
oh my grasping breath, barely eternal
since I only still wear the lungs of a human.

I will no longer awake
except in softly shrieking silk
or crying in the neck of a velvet star.

I say. I feel a wall enough.
You, dry plant in which I live,
In which a black lamp loves me
With her safe holy light.

I am my son, my own sea
My life that wears the old glitter of churches
And walks, tottering among the sleep of the late roofs.

And of a prince, is my love the night's rest.
His wrestling muscles opened red
on the cool floors of sadness.

How I get out of my body like a bed
and turn plural and breathe in my earthen temple,
sleeping on the hard pillar of the truth.

I call a dream. I seek my sustenance
in the silence of a cactus field.

Tonight my wolves melt and God smiles.
Yes, I whinny in the white wind.

They who feel where the women are graceful and tired
Carry good grain in their breast,
Suck on the sweet fruit that depletes
Search for the skin that eternally dies out

And know they are chained to their heart muscle,
Until the flowers become uninhabitable
And beasts barely still able to be named with a name
Whispers in the water.

I am the sun, not the summer. I wear
a film of love on my heart, like gold its glow,
or wood its axis and this is a given.

Also fragility, but not of glass.
Finally, the moving with fingers and veins
of the entire silence of waters.

The surf I know not. I am the sea
and bearer of the perfume of embrace,
a fine fluid. Name me friend, dispersion:
the orchard of my breast is large.

As the sun in a sleeping dripple,
so too, I tenderly embrace with water
the smoldering shadow of the truth.

My hand, she became a refreshing flower
and yours, the fire-catching insect.

Therefore, I bend my wonderful cheek
on the cheek of an angel
and sleep in a flowing vein
and swing eternally further, bleeding like an echo.

*

Paul Snoek was the pseudonym of Edmund Schietekat, one of Belgium's best known post-war poets. He was born in 1933 in St. Niklaas, Belgium, near Antwerp. His works consists of twenty volumes of poetry published between 1954 and 1982. He received the Ark-Prize of the Free Word in 1963, the Triennial State Prize for Poetry in 1968, the Jan Campert Prize in 1971, and the Eugene Baie Prize in 1972. He was a director of the Flemish PEN Center, and was also well known as a painter. In his private life he was a sales agent for the family textile company, a part owner of a cement pile manufacturer, and arts administrator for a children's hospital, and an importer of furniture to Saudi Arabia. In October 1981 he was killed when the sports car he was driving rear-ended a slow-moving vehicle on a country road in West Flanders.

A member of the second experimental generation in Flanders, Snoek began his writing career in 1954 with the publication of Archipel (Archipelago), *a book of experimental poems influenced by Flemish expressionism, French surrealism, and Snoek's Dutch and Flemish contemporaries. Throughout the fifties Snoek continued to develop his style, publishing six volumes of poetry which culminated in* De helige gedichte (The Holy Poems), *a book with much social satire, influenced by the German Dada movement with which he came in contact during his military service in Cologne. He was also a founding member of the avant-garde magazine,* Gard Sivik.

In the sixties Snoek's work took a more inward turn with the prophetic trilogy, Hercules, Richelieu, *and* Nostradamus, *which*

Sun & Moon Press will publish. The end of the 1960s marked a darker period with Op de grens van land en zee (On the Border of Land and Sea) *and* De zwarte muze (The Black Muse), *after which he returned to social satire and a more narrative style in* Gedrichten: gedocumenterrde aktualiteits poëzie en/or alternatieve griezelgedichten (Ogrems: Documented actuality poetry and/or alternative horror poems) *and* Frankenstein. *In 1978, after a five-year break from poetry, during which time he painted and tried his hand at short stories and a novel, Snoek published* Welkom in mijn onderwereld (Welcome in my underworld). *His final book,* Schildersverdriet (Painter's Grief), was published posthumously in 1982, and his collected poems appeared in 1983.

Sibila Petlevski

Turtle Dove's Sonnet,
Carnal Sonnet
AND
Dog-sick Sonnet

Translated from Croatian by the author

Turtle Dove's Sonnet

Lips turned turtle. Doves stopped cooing
Their words this time giving us the rough
Side of the tongue and rags for chewing.
We've got the jetsam off the chest. Tough

Luck, low latitudes. A triangular figure
Contributed to make this geometry eternal.
Well adjusted parts. Long live the rigger!
"We should scuttle the ship" said the colonel.

"Here is the saline solution to any problem
That could crop up like a coral reef."
Swamped with emotion, survivors stick to an emblem:

This crepuscular creature, a fallen five-pointed
Star has taken on the form of a sea anemone.
A bunch of short-winded whelks and a single jointed

Doll makes the most precious flotsam. A big hug
For a big girl. Atonal music. A salvage tug.

Carnal Sonnet

Siamese twins are fighting tooth and nail
To get separated. Later they will spend their life
Knitting bones together. Woven up into chain-mail,
Umbilical chords suggest harmony through brotherly strife.

Rubbing against each other until there is little left
Except the joined body hole with a pinky ring of flesh,
They are undoing the texture of time. The warp and the weft.
The body machine propelled by the sweat-engine. A heat-rash

On a piece of skin. And then, the need to remove tattoos
From the surface of reality. Rib cages reduced to rubble
After long years of holding breath. Liquid gases starting to ooze.

Children's voices orbit the radiant sun from the picture
Drawn by an untrained hand, bringing the music of the spheres
To their inner ears where it strikes the membranes prone to rupture.

The heavy-duty conscience of those who have their excuses pat.
Sentimentality put to the test. Sturdy fabrics. Tit for tat.

Dog-Sick Sonnet

Returning to their vomit, dogs
Bark our heads off again. Tomorrow's
Another day, we say, emerging from the bogs.
Sweet with ammonia this airless evening borrows

Its amphibian vehicle from the full moon's tenor.
Drugged out heroes and stoned metaphors have gone
Bell-wavering by the road to the cemeteries. Poetry's manor:
New voices in the field. Resonant elm-trees, a dug out bone.

Dead stock. A school of slippery hands
Going right to the mouth of the river. Shall we enter
The stiffs in an inventory? A muddy stream of ideas ends

In a trail of mucus. Too late to establish the identity.
What a legacy of hideous genes passing on to offspring!
A cluster of names sticking like leeches to an entity.

Old carriers resting on the lorries except for helmet pigeons,
Each with an inborn homing guidance system. The lower regions.

*

*Sibila Petlevski is one of the most established writers of her gen-
eration in Croatia. Born May 11, 1964, she began to write while
still young. She was soon recognized by the critics, winning the
first prize of the Young Croat Poets' Competition in 1978. Since
then she has published two books of poetry, one of them translated
into Macedonian:* Crystals *(1988) and* Jumping Off Place *(1990).
Her poems have also been translated into German.*

Petlevski also writes fiction and literary criticism on Croatian and American poetry and theater. She translated from English and Macedonian, and recently edited and translated an anthology of new American poetry, titled Spin Off—Mala antologija novijeg americkog pjesnistva.

A member of PEN International and the Croatian Writers' Union, Petlevski graduated in Comparative Literature and English Language and Literature with an MA from Zagreb University. She is currently preparing her doctoral thesis.

Kurt Schwitters

Bildgedichte

Realized typographically by Guy Bennett

In a letter dated September 13, 1922, Kurt Schwitters sent Theo van Doesburg three *Bildgedichte* or "painting-poems" with the hope that van Doesburg could use them in his magazine *De Stijl*.[1] Like the single-letter poems "Das i-Gedicht" ["The i-Poem"—1922] and "w" (1924), the painting-poems represent a radical reduction of Schwitters' already minimal phonetic poetry, moving beyond the syllable and focusing on the letter itself. Unlike "The i-Poem" and "w," however, the painting-poems effectuate a significant shift in that focus from the phoneme to the grapheme, the aural character of the poetic text being removed to the background while its visual features are brought to the fore. The emphasis on the visual aspect of these works, evident in their collective title, is accentuated in their compositional structure which denies the possibility of a strict linear reading, thus transforming the reader into a spectator who must look at rather than read them. While van Doesburg declined to publish any of the painting-poems, Schwitters himself eventually did, including a slightly altered version of "ao" in a collection of poetry that appeared later that year under the title "Gesetztes Bildgedicht" ["Typeset Painting-Poem"].[2] This was, until now, the only painting-poem to have received typographical

treatment. I have reproduced it, and rendered the remaining
three into type as Schwitters might one day have done.

—G.B.

1 These poems can be found in Kurt Schwitters, *Das literarische Werk* (Köln:
   Verlag M. DuMont Schauberg, 1973), 1: 200–201, and in Kurt Schwitters,
   Poems Performance Pieces Proses Plays Poetics (Philadelphia: Temple Univer-
   sity Press, 1993), 50–51. The letter appears in Kurt Schwitters, *Briefe* (Frank-
   furt/Main; Berlin: Verlag Ullstein, 1975), 70–71.
2 *Die Blume Anna: Elementar. Die Blume Anna. Die neue Anna Blume* (Berlin,
   1922).

Gesetztes Bildgedicht

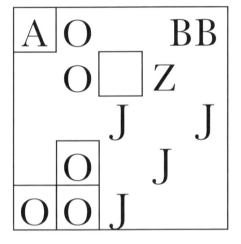

A-A Bildgedicht

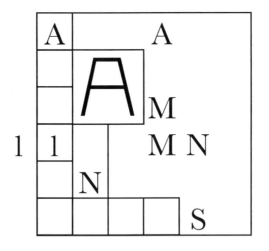

AO Bildgedicht

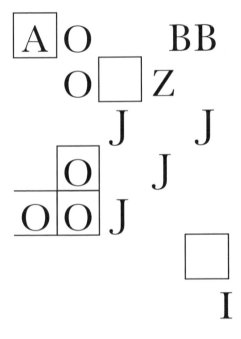

S-S Bildgedicht

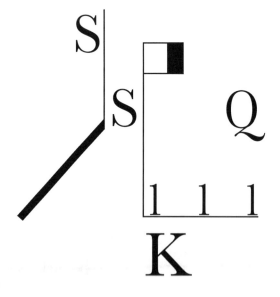

Although Kurt Schwitters is increasingly recognized as one of the great visual artists of the twentieth century—a recognition reconfirmed in 1985 by a highly acclaimed retrospective at New York's Museum of Modern Art—his achievement as one of the major poets and theorists of Modernism has so far not received the same degree of attention in the English-speaking world. Jerome Rothenberg and Pierre Joris's award-winning translation of Schwitters works, pppppp *(1993), has helped enormously in the effort to change that.*

Born on June 20, 1887 in Hannover, Germany, Schwitters began working in 1918 as a commercial artist. But with the German revolution of the same year and his parents' sudden inability to help in his support, he gave up the job, living on income received either through freelance activities as a graphic designer or through monies he could generate through his art work and public performances.

He soon came to describe the pieces of "garbage" which he glued and nailed together as Merz works, a word derived from a collage of the word Kommerzbank, *"merz," which came from the German verb* ausmerzen, *denoting a process of discarding or weeding out. Since a great deal of Berlin was already in ruins, the young Schwitters took things from the shards, painting upon them, nailing them together, gluing them, and writing across them to represent and recreate a new Berlin. With new found friends such as Raoul Hausmann, Hans Arp, and (through correspondence) Tristan Tazara, Schwitters began to publish his work, first in the last of Zurich Dada magazines,* Die Zeltweg, *and then elsewhere. In 1919 a small Hannover avant-grade publisher, Paul Steegemann, brought out a collection of Schwitters' work titled* Anna Blume, *which put him in the forefront of the German and international avant-garde.*

In the early 1920s Schwitters began on a series of travels and poetry readings that would make him known throughout Europe.

From 1923 to 1932 he edited twenty-four issues of a magazine, Merz, *which would serve as the main platform for his own works and poetics. The magazine also published a wide variety of artists, including Tzara, Georges Ribemont-Dessaignes, Moholy-Nagy, Theo Van Doesburg (under the pseudonym of I. K Bonset), Man Ray, Francis Picabia, Picasso, and others.*

With the gradual rise of the Nazi regime, the energy of Merz *and other movements began to die out in the early 1930s. In 1937, the infamous* Entartete Kunst *(Degenerate art show) included works by Schwitters. He left Germany for Norway with his son, Ernst, in 1937, only a few days ahead of the Gestapo. In Norway he settled in Molde on the island of Hjertøy. Although he kept his international contacts, he grew more and more depressed during the first years of his exile, and fled Norway again, this time to England, in April 1940, again only a day ahead of the Gestapo. For a while he was detained in a prison camp, but he gained release in 1942 and moved to London. He died in England in 1948.*

Juan Goytisolo

To Read or to Re-Read

Translated from Spanish by Peter Bush

ABOUT a year and a half ago, a functionary phoned me from our ineffable Ministry of Culture and invited me to participate in a writers' colloquium that was to be held in Lisbon. As his proposal didn't fire my enthusiasm, the well-meaning civil servant added in the hope of convincing me: "More than 45 writers are going to be there." Rather than delighting me and transporting me to seventh heaven, this figure took me aback: "How on earth, I muttered to myself, can there be 45 writers in a single country at any one time?" If we were being optimistic, such a figure might perhaps be plausible for the entire world. But in a Spain where, for instance, there wasn't a single real writer in the whole of the eighteenth century, this was to scale absurd heights of absurdity. Extremely fortunate is the nation which can assume that three or four writers at a particular moment in its history are destined to survive. The qualitative leap made by our man from the Ministry of Culture did not however arise from illusions of grandeur or patriotic chauvinism: it reflected a misconception widespread in the would-be critical field of the printed page and other news media.

In Spain and all countries with a more or less thriving book publishing industry there exists a deplorable confusion of literary text and publishers' product and, even more worrying, a tendency on the part of reviewers and cultural programmers to ignore or silence the former in favour of the latter. Whenever I raise this issue in public, some critic or reader quite rightly asks: "What are your criteria for distinguishing one from the other?"

Although the answer is quite complex, it can be formulated starkly and simply: whether or not the writing begs to be re-read. The publishers' product, particularly the carefully concocted variety, immediately satisfies the reader's appetite and can be consumed, digested and expelled like a hamburger from a fast-food outlet: manufactured to entertain a passive reader, it departs his consciousness as easily as it went in. The best-seller is the desired goal, what the publishing industry and a great many authors have set their sights on: the conquest of the greatest number of readers.

Well, as André Gide lucidly remarked, "what can be understood in the blink of an eyelid usually disappears without trace": and this publishers' product for instant assimilation is usually condemned to oblivion, except in those cases where a fortunate blend of ingredients allows it to soldier on for years and decades in the honours list of subliterature.

In total contrast, the literary text doesn't aspire to immediate recognition or to the instantaneous seduction of the reading public. It goes in search not of readers but of re-readers and often, when the latter don't exist, is obliged to invent them. Rather than operate in an area that is known in advance and keep to rules familiar to the usual recipient, the writer whose ambition it is to leave some trace and add something to the leafy tree of literature will not hesitate to destabilise the reader, force him to head into unknown territory and from the outset present a completely new set of rules. The reader's initial sense of shock, his tentative journey across an unexplored land that lacks the usual sign-posts, his need to turn back in order to uncover the secret laws determining the new space opened up by the book, will stimulate his enjoyment as a reader, drive him to collaborate with the author in the appropriation of his innovative artistic project. Imperceptibly, the reader will be changed into a re-reader and, thanks to that, will actively intervene in the siege and scaling of a text to be read and re-read.

As a reader, I have been forged by dozens and dozens of authors whose novels or poems rebelled against previous literary experiences and forced me to tangle with them in unusual, painstaking hand-to-hand combat. My mettle as a new reader, created by texts of substance like the *Book of Good Love*, the *Spanish Bawd*, the *Lozana Andaluza*, the *Quixote*, the *Spiritual Canticle* and *Solitudes*, has been a determining factor in the development of my own writing. What I have demanded of them and their authors I have in turn sought from myself, thus forcing myself to change the ideal target of my books: from the reader ordinarily satisfied with a single reading to the re-reader constrained to grapple with the text, to lose himself in its twists and turns, trawling its elusive path in a compelling process of reconstruction. Repeated experiences as reader and author over the last 25 years of my life have turned my life and my conception of the written text upside down: a move from the novel manufactured according to the canons of the genre to the kind of work that creates its own laws as it develops. Several months ago, a young man came up to me and said: "I've read your last novel and really liked it". "Have you re-read it?" "No." "In that case, either you're a bad reader or I've written a bad novel."

From the time of *Count Julian*, writing for me has been an adventure of the same order as the creative reading I was referring to. Whilst in my youthful novels I started out with ready-made plans, credible, well-defined characters and situations, the ones I have written since are real shots in the dark: I start the text from a phrase or image and don't know where my pen will lead me. Creative uncertainty that allows the novel to grow and develop organically with minimal intervention from the author, in line with Genet's lapidary dictum on the writing of his time: "If you already know your starting-point and destination, you should talk of a bus journey rather than a literary enterprise." Thanks to my voracious appetite as a reader accustomed to probing texts that are substantial, difficult and, at first sight, opaque, I have moved on from writing that I have inherited to writing conceived as an adventure prolonged in the hands of the reader, of that new re-reader, the product of every rich, provocative work. For while the immense majority of books apparently find a ready-made audience, the texts I stand by cut a slow path until they find or invent their readership. Who could read *The Songs of Maldoror* or Joyce's *Ulysses* when they were written? Years, even decades, have gone by before readers/re-readers finally emerged able to understand them, in a logical continuation of the process unleashed by the writing. After an interlude of ten, fifteen, or forty years these works have nevertheless found their target audience!

What separates the atemporal pleiad of creators of texts from the general run of writers acclaimed by critics and applauded by the public at large, is the fact they perceive what the latter reckon buzzes with life to be either worked out or dead. The innovative author insensitive to the applause and reproaches of his contemporaries, knows he is surrounded by colleagues who are dead—whatever fuss these people make accumulating honours and prizes and aspiring, in the manner of some second-rate academics, to the glory of immortality. If I can paraphrase José Bergamín to describe the

former, their world is not of this kingdom. Mine, for ex-
ample, is scattered over a constellation of literary anomalies
and exceptions outside the fashions and laws of the day; in
cemeteries where the writers who remain exuberantly alive
illuminate my steps with their light after centuries have gone
by—not on the stage of the great traveling theatre of incon-
sequential shadows all vestiges of which will be mercilessly
swept away. This communion with the living via the written
word ignores frontiers and epochs. It unites me with the
writers whose works I have mentioned and others from di-
verse regions and cultures: with Ibn Arabi and Ibn Al Farid,
with Rabelais and Swift, with Flaubert and Biely, with Svevo
and Céline, with Arno Schmidt and Lezama. Their brilliance
accompanies me wherever I go in the universe of fleeting
spectres that is the raucous mediocrity of contemporary lit-
erature. Only if one penetrates the shell to reach the "kernel
within the kernel" and enters into possession of that truth
paying no heed to the values of the tribe, will one find this
unique, irrepeatable voice, that is distinguished from the oth-
ers by its strangeness and discourages imitation or alter-
ation by the customary retinue of epigones. The history of
literature, of each literature, is the history of these unmis-
takable voices which through the centuries speak to each
other and captivate us with the magic of their singularity.

Having reached this far, I now have a confession to make:
I haven't read or hardly read for a good number of years—is
it ten or twelve?: I re-read. Harassed by age and awareness
of the need to divide my time between the things that are
most important to me such as writing, friendship and travel,
I know I have only a very limited interlude to dedicate to
books. How then can I waste it on works whose interest is
exhausted in a single reading, which are consumed without
profit? Re-reading and only re-reading accompanies my

hours of relaxation, when, obliged to travel for professional reasons for weeks or months I have no choice but to select a small portable library. I'll tell you what I took to Iran and the Soviet Republics of Central Asia on the last filming of *Alquibla*: the *Quixote, Bouvard and Pécuchet, St. Petersburg, Terra Nostra, Oppiano Licario*, the *Spiritual Canticle* and an excellent English anthology of Sufi, Arab and Persian poets. Does that mean I have shut myself off completely from reading works that are published today inside or outside Spain? Not entirely. When someone I trust recommends a book, assuring me I'll re-read it, I take a risk and bury myself in it, but if my interest doesn't extend beyond this reading, I consider it's been a waste of time and withdraw my literary trust from my adviser. As the saying goes, for that journey, no saddlebags needed!

Writing to be re-read imposes on the author a particular morality of pride and sacrifice the principal elements of which I shall now set out. Renunciation of vanity, of wordly glories and rewards. A secret pride in the knowledge that one is creating something new and returning to the culture to which one belongs, as I wrote some time ago, "a language different from the one received when starting out on its creation". Immunity to the jibes of critics, accepting these in one's heart of hearts as indirect praise of fertile deviation. Closeness to the morality of the malama, of those Sufis who, in order to escape praise and maintain their pursuit of secret perfection, behaved in public so as to arouse disapproval and condemnation. "If you can get into a situation that turns you into a suspected thief, do all you can to do so," wrote one of their teachers.

Didn't the author of *The Balcony, For a Tight-rope Walker* and *Our Lady of the Flowers* steal, praise betrayal, and proudly assume his homosexuality when he undertook his rigorous, masterly work, a man whose example has illuminated me at crucial moments in my life?

To re-read a book is to accept joyfully the author's contagious project. No creator could capture this immanent power of literature like Cervantes, able to transform the characters in the Quixote into distinct beings, infected by the novels they read to the point of wanting to rival their heroes and throw themselves into the first preposterous adventure. Unknowingly Cervantes secularised the persuasive power of religious discourse, of the word revealed to the prophets, transmuting literature into a kind of lay religion, of purely human creation, though endowed with a very similar transcendence. His exemplary experience, like that of the great mystic poets from Ibn Arabi to Saint John of the Cross, has radically modified my writing and my life, fused them into a single entity and made of both a text that only awaits bodily decomposition before assuming its definitive form.

Re-reading and the involvement of the reader in the creative offering of a book is the best means known to me of reactivating our spiritual life, impoverished by the continual aggression of the new Leviathan of uncontrolled modernity that obstructs and obscures the human horizon in this imminent end to the millennium. To propagate the vision of diverse worlds, spread the gift of ubiquity by dint of poetic-novelesque recourse to distopy and anachronism, to re-invent the eschatological visions that console or torment our perennial desire for transcendence in a universe that scientists have cruelly deprived of a metaphysics of nature, are enriching projects in accord with Blanco White's defense of the "pleasure of unlikely imaginings" and turn literature into a most useful weapon against the rational tyranny of an epoch impermeable to spiritual realities, atrophied and nullified by continual technological "advances" and the implacable fun-

damentalism of science. If only my works could infect the
odd one of you as I have been infected by the works of the
authors I admire! What more could an author/re-reader like
myself aspire to than this small but cherished reward?

*

*Born in Barcelona in 1931, Goytisolo has lived for many years in
France. Some of his early works, accordingly, have been influenced
by the French new novel, but the injustice and moral outrage con-
cerning Spain under the Franco government represent a unique
trajectory of 20th century fiction which has made Goytisolo one of
its most outstanding practitioners. Among his novels are* Fiestas
(1958), The Party's Over *(1962),* Marks of Identity *(1966),*
Count Julian *(1974),* Juan the Landless *(1975),* Makbara
(1980), and The Virtues of the Solitary Bird *(1988).*

Osman Lins

"Lost and Found"
from *Nine, Novena*

Translated from Portuguese by Adria Frizzi

To
Alvaro de Souza Melo Filho
Antônio A. Macedo Lima
Ernâni Bezerra
Lauro de Oliveira and
Roderico Queiroz

THE BEACH is a no man's land that the waters surrender and reclaim. Governed by the cycle of the tides, the creatures which in the beginning lived in the sea and now inhabit this frontier have long accepted the hapless condition of being fought over by the thalassic and terrestrial worlds. If some dig tunnels to escape the invasion of the rising tide, others cling to pebbles, lie still among damp stones, take refuge in tide pools. Some absorb excess water and will dry up and die if they are exposed to the sun too long. The creatures that live inside shells shut them tight; many burrow into the damp sand. The tide rises, invades the tunnels, floods their inhabitants, brings in the big fish, agile reapers, alert eye and greedy tooth. When everything has been turned over,

the ebb tide comes, the loud crashing noise of the waves sub-
sides, the fish leave. Then, upon the anemones hidden among
the rocks, upon the small mollusks and crustaceans which
have taken shelter in the dead waters of the beach, upon the
fugitives of the countless tunnels surfacing, full of fear, among
empty shells and debris spat out by the sea, then, more rav-
enous than the fish, descend the shadows of the coastal
birds—sharp beaks, terrestrial eyes.

—Where's my son?
—I don't know.
—How old is he?
—A little over seven, blond, green trunks.
—No, I haven't seen him.
—He was here only ten minutes ago, playing with a ball.

∅ Sitting there in the sand in my swimming suit, next to
the big blue canvas tent we—the clubmembers—put up two
and a half hours ago, I watch Renato, three meters away from
me, as he says the last sentence. He is barefoot, in black trunks
and a red shirt, holding his right hand out to show the height
of the boy. Is it because I have lost so many precious things,
and I do not have the strength to live through what I have
received in exchange, that a bitter joy, sponge of honey and
ammonia, fills my mouth? Remembering the night in which
I was stripped, one by one, of everything I had with me, only
to lose even more cherished possessions later, I watch his
face crack with a sharp sound, the way framed sheets of glass
do on days of intense heat.

▽ Lying in the sand, the color of sand myself, beneath
the umbrella with yellow sections, I observe the man sitting
in the shade of the tent. When the other one inquired about
the child, some mechanism began to work in his eyes, sud-
denly transformed into piercing instruments completely de-

void of compassion, like the eyes of animals of prey. I barely
remember my father, I only saw him a few times, perhaps his
real home was the small or medium-sized ships he sailed, his
visits were not very frequent, nor long, but he looked at ev-
erything in the same way: as if he were about to jump on it.
A strange face. It was worth seeing at least once in your life.

∅ Watch him. As much as possible, follow all his steps
and words with the utmost rigor, record the evolution of his
despair. Observe, like a condensed version, in a few minutes,
what sooner or later happens to everybody, but usually over
a period of years: the realization that something essential
has been snatched from us. He is still very far from this. Hesi-
tant, one face gazing at the sea, another searching the av-
enue, two more trying to look as far as possible down the
sun-drenched beach full of tents, swimmers and vendors, his
mind, overcome by the idea that his son is dead, and com-
forted by the fleeting hope that he'll soon find him again,
resembles the beach, which the waves reclaim and surren-
der, then invade again. Embarrassed by his own question,
because asking is like divulging his fear and giving it sub-
stance, he approaches various people, smiling, holding out
his hand where the top of his son's hair would be, but the
answers are always discordant, one pointed north, another
south, there were vague gestures, negative answers, some-
one holds his arm out toward the sea.

⦾ In the same way that a droning sound born in the
heart of many other noises passes through them, without
history or destiny, I will appear on my bicycle, pedaling slowly
along the beach, the high waves on my left, on the right the
cars in the avenue, the buildings, the consulates with their
big flags hoisted. I will violate, among curses, the area where
the young men are playing soccer, I'll see the jangada sailrafts
at sea and ashore, the ships at anchor, the motorboats, the

woman swimming among the waves, children floating in-
side plastic animals, old men drifting in their inner tubes,
the jets performing acrobatics in formation; I'll pass ven-
dors selling their baskets of mangabas, braids of cashew fruits,
coconut stands, clusters of tangerines, soda and ice cream
carts, parasols, straw mats, towels, wicker baskets, couples
playing paddleball, groups with a feather shuttlecock, vol-
leyball teams, sunbathers lying in the sand or swimming,
other bicycles, hats in the shape of dahlias, cones, birds, boxes,
lovers writing in the sand, mothers chastising their prog-
eny, children looking for shells or making sand castles. I will
pass through it all, I will record it all, completely unnoticed,
before I vanish the same way a buzzing sound ends, never to
be remembered again.

—Hi, Renato. How's it going?

—ok, I guess.

—What do you think of the planes?

—I wasn't paying attention to them. I'm worried about…

—Did you ever get to see the Zeppelin ?

—Just the picture. It came out in the papers.

—I was very young then, but I remember. That was re-
ally something. I wonder why they don't keep making zep-
pelins.

—Me too. My son…

—That's right…everything changes. Just think what our
children will see.

—Where are yours?

—Over there, in the water.

—Did any of them want to see the Independence Day
parade?

—No.

—Mine did. He loves parades. You haven't seen him
around, have you?

—No. Mine took after me. They like mechanics and the beach. Shall we go into the water?

—Later.

—Why later? It's 11:40. In half an hour the bus will be here. We don't have much time. Let's go. They say that life began in the sea. Let's return to our origins.

△ It began in the sea? Where exactly, if ancient mountains lie under the oceans and marine skeletons are sometimes found at great altitudes? I do not know how I could give in to his insistence, even though he did insist a lot, and how I can be swimming now, when I cannot see my son, when nobody is telling me anything about him, when maybe he is only a few meters away from me, his face in the sand. Throughout the long Cambrian Period the earth was uninhabited: life was present only in the water, which was fishless. No vertebrates. Mollusks, sponges, jellyfish, long trilobites drifted, sounding the marine depths. The swimming animals had not appeared yet. Bald, sterile and dead, as in times not even fossils can remember, that is how I see the earth now, without my son. I must get out of the water, shout, run around the beach, accept once and for all the condition of a man upon whom the beak and claws of misfortune have descended, so that everybody will know and help me. Even if this search may be vain.

∅ Are adversities sent to men from heaven? No, we plunge into them, in our blindness, like someone who throws himself into an abyss. We are never extraneous to the things that befall us. Could I imagine, when I took my daughters out for a stroll on Sunday afternoons, and picked poppies from the brick walls for them, or sat in the grass with a volume of Horace while they played in the sun, could I imagine then that I was already moving toward the still remote moment in which I would suddenly lose them? And how could

I guess, upon leaving home that afternoon, to celebrate Z.I.'s birthday in secret, that I would lose everything, salvaging little besides my own life and receiving in exchange something that my half-heartedness doesn't allow me to accept? Completely unaware of everything, I added weight and purpose to my own movements, carefully preparing, step by step, that catastrophe, without even realizing that I was in the midst of a disaster when it had already been consummated. Destiny carefully conceals its machinations, and to discover them it is almost always necessary to peel off many layers of ignorance. Ahead of Renato, I ripped them open faster than anyone else: I precede him in the knowledge of his destitution. Experienced, wise, and yet merciless, I will follow his struggle against the acceptance of what has happened. Like an invader in the antechamber of the future, I will wait for him, alert, I won't miss a single step. He will forget almost all he did or will do in the next moments: the conversation about dirigibles, his extemporaneous swim, everybody's indifference, all this running around: he goes to the left, retraces his steps immediately, rushes off to the right, stops, raises his hands to his face (the first gesture of affliction), climbs to the top of the sandbank and surveys the festive beach, then starts toward a child playing in the distance, only to realize that it's not his; which exacerbates his movements, is followed by a moment of stupor, then a sudden progression toward the evidence. I will record in detail his goings in the darkness, his comings. Who knows if this will not help me? He is walking toward the jangadas.

▽ Our father, who also disappeared in the sea, never saw his last child, born three weeks after his death. The captain of the cargo ship comes to see us: "He could swim well, despite his age. He must have gotten dizzy, stumbled. Anyone can have an accident. We looked for him, it was a beautiful day. Only ten minutes earlier he'd been seen paring his nails with a knife, between the deck and the lifeboats. We looked for him quite a bit. I decided to come in person to give you my condolences. If I can do anything…" That is why I know what this man's search is like. He has not given the alarm yet. Silently—or talking to himself—he is tracing concentric ellipses, widening his search around the area where he first noticed the child's absence and which in his mind took on the function of the imaginary center of his anxiety. That is how I picture the cargoship, describing a spiral with its bow, because of my father dead in the Atlantic. All his papers disappeared with him; the administration did not keep any pictures, and we did not have any at home either. Twenty years later, my brother, compelled to fix on a face his sudden love for the father he had never seen, would begin another search; for a picture he had learned existed in Serinhaém, Goiana and Flores do Indaiá, my father's birthplaces where half a century earlier he had received his first communion with several other children. This event had been captured on a sepia-colored photograph, twenty-five boys in white, almost all dead by now.

$\wedge$ Peacefully, the jangadas came back, all of them, from the open sea. And my son sucked in by the waves? After the Cambrian, as big as men, and even bigger, came the marine scorpions. They multiplied, established their reign in the salty depths. They swam slowly, with their legs wide, like big aggressive seraphim. Millions of years later, the cycle of their flagellating passage consummated, they moved to salty or fresh waters and, their powers already declining, sought refuge in estuaries, rivers, lakes and lagoons. By the Permian they had disappeared. But in the previous era, when the marine fauna had become diversified and amphibious fish dragged themselves across the bottom of swamps, they still dominated. This sea which perhaps has already taken my son is for me like the waters after the Cambrian, filled with huge scorpions with irate stingers, looking like angels with dried-up wings.

—I'm starting to get worried. I can't find my son.

—He must be around here someplace.

—I'm going to look around with you. Should we go too?

—Where?

—Renato's son has disappeared.

—When?

—More than half an hour ago. What do I do?

—Keep going this way; I'll look the other. Don't go alone, though.

∅ What is about to happen will be important: the disclosure and widening of the search, the precipitous onset of panic. I must witness these things. I walk down the beach with Renato, the black sea on one side, on the other the buildings with their lilac glass, the avenue with glittering cars. There we are, side by side, in the salt-colored sand, among people who have also lost their children or their wristwatches, youth or opportunities, courage or their teeth, their parents or their money, confidence or an arm, ardor or assets, or their identity, or their job, or their minds, or the way, or strength, or life—there we are, following the scent of a dead child. Somebody looks at his watch, 11:48, on this same beach Z.I. and I met to watch the moon rise. I bring her roses, we have been meeting in dark and deserted places, in a sort of sterile lyricism, for four years. We have not even become lovers, we have limited ourselves to discussing that possibility. Our trysts are tender and heart-rending, our kisses passionate, dramatic our good-byes. But what have we done to change our situation? We couldn't bring ourselves to break up, nor to make a commitment. We blamed it on our sensitivity, re-

peated that we would never be happy at the price of some-
body else's suffering: our passion feeds on the indulgence
with which we look at each other. A painful game in which I
am getting caught more and more, gradually losing sight of
what is imaginary in it. Z.I. did not come to the beach. Not
to show up occasionally, out of coyness or remorse, for long
expected trysts is part of the pleasant ritual we have estab-
lished. To arrive very late, thus manifesting our hesitancy, is
another ceremony. At times I have waited two hours for Z I.,
only to leave in the end, or see her come, ecstatic in both
cases. We breathe cultivated pleasures and torments that do
not affect us deeply. I need Z.I. to feel alive, it is indispens-
able to the economy of my being that the secret encounters
and the whispered telephone calls between which weeks and
even months often pass—occur on the placid and safe stream
of my days, and that I evoke them among my family—my
three daughters, my prosaic and affectionate wife—the five
of us in the light of the lamp, around the table set with china,
silver and crystal. Alone, I watch the moon rise, throw the
roses in the sea. Not in vain: I will tell Z.I. of my gesture.
Touched, she will ask me to meet her on the bank of the
canal, to celebrate her birthday, and that will be the end of
my comfortable and two-faced existence. Renato's nerves are
beginning to fail him. I can tell from the self-assured way in
which he is acting, like those people who are more composed
when they are drunk than when they are sober. His despera-
tion increased, multiplied, all of a sudden walking seemed a
precarious recourse. He took a bicycle whose owner must be
in the water swimming, fell twice, finally gained some bal-
ance, is pedaling sinuously now. I stay here, to explain what
happened in case the owner gets here first. I will apologize
to him.

$\wedge$ Real scorpions, ancestors of those existing nowadays and precursors of life on the deserted continents, appeared in the Silurian. Then, out of mica, mud, refracted light, darkness and salt, the fish are formed, voracious from the beginning. They devour each other and every millennium they are more numerous. Great convulsions transform the earth, promontories are submerged, lakes dry up. Seas empty out.

∅ The canal runs through Recife, from the Derby to Santo Amaro, like a blind and powerful animal. Slow and obstinate, it advances, goes around Boa Vista, almost without meandering, cuts across streets, plazas, avenues, with its putrid waters, moat without end and more devastating than time. Both sides are covered with undergrowth, wild shrubs thrive, shacks proliferate. No light, except on the ten bridges: Paiçandu, Fronteiras, Derby, Amorim Park, Espinheiro, João de Barros, Maduro, Tacaruna. Z.I. and I meet here many times, in the shady areas between those bridges, like many lovers whose silhouettes pass by, furtive, with their faces lowered, among toads, reptiles, grazing horses and clouds of mosquitoes. Renato is back. With extreme care, he puts the bicycle back and doesn't tell me anything about his expedition. His face has shattered into a thousand pieces. His eyes are glassy, his shirt in his hand, his trunks damp. Some children are playing. The ball, thrown up high, hits his shoulder. He turns, violently kicks it toward the sea, yells at the children. Then he begins to call his son's name aloud. The children, frightened, run away, he continues to throw the boy's name to the wind, asks me to do the same, I call out without conviction. That is how I call Z.I., that night, watching her walk away certain that she will not turn to look at me, ever again. A siren vibrates somewhere, it is noon, the jet formation is back, they fly low over the beach, with a deafening noise, while the warships fire their cannons, the horizon fills with smoke, the simultaneous detonations shake

the ground and the houses, Renato continues to shout, no-
body hears his call, I stop.

▽ Two of the town's pious old women, Anita and
Albertina, one of whom plays the fiddle and the organ, have
the picture: our father and his companions, all in white, the
extinguished candles. This is what my brother heard. In the
sitting room, next to the parish church, among old furniture
and a lit lamp of blue glass, he inquires about it. ▽ Mothers
running after their children in the water or in the sand, drag-
ging them by the arm, some by the ear. You can see the pride
shining on their faces: they snatched their children from
death. Resented words, words of fear crackle among them.
▽ The two whiteclad virgins know almost nothing, they
confuse our father with other boys. One of them has gray
hair, the fiddle-player's, despite her age, is still yellow, the
color of old paper. Every now and then, without any reason,
she bursts into a little laugh, hoarse and croaking, like a par-
rot or a snipe. ▽ One of the zealous mothers didn't find her
daughter and ran to the tent in tears, everybody rushes over,
talking excitedly. A member of the club who got drunk dances
around the agitated group, handing out cashew fruits that
only the children will accept. ▽ The old women's walls, cov-
ered with sacred images, the fiddle case on top of a console.
Both wear rosaries of white beads around their wrists. They
say they never saw the picture. They limit themselves to
describing to my brother our father at thirteen or fifteen, a
description that could be of any other boy. The church bells
strike nine, they cross themselves, the yellow-haired one cack-
les again. ▽ The news that a child is missing and that his
corpse might suddenly appear on the beach, brought in by
the waves, has spread. This part of the shore, turned into a
mourning chamber, begins to empty. People talk, look to-
ward the club's blue tent, some come to see what is going

on, others have already left. ▽ The gray-haired one says to my brother that it is Jovina Veras who must have the picture with our father. But Jovina has moved, lives with a brother, on a farm. Where? They do not know exactly: out of town. They will pray that my brother finds what he is looking for. ▽ The light has risen from the ocean like a giant amphibian, emerged from the abysses. Daggers gleam among the waves. With its keels of silver, oars of fire and enormous resplendent sails, hundreds of galleys slowly move across the horizon, reflected by the sea. The amphibian has grown, is advancing, invades us, fills me with light, I close my eyes and see myself the way you see an egg against the sun. Even the closed up houses' lights have come on, even the basements are lit up. Brief dialogues, in this light so intense and absurd that for a moment I cannot see anything: "When's the bus coming?" "In ten or fifteen minutes." "How many teeth does the Leviathan have?" "Four in the upper arch, twelve in the lower, twenty-four in the middle." "What about Renato? Shall we wait for him?" "Of course not." ▽ The sulphur-haired woman cackles again. The other has placed a drawer next to the lamp, and is showing us the pictures she has. Daughters of Mary grouped around the vicar, death notices, Guy de Fontgalland, white dresses, black dresses, high boots, curls, wicker seats, iron gates, dogs, chairs, bouquets. She doesn't know the names of these ghosts, does not recognize anyone. The fiddler has also bent over the pictures, but cannot add anything to her sister's uncertainties. They weep, the two old maids, over that world they've witnessed and of which they know so little. "We can't remember anything. You can have the pictures if you like." ▽ The morning quivers with explosions and lamentations. Piercing constellation, seven airplanes tear through the winds. Bottles, dishes, cups and glasses dance in the cupboards, knives and ladles rattle in the drawers, clocks stop, pictures swing in their hooks, crystals shatter. The relationship between the fuselage of airplanes and the deafening noise filling land and sea seems to me identical to that existing between the bill of a peacock and the fan of its feathers.

There is, fringing this no man's land, a strip which is never uncovered by the waters, as low as the tide may be. A fauna of indolent beings, averse to adventure and reluctant to change, undecided between animal and plant, sea and continent, has inhabited it for millions of years. A fish, covered with long vibratile cilia, with tentacles like ferns and heads like calices, invades this archaic and mortal land. Suddenly, it is pierced by arrows and can no longer move. The killer does not come out in the open: it waits until the waters bring the victim within reach of its apathy and, without hurrying, brings it to the opening which serves as a mouth. Sometimes it happens that animals once diligent come to this sad zone and here multiply. They lose their agility, color, initiative, skeleton. They take pleasure in imitating the indolence of anemones and jellyfish, with time they begin to resemble them and eventually become indistinguishable. They cast off everything, seek nothing more.

$\wedge$ The plants of the earth, preparing the terrain for the coming of animals, appear in the Devonian. My friend Albano has just arrived, I see the fenders of his bicycle. He does not greet me.

—What is it, Renato?

—I don't know what to do any more. He's gone.

$\wedge$ Deep lakes and big lagoons formed at that time. The first insects, similar to fleas, leaped in the silence, lords of the birdless spaces.

—Where did you see him last?

—That's the problem. I can't remember.

∧Those who went to look for my son at the other end of the beach have already returned. In the Carboniferous, the trees and the giant insects grow, beetles, ants, forests prolif-erate, butterflies with wings as big as palm-leaf fans graze in the prairies.

—I can't remember. I think it was when he was playing in the sand; but then again, it seems that he called me and I didn't turn.

—How could you let him out of your sight with a sea like this!

∧The sea claimed again the land it had lost, fish swam among tree branches, other forests were conquered, drowned, became petrified. The fish were the birds of those black woods.

—It just happened.

—Go get dressed.

∧ Many people have already changed their clothes and are sitting in the sun or in the shade of the tent. Is it that late? Soon they will all leave. I will be alone.

—When?

—Now. We're going to the police station.

—It's a waste of time. (The glaciers and the deserts). My heart tells me that he is dead. (The reptiles evolve in the Permian). What have I done to deserve this?

∅ The naive question. The same one Z.I. asked so many times, when the situation in which we lived, torn as we were between adventure and doubt, seemed to cloud her mind. "Before meeting you, I lived in peace with my husband and children, they were my whole life. I haven't done anything to deserve this misery, this exhausting dream. I don't know for what sins I was condemned to nourish this cancer within me." "Nothing keeps you from leaving me." "You know that I

can't. I'm expiating some evil deed." In the tent, Renato gets
dressed to continue his search. Why should human destiny
be a punishment or a reward? A fire burns down the walls
and roof of the just man, all his children die. The floods wash
away plantations irrigated with honest sweat, hard work and
prayers. The sinner's fortune grows larger and, in his old
age, after a short and placid end, his children and wife be-
moan his death. Life doesn't give any marks for good behav-
ior. What appears to be justice is only disorder and chance.
There must be a God, since the Devil exists. Does this mean
that I must see in what happened to me a sentence, a punish-
ment, the wrath manifested by some sovereign entity? The
bus has just arrived. Before it turned around, a lot of people
got on and took all the seats. For a man in this condition,
going in and out of the tent looking at the bus, confused,
maybe even hiding in the dressing room for some difficult
act carried out with modesty, this is like facing a dreaded
goodbye. As long as familiar even though indifferent faces
surround him he can fool himself or his fear. When they leave,
he will have to face his despair. He will find himself alone
and his misfortune will seem like a handicap, something like
those gangrenes that force fugitives to abandon a man to the
wolves or the ants. That is how I feel that night, on the bank
of the canal—gangrenous, with nobody by my side, waiting
to be thrown into the stagnant water.

▽ The blue tent measured four meters by three, and it
was three meters high. Once the canvas was rolled around
the poles, and the ropes and iron hooks were gathered, a
void opened up. A few people are still standing around the
man who lost his son, who is now wearing sunglasses, most
of them got on the bus, the driver is honking impatiently. A
few couples, more affluent perhaps, brought their own um-
brellas and set them up far from the others, so they would

not look as if they had come to the beach with everybody
else. They approach looking very distinguished (or so they
think), the men carrying fishing gear under their arms, the
women wearing colorful straw hats. They march on, haughty
and full of disdain, indifferently pass the man with the sun-
glasses, ignoring the honking and the square of empty space
left by the tent. Our father, when he is at home, during the
intervals between his travels, works as a cooper. He shapes
the oaken staves with care, fastens them with strips of steel.
When he leaves, the tools and the materials he works with
remain in the yard. His presence, like his absence, has the
same forest smell. Which is also the smell of his voice, of his
unexpected arrivals, of his sudden goodbyes, the smell of noise
and silence, of death and ships. When we're told that he will
not be coming back, our mother gets rid of the tools, sells
the leftover steel and wood. Then the yard dies: and it is in
this emptiness that the man with the tense expression on his
face really disappears for me. From repeating so many times
to my brother, who demands more and more details, that
look, the face, the body and the voice of our father, I lose
him. His memory, on which my own words as well as my
brother's desires or suppositions begin to impinge, dies out
little by little, so that, because of his eagerness, my brother
destroys the only clear image of our father. All that is left to
me is the expression of his eyes (not the color, not even the
shine or the shape) and the oak smell in the yard. As for our
mother, she was never able to talk about her husband. To
the point that I sometimes wonder if she actually ever saw
him.

—You're really leaving, then?

—I'll make an announcement on the radio, if you want.

—It's not necessary. Are you coming with me, Albano?

—Of course!

—It'd better to take a cab.

—I'll drive slowly. Look on both sides, maybe you'll see him.

—See you later, Renato. We'll ask the driver not to go fast. Well keep an eye out. If you find the kid, you can stop a car and catch up with the bus. If we do, we'll wait for you.

▽ Everybody has left. The two friends, each with his back turned to the other, look in opposite directions. Now they turn, exchange some words I cannot hear, they walk away. It is when invoking God's name is no longer natural for him that his plans begin to take on the aspect, in his mind, of an absurd compromise between his own strength and chance, it is when the old certainties disappear and certain interrogatives he did not even dare to voice before turn into dogmas, when certain questions previously answered turn into their own answers, it is, in short, when he loses his faith that my brother becomes obsessed with my father's face, to substitute it for God's, now hidden. His search is different from this man's: it's not for another encounter that he's preparing; he is trying to claim the invisible, the unknown, to reach, through intricate labyrinths, a remote being and his halo. First I have to recreate the way in which that sailor makes vats and tubs, shapes barrel staves, rounds the hoops and arranges each piece: the barrel staves of the casks, joined by the first steel band, are petals forming a big oaken flower, which is born open and closes later, bound by the last hoop. Then I have to evoke the instruments of an art practiced without compass or ruler, by an expert eye and hands that know the right measurements; I have to soak the wood to make it more docile to the camber, I have to warm it up in a fire of wood chips and compose again the music, the rhythm our father invents when he hammers the boards during the last phase of each piece, a rhythm subject to countless variations, always new and always identical. Then, my brother begins to demand that I make our father visible to him and, with time, his questions become statements instead; he has engendered within himself a figure born of who knows what molds, and while he pretends to be asking, he instills in my memory his own version of the dead. Could these two images have destroyed each other in me, like two ferocious fish or gamecocks?

∅ One night I come to the beach with Z.I., in a cab. The car moves as slowly as this bus, we are still at the beginning of our relationship, I watch her with fear. I have just felt, in her hands, a quivering, a fluttering of wings immediately suppressed. Her face, in the shade, has something of a bristling animal. ∧ In the Permian the reptiles appear, thick layers of ice cover the south of Africa. The police officer in Boa Viagem knows nothing about lost children or salamanders, none was reported to him this Sunday. During the apogee of reptiles, mollusks protected by shells appear everywhere. The design of the shells mirrors, with increasing rigor, a definite rhythm. ∨ My brother continues his search for the picture. He goes everywhere he knows or imagines there are relatives of the cooper—the seaman: Porto Real do Colégio, Igaraçu; Cabedelo, Barreiros, Coruripe; Penedo, Areia, Porto Calvo. Years of search, all in vain. ∧ A varied species and absolute lords of the plain, some on two feet, others on four, the dinosaurs dominate the planet for a hundred million years. Crocodiles, tritons, turtles, serpents and dragons go back to the sea. There are so many that the level of the water rises. In the Cretaceous the flowers, the Pyrenees, the Rocky Mountains, the Caucasus, the Himalaya, the harmonious skeleton of fish bloom. ∅ Z.I. and I walk in silence, looking at the distant lights of the ships in the dark. She brought me a bilingual edition of the *Sonnets from the Portu-*

guese, says she underlined E. B. Browning's verses: "I will not let you come near me, for fear you would suffer my pains." ▽ He has moved to the south of Bahia, keeps writing to all the relatives. In Serinhaém, in Goiana, in Flores de Indaiá. He asks them about the alleged picture of our father. Insistent letters, which go unanswered most of the time. ∧ Seals? Sea elephants? Walruses? Amphibious children? The police officer at Pina wrings his hands regretfully. Albano pats my back, I lower my head. Shall we come back? Shall we go on? In the ocean a cold, black saddlebag bursts open, and out of it leap all the toads and frogs that inhabit nightmares, swamps and hollow trunks, with their long hind legs, their drunken eyes, their slimy skin. Some, like silkworms, hibernate, then they break out of the cocoon, become bats, soar to the heights of the night. ∨ Our aunt writes to my brother. She found the photograph, it is in her hands. He wires: DO NOT SEND PRECIOUS FIND BY MAIL. WILL COME GET IT AS SOON AS POSSIBLE. ∅ I kiss Z.I., it is the first time. Her mouth is as warm as a bird in the summer sun. Was there, when I kissed her, a muffled trill, the hint of a cicada song in her hips, in her shoulders? ∧ With the bats, the lemurs also venture forth. The skeletons of some beings become lighter, feathers cover their bodies, they fly in the air. Fearless fish rise above the water. Some bird, frightened by its own voice, begins to sing. ▽ The reply to my brother: "Unfortunately I don't have the picture any more. Isabe Veras, Jovina's sister, came to take it back. She says that it's precious, because one of the children in it is in the family. She doesn't know which one. But I recognized your father. When you come, we'll go to Isabe's house together." Years pass before he comes to Pernambuco. I cannot tell whether he has come to resemble father more, or whether the face I remember then and think is the Deceased's is his. ∅ I've chosen, to celebrate Z.I.'s birthdays, a different date from the day on which she was born, like the sovereigns of England. She wears a new dress, comes to meet me (always in solitary places), I give her presents, inexpensive but meaningful. ∧ Continents coalesce and separate, ice and fire appear, stones turn into rhinoceroses, wind into horses, gourds into armadillos, the shadow of foliage into tigers, dawn into lions, sponges into three-toed sloths, tree branches into deer and caribous, the earth is filled with roars, howls, whistles, neighs and bellows and suddenly there is a silence, the hour of humankind has come. ∅ For this birthday, I bring Z.I. an album with drawings of roses in the center of huge leaves of paper, below the Latin names, *fusca superba, corona rubrorum, gemma rubra, omnium calendarum, glauca, virginalis, scandeus, balearica, reclinata, rubra, hispida, sulphurea, corimbosa, mutabilis. Mutabilis.*

∧ And him? The eras past, the fossils of cyclones and of eruptions, the freezes and fires, the arid millennia, the floods, the cataclysms, exoduses, submerged mountains, the pulsing of blood, the trajectory of the arrow; the seed in the ground, the fruit ripening, everything happened for my son— not a bird or a fish—to be and cease to be? Like the earth in space, in the depths of space, atolls are born in the ocean with their illusion of tranquillity and their shipwrecks. ∅ The bus stops, some people get off, they think they saw the boy wandering along the beach. They come back. We all turn into stone and silence.

Four hundred meters below sea level darkness begins, and the only lights are those of phosphorescent animals. The ebb and flow of the water above still reaches this darkness. Six hundred meters below all movements cease: in the heart of this invisible, obscure and dense universe creatures with cylindrical bodies, not very large, spy on each other. Their sin-

ister eyes, placed on the sides of their head, see in all direc-
tions at the same time. Some have separated their blind eyes
into threads and sound the black depths with long tactile
filaments. They are all carnivore and equipped with steely
teeth. If elsewhere the destiny of fish is to be eaten by en-
emies of greater strength, in these abysses the law is inverted:
with their enormous mouths and their dilatable bodies the
pelagic creatures devour prey four times bigger than them-
selves.

▽ Soon I will take the umbrella apart, pick up the straw
mat, oils, towel, the shade, and I will leave. Almost in front
of me, bathers—men and women—excitedly exchange words
and gestures I do not understand, they all run out of the
water, to the beach. They pass by me, I hear the words *leg*
and *shark*. The tide comes in, the waters expand again their
movable frontiers. From the ocean, from its depths, comes
the continuing cry of a swallow. This bird does not exist in
Pernambuco. My aunt, my brother and I around the small
table, the lamp hanging above our green heads. Two candles
burning in the oratory. Pictures of saints on all the walls,
behind the doors, statuettes on the furniture. "Isabe Veras
died a week ago. Even less." "What about the house? Her
things, the pictures? Did you go there?" "It didn't occur to
me." "You pray so much that you don't have time to think
about anything else. You should have kept the picture." "It
was hers. What could I do?" "You should have told her that
you had lost it." "Maybe we can go there tomorrow. Jovina
Veras may be able to help you, if she still hasn't moved."
"Didn't she live on a farm, with another brother?" "Isabe
and Jovina were living together again. Had been, for many
years. I'm going to find out where the house is." My brother
cannot wait an entire night, he drags us around the three

silent towns. We find the house, which Jovina Veras is still occupying, we bang on the door. Even our aunt knocks lightly with her bony knuckles, smiling, surprised at her own boldness. Nobody answers. My brother, with bleary eyes, and like someone who is very far, on the other bank of a big river, looks at the images in the oratory, blows out the two candles. Closer, distinct, the screeching of the swallows.

∅ We had to stop for the fourth time, this time to pick him up, and not because someone thinks he saw his son. All he said was "No." He sits down quietly, without looking around, his gangrene invades us. On the bank of the canal, the album with drawings of roses in my hand, I wait for Z.I. to show up. For some of the clandestine lovers the time of their hurried encounters is up, they part, each goes in a different direction, on the paths cutting through the wild growth. From the stagnant waters rises a smell of trash, rotten fruit, human waste and burning sulphur. Two things are nagging at me: the album, which I took the precaution of hiding among my shirts, was not in the same position, and it is almost dinnertime already, my family must be waiting far me, I do not want to be late. If throughout these many months Z.I. had not managed to incorporate her delays with my waits, much longer than normal, I would have left. But this pleasure a vice—she feels in always appearing to be struggling with herself, infected me, dissolving within me that more or less brief moment in which, our patience at an end, we decide that the person we are waiting for will not come, and leave. I look at my watch in the light of the lighter. Later than I thought. All is set for my ruin: the thickness of the night, the propitious hour, the absence of stars, the dim reflections in the water, the pit in which I will fall. Now at the core of the event that has been brewing for three years, imminent the gesture for which there will be no mending, I get up, cautiously move a few steps forward on the wide wall of the canal. In the sooty field, which, in this night of few lights, is the putrid place Z.I. and I transformed into a river, I make out a small roundish area to my left. I feel with my foot what I think is firm ground, lose my balance, plunge headlong into a watery world of worms and debris, sink to the bottom, fling my arms about in that noxious paste, tumble with my arms wide while my cry gets muffled in the mud; I sink in the swamp, fall wondering why this is happening to me, roll like a stone into the darkness that invades my nostrils with its creatures and weeds. The album with the drawings of roses—the *Président Carnot*, the *Niphetos*, the *Souvenir de Wooton*—will never be found. In the almost empty bus—since many, including Renato, have joined a consternated group of people in the center of which a child was crying, a boy everybody believed to be someone he actually is not—I wait for their return.

—It's not him, Renato. But this old man saw a kid who'd gotten lost half an hour ago.

—How old was he?

—About eight. Two women were leaving in their car.

—And?

—They took him home. He knew the name of the street where he lives.

—His hair…what color was it?

—Black. Long. He was wearing something red.

—Red?

▽ My brother and I knock on Jovina's door again. We are told that she went to the city hall with her brother. We do not find her. They must have gone to the church, to take care of matters related to Isabe's death. My brother refuses to enter, I inquire in the sacristy. We find the two old people at the civil registry, she staring at the walls while he signs papers. Men in the waiting room, all looking sad, even the ones who came to register their newborn children. My brother approaches Jovina, tells her in a low voice about the picture in which our father appears. She looks at him, frightened, without understanding. The same people who ran out of the water are coming back with others, some dive in, others get out quickly, the curious draw in faster than the shadows, the cries of the swallows multiply. My brother looks at me. It is difficult to talk about such an intimate matter. He speaks a little louder, hints at our father. Jovina remains silent, does not answer, smiles, my brother shouts and suddenly stops, the old woman is deaf. "Oh God, she's not going to understand anything!" The old man has finished with the signatures, gets up from the table, it is he now who is asking questions. My brother and I try to explain, the old man translates our confused words, Jovina Veras confuses our father with someone else with the same name. "Where are Isabe's things? Her pictures?" Who answers? "We're scrupulous people. The deceased has a son in Rio, another in Acre. Death is always followed by disorder. The pictures were scattered on the floor, on the chairs, the neighbors' children even ripped some up. We gave some away, four or five went to the farm, then we made two packages of the others and sent them to our nephews." "Wasn't there one of a first communion, a group of boys?" "Who knows? It's possible." "Are there any left?" "No." They fished the child's body out of the sea, the shadows of the people who are approaching recoil in fear, the shadows of those who prefer not to see form a circle around him, I get up and look at the find, the sea advances on the beach, a few steps from the dead child I hear the birds crying inside him, hundreds of swallows (trapped, hungry, irate, cruel) wounding each other with their wings, devouring each other with their beaks, screeching inside his body.

∅ Renato and the others come back, sit down and argue, we start moving again. They are hopeful, someone said he saw a lost boy, the description does not correspond to Renato's child but everybody thinks it is inaccurate and even wrong. I have come back to the surface, I struggle in the mud and manage to lean against the high bank. My body feels heavy, I barely have the strength to pull myself up, with all the water and dirt I have in my pockets and inside my shirt. We get to the bridge over one of the branches of the Capibaribe, here made bigger by the waters of the Pina and the Tejipió. My companions look at the river in silence. Several children have fallen asleep against their fathers' shoulders.

∧ The coral formations come together little by little. I will open the door. Following the line of the equator, but never going beyond the tropics, and always where the water is shallower, the mother-of-pearls spread in the sea. I will open the door, maybe I will see my son. Drawn by that sort of city which every day becomes more luminous, turbulent and ferocious, many animals migrate to it. I'll open the door, maybe I will see my son and laugh off all my fears.

∅ I have managed to climb the wall—almost losing one of my nails—and throw up kneeling on the ground. My shoes are floating, one is upside down. I try to take off my tie, which is choking me; I get it, throw it in the mud too. I pull out of my pocket a handkerchief half-dry between the folds, wipe my face. I want to wipe my hands but the handkerchief has vanished, I do not know where I put it. My hair is full of dirt, twigs and shreds of vegetation. I look for my comb, but I do not have it any more. My wallet is swollen, I pull it out with difficulty, squeeze the water out against the wall. It looks like a sponge. Z.I. is still not coming, nobody else is either, no help. I wonder what time it is. I run my hand down my wrist: I lost my watch. Go home, tell some lie, or say nothing at all, wash out my guts. I look where I think I put my wallet and cannot see it any more. Nobody has walked by, not even a dog. A rat maybe? A gust of wind? There is no wind; it must still be where I left it. I feel my pockets for the lighter (with a little light I will certainly find it) and discover that my thirteen pockets are full of mud, and mud only. My money, I.D., lighter, comb, handkerchief, glasses, watch, a gold chain, the wedding ring, it is all gone, I cannot even see the album and the shoes floating in the black water. One night I woke up and lay in bed without moving, I distinctly heard a rustling of wings against my shoulder, dried-up and short wings. "Is this the Devil who, deceived, thinking that I'm asleep, is hovering in the dark?" I fell asleep almost immediately, life went on. On the bank of the canal, stripped of everything as if by some malicious power, I believe in that wing again and begin to cross myself. I do not have the time to finish: my wife, two steps away from me, is there, looking at me. After having made sure that the ghost in front of her is me, she turns and walks away without saying a word. I see myself hugging her, covering her with dirt, sobbing and biting her dress at the height of her shoulder, while she remains silent and stiff, untouched by my affliction and my pleas. Finally she says: "Don't you ever come back. You'll never see my daughters again. For us, you'll always be as filthy as you are now." I move away nauseated by my own misery, my head hanging. When I raise it, I see the silhouettes of two women moving away, and one of them is Z.I. I holler her name, go after her wounding my feet, they both begin to run, I advance resolutely, grab her by her arm. "I love you!" She turns, spits in my face. Then I see—I saw—I see then that she is made of animals put together. I hear a muffled sound, a fluttering of wings, Z.I. comes apart and turns into night birds, wasps, butterflies, beetles and bats.

∞ We, who have lost so much, form a circle around this boy. We, who have sought so long, found this dead body, a victim of the sea in a city wrested from the sea. Here we were, come from all points of Recife, a fluviomarine plain, surrounded by hills of sand and clay, left by the sea in the Pliocene, when it withdrew from the continent. How many times were the streets we live on and where, in moments of delusion, we imagine we live safely, how many times were they flooded by the sea—once curbed by the hills that nowadays surround the city? Were not those reefs, whose sharp edges rise in the middle of the ocean, littoral cliffs, snatched from the continent by marine assaults? Here we are all around the boy, half-naked, soaked with sun and compassion, breathing the salty air and the light of the early afternoon. We know that we are vulnerable and fragile like him, that our ears are as deaf as his, our eyes as distracted. ∨ My brother visits all the houses on the street where Isabe lived, one by one. Few of the old pictures are left, and none is the one he is looking for. He asks the women, the children, gives out money. Intermingling descriptions arise, all imprecise. Finally, those minds yield to his desire and his frenetic entreaties and someone describes, in great detail, the group of little communicants. This description, which is his own doing, encourages him to continue the search. ∅ On the bank of the canal, I await the return of the perverse entity that has deprived me of almost everything. It won't be difficult for it draw close, throw me down to the bottom, this time forever. Perhaps complying with some inflexible code, it demands that the final gesture, that which will consign me to its power without appeal, come from me? I stand with my back turned to the silent waters, looking at the lights of Espinheiro Bridge, shivering with cold, revulsion and misery. Nothing happens. ∧ I'll open the door. In hot waters, polyps secrete their hard skeletons. I'll open the door, maybe I'll see my son. The skeletons form coral reefs and these grow and reach the surface, with their opposing characteristics: refuge and threat. I will open the door, maybe I will see my son, I'll laugh off all my fears. Many of the coral reefs form a lagoon, bays, inlets, bristly traps lying in wait for ships; many coral reefs stretch into cordons and fringes, imitating or altering the coastline; many coral reefs take the shape of circular islands, exuberant atolls, oases of green, shade and tranquillity, with their central lake silently responding to the pulsations of the sea. ▽ He goes to the farm of the old man, Isabe's brother. The version according to which some pictures would be there proves to be inaccurate. There is only one: of a French soldier, from the First Great War (Hiquily, Lucien, *brigadier*), with a dedication to Isabe, his unknown patroness from overseas. The rest are color prints, magazine clippings, birthday cards: couples with smooth faces and well contoured lips, with their foreheads touching, in a benevolent world, where petunias blossom in the lovers' hands and plump birds hover above them with an air of complicity. ∞ Let us weep for the child, we, half men and half fish, docile amphibians, creatures of uncertainty, as if we were crying for ourselves. In the course of time, following the regressions and transgressions of the sea, the contour of the bay of Recife, changed many times, altered by the floods of the numerous rivers (Capibaribe or of the Capybaras, Tejipió, Jabotão, Pirapama, Beberibe, Pina, Jiquiá, Camaragibe, Jordão), coming from far away, or born right here, tributary of other streams, inscribing and erasing interlaced deltas, many islands, numerous beaches, worlds of sand banks, kingdoms of crescent-shaped beaches and who knows how many more deltas. To escape the destiny of fish, we have been building on the deltas, out of cement, steel, wood, a system of bridges: Maurício de

Nassau, Santa Isabel, Velha, Giratória, Buarque de Macedo,
Boa Vista, Pina, Limoeiro, Derby, Madalena, Lasserre, Torre,
Caxangá—all ten over the canal, and many others without
name or future, collapsed by time, carried off by the floods
along with trees and animals, doors and furniture, roofs and
dead people, pieces of us all. Let us weep, then, for ourselves
and for the dead. ∅ We have almost arrived. The Alfândega
quay, the Santa Rita quay, the old boats, church steeples and
carcasses of trains in the freightyard. Flags blowing in the
wind. In the same boarding-house where I used to live when
I was single, I bathe, get rid of all that filth that hurts my
eyes and got even in my pubic hair. They lend me a retired
colonel's clothes, socks and shoes left behind by an old priest
in transit, some money. They ask questions. Without an-
swering, and repeating to myself that if the Devil exists there
must be a God too, I wrap my wet clothes in a newspaper.
I'm going back to the canal. ∧ I will open the door. A color-
ful world of sponges and actinias lives under the water, among
the pillars, arches, beams and porticos of mother-of-pearl;
crustaceans nest between the rifts of the caverns, in compact
groups; this moveable submarine garden is lit up with red,
green, violet and golden reflections; small fish—aquatic
butterflies—perform evolutions in cloudlike formations. I will
open the door, I will see my son. Starfish patrol that hunting
area and eat the fish, the fish eat the flowing manes, the manes
eat the crabs, the crabs eat the feathery sea fans, the fans eat
the lobsters, the lobsters eat the sunbursts, the sunbursts
eat the seahorses, the seahorses eat the boughs, the boughs
eat the tip of the stars. I will open the door, I will laugh off
all these fears. ▽ He continues to look for the picture, which
perhaps got torn or eaten by moths, or lies face down at the
bottom of some drawer, among useless papers (in what part
of the world?), surrounded by shadows, like our father and

the fish that despoiled him of his seaman's garb. ∅ "If the Devil exists, there must be a God." The package in my arms feels like a dog, like a pig. I walk, in these clothes that are not mine, in these shoes worn by other feet, as if another, a usurper, had appropriated the space occupied by my body. I throw the dirty clothes into the channel with anger, thinking that with this gesture I am getting rid of my weak and hypocritical soul. "Now I'll wait until another is born within me, blown by the winds of truth." So many months have passed, and I am still waiting. And those intimations of truth have not coalesced. It is difficult to apply an incandescent iron to our own tumor. ∞ Let us weep hand in hand around the dead boy—in whom we see ourselves—let us weep our salty tears. The water always at our side and always about to come back and submerge all that is ours, reaches the names of the places we inhabit, few of which are not familiar with this presence. This is the way the section of the Afflicted is, this is the way the Beberibe or river of the parakeets is, Recife the reef, the island of Refuge, Milk Island, the Jiquiá or fishing basket, the island of Good Views, Long Waters, Ibura or the source, Iputinga or the place of the clear fountain, the Uchoa bridge, the sections of Lowlands, Sands, Cold Water, the island of Santo Antônio, small river Parnamirim, and the Little Fishes, the Well, the Drowned. How many times have we been invaded, flooded, ravaged by seas whose names we do not know? How many times have we disappeared and, always stubborn, rebuilt city, cape, dune, reef, swamp? We have lost much, losing we live, letting go of what we have, earn and own, breaking, squandering, putting away, not finding, using, shattering what is fragile, shredding the hardiest possessions. For us from Recife, there is no security, as much as we hold out our arms, trying to preserve the tranquillity of our street. ∧ I get off the bus and many follow me. How many hours pass, between the beginning and the full blooming of a reef? I will open the door, those who are coming with me will wait. Nothing gives away the barrier developing, the structure rising. I will open the door. Will I see my son? Will I laugh off all these fears? While this is happening, the sword is being sharpened, the trap set up, the refuge comes into being, the flowers of coral are being born in the sea. One day, along the route followed for so long and where, for many years, it sailed undisturbed, a ship wrecks; one day, preceded by moss, by grass, by ants, by spiders, by grass-hoppers, birds, bees, rats, rains and palm trees, a couple of fugitives brings fire, domestic animals, some tools; with them disembark the legions and the invisible choruses that follow or haunt all human beings. My hand is reaching out, my eyes are lowered, in the attitude of someone who's going to open that door. I do not hear the slightest sound.

*

Osman Lins (1924–1978) is one of the most important and inno-vative writers of contemporary Brazilian fiction. His work has received considerable critical attention both in the United States and abroad, and has been translated into several languages. His major works have all been translated into French, German and Spanish; however, only Avalovara *(1973) has appeared in En-glish to date.*

*Although Lins began in a more traditional, realistic vein, his later work—*Nine, Novena *(1966),* Avalovara *(1973) and* A Rainha dos Carcoeres de Grécia *(1976) is characterized by for-mal innovations that reflect the evolution of his poetics and put him on a par with the masters of contemporary Latin American fiction. In addition to his better known fictional works, Lins' pro-duction includes several theatre pieces and essays.*

Nine, Novena, *a collection of nine stories, represents the turning point in Lins' work, the passage from a fairly traditional approach to literature to a more experimental style. It is a book characterized by an extreme rigor of construction and a profound lyricism. The recurring themes of entrapment and search for self, art versus life, and the mythic aspect of existence are presented against a background of rural and urban life in the northeast Brazil. Other noteworthy aspects of this work are the frequent use of graphic signals to identify the multiple narrators, ornamentation, and the lack of a central perspective, strategies that serve as part of Lins' aspiration to reinsert man into the universe with which he has lost touch.*

Sun & Moon Press will publish Nine, Novena *in 1995.*

Maggie O'Sullivan

from "Doubtless" / *Palace of Reptiles*

In the tattooed
Repetitions, the Poet
Repeats

7 steps of the stairs
one for each
lap
across her knees—(laps of air)

              gaps of cloak

                (the Voices

                          /

                              Voices halted)

halted, immobiled, Perished—
the small water
minded w/straw—
half & full in firm
on the Brink of

Sea,

(Stayed, Strayed, *Beyonded*)

rushless

to Water

She Floats a Moss—sashes & bends
the White Willow
to a Triangular Mantle of
Seeing—

3 is for
Pond
Marsh
Bog

Ocean
Spring
Sea

3 is for—

                    (riverrun,

                              /

                                        Spirally & Counter—)

1. By the Smallest Eye, she places
    Pot's Inching
    Counters of Vermilion
    governances,
    that intention
    Severally—

2. By the Middle Eye, she places
    a fistful of skull's
    uneven starings.

3. By the Largest Eye, she places
    little huts, little light—
    Heart
    Arrivedly of
    web, stars.

The Poet spools a south feather to string—
Dictions a big land in landless wandering cobalt.
Airs Ounce & Strand
Evictions.
Absconded morsels
gabble & whistle
random spurges blood along
her tongue. Blood rush of spit shot
away. The pupil of each
Eye
Weeps
the spoils
of Excavation.

The rest of it, spared scavenged fiscal inking.

The Dancer—

Jink—
Jointed
Uprised & Birth—

Stretching, Strung

Plover, low lowing in a far field
AY—PR—PRO—LONGED, LESQUING—OFF—OFF
(fell, fell, soft)

An Oar Broken—
Axis
Drove Out—

(Recede, Approach, Recede)

(splotched, traction, trashing)

I ALWAYS IMAGINED
I SAW HIM—

BUT I NEVER DID—
HIS LYRIC
VOLUTED, CONGRESSED
INTO GOING—

GOING THE WAY
& THE MAPS ALL GONE,
GONE-IN NOW,

GONE-FROM,
GONE-BY

GO—

HIS JUMP / HIS FALL / HIS LEG /
BROKEN
LUMINOUS, CHARRED IM-
POSSIBLE

THE COOL SHADES OF EVENING THEIR MANTLES
        [WERE SPREADING,

HE SANG—

STIFFENED CROW
TO THE HAIL—
GARNET
AS HE AROSE—

AROSE, FRACTURED

PRECIPICE AJAR

HIS THROAT'S
WEPT
SEMI-SUNG
HALF-SUNG / HALF-SAID
SPOKES

HE SHOOK THE AIR—

(WIRE
ON ALL SIDES
UNFIXED
& THE VAST
CONVULSED
GALE
ASHORE—
A WIND
SUTURED—

A WILD BOAR—
A TAR
OF
RISING
ROOKS—
HIS TONGUE—
MUTINOUS
ASTRAY
ON
BREAD
&
THIRST

LIVERING—
CRACKING, PUNCHING
THE WORDS—

WINGBENT—
SHE—
SHRED HIND
PAPERING HAZEL
PICK
OF THE

BLUE FUSE
I HUG
TUMBLING TO
BLISTERWAYS &
LIP. LIPLING
LEAP HER AMONG HER LEAPT LIT——
SHE——
HER
SEVEN RAINBOWS
CANDLED
INTO
THE TOILING——

      ELEGANCE——ELLEN DANCE——ELLEN SOUL——ELLEN SPEECH
                        ELLEN SONG——
                 ELLEN, MY NAMESAKE——
                     NAME'S ACHE——
                  SELF'S OTHER SELF——
            ELLEN, HEARTH OF MY NAME——
                  HEART'S ACHE——

OF THE
LAMP'S
ROVED THREADS
& SMART
OVER FIELDS, HER PASSAGE
TIPPING THE GROUND——
HURTLE,
SCATTERING——

LOW BLACKISH
THAT——

MY SKULL'S
CAPE—

DRIVEN
IN THE RIP OF HER STOOPED HEAD—
HYMN
OF SICKLE—
STRIKING OUT OF ME—

CROOKED
RUPTURES IN A SOCKET
& BURSTING—
DOCK, DOCK,
OF HER HORIZON'S VEXED
COGNATORIAL
PITCHES—

STOUT RAVEN OF A PAIR—
CHIMNEY
CRUMBLING—

LEAN THE MONTHS ARE HARD—

APART, NOR NEEDED—

& WE IN THE LOFT
OF THE LONG FIELD'S CORN SKY
TO A BLUE
CHURNING—

FREQUENCIES—

THE MOUTH'S HEN RIBBON—
FLOOR
FLOOAR

WHISPERED FLOOR—
SODDEN
EVERY POCKET.

The Dancer
withdraws, draws
with her sticks in Dandelion wing the loop
of her Pink &
Gouged
banners.

In the West
the Painter throws Indigo rods
on a black bough.

5 Moonlight spires
him up
His palm & heave
frail, immense

broad

Victuals beat—
Gridlock, Tumuli—

Slantly—

Wheel of Opposites—

Loosely Cones & Purple margins
bleeded w/dream's responsorial palette.
Sticks & Wall.
Agogving, fibrous filters of
wet muslin
cross his chest.

On his back—
crevices, caves, ear's flow—

small processions—

(look-on & visit)—

Oboe—
drag-along ascensions in chalk blue
loud
brim
his tracks there.

*

Maggie O'Sullivan is a artist, poet, publisher and performance artist living in Hebden Bridge, West Yorkshire, England. Her poetry is known throughout Britain, Europe, and the United States. Among her books are Concerning Spheres *(1982),* An Incomplete Natural History *(1984),* A Natural History in 3 Incomplete Parts *(1985),* Un-Assuming Personas *(1985),* Divisions of Labour *(1986),* From the Handbook of That Furriery *(1986),* States of Emercy *(1987),* Unofficial Word *(1988), and* In the House of the Shaman *(1993). Sun & Moon Press will publish the work she is currently completing,* Palace of Reptiles.

Norberto Luis Romero

Pitcher, with Swans

Translated from Spanish by H. E. Francis

IT WAS the spontaneous gift from a friend.

It was so dirty that the white porcelain on which the figures insinuated was barely visible.

"I just bought it. I saw it and thought you'd like it," he explained. "It's one of those bathroom pitchers from early in the century—ewers I think they're called. Once cleaned up, it may be pretty. It's decorated by hand."

In fact, washed, it showed a small pond with swans: an elegant white swan leisurely looking at another which, with its head raised, seemed to be singing. I remembered the legend that the swan is silent and sings only before dying, emitting a disagreeable sound, not at all melodious, similar to a crow's caw. I found a number of reddish hairs stuck to its dirty base. At once I thought, "The dead girl was a redhead." As I rubbed the inside with soapy water and clorox, I went on rambling, "Perhaps she died of tuberculosis in a miserable pension attic, the cheapest room in those days." And I pictured her thin and unkempt, with sunken, colorless cheeks, in a threadbare nightgown, pouring water from that pitcher into the basin to wash her sleepy eyes. A certain apprehension and compassion simultaneously came over me when I took it between my hands. The painting, although mediocre, was interesting. The birds were of a blue rare in the porcelain of that period. I definitely liked it. I set it on the hall table to use as a flower vase.

The red hairs, after washing and tying them together with a fine ribbon, I preserved between the pages of a book.

Since that day that unknown woman, with her fragile, bloodless body floating in the atmosphere of the house, interrupted my thoughts. Often I imagined her pouring water from that pitcher to refresh her face, abandoned by her lover, alone in the summer heat, far from her own if she had any, with no man to make her illness and her last days less painful, re-reading her diary filled with dreamy love poems, unable to go out because of weakness and attacks of coughing, leaning out the window to hear the robins' morning songs, seeking a ray of sun to connect her to the world outside. And I imagined a fat, breasty landlady, stupid and dull, incapable of saying a consoling word—not a bad woman, but tactless, who said as she looked her up and down, "Poor girl …in the flower of youth…," and left the room emitting a heavy sigh more like a croaking.

After that night I kept dreaming. In my dream I saw her combing her hair in that mirror with the peeling quicksilver, where she could barely distinguish her face from the reflection of other girls equally solitary and sick who had looked at themselves there. The dream revealed an attic in the Madrid of the Austrias (more precisely, on Almendro Street), and in its dark interior her re-reading her diary, perhaps worn pages which spoke to her of happy moments, of deceiving loves, of furtive kisses not so distant in memory. She raised her head and her wet eyes reflected the wretched coin of sun that fell like alms through the little window. White as a swan, with the same beauty, she cried silently. The number of the tenement did not appear in the dream.

The images were so alive and clear that I was certain that attic really existed. And the dream was, no doubt, the beginning of the search. From then on, many afternoons I went up and down that short street, looking toward the roofs, trying to locate the window where she leaned out, seeking the midday sun and the robins' song; but the height of the house and the narrowness of the street defeated me. I also stood at the mouth of the nearby streets, hoping to run into the landlady, the fat woman whom I had imagined. Often I imagined a dialogue with her, which I know by heart. At the end of it, I always ask about the girl, about her health; but I avoid finding out her name because I feel that if I named her she would cease to be who she is and become a real woman, or a memory; and with the loss of the daydream, the attic, the gable with its sunstruck window, the pitcher with the swan, and also the red strand of hair which I treasure in my book—all would disappear.

One afternoon I identified the house. In the past they had made some modifications on the facade which, although of little importance, kept me from recognizing it earlier, despite having passed before it numerous times. She was nearer now.

And I did not want to lose her. Her twenty years belonged to me now, her romantic suffering and her agony. Her secret, evanescent, anacronistic image, emanating from an old postcard or serial novel was mine: an indolent swan on the pitcher.

The dream, with its constant repetition, did not grieve me, but disturbed me because I did not know its true cause or understand its rigorous logic, unusual in a dream. The image of her I evoked when I found her strands of hair returned her to this world a captive in the pitcher, prisoner of a pitiless genie awaiting his Aladdin to free her. My dream was but the anticipation of her desire to escape. My dreams were her tender trick, but I did not know how to save her. I knew no magic I could perform. If these were the arts I needed, I was no Aladdin, although I would give my life to free her from her nightmare.

The pitcher is almost always filled with flowers in season, which I change the instant they begin to fade and wither. I have observed that when they are fresh they make my dream more real and the girl seems to recover a bit of color in her cheeks, as if they had the power to cure her, transfer their colors to her body. and with their perfume inundate her breast with balsam, reviving her love of life. It is then when she abandons reading her diary and leans out the window with a glow in her dark eyes, looking avidly out over the neighboring roofs.

It is curious. With the arrival of the pitcher, two things happened simultaneously: one is the dream, the other my assistant's talk of leaving me because, she said, a permanent job was about to come up—an excuse, I now realize, since one morning she said: "Excuse me. I don't dare throw the flowers out, although they're dried up, because that pitcher makes me nervous, I don't dare touch it."

I said I would do it. I'd change the water and the flowers. That seemed to relieve her. In any case, when she dusted the waiting room, she dared not even touch the pitcher and dusted around its base without even grazing it. I asked her why the pitcher caused such repulsion. She stood staring at me in amazement. "The vase," I corrected at once. She said she did not know, but could not look at it even from a distance. Two days later she asked for her pay and left. Before going, she advised me to get rid of what she called "the pitcher." I was hurt.

A desire as powerful as a serpent's gaze each day made me verify the presence of that strand of hair inside the book;

its copper shine bewitched me, provoking indescribable day-
dreams, fantasies which, at other moments of my life, would
have seemed intolerable.

With a trivial excuse, one afternoon I got into an empty
apartment on Almendro Street and from one of its windows
saw the roof of the building opposite, which I had identified
as the one in the dream. There above I located the gable. I
had no doubt that was the one, despite its looking abandoned.
The window was closed. On the narrow sill was a pot painted
red and a dry plant with only a twisted, fragile stem.

I had the unexpected luck of learning that an attic was
for rent in that building, an attic recently renovated, which
also had a gable giving onto the street. I rented it at once
although the price was absurd and the contract was so one-
sided it nearly bowled me over. Now I could be there day
and night, if necessary, observing the window opposite, await-
ing her.

I moved right away, taking only the necessities. The
pitcher I set on a low table. I no longer put flowers in it since
fresh ones lasted only a few hours and without them the
dream remained constant and clear. I bought opera glasses
to be able to observe her opening that closed gable in which
(my heart knew) sooner or later she would appear. I hired a
cleaning woman to keep my quarters clean and take care of
my immediate needs. She was very fat, clumsy, and slow, but
good and very clean. She came every morning, shopped,
cleaned, washed and ironed my clothes and went off after
leaving my meal ready. While she was in the house, I went
wandering through the street, trying to quell the anxiety
caused by not being able to watch for her apparition, or I
went to a bar from which I could keep close watch on her
front door. But suppose she looked out just when I was not
there and it was my cleaning woman who was lucky enough

to see her or even exchange a few words with her? At two sharp I returned and moved the table close to the window, ate, and no sooner finished posted myself to watch with my glasses.

Each roof tile, each crack in the dark wood shutters, each chip in the red pot, were tattoos in my memory, open wounds in my chest. Every morning I examined the tiny overnight changes as signs, as a language which bound me to that roof, to the gable and the window closed to hide an object of desire capable of driving me mad, a dialogue substituted for the one I longed to have with her, I spoke with the vestiges which night and day let fall over that wasted architecture.

I had been living there for more than a month when my cleaning woman, arriving one morning, stood staring at me:

"You look bad," she said.

I paid little attention to her and excused myself by saying I had spent the night reading. She did not believe me and insisted, adding that she had noticed it for some time:

"You're thinner."

Despite having paid no attention, I knew it was true—I was thinner. Perhaps weariness, bad food, and lack of sleep had taken their toll on my face. It was also true that I felt a little weak, but I was sure that when I saw that girl lean out the window seeking sun and the robins' song, her image would be a miraculous bulwark against my illnesses.

I dedicated all my time to that obsession. Waiting was bitter and fruitless. What would I say to her if I saw her? Knowing my timidity, surely nothing—only stare at her, captivated. Perhaps I would be able to greet her, making an effort, blushing. She would ask me to sing to her like a morning robin. And for her I would be able to sing like a bird, inundating her soul with my song, the notes penetrating her breast until curing her.

One night I felt still weaker, more feverish with desire to see her, and sat almost all night long at the window under the moon which filled the window, exposing myself to the night dew of winter. I must have dozed for a few instants. When I woke, terrified, I saw her: the sun appeared over the roofs and an intense ray fell obliquely over the gable window, tinting the old wood gold. There she was, offering her pale face to the sun, seeking its warmth, seeking the robin's song. An intense emotion invaded my breast, like the sharp pain of a dagger. I wanted to sing like the robin, but I had a slight fit of coughing which turned my song to a croaking, and when I stopped coughing and opened my eyes, she was no longer there. The window was once more closed as always.

The painted pot is losing its color, and the dry clay is exposed. The intense noon sun makes deep cracks in the wooden shutters. The fierce autumn wind carries off a loose tile from the gable—frames and tattoos which are now brash remarks and no dialogue. Every day I open the book where I keep her hair and long I contemplate its copper reflections. I submerge myself in them, hypnotized by the witchery which makes me faint. Until just a short time ago, like a ritual, I have again put fresh flowers in the pitcher mornings, and afternoon I throw them, stale, into the garbage.

Since that feverish morning she has never again appeared, nor has my song stirred her to look out. It is as if enjoying the sun or listening to the robins no longer matter to her, as if she has lost all desire to live, as if my dream no longer revived her. And I imagine her going back to reading her diary, shedding tears over her happy memories.

Meanwhile, I had many cleaning women and all of them abandoned me. Fortunately, for some time now I have had a very loyal nurse who comes to care for me, give me shots and administer some bitter medicine which I accept without a word. She goes down for fresh flowers every morning, selecting the most beautiful. She writes the diary I dictate, admires my poems, and on hot days also helps me to the window so I can stick my head out and feel the sun as I sing. She is a fine, vigorous woman. What most endears me to her is her ingenuousness since she does not know that I realize she is in love with me. I have seen her collect my fallen hairs and put them in a pocket. I also admire her impassive character and her lack of apprehension when she empties my vomited blood in the toilet and washes out the pitcher without disgust.

*

Norberto Luis Romero lives in Madrid, Spain, where he has published two collections of short tales. Sun & Moon Press will publish a selection of his tales, The Arrival of Autumn in Constantinople, *in 1995.*

Clark Coolidge

Better the Man the Woman Had

The man has no use being in trouble
when he has to stand for the planet on a veer
his veins show
for the moment he has no ribs
the placement is back in a sentence of some argument
a pan of the anatomy augments
he has to watch the birds
a fan at the window, a liar in the lab
three similar pots of tea, all for the glory of him
slung as long as wet hair and caught
slender a while
out on a lie

The mirror has brought the trees
to a further pass
than he have no face
in this mix a parade
coping in vesture
he wracks his brains for a woman's gear

No flow this year
bare speech but stopped dawns
the corner is of talk by seeing
a stripping of the barks from the drip panorama

hallway by a bad Modigliani
time by hands on the fridge
and the walls come out of a dream of kilter
and the thighs reach a spread of one hour

That lasts
thanks to lights
speed of entry of a particle thought
pins in a bar of soap
all his wishing weaves, all his done with
bruises in the uncarved block

dreaming then that lasts
applause through the center of a pool
made antenna mound of social bugs
could cross them off a list, singly at their use
trouble and trouble repeats

The problem is a dancer
solution is a bar
the man has no use for planetary moves
scowling as an answer to his aisles
the dancer is a woman
stern of little use
throttleless as a glass pancreas
thinking on thrown seas of a dial sun
she shocks and draws away

Thought draws near an alarm mist
again he stood
the window to a perfect solution
prism of Picassos intermittent
other throws down the side
spreading of the leg is the thigh

heating from here
who are you

Whose thought is a man
responsive to the hilt
own throat of a view
predicts the long night of high lights
swallowed is not carried
long and static velvet swimmingly
chokes of her neck

The motions a man stops
his sits and stilling slices
giving away what actuates
giving the window to the sun's alarm
man's turns are an amateur
rides in the sole car

meets in place of avenue
dates on the side
bottles the thoughts of the woman stops him
crushed in embracing wheel
the notions off to the death by silencer

The man is the problem
of the woman sides with whom
balancer in a taxing stroke
lapping against music the kissing of the bright
step backward and step in advance
of the thought to replace the better
with a honking horn a pacing light
she met with
he admits

The problem peers from
high in a woman's leg
the buckling fluid circles a day
time to say pounce
and delimit and hedge
the bottle once drunk
the member of which stands
the sun better than the member
with the fraught skin
a decimal buzzing
not with meaning

He thought how
she thought what
he meant to say
back to her
many a day
and the windows gain suns
the thoughts then veer
the man gains a woman
this year gains on him
a stare

*

*Born in Providence, Rhode Island in 1939, Clark Coolidge has
lived in the Berkshire Hills of western Massachusetts since 1970.
In his early works,* Flag Flutter & U.S. Electric *(1966),* Space
(1970), The So *(1971), and* Suite V *(1973), Coolidge worked in
what some have described as a reductive syntax in order to open
the poem to reveal its visual order and the abstract, but quite mean-
ingful, structures of sound. During this period, Coolidge was con-
nected with the so-called "New York School" of writers, and his*

worked appeared in An Anthology of New York Poets *published in 1970.*

The publication of The Maintains *in 1974 had a significant impact on the rising group of young poets who later would be described as "Language" Poets. Taking seemingly random words, Coolidge created syntactical units that lead to completely new associations and possibilities in language. This book resulted, in part, in a close relationship with Coolidge and some of these poets, which has continued through the present.*

Polaroid *(1975) and* Quartz Hearts *(1978) followed in the same vein. But in* Own Face *(published the same year and republished by Sun & Moon Press in 1993), Coolidge shifted his focus to a more seemingly biographical and lyrical writing. In this sense,* Own Face—*with its focus on authorial events, friends, and real-life figures—marked an important change in Coolidge's writing, which was to continue through the 1980s in books such as* American Ones *(1982),* The Crystal Text *(1986, scheduled to be republished by Sun & Moon in 1995), and the large collection* Solution Passage: Poems 1978-1981 *(Sun & Moon Press, 1986). The last three books received major critical attention, and helped to expand Coolidge's reading audience.*

A jazz musician throughout his life, Coolidge has continued to explore over the past few years the relation of words and sound much in the manner of a musician; but for Coolidge it is the meaning *of these word and sound associations, not merely their formal patterns, on which he centers his art. Recent works include* Sound As Thought: Poems 1982-1984 *(Sun & Moon Press, 1990),* Baffling Means *(a collaboration with the artist Philip Guston, 1991),* Odes of Roba *(1991),* The Book of During *(1991), and* The Rova Improvisations *(Sun & Moon Press, 1994).*

Liliane Giraudon

The Man Who Had Trouble Defecating

Translated from French by Guy Bennett

ONE THING canceled out another. The weather was nice. I was watching a piece of incense paper burn up on the table's edge. I was trying to attenuate that which permeated the air at times by burning little packets of the stuff that I bought at a hardware store. Not only the air in the bedroom where I spent most of my time, but also that which enveloped the grasses and plants in the little garden behind the iron door.

If I thus come back to that former era, it is so you will know who I am. Or more precisely, the one whom I have become since that past adventure that you alone will know from my mouth.

It is curious that *my* mouth appears here, at the end of this sentence that I address to you and which, turning over in my head, floats at the tops of the trees where my eyes would wander at the precise second I that attempted to formulate my proposal. It is strange that this half-opened, pinkish gray into which you occasionally like to stick your own tongue is as if drawn here, yes, suspended and drawn; I see, yes, I see the thing called "mouth," at the edge of a dentate leaf, between the pure, very blue sky and the green thickness. I see my mouth talking to you while seemingly chewing at air so that you will learn what follows.

"My mouth" means *no other*. From me alone will you learn what you are going to learn.

The sunset is there for everyone. Thus, I was prey to what I later called the odor.

I was the only one to smell it but I can assure you that it was unbearable. A considerable odor of shit. Precise. Regular in its intensity.

We must know how to leave each thing to its station. Certain poetic extravagances make me think of trained dogs become rabid. Thus, at that time, aside from the incense paper that I was burning everywhere I happened to be since the odor seemed to move with me, I spent most of my days trying to write vertically. I really don't know what I meant by that any more, but, corporeally, I had a rather precise idea of the thing. At the same time, I was becoming anorexic. Boy, can you go without food! I fed myself on water. I was satisfied to lap it up as it dripped from the faucet. And only at nightfall. I would urinate considerably, and I had begun to do so sitting down, like a woman or antique Egyptian, or like an Egyptian antique, I don't remember.

One after another I published three little books of poetry illustrating the fact that, large or small accumulators, it's loading and unloading that count.

The perception and choice of relationships vary from subject to subject. Solange left me. Snow or leaves on the ground, everything is earth. Not because of the odor, which couldn't have bothered her since I alone smelled it, but because one morning, she decided that I had become, as she put it, a man with a frozen heart. It is true that I hardly ever touched her any more. And then, there were my friends. It is difficult to get rid of one's friends. I managed to, however. It took me a while. Their wives helped me. They all wanted to smell the odor. They never stopped coming to see me, amassing pre-texts. I took to fucking them. Systematically. Before throwing them out. Their wives. Some of them sought the odor on my body, in the most secret wrinkles, murmuring hungrily: "*The next poem's for me, isn't it? Just for me?*" But since what I called the piping was empty, they were very disappointed. Essentially, everything is made up of elucidations. All the more so, since I always took the most extreme care of my skin. It is only on the outside that a being or work discover what makes them live. It's what's in the skin that gives a body its shape.

Your dead husband knew it, dearie. He knew it all marvelously well. Since with his own eyes he saw us kiss behind each door of the Villa.

A cripple such as himself was undoubtedly amazed that I didn't go any further. You yourself were undoubtedly disappointed about it at the time. I was not able to. Not from lack or absence of desire, on the contrary, not even from inability (the way in which I probed your mouth must have proven this to you), but because the odor had left me. I was wrapped in a void. A sort of material, palpable void. As alive as the grasses and trees that I spoke of a moment ago. It was the creation of this void, as enveloping a case as an invisible coffin endlessly drawn around one's members, which made certain of my actions impossible.

Still, in the month of November the sea was calm and the wind very light. I noted the temperature each morning. In short, I was enduring a superficial test. I never stopped telling myself that. And I didn't know how right I was. Besides, I never finished my sentences any more. There was a squall, and I opened the window; I had been experiencing strange itching sensations for several days. That night, November

24th, I grew a tail. Exactly like the first one, only that, erect, it seemed longer, and I thus had to sleep on my side. The colorless boundaries date back to that period. The little book with the salmon cover dedicated to you alone does as well. I wrote it with neither mouth nor tongue. Nor sound of syllables. That is undoubtedly why, at the beginning of my confession, my own lips shone at the top of the tree.

*

Liliane Giraudon was born in Marseilles, France in 1946. Giraudon has been active in French publishing, and was a member of the editorial board for the noted magazine Action-Poétique *from 1977 to 1980. She was co-editor, with her husband Jean-Jacques Viton, of the magazine* Banana Split *and is currently editing the Marseilles based magazine* If.

She has written numerous books of poetry and fiction, and has been translated previously into English by British poet, Tom Raworth. Among her books of poetry are Je marche ou je m'endors *(1982),* La Réserve *(1984),* Quel jour sommes-nous? *(1985), and* Divagation des chiens *(1988). Among her prose works are* La Nuit *(1986),* Pallaksch, Pallaksch *(1990, published by Sun & Moon Press in 1994) and* Fur *(1992, forthcoming from Sun & Moon Press).*

Vladimir Mayakovsky

Vladimir Mayakovsky: Tragedy in Two Acts with a Prologue and Epilogue

Translated from Russian by Paul Schmidt
Drawings by Vladimir and David Burliuk

Cast of Characters

Vladimir Vladimirovich Mayakovsky, a poet, 20-25 years old
An enormous woman, friend of his, maybe twenty feet tall,
  never says a thing
An old man with scrawny black cats, a couple of thousand
  years old
A man with one eye and one leg
A man with one ear
A man with no head
A woman who cries ordinary tears
A woman who cries little tiny tears
A woman who cries great big tears
A man with a long face
An ordinary young man
Little paper boys and girls
Little baby kisses, etc.

Prologue
Mayakovsky

Can you understand why I am **silent**

In this whirlwind of sneers

And carry my **soul** like food on a platter

Toward the coming years

On the stone **stubble** of the public *p*avement

I slide like unnecessary **te**ars

I am a **poet** and I am possibly
alon**E**.

HAVE YOU SEEN the bruises on the faces of **boredom**

Hanging over **pathways** of stone

And the iron arms of bridges that arch and twist

Through soap-sud rage on the slippery necks

Of foaming streams?

Above me the heavens weep harshly

They jangle above me!

And a **slit-mouth** cloud has the twisted look

Of a woman **expecting** a baby

When what she got was a mongoloid from God.

You are stung by the sun with his great fat fingers!

They are covered all over with little **red** hairs!

They are worse than the whine of sadistic mosquitoes!

Your *souls* are his slaves, his kisses have killed them!

I hate the **light** of day, I always have.

My hatred is fearless, my hatred advances,

My soul is a filament, stretched like the **nerves** of a wire:

I'm the **king** of street light land!

Come unto me all you *WHO* shatter the silence

Who scream at the nooses of noon about your necks!

My words are simple as a blow-job,

Self-evident soul-suck, with sounds

That burn **LIKE** street lights.

Feel my fingers move upon **your head**.

Your lips will swell for **g**or**g**eou**s** kisses

And the **TONGUES** of all nations will be as your ow N.

And what about me, bright, shining me?

I'll dissolve in the distance

Like a little lost soul,

Descend to **my** throne through crumbling vaults

With holes full of stars.

Bright, shining me!

I will lie down lazy in a **LINEN** sheet

I will make my **b**e**d** in the **shit** of the street

And quietly kiss the knees of the track

While the weight of a freight train

Caresses my back.

Act One
Happy
A city. A spider web
tangle of streets.
Poor people hav-
ing a holiday. V
Mayakovsky alone.
People carry on
food from store
front advertise-
ments. A tin her-
ring from a sign.
A huge gold bagel.
Big pieces of yel-
low velvet.
Mayakovsky

Ladies and gentlemen!

Sew up my soul

So my nothingness won't leak out.

If somebody **spits**

I don't know if that's good

Or that's bad.

I'm as dry as an overworked **w**et **n**urse.

Ladies and gentleme**N**!
YOUR ATTENTION, PLEASE!

A rising young poet will now do a dance

For your entertainment.

*Enter the Old Man
with Scrawny Black
Cats. He pats them.
He is all beard.
Mayakovsky*

Ransack the houses, drag out the **fatties**, the
ones who sit sloshing in their greasy shells,

Beat me out a **RHYTHM** on the drums and the bells!

Gotta tackle the **dumb ones**, the ones that
can't hear

You gotta WHISTLE down your flute and tickle
their ears!

Watch me gobble down the brand new bagel of
a hot idea

And kick out the bottoms of barrels of badness;

Shout congratulations to me loud and clear

Today **I'm** getting married, and I'm Marrying madness!

The stage slowly begins to fill with people. Enter the Man with One Ear, the Man without a Head, etc. They move like doped-up druggies in a daze. Everything's a mess. Everybody keeps on eating. Mayakovsky

I'm a **barefoot** jeweler, and I Polish my poems

The way you polish your diamonds.

I fluff **feather pillows** in strange people's houses.

I push a button and presto!

Holiday!

All the rich and ragged beggars in the world

Can celebrate **t**oda**y**.

The Old Man with the Cats

I'm an old, old man, **I'm** a **th**o**us**a**nd years** old

And I see you, sonny, I see what you are,

You're a cry of anguish crucified upon a cross
of laughs.

Over the city one enormous sorrow floats

While a hundred **p**iddling little ones spot the sky;

Street lights and head lights meet in a rush,

A clash that **covers** the hesitant hush of dawn.

These flabby old moons have lost their charm:

Street light now is the trenchant fashion,

Its wit bites harder. Things are in charge.

In the world of cities, **things** run the show.

And things have no souls, they **w**an**t** to wipe us
out.

A god gone mad l**oo**ks down out of heaven

At the howls of his **hu**m**an** hordes,

His hands in his beard and his beard in tangles,

White with the dust of dissolving **roads**.

He warns you himself of his **C**ruel retribution

But you only sigh a silly sigh and scratch your
    scabby s**ou**l.

Get rid of him! Go pat cats! Pat skinny black cats!

Grab their great big bellies and boast that you've
    done it!

Pop the bubble gum bubbles of your **ci**ty **sli**cker
    cheeks!

Only in cats with rainb**o**w c**o**a*t*s

CAN YOU FIND the true flash of electric eyes.

Pat them and haul in the harvest of flashes,
    streaks

of abundant **electric fire**.

Let it all stream out! into muscle-tight stretches
    of wire!

Streetcars will jump and **s**ignals will flame

Night will flare brighter than victory parades!

Amazed at its face in such *radiant* make-up

The world will *sh*udder slowly into action.

Flowers in every window will flash their
peacock tails!

People will travel on **c**able**s** and **r**ail**s**,

And after them hundreds of ca*t*s.

Great fat blue black cats.

This cat and that cat! Pat that cat!

St*i*ck **st**a**r**s all over the people you love

And decorate dresses with comets and planets

And cats! cats! fat black cats! skinny black cats!

O, **forg**et your apartments and go **pat**

Cats! Go **pat fat** black cats!

*The Man with
One Ear.*

Oh, it's tru**E**! look up in the air!

High above the city where **W**eather-vanes
spin

A woman has eyelids darker than caves.

She **covers** the sidewalks with gobs of s*p*it

And the spit goblins grow into great big cripples.

High above the **city** somebody's guilt thickens into revenge.

People gather in groups, they STAMPE*DE* in the streets.

And there, where win E-stains pattern the skies,

An old man slumps at his keyboard and cries.

A crowd gathers.
He continues.

High above the **city**, nothing but suffering, far and wide.

You reach for a note, your hands get all bloody.

A piano player's fingers were bitten bad

By the rabid white teeth of a snarling keyboard.

Agitation and alarm.
He goes on.

And now **today**, ever since

This morning,

A fast fandango has *razored* a mouth

In my soul!

I go around twitching with my **arms** raised to
    heaven

And the rooftops are covered with chimneys that
    dance,

All bent over like the number **7**.

Ladies and gentlemen, stop!

Is th*is* right?

Even the sidestreets are ready **for** a fight.

And my **longing** for something keeps growing,
    I don't know what.

I feel like a tear on the **nose** of a beaten pup.

*Everybody gets
more upset.
The Old Man with
the Cats*

Now **listen** up, folks, we've got us a problem.

We've got to get rid of our **things**.

I told you they weren't to be trusted,

They pretended they loved you
And now look.

*The Man with a
Long Face.*

> But may**be** we just didn't love them enough. You
> gotta
>
> *Love* your things, so they'll love you back.

*The Man with One
Ear.*

> **B**ut lots of things aren't put together ri**ght**.
>
> They can't feel a thing. they've got *blocked*
> emotions.

*The Man with a
Long Face, joyfully
nodding agreement.*

> See, on your face, **where** you have a mouth,
>
> **Lo**ts of things have an ear! That's where they
> hear!

*Mayakovsky ap-
pears in the heart of
town.*

> Don't heat up your hearts with the oil of anger.
>
> *You* are all my children. Come learn your lessons.
>
> I am your stern teacher; I spare not the rod.
>
> Remember your places, you people. Who are
> you?

You are tinkling bells on the **fool's cap** of God.

My feet are all swollen with searching.

I have trekked your *country* from end **to** end

I have crossed over other lands as well

In a mask and a cloak—the domino of
        darkness—

I have sought out her **unseen** soul.

i wanted to wipe my wounded lips

with the softness of her healing flowers.

Pause

I have crouched like a slave dripping

Blood and sweat, and rocked
        my wracked body

In mad, mad motion, weeping in misery—

And *one time* I actually found her, the soul of this
        country,

I mean, but she was wearing a dirty blue house
        dress and she **said hi** glad to

see you sit down you **want** some tea?

Pause

I am a poet and I've wiped out the spaces

Between my own face and *other people's faces*:

In the pus and abcesses of city **morgues**

I've gone to discover my soul's sister;

I've covered sick people with passionate kisses

And today on a bonfire's yellow flame

Deeper than the hid**de**n tears of the **SE A**

I will throw my sister's secret shame

And your gray-haired mothers' wr**in**kl**ed** faces.

And on plates licked clean in fancy places

We **will** gorge on the meat of eternity.

He rips away a veil. The Enormous Woman. Everyone crowds around her in a panic. The Ordinary Young Man rushes in. Much ado. Mayakovsky continues.

Ladies and gentlemen, don't get hysterical.

The word is out, and the word is this:

Somewhere—I think it's in South America—

One happy man r**eall**y d**oe**s exist.

The   Ordinary
Young Man.
He runs around
grabbing people by
their lapels.

Listen here, **everybody**,

Li**st**en, lady, listen, miste R,

Wait a minute, wait a minute,

What the hell is going on?

Is **this** the place I heard of

Where you're all opposed to motherhood?

Listen, that's downright illegal!

You think you know all the answers

But you're **nuthin** next to nature.

You people—

You just wanna start a riot

And destroy the things we've worked for!

Listen here, I been to college

—that should prove I'm not a dummy—

Wanna hear what **I invented**?

A machine for slicing meat-loaf!

And **I g**ott**a** friend who's working

On a trap for catching fleas!

Well, all *right*!

And I gotta little **WOMAN**

And we're gonna have a baby,

So let's not have any trouble!

Now to me you **DON'T LOOK STUPID**

But the things you say are craz**Y**—

And it really is a **goddam** shame.

The Man with One Ear

Young **man**, why don't you get up on this

soap-box here...

A voice from the crowd.

B**etter** he should go down on it!

The Man with One Ear

...So everyone can see yoᴜ.

The Ordinary Young Man

What's so funny? What's so funny?

Look, *I* gotta little brother,

Just a baby, but you people—

Whaddaya want? Whaddaya want?

You'll go gobble gobble gobble

And you'll eat up all his bones.

Alarms, automobile horns, crowds murmuring:

Pants

Pants

Pants

Pants

Pants

Mayakovsky

Knock it off!

*The Ordinary
Young Man is
surrounded.
Mayakovsky*

If you'd lived as I've lived

You would leave off living.

You would hunger for horizons—

Crack east and crack west

Like the smoke-smeared faces

Of factories cracking

The bones **of the sky.**

*Ordinary Young
Man*

Whaddaya mean? Whaddaya mean?

Doesn't love count for something,

Doesn't—think of little Sonya,

She's my little baby **siste R !**

On his knees

Look—let's not have any trouble.

We don't want to have a riot!

The alarm increases.
A shot rings out.
Sewer pipes slowly
begin to sing a
single note. Metal
rooftops rattle.
The man with a
long face

If you'd loved as I've loved

You would live without love.

YOU would liquidate LOVE

In the public squares

You would rape the sheepish heavens

And the milk-tooth innocent stars.

The Man with
One Ear

Y our women don't know how to **love!**

They're a bunch of swollen sponges!

*A thousand feet
stomp on the belly
of the public square.
The Man with the
Long Face*

AND LISTEN HONEY, if you're interested—

You can cut up my soul and make a *gorgeous*
  skirt.

*Boundless agitation.
Everyone crowds
around the enor-
mous woman. They
hoist her onto their
shoulders and head
for the door.
Everyone in unison.*

We will go

To the place

Where they crucified our

Good old lord

We'll go crazy with the strip-tease

And we'll dance in the street

And on sin's **black** stone

We'll raise a monument to meat.

They drag the woman to the doors but the madness finally breaks all bounds. Enter The Man with One Eye and One Leg, bursting with joy. People throw with woman into a corner.
The Man with One Eye and One Leg

Stop!

On the street everybody wears a face like a
    burden

And the faces are all the same.

Time's an old lady, but she just had a baby,

A twisted terror. And it's starting to grow.

As the snouts of years came wriggling out

Old men went mad and **w**ould **n**ot **s**peak.

Evil thickened the *city*'s wrinkle**S**

In veins like rivers a thousand miles long.

Slowly *a horror* of rockets of hair

Were raised on the pad of time's bald head,

A^{ND SUDDENLY}

All of the things in the world went crazy.

They tore up their voices and ripped off their
    rags

As they ran, they threw away their worn-out
    names.

The windows of wine-stores splashed by
    themselves

Like Satan pawing in the bottom of a bottle.

Pants in pairs **ran away** from their tailors

Who went into shock when they saw them move

By themselves! Without butts!

Dining room **Furniture** stumbled away

Opening its twisted blackened drawers,

And underwear wept, afraid of falling

From signs that said fashion modes.

Boots looked strict and untouchable.

Stockings wiggled their holes like whores.

I *ran and ran* like a wallfull of dirty graffiti.

I lost one leg a block away—

It's still trying to catch up with me.
Why do you all of you call me a cripple?

I hate you. You're **fat-gutted**, flabby, and old.

Remember: nowadays nobody's left alive

Whose legs are identical.

Curtain

Act Two
Depressed
A public square in
the city of the fu-
ture. Mayakovsky,
who is now wear-
ing a toga. And a
laurel wreath. Be-
hind a door, the
sound of many feet.
The Man with One
Eye and One Leg
Ingratiatingly

Poet, poet.

They've made **you** a prince.

There's a crowd outside the door.

They're licking their fingers and asking for more.

And they're carrying containers

Of something strange.

Mayakovsky

WHAT THE HELL. Let them come in.

Enter women with
bundles, all of them
shy. Some of them
curtsey.
A Woman who
Cries Ordinary
Tears

Here.

I don't need this any more.

It's a tear.

Take it, go on.

It's absolutely *pure.*

It's absolutely *white.*

I wrapped it in silk made from the **ligh**▜

That shines from melancholy **eye**s.

Mayakovsky
He gets nervous

I don't need it. I don't want it.

I don't get it: what's this all about?

To the next woman

Look at you. Your eyes are a *mess* too. Just like
hers.

A Woman who
Cries Little Tiny
Tears

So what? Why should I care?

My baby boy is dying, do you think that's **fair**?

But I don't care. Listen here,

Here's another little tear.

I wept it specially for you.

You *can* sew it on your shoe.

It'll be real pretty, don't you think?

Mayakovsky is afraid
A Woman who Cries Great Big Tears

Don't look. I must be a mess too. A wreck.

Next time I'll be in better shape, I promise.

Anyway, **here's** a tear from m**E**.

This is not one of your everyday drops,

This is a **professional tear**. It's twice as effective.

Mayakovsky

That's enough. This is too many tears

For a man to bear.

Anyway I gotta go now.

But say—who's that over there?

Who's the good looking number

With the dark brown hair?

Paperboys enter in single file, shouting

Figaro, Figaro, Figaro, Figaro, Times, Times, Times!

A crowd gathers begins to shout

Oh, look!

What a wild man!

Move back a bit.

Give the boy room.

Young maN, *stop that hiccuping.*

The Man without a Head

Eee eee eee eee!
Eh! Eh! Ehhhhhhhhhh....

The Man with Two Kisses

Look at the clouds, they're melting in the gold of the sun.

They're **frivolous**, they're fragile, and they're fading fast.

The day is dead. All over and done.

Even the daughters of heaven are gold-diggers too.

All they want is money money *money.*

Mayakovsky

What? What? Who?

The Man with Two Kisses

All of them do it for money money money.

Voices from the crowd

Quiet! Quiet!

The Man with Two Kisses
He dances with a ball full of holes

Somebody gave two kisses to a big and greasy man.

He was all upset and he just **didn't kno W**

What to do with them or where to go.

It was a high old time in the CITY

Everybody singing holy *hallelujah!*

People were dressed up in beautiful clothes.

But the man *was* cold,

The s**ol**es of his shoes had *oval holes.*

He *took* the **biggest** ki*s*s

And he *put* it *on—*

A kiss GALOSH.

But the cold got wise, still STUNG his toe S .

"Oh what the hell," HE said.

"I'll throw them away.

These *kiss*es are good for nothing anyway!"

And t**ha**t's w**ha**t he DID.

Then all of a sudden

The little kiss **grew** ears

And started fidgeting around:

 t made a teeny-weeny **sound**,

I t said: "*mommy*".

The man got scared.

He wrapped the poor thing up in a piece of his
    soul

And he took it home to keep it

In a sky-blue bowl.

For a long time he poked around **in dusty
    trunks**

He was looking for the bowl.

Then he turned around—

The kiss was sprawled out on the couch!

It had got fat!

Fat!

It laughed a fat-mouthed laugh.

"OH GOD,"

The man cried,

"Who would have thought I'd ever get so t**ire**d!

I'll go and hang myself."

And that's what he did.

And while the poor man hung

And stunk

Women in bedrooms everywhere—

Smokestackless factories—

Kept **G**RINDING OUT millions of kisses:

Big kisses

Little kisses

All kinds of kisses

With the fat-flesh levers of their smacking lips.

Enter a crowd of kids dressed as kisses; they speak.

They sure made a lot of us kisses! Hooray!

Take me, I'm yours!

Hey! There's more of us coming, hundreds every
    day!

HEY! MY NAME IS MICKEY!

Let's make it. ok?

They pile up a heap of tears in front of the poet Mayakovsky.

Mayakovsky

Ladies and gentlemen, I'm just about through.

This is **breaking my heart** again and again,

Taking these tears.

If you only knew.

None of this seems to bother any of you.

But what about me and my pain?

Shouts from the crowd

That's *your* problem!

You keep it up with the fancy *talk*

And you'll always wind up in hot water!

The Old Man with One Skinned Cat Left

Sonny, you're the only one left who knows
    how to write a poem.

So you just take up your burden. Haul it all back
    to your god.

He points to the heap of tears.
Mayakovsky

Just let me rest for a minute.

They don't. He awkwardly packs up the tears in his bag. He just stands there, holding the bag.

OK, I'm done.

Just let me say goodbye.

I thought I could go on having fun forever,

I had such great big beautiful EYES—

I **thought** that being a prince would be heaven.

But no. It's back to gray skies

And the open road. You roads, I'll remember you
        forever—

Sk*inny* **LEGS** moving

Toward the long gray curls of that northern river.

So this is the day

Of my great GET-AWAY!

Got to get out of this cit**Y**!

I'm leaving my soul in rags and tatters

On the sharp hard edges

Of your nitty-gritty.

The moon will go with me

As far as she can; to a place

Where the arches of heaven crumble

And the sky falls flat.

She'll gl**ide up** bes**ide** me and idle for a moment

While she tries on my derby hat.

Then I'll shoulder my bundle and keep on **G**
haulin

I may fumble and fall and wind up crawling

Just a stumblebum with a heavy burden

But I'll keep on moving further and further

North,

Where the world is locked in a vise of ice,

In a frozen spasm of e*TeR*n*A*l despair,

And the icy fingers of fanatical oceans

Claw for the heat of its heart. And I swear,

I swear, I'll make it there.

I may be **ExHaUsTEd**

But my last mad gesture

Will be for you all: I'll throw your tears

In old grim-god's face

In his primal prison,

The source

    of the sign

       of the beas*T*.

Curtain

Epilogue
Mayakovsky

LADIES and *gentlemen,*

I wrote all this myself.

It's about poor suckers

Like you.

Too bad I don't have tits.

I could gi**ve** you a mouth**ful**

Like your **G**ood old mama used to do.

But I'm really sucked dry.

And *now* you know why.

Anyway, I'm through.

I may seem like a simple-minded idiot to you.

But on the other hand, think of it this way:

Who else could provide

Such a **SUPERHUMAN** avalanche of
    argumentation?

What happened was, God opened his heavenly

MOUTH

And I put my foot right in it. Told him

I was his greatest creation.

There are times when I think I'd like to be a
    great artist—

You know, like Rimsky-Korsakov,

Or maybe become famous overnight, like
    Tchaik**o**v**sk**y.

But whenever I really think about it seriously

I like my OWN name best—

VLADIMIR MAYAKOVSKY

*

Vladimir Vladimirovich Mayakovsky was born in 1893 in the village of Bagdadi, near Kutayis (now renamed Mayakovsky) in the Republic of Georgia. At the age of twelve Mayakovsky experienced the first Russian Revolution and the death of his father. In June of 1906 his family moved to Moscow, where he entered high school and was brought into political work with the then Russian Social Democratic Workers' Party (Bolsheviks). He became a member of the party the following year.

The next years saw a great deal of political activity, as he was arrested and released several times. In 1911 he passed the entrance examination for the training college of painting and fine arts and entered a class for figure painting. Over the next few months he met David Burliuk and several poets of the Futurist Group, including Velimir Khlebnikov, Alexei Kruchonykh, and Vasily Kamensky. In 1912 he joined Burlyuk, Khlebnikov, and Kruchonykh in the manifesto A Slap in the Face of Public Taste.

In November of the next year he rehearsed and presented his first play Vladimir Mayakovsky: A Tragedy *at the Luna Park theatre in St. Petersburg. Over the next few years he wrote some of his major works, including "A Cloud in Trousers," "Man" and his play* Mystery Bouffe *(1918). Most of these works were written in support of the new Soviet order, but Mayakovsky's later works, such as* The Bedbug *(1928) and* The Bathhouse *(1930) were satirical criticisms of the new order. He grew increasingly disillusioned with Soviet life and committed suicide in 1930.*

Armand Gatti

Your Name Was Joy

Translated from French by Teresa L. Jillson

1

LOOKING FOR YOU with a camera what a paradox!

You, who both times you went to the movies with me fell asleep before the opening credits had hardly gone by. I remember the images that paraded past, your head leaning forward and my fear that the sound would wake you.

But paradoxes have built, constructed, lifted your entire life. And no doubt in order to lift it further yet, it would be necessary to give to the images of a camera quest on the hills of Montferrat a sound only composed by whales. But the paradoxes from which I orchestrate you are always short-lived paradoxes which at your touch become normalcy.

For the image, you come just behind Mélies, one of the inventors of the cinema of the imagination. But alas, barely uttered, the words break the magic of what I must call your solitary filmings. For the sound, the whale is easier to identify. It is the animal with which Auguste, your man, established relations of time, space, sympathy, and to say it all, of permanent marriage. His only decree—as one of the twelve leaders of the libertarian republic of Patagonia which only lasted fifteen days before being drowned in blood by the Argentine troops—was for the universalized invention of the whales.

From that moment the song of the whale has accompanied your entire life. You survived the death of your man but not the whale—at least the one your son had reinvented and which was dragged by the revolutionaries through the streets of Havana on the pretext of celebrating Carnival—in the parade of the century's vanquished. Your house, empty today, is yet again the whale. Once a year your grandchildren and your great-grandsons come play more or less conscious Jonahs there.

And now here is its song at the meeting with the camera—and with the landscapes it intends to glean from what you were.

2

Even before the hills, you must be sought in your name: Laetitia. You had the name of joy, mother—against all evidence. You still had it at the age of 81 when in greatest secret you went and joined a revolutionary party, because, so you said: it makes the rich afraid, and without that fear the poor would never advance. You were preparing tomorrows which sing. Nevertheless you were not communist like Uncle Rainier who almost died of hunger under Lenin's portrait because he no longer wished to accept the exploitation of man by man.

You weren't an anarchist either like Auguste your man, stabbed thirteen times by the Pinkerton police, put in a sack, and thrown into Lake Calumet in the south of Chicago. His militancy was the black scarf around his neck.

Yours, the cord of the third order of Saint Francis of Assisi around your waist. Those are the only identities to which you laid claim for your last journey, he in French soil, you in Italian soil.

They die with you at this moment.

Your name spoke joy. It continues to speak it but with you, a joy as tragic as all militancy put together. The whole, like a Beginning, meant to reform the sky in hard human dimensions: the hills of Montferrat.

3

What can Montferrat say to someone seeking his mother with a camera?

First that it has a center. This center for all your piedmont years written in the official record is the Will-o-the-Wisp farm. It has changed a lot since but it remains a few steps from the cemetery. There you watch over (you continue to watch over) along with tens and tens of women in black like you—all having made the universe larger through their way of seeing it—and sometimes completing it with their hard, tired and creviced hands like yours. Around the Will-o-the-Wisp farm, always the same scenario in the round: emigration, catastrophe, return. More than eleven times. Age two years, the age at which one discovers the world. For you the age when your father, Salvatore the Magnificent, mason, falls from a roof and is crushed in a street in Marseille. Your mother brings you back. The farm doesn't yet exist. And Montferrat is no longer anything but a long furrowing of walks—with doors at the end. All closed. You were one character too much in the landscape.

What to do with a daughter with no father? And from

refusal to refusal halfway up the hill above the valley appears the Will-o-the-Wisp farm . With it appears Francesco, knight with a cart for transporting fruits and vegetables on the route Turin, Casale, the Valley. He offers you his protection and marries your mother.

Eleven times this same scenario.

The foreign countries change, the catastrophes are not the same. But the closed doors of Montferrat remain. For a long time. Variation around a never-changing peripetia. What other scenario could the camera seeking you invent for itself.

They said you were like an ant. Was that because of that eternal return with which you bestrode the language of the star, and misery? For these returns home only the Will-of-the Wisps had the possibility of flight.

Everything else dragged along at ground level, at hunger level.

They said you were small like an ant. Your first school was your gaze upon the ants as if it were a question of knowing yourself. Many words of the ants in the hills were said without your ever knowing for whom nature turned green in these springtimes which were those of your return. Elms and yet more elms which shaded your entire childhood— elms made to make it tutelary—Elms which disappeared within a few years from the same sickness as you within a few weeks.

May the oak ally itself to the birch, ally itself to the beech inside the multiple frames that an emigrant can imagine for them, there will always be in that first return home (like in the votive offering of Crea) the image of the Mother carrying you. And at her feet the hills.

4

The votive offerings have always been tied to you. Through them the world found a probability.

Faces of Montferrat which the earth goes to meet, you are marked by the returns and departures to the four corners of the century and of the planet. Each time part of you dies with your dead, because mourning can only come from old joys.

Where are these joys?

But Auguste had survived. Not able to come into the hills because of the fascism in power in the whole peninsula, he gave you a rendez-vous just beyond the French border.

In front of the house of the Whale.

That time it was only a skeleton in a museum but Auguste knew how to fix it so that it was still the Whale. Since then its song has never left you. It was born at the same time as I.

5

It continues solitary, still today in the station at Turin. You were thirteen. A sign around your neck said: "I'm looking for work," not even a bundle like all serious emigrants. In a handkerchief a crumb of bread, and that's all. Work you find and you sell newspapers on the quay of the stations. The miserable money of underpayment, and of exploited children. What can the Turin station say to a man of more than half a century searching with his camera for his mother who is not yet thirteen. You said yourself: there is only the crying of empty men—and this wake of broken odors they drag behind them that nothing can erase.

Turin became a long uncensored sentence, forever unintelligible. Thoughts of a common spirit which go to ask asylum in the gazes of the statues at the historical center.

Behind which block of houses might this disappeared world (refugees, door-to-door salesmen, public soup kitchens, sellers of shams and of Tuscans, carters, blacksmiths, metal workers, seminary students, sellers of coffee and all that can be put in the mouth, ever-busy sewing machine representatives) still exist?

Because it continues to exist among the men at the foot of the mounts where flows the river Po.

Of the Turin of that time you kept only a slaughterhouse scream. The war of 14. Its hells fallen into disuse, its men stuffed into the language of ancient catastrophes—even if some days Turin rang loud like its mountains whose advanced history it was. It remained backward, Turin. Turin hospital with an internal architecture where crossed, ran parallel, went astray, ideas, banks, football players, worker thought and automobiles... The labyrinth.

Never did a labyrinth, even haunted, for you, by the parish saints (as was the case) return a world to a child spitting her lungs on the quays of the central station. She was no more than solitude crossed by a screaming locomotive. In its cars all the travelers are dead.

You were always dressed in black. Not Auguste's black planted on the pyramid of the living and the dead in order to sing the Social there. You only wore the black of which the Mediterranean sun is made, a sea onto which the hills were never able to open. Beginning with the death of the Magnificent crushed at the bottom of a Marseille building, you were the woman in black.

When the circular wind blows, Montferrat leaves the now-touristic maps and goes around the world. At that time, it is no longer made up of solitudes which add to those of the emigrants. Families from the top of the hills, they are today the Montferrat of the end of the world. Reconstruction of the lost world: the travels of emigrants spread out on the world map are always a nocturnal vigil. The Chicago in which you lived no longer exists. Only in the albums and documents of the time. What you brought back of it is falling apart with age. Chicago was only a resurrection of the scenario inaugurated by the Magnificent but with Auguste, this time.

Capital's killers had thrown him in a lake after having stabbed him thirteen times. And you left with me in you, in the direction of the hills.

You were brought back into the hills to die there of tuberculosis, the illness of the poor then. Your transportation was the fruit and vegetable cart.

6

The rice paddy looks at the camera, and the camera accepts this gaze. In it you have come to set yourself down after two black years of sickness, bent over the flatness beyond the hills, your weight calculated in sacks of rice. The birds of your trees were never poets of the storm—they always spoke labor, patience and waiting above all. And if the moon has been invented above the hills, it is most often so one could fast there.

Here rival stars (from top to bottom) mix their knowledge which at night maintains on the rice paddy the uncertain, the fragile, the contradictory. Dawn dissolves it as if she only wanted to show the laborious part of things. That is what the old from those years' paddies still sing. On each kernel of rice, companion of many silences, the universe becomes an ensemble of metaphors.

Reunited under this light all your young years (waiting for the excess which washes secular usury) say that all emigration from Montferrat began there. The map of the world was the work contract for the rice paddy that reproduced it. The map only, because Turin, Chicago, Paris, Monaco, Barcelona and even Casale remain an enlargement of a piece of hill. Everywhere the hill remains fundamental. Love is the gaze open on the being of the beloved, but which passes through to reach the depth of being of those who love.

7

Macaronis—(the names given to émigrés are mostly culinary) Macaroni—they said it of the men who in the emigration were, they too, from the hills. Auguste (the one who had chosen you) was one of them.

He came already leaving. I never saw him as big rather tall...He took me and I followed him all over the world.

He had red hair, blue eyes (when the blue is liquid), the south of the bells which answer each other in a smile, and the swarming of stars over his head.

Macaronis are these vast, elementary beings who live far from the Hills while continuing to walk toward Them.

Mixes, weavings, fascinations, chromosomes, life's moments—always end up incarnated themselves, jumping from one life to another. During the last years of your life you systematically visited all the churches of Italy or of anywhere else, you went on all the pilgrimages, you haunted all the museums. I believed you were searching for the time of Faith of which you remained one of the survivors. You said you were seeking colors which would uphold the world and I called you "My unworthy old lady"…

There is always a moment when the birds of Giotto to whom Saint Francis of Assisi speaks become the birds of our own garden, the dog of Saint Roch becomes the very character of destiny, the old man of the last judgement high in the Sistine, our neighbor, and Botticelli's Springtime our own springtime.

8

All this you had known for a long time, and you would say, showing one of the characters from the chapels of the Sacred Mount: "That's one of them…!"

And "one of them" took her place in the Turin station, plunged into the mud of the rice field, or took a few hours of forced respite on the emigrants' boat.

Sometimes the dawns and sunsets on the hills became a long wait for THEM and ONE OF THEM made a path through lives juxtaposed in space by the Tabachetti or Moncalvo brothers.

Complicities and communions crashed into everyday objects, sometimes died of it, sometimes culled evidence of civil status. Before them, other characters, in other forms of expression (from what other chapels?) dressed their silhouettes (foreseen for another story) on your work places—around the world.

To add them up is to tell the Story of the Century. Hands of my mother you were at the edge of each of their gestures. They constructed the world in the two hemispheres. You were part of THEM.

Sometimes you were the question. Sometimes, the answer. You said—With the father it was as if the marks he left behind him were wolves. They cried after his passing, with the voice of the dead. I never knew if you were talking about Auguste or the Magnificent. But the father was one of THEM.

And "they" in their chapels gave dream and reality to all those absent from the hills. Whatever the season, they knew how to greet one another smiling. There would begin yet another adventure altogether.

9

How do these dialogues that we are begin? Who is it then who grasps in hairy, clawed (and always ephemeral) time something which remains and which the word makes persist. You were always invested with the Fourth Word, and all the animals always gave you (in the sense of gift) the answer.

There were dogs at each marking period of your life. The one of your burned lungs to which (not without reason) you attribute your healing, the one who witnessed your marriage, the one who would go salute the hanged of Chicago in their next to last refuge, the one belonging to Auguste which died the same day as he, the one of your death who entering into the church put himself in front of the first row as if he had come to demand your final resting place, and as if it belonged to him.

Since they were all named Pinot, I now have the impression of one and only one dog who accompanied your entire life.

The Fourth Word made Pinot into a chronicle, an epic, a tale of giants.

Good are the legends because they are a memorial. But for what Most-High, and by whom will the legends be interpreted?

The camera is set there where I was born of you on the middle ledge overlooking the Monegasque oceanographic museum. But it is set at the same time on one of the infinite chapters of the saga where it is told how Pinot succeeded in leading you to the middle ledge at the oceanographic museum where Auguste the miraculous from Chicago awaited you...

In the museum there was a whale and it was there that six months later you donned—for the only time in your life—uniform: you became guard of the fish.

That whale has always gathered our destinies together as a mountain chain groups mountains. It was the fundamental trait which originally confers unity and determination upon the gifts of destiny. Your gaze resting each day on the History of the Oceans—and the remedies that must necessarily be brought to them for it to continue to be history under the visitors' eye—was the great moment of your life. There was a Laetitien era—as there was a Victorian era—At the end catastrophe (the great fire like in Chicago). But this time, there was no return.

The scenario of the Magnificent was broken.

10

What is it, for you to be absent in the landscape?

Without you, the possibilities of sky, of trees, of birds, of dramas, of catastrophes to which only you had access are lighting up with stars.

The owl from the roof over the sundial has gone.

On the roads of the hills still guarded by the dog of Saint Roch, the storm continues to call itself a native of the sacred chaos in which you are now a character.

11

The return upon the hills which was to be the last—made of these hills the place of exile for an entire life. The Piedmont speech (whatever the rotation of the earth) emigrated by you across the world—was dying there "Like Garibaldi died" and in your mind it was one and the same character. You needed their words where the mountain responded by echo to brotherhood, and the river to conquest. But how to find them again with a fleeing life inflicted with more knife wounds than Auguste's sack in Lake Calumet? Those of Aunt Madeleine's return, of the strikes of '36, of your mother's death, the commemorative to Sacco and Vanzetti...the commemoratives of a comet whose multiple powers you set yourself to boast and even those when you left for the Americas (and elsewhere) who knew how to be there to give you the same wink as a work contract.

Only Auguste and the dynastic Pinot passed through other jurisdictions. Saint Roch for the Dog—Saint Francis of Assisi for Auguste ("He's the only one I salvage from all your paradise which is like a pack of reactionary fiefholders, and even Stalinian reactionaries like that Saint Anthony...")

They had above all that silence which finds its source at the top of the hills and which always ends up asking questions of the valley. You, you were between the two.

The route from your house to Crea, almost always taken on foot, you called it the route of the tree's gaze...but with double vision.

Was it the times of the Old Testament that invented the space Montferrat. Was it the space Montferrat that invented the times of the Old Testament?

Behind each chapel there is a cosmic passageway which makes men and animals of stone or of terra cotta omnipresent: the temptation to participate in the why of their gazes.

You brought us a new Laetitia, the one of the flowers. On your hill the garden always took up more space than the house. A day and night vigil, waiting for destiny. Every summer the flowers became the arrival of the art of prediction. It lead to the Sacred Mount.

They of the hills know in returning there that the characters of the chapels perpetuate themselves (like the realization of a prophesy) from one village to another, across seasons and years. Continue with the Virgin and the Christ carriers of that Kitsch which your poor dote on. They inscribe their piety around it, even if it is always through lack that God acts. On the Sacred Mount what he cannot refuse to accept is his belonging to the earth. Those faces with which the Franciscan recreated all the paths of the Bible, you always knew how to recognize your past there.

As many angels as events in your life
those of the dead of the Great War
those of the imprisoned of the Resistance
those of uncle Angelo
those of uncle Armand
those of fascism
those of the assassination of the Rosselli brothers

They came from the depths of the ages, laden with messages unknown to themselves. When night equals day one has the impression that the Sacred Mount is the result of the just thought of the trees.

Even condemned the elm lives its last commitments to

the history the chapels would like to tell. Each tree there is an enigma and more, a celebration, origin of all the events which have spread in the region since the dreams of Saint Eusebe.

12

Saint Eusebe who dreamed Crea begins to sing, in the slightly overlyrical mode which is his own.

—Celebration is the origin of the story of humanity. The name Laetitia comes out of the celebration. So the gestures of Laetitia become founder of a story of humanity (Which one? It matters little...We are happy to be part of it).

13

Saint Francis who usually did so also sang

—These hills which seek to share the suffering of a god to the point of inventing one in 21 chapels—are like so many gestures of the world entering into the light...

The dog of Roch who did not usually sing simply added

—They are not the world. But one without the other they can no longer be.

14

You did not respond. But a long time later you asked (and my heart melts within me to remember it...)

—And if the whole was the Virgin of the Sacred Mount?...

15

Once. Only once you preceded the eternal return, after the catastrophe: The Magnificent crushed in the streets of Marseilles, Auguste in his Chicago sack, Angelo of America who killed himself for love, the blade of the scythe beating as in an allegory on the head of Dionigi the absolute ancestor...

Characters without traits without photographs, but of whom places remain, and even whole faces to tell them: Monbello, Castel San Pietro, Camino, Castello Merli. And uniting them all like a mausoleum built against the death of the century: the Will-o-the-Wisp farm.

Woman in black, like all your ancestresses.

Uninterrupted black, like, most of the time, the mourning was uninterrupted.

Time of the Resistance: woman in black. Harmony of the times.

Your son had just been condemned to death. You had received the announcement from a police inspector with a Corsican accent. Of that announcement only emptiness stayed with you, and the accent in which that emptiness was dug.

You came to ask grace of your own—In Piedmontese— Of those to whom you knew why to speak. Because for centuries the trembling light of the candles said on the Sacred Mount that these characters were foreseen.

I still have, the way I imagined them in prison, the form of your hands, the color of your eyes, of your hair knotted by a chignon behind your head—more than the unbelievability that words bring to any reconstruction outside your presence.

16

The saints are part of the things of the earth.

They must keep their feet on the ground if they wish to remain saints. It is on this earth that you join them. Hardly set forth, the clock of the Crescentino station was saying that your gait was as right as the hour it was trying to give.

The black scarf which covered your head, but which what's more came down to knot around your neck (like Auguste's for serious decisions) indicated family business, and that it was a question of descendance and of the future of the whale man.

17

Auguste, when he put his black scarf around his neck never went to those he confined to one vast word, a universe word (the reactionaries). He had his place—and it still is, in a way, today: Montalero...The days and nights of the Great War (the one that put an end to country civilization) are also a piece of hill. But a piece of hill where disappeared soldiers are trees finding it strange on the weavings of memory, and of the sky, to be mixed with the ease of the day.

The officer, the under-officer, the soldier, the soldier again as at war, but this time carriers of the silence of things. Surveying this monument to the dead, vegetal, Auguste named the enigma: A continual movement of gestures and actions of which he alone had the adjacent parts. It is toward them that he went the night of your wedding—to the assault of one never knew what enormity—They hunted for him all night and at dawn they found him unconscious, at the foot of these commemorative trees. (Auguste the Pacifist was the place of violence—He awakened it around him—His confrontations tasted of thunder, and speech—in his sentences—the presence of the broken storm).

For you the mounts of the war were the blue hour of the hills. Even if at certain moments it filled the earth, they remained hidden somewhere in the century with your twenty years.

18

To name you, that day, one would have to pass from joy to its excess. Superfluity (a flux which runs over, and which by that very fact surpasses itself) that was you. Through you the chapels of the Sacred Mount became that superfluity in which the painters of all times have always assembled the thoughts of the earth. And it is with that thought that you the daughter of the Magnificent were going to enter into dialogue (even if it was only a long monologue).

Behind you cried all the faces of your life. With them the whales sang somewhere the same rendezvous. Despair belled like a deer in the midst of the trees of the Natural Park. And in the cloister the votive offerings threw off their habits of suffering humanity. Of a certainty, the dogs of memory—Is it enough today for the camera to surprise a descendant of the Pinots (with his scarf, he too) to say how those things happened.

On your knees (advancing on your knees) meter by meter, the chaplet in your hand, you made the journey of the twenty-two chapels. At each one you asked for the life of your son.

19

For how long (how many centuries) had the discussions been silent in the chapel of the twelve apostles? They began again, as if they had ceased to be another planet and as if it really had to do with characters from Montferrat. Your books of piety (Franciscan nonetheless) were full of exterminating angels. The Nazis who had condemned your son were part of them. But for the serious things of this world, it was the apostles, those saints covered with dust and begging for restoration, who decided them. And on what remained of their ceramic colors were born requests and answers.

You told them that emigrants were always searching somewhere for a trial by fire, that they persevered in seeing it as the rising of the sun—that sun which is ever lacking for the making of a full life—and that was speaking of the poor.

You told them that bread was the fruit of the earth but the benediction which gave it meaning came from the light.

You told them that men were the primary directions wandering around the earth and that it was their space-sickness which made them die in time.

You told them that the men of your time, their memory and their sometimes inexplicable designs, were part of the same poor, the same unprovided for as you, that we were fragile, supremely fragile and that inside that fragility there was an obstinate dim light which could not go out because it was the trial by fire among us. The wedding of Cana, given the abundance of the witnesses and their lack of care, you wanted to make them enter into that hope which oozes across the world, runs under each prison door and which one perseveres in calling sickness.

You told them that you wanted your son exactly as you yourself had given him to the world on the day of his birth, menacing to make of the Sacred Mount the Burning Bush burning on High.

So many washed parquets in your life as a domestic, scrubbed on your knees, so many stairways (the fourteen floors of the Beausoleil castle, washed every week) made this ascension an everyday journey. It was one way to continue the work. And that work without your knowing…

20

Several years later the one in question that day would say— Imagination (and the cinema of which it is capable) should start from the struggles and realities (hopes, joys and pains) of its time, install them in a frame and dialogue with them. Its adventure: that of images, words and sounds born of that dialogue. Maybe that day across time and space you heard your son say it…In fact he did nothing but copy what you had traced that day on the Sacred Mount. He took the message up again.

You were not the author of films, you were their source, that is why the camera is searching for you on the Sacred Mount.

A cinema without film, with nothing but frames, shots or sequences (but everyone knows that for the cinema everything that is outside the frame doesn't exist). And you at each of these frame-chapels you brought the hows and the whys of your century (who more than a chapel of Crea, through its destiny in space can pretend to the eye of the camera?)

21

You said:

—That day before arriving at the last chapel, I knew that they had listened to me. But they remained silent...Climbing the stairs of the crown I had the impression that one of them had answered me—And it was true.

22

Aimed at these hills, they too engaged in the debate with the invisible of the things of our History, the camera (against all its references as camera) speaks.

It is evening, pronounced by the Alps. In two hours the hills go through five different colors, and the camera says— it is the daughter of the Magnificent who makes the essays of her film in colors, always in the breach of the universe.

Before your empty house: the only tree on the hill that knows the song of the whale.

You planted it.

*

Born in Monaco in 1924, Armand Gatti graduated from the Monaco lycée in 1941. In 1942, he departed Monaco and took up with the French resistance. In 1942 the G.M.R. (the Garde Mobile Régionale, the national police under the German occupation) arrested Gatti and condemned him to death. He was reprieved and deported to the Linderman camp near Hamburg. The same year he escaped, managing to get to Great Britain, where he joined the parachute regiment of the Special Air Service.

Gatti participated in the battles of the liberation and was deco-

rated after the Arnheim battle. But upon returning to France he was arrested and jailed in a military prison for "lack of respect to a career officer." He was discharged to Monaco in 1945.

The same year he moved to Paris and began work for the Parisien Libéré. *There he met Pierre Joffroy, Philippe Soupault and, over the next couple of years, frequented the salons of Suzanne Tezenas where he met Henri Michaux, John Cage, Pierre Souvtchinsky, Yves Benot, Paule Thevenin and others who led him on a career of theatre and writing. In 1948 he began a theatrical project,* Les menstrues, *with music by Pierre Boulez.*

Over the next years he continued his journalistic career, becoming, in 1956, the star reporter at France-Soir. *The same year he became a French national. From 1957 through the 1960s Gatti wrote and directed several films and dramas, among them* Morambong *(1958),* Le crapaud-buffle *(1959),* L'Enclos *(1960),* Le château, *an adaptation of the Kafka novel (1960),* L'enfant rat *(1961),* La seconde existence du camp de Tattenberg *(1962),* El otro Cristobal *(1962), and numerous others. His play,* Les 7 possibilités du train 713 en partance d'Auschwitz (The 7 Possibilities of Train 713 Departing from Auschwitz), *was performed in Vienna in 1987 and at the University of Rochester in 1988. Sun & Moon will publish the play in 1995.*

Rosita Copioli

White

AND

Tree

Translated from Italian by Renata Treitel

White

Fruit-tree lined avenue albescent with wind that blows
corollas in midair, bundle of mists and rare objects
between sky and earth, petals that evening flings down.
      Branches, mists
from the bellies of the wood already fruit—plane of the white soft
flow of drifting petals.
Cherry-tree lined evenings, when darkness
      flings down the features of the rare objects,
the embrace of the wind holds weakly and
the sunset broken by the ripe blossom
unravels on the leaves of grass.

Tree

To speak, if to speak of trees is to speak of you
to speak, to see and to know, if to speak and see
is to know that the trees are still the ones with the flowery names
that their end can be seen down the roads
and gardens of signs and rotating tall tufts
disturb the image of our garden.
That behind every sign remains the image
of the tree, the one which neither a Middle Ages of paradises
nor any enchanted garden has ever wanted; a plant
which in itself hides only itself and values only
                                        its woody flowering.
An unfathomable disdain knew how to speak
                        of the tree
of this tree which is
which does not flee, and one can see and speak of it
and one sees and knows it.
The tree which is and whom disdain cannot touch,
which is not on the bright path of Eden.

*

*Born in Riccione, in the province of Emilia-Romagna, Italy, in
1948, Rosita Copioli studied Humanities and received a degree in
Aesthetics under the guidance of Luciano Anceschi. Her disserta-
tion on Leopardi represents an interest which she carries with her
to this day, and she has continued in her research on Leopardian
poetics.*

She currently teaches in a technical-commercial institute. Her book, Splendida Lumina Solis, *was published by Generazione in 1979, and will be published in a bi-lingual edition by Sun & Moon Press in 1995.*

Heimito von Doderer

from *The Merovingians*

Translated from German by Vinal O. Binner

The Total Family and the Origin of the Beard Regalia

CHILDERICH VON BARTENBRUCH had spent his childhood
and youth in ancestral castles in Central Franconia. He still
kept tight possession of the Bartenbruch estate, although
after he came of age he lived more in the city than on these
properties. Childerich got himself married very early, the first
time when he was just twenty-five, and to a forty-five-year-
old lady.

His youth merely oppressed him. Among the numerous
Bartenbruch brothers he was the oldest, it is true, although
the least in appearance, small and softish, very early already
wrinkled; meanwhile, the other fellows grew like fir trees.
At that time he enjoyed not the slightest authority over his
younger brothers—at an age, that is, when the question de-
pends primarily on physical superiority, although Childerich
in his youth had a considerable advantage in years; three
years separated him from his next oldest brother. Even so,
Childerich frequently received a dubbing, and for a time slaps
and kicks were bestowed almost daily. Heaviest frays among
the young people were the rule at Bartenbruch, against which
not even the father had any influence (Childerich's mother,

an English lady, had perished a few years after the birth of her youngest son, Ekkehard). Only the fist could assert itself here. Therefore, in his youth the future master of the estate led a completely repressed, crushed, and crestfallen existence.

At fifteen he looked like a sad little bag. The face was old, the cheeks slack. However, he was never sickly. Also in his later life Childerich almost never fell ill, nor was he under medical care, with the exception of the care of Professor Horn—a care that really, though, nearly presumed a stable state of health.

Yet, there was strength in Childerich, too, of a beaten-back, frightened-back sort that had had to turn inward, where it collected. Though he never, in the slightest degree, took more than the minimum interest in the arts or sciences that was dictated by his station to be the obligatory cultural amount, Childerich's spirit sharpened itself just in his early youth, to be sure on completely other matters; especially his memory was strengthened through the registration of the chain of the insults and abuses he suffered; and thereby there developed in him a cultivated system of the most painstakingly noted resentments of rare subtlety. He "took his punishment well," as a boxer would express it. But with all this— and this formed the significant content of his youth—there dwelled in him an untested and irrevocable certitude that his hour was yet to come, that he need but be ready with assorted registers of the tortures inflicted on him to open then at the right moment a campaign against World and Life that, following the most careful preparations, could do nothing but lead him from victory to victory.

To acquire importance and power—about these things the mere fifteen-year-old brooded and meditated. We said that he meditated, and by just that way of expressing it we

also meant that he did not dream. The unequaled attacks of
rage—that some day would violently rock his mature years—
remained then for him, in the face of the extreme external
pressure, pushed deep inside himself; and how violent this
pressure must have been, to frighten such fury into secret
caverns! However, also in the later, the already raging
Childerich III, we could see that the thick-as-hail applica-
tion of powerful slaps by the attending doctor, Professor
Horn, was not without effect. But such a hail had been in his
early youth his daily bread. If the brothers saw the slightest
sign in him of that deep resentment, then they punched at
him. So fury pierced Childerich during his youth like a deep
nail, yes, like a nail—with its head driven deep into the
wood—that one hardly sees. His luck was that the further
and higher education of his younger brothers was consum-
mated in England, by which an earlier expressed wish of
Childerich III's mother was piously fulfilled, a wish that she
could naturally not extend to the oldest, the heir to the es-
tate, for the fellows were to remain over there to inherit their
properties, at least the three younger ones after Childerich—
Dankwart, Rollo (Rolf) and Eberhard. Of course the late-
born Ekkehord was not yet under consideration.

To acquire importance and power: Childerich meditated,
completely lucidly, completely without self-deception, on how
to do this. That is, he was not only aware of his hitherto
prevailing powerlessness, but it was also clear to him that
there was a good reason for it, and this reason lay in himself,
in his insignificant, miserable weakness, wretched as a sad,
senile little sack: had he not been like that, the external cir-
cumstances alone would have enabled him—indeed, almost
made it natural for him—as the oldest and as the future
master of the estates, to conduct a reign of terror over his
younger brothers and sisters (there were also sisters). Ulti-

mately, in the house of those of Bartenbruch, there were not many other possibilities of carrying on relations among the members of the family except those of beating up or being beaten up: the father, however, avoided the first, well knowing that right off and forthwith his sons would have made him the object of the second. And with Childerich III it happened, even when he was already fifteen years old, that the sisters, too, Gerhild and Richenza, did not refrain from delivering him slaps and kicks.

Amid such tortures and the sundry other vexations and hard times he was given, Childerich quietly discovered that single vehicle that could lead him to fame and revenge: his male potency, far surpassing normal standards. In his twentieth year he attained his full power. At the same time there appeared on him an enormous beardedness; he could hardly shave enough, and still his flabby hanging jowls continually wore a deep blue shadow.

Here did he then erect the axis of his life. Not yet twenty-five, he married, in her forty-fifth year, the rich widow of a Kulmbach beerbrewer (named Christian Paust), a lady born a von Knötelbrech, a passable if not exactly old line of nobility. This person, a sturdily built, pretty woman with smooth black horse hair, experienced such excesses in her marriage that after four years she gave up the ghost. Not seldom did it happen that Childerich, deep in the night, raced into her bedroom as though shot from a cannon.

In spite of the relatively short duration of this marriage, his first wife left him two little girls, and also with them some grown or nearly grown children by the brewer, Paust. The oldest of these grown children, Barbara, a tall, unusually beautiful female, married in the same year of the second marriage of her mother (who, by the way was named Christine, the female form of the late brewer's baptismal name) the district judge of Kulmbach, named Bein. Barbara's marriage developed happily and rich in children, but it found a premature end after but fifteen years through the decease of the husband: the judge set himself out in a cold mountain wind in Upper Bavaria, sweating heavily, and did not arise from a bout with pneumonia.

About the time that the von Knötelbrech by birth, now Baroness von Bartenbruch, gave up her ghost, there was in the House of Bartenbruch a perfect scandal of considerable dimension.

This was the second marriage of Childerich's grandfather, known as Childerich I. This old and extremely rich malady in the family—a thin, boorish old man with a twisted mustache and the malice of a baboon—began (when he was nearly eighty-five) to lose his head in such a way that he fell madly in love with and lusted after a pretty twenty-six-year-old person. This Childerich I was, by the way, the only Bartenbruch to have chosen a business beneath his station: he owned large factories for toy-making in the Thüringen country, where it is known that such industries are indigenous. But in matters concerning his later love inclinations, the old Bartenbruch "moved" not at all beneath his station— for example, like some old man driven out of his mind by some ordinary gadabout woman. On the contrary, his second and so very young wife was a countess, Countess Cellé; and, in addition, she was wealthier than he himself, was of age, and was nearly alone in the world.

There is no sense in here writing around all these things in order to make a monstrous fact agreeable by describing motivations. It is clear, rather, that this bond had some kind of hardly understandable, repulsive, background. But in this case the ghost gave itself up on the Bartenbruch side, and the Baroness Clara, born Countess Cellé, one morning found the remainder, or little crust of what was left of Childerich I, already cold beside her in the second bed.

But that was for Childerich III, more than ever, a stoking of the fire. The baboon, angered by the disapproval that his second marriage found in the furthest family circles, had reduced the inheritance of his son—that is, Childerich III's father—to the lowest legitimate portion, disinherited all the other hopefuls, and made his young wife his sole heir. It was easy to see in advance that the Baroness, nee Cellé, would not long remain unwed, and that sooner or later one could expect a branching off of a considerable portion of the Bartenbruch fortune to alien lines.

Childerich III broke out in the most extreme fury. By his merely imagining that things could take that turn, there occurred in him for the first time one of those mighty, one could say comprehensive, attacks of rage with which, much later, Professor Horn would have such great trouble.

Childerich had not so much as become personally acquainted with the Baroness Cellé-Bartenbruch, for he had taken part in the nearly complete boycott that the Bartenbruchs had hung over the baboon's house even at the news of his engagement, and the more so when the old one then made no secret of his will's disposals. Now, not too long after his grandfather's death, as Childerich (at that time already a widower) found himself alone in his city palace on an afternoon in June, the servant announced to him the visit of his step-grandmother.

Childerich III, at that time in his thirtieth year, looked (at least considered by normal eyes) downright loathsome. His inferior bodily height, the lightly forward-bent posture, the flabby, limp, drooping countenance with the blue-black shadow of a beard gave an anything but advantageous impression; added to that was a certain protrusion of the eyes, a pop-eyedness, that one not seldom finds in those persons of an extremely choleric nature. All the same, it must not be kept concealed that in spite of everything one somehow saw that a descendent of a distinguished old family looked out through all the cracks and wrinkles. He was in his behavior often less than aristocratic, our Baron, but he did look aristocratic. The virtue of noble ancestry still showed, although mostly only on the visible surface. This surface still remained intact; and where there was no longer any indication of an inner strength, still there was always this curtain, thick enough to conceal the abominable.

One has to imagine Childerich as he raised himself from the corner of a sofa to confront his grandmother. These hyperthrophic eyes had had, after all, their forefathers, whose somewhat outwards hanging glance had rested on generations of small peasants and serfs, menacing forth out of a security which was a forgone conclusion, which had never been disputed; oppressive, suppressive. Childerich wore a very expensive summer suit of a dark color, of that pattern that one calls "salt and pepper," and—as we wrote in 1920, but even for that period they were somewhat old-fashioned— white spats over light brown shoes. The cravat was white, too; this latter constituted a regular, customary idiosyncrasy of Childerich's, distinct from all fashion. Just recently, too (and a bit early), he had again laid aside the mourning clothes of a widower.

What caused Countess Cellé to pay a visit to a member of the hostile family, and besides that, precisely to the grandson, remained entirely unclear to the Baron, and just now he did not have much time for consideration; objectively speaking, it lay completely out of the realm of possibility for him to discover the truth, which was as simple as it was paradoxical. Clara Cellé had already seen the Baron, often and

long since, for the first time at the famous race track at
Auteuil. Someone had pointed him out to her. And she had
taken a liking to him—a greater one, indeed, than later to
the baboon. But that one was dead now

Her visit here was made possible by a peculiar excuse.
She bore this excuse literally athwart her arms: a long, nar-
row package in brown paper.

Her grandson easily guessed what the thing was; how-
ever, that she brought it to him instead of taking it to his
father—to whom it was, rather, due—enfeebled the excuse,
caused the appearance of Clara Cellé here in his house to be
now really mysterious. Why on earth did she bring this family
antiquity personally instead of availing herself of her lawyer
or simply of a messenger? Had she not wanted to do it her-
self for some reason or other, then the way to the father should
have been easier for her. Childerich ii's participation in the
boycott against the baboon was half-hearted and had been
but forced because of the wild threats in correspondence from
his younger sons. One might think that he behaved as he did
because he loved his sons. Later it will be shown that he
offered (due to the similarity of his own slumbering inclina-
tions to amorous madness) the old one a forgiving under-
standing. Besides, Childerich ii looked very much like his
father. There was also about him something that was posi-
tively baboon-like. However, had the one been from spite a
madder, so was the one here a sadder Cynocephalus.

After the death of Childerich ii's English spouse—that
may have been about 1908—he moved completely back to
his subsidiary estate in Franconia; gave then his oldest son
(whom he let be declared of age shortly after 1910, that is,
prematurely) the major country property and city palace;
and now lived, since Dankwart, Rollo (Rolf) and Eberhard
were happy in England, completely alone with little

Ekkehard, a good-looking, good-natured boy who was abso-
lutely healthy and quick. Otherwise, Childerich II appeared
to have enough of all and everything; yet this appearance
would prove itself misleading—albeit, much later. After
Ekkehard had departed, shortly after the First World War
at the age of about fifteen, to an expensive Swiss educational
academy, Childerich II remained alone; and it appeared then
as though he pupated. Ekkehard later became flag-bearer and
then an officer in the small German army. He avoided his
oldest brother as well as those in England.

So then Childerich III, a young widower with his two little
daughters, lived alone in an immense palace. Its extensive
garden greened under old trees from the rear of the house
outwards, a house that opened itself out to the park in balco-
nies and porches. Here, in a little hall, Childerich received
Clara Cellé.

Two pairs of eyes hung toward each other; also Clara's
showed a what one might call protrusion, and in addition an
unusually strong curvature, somewhat of a kind possessed
by the eyes of the famous King of Sweden, Gustav Adolf;
remarkably enough, that heroic and unhappy sovereign ac-
tually found himself among the ancestors of the Countess's
family. The remainder of Clara's countenance was frugally
endowed, quite suiting the modest size of her head. But above
this raised itself a thick, vast crown of hair, erected like a
tower or a pot, slanting to the rear like that of a lady pha-
raoh. Therewith, indeed, she towered over Childerich III by
at least ten centimeters, so that the Baron stood small before
her. The face of Clara Cellé now appeared reduced almost to
a minimum, whose single parts were, however, plump and
firm: smooth prominent little apple cheeks; a round chin;
and a throat—Childerich could see it well from below—of
the taut plumpness and tenderness of a frog's belly. But oth-

erwise this whole little face gave, as it were, the impression
of shrinking back again into the head. The turned-up nose
tiny, with very evident nostrils; that is, almost a snub nose.
In all: a young, pretty little skull. A broad mouth and huge
snow-white teeth.

Two pairs of eyes hung toward each other, and with her
it was really and strictly speaking the case, for she looked
down from above, while Childerich III's look welled up to-
ward her from below. Here it was, as is often the case in such
matters, that probably everything crucial occurred in the first
seconds: indeed, one may suppose that during them
Childerich III's actual life's plan originated.

He received the heavy, long and broad Franconian
sword—for such was contained in the package across her
arms—and bore it now in the same manner across his own.
From the deep green cavity of the park one heard in a high-
pitched woman's voice a few words called in English, and
then the pattering steps on the gravel and the laughter of a
child: it was the older of Childerich III's two small daugh-
ters, who were borne him by Christine, the von Knötelbrech
by birth; and just then the English governess passed by be-
low with the little one. After that, the silence returned. It
became ever stiller. The droning of the stillness and of their
silence increased by leaps and bounds. And the two here,
from within the barred cages of two ancient noble families,
with eyes welling toward each other, still retained enough of
their heritage that they now, in spite of everything, staring,
supported this silence that disclosed enormous depths, with-
out any useless attempt to fill the ripped-open canyon with
the sand of conversation—something that usually prohibits
the prospect of a true meeting of two human beings. Yes,
they remained standing, just where they were; Childerich
made no move to offer a seat to Clara at once; that would

have led to conversation. One could dispense with that. And
so they bore the silence quite easily, much more easily than
Childerich was able to bear the mighty weapon, from the
time of the Franconian kings, across his weak and ridiculous
little arms.

Yes, she had brought him—and just him—this ancient
symbol of his clan. A legend was attached to it that had sur-
vived; though, at closer scrutiny, there seems to have been
little truth in it. This sword was supposed to have belonged
to a warrior, a stiff-necked champion of privilege for the old
German common soldier, who at Soissons prevented the still
heathen king, Chlodwig I, from removing a precious church
receptacle from the collected booty of war before the appor-
tionment, in order to return it to an episcopal church whose
head had requested it of him. The wrathful Chlodwig con-
trolled himself in spite of the audacity of this common man,
whose act, however, but represented the then valid rules of
war. Nevertheless, all the other men had servilely agreed to
the exception desired by the King. The next spring, at the
assembly of the Franks, the King found fault with the condi-
tion of the equipment belonging to this very same man: "Not
thy lance, nor thy sword, nor thy battleaxe is suitable!" And
he pitched into him and threw the last-named object—*la
francisque* it is called in French—before his feet. The man
bent over to retrieve it. At that moment the King jerked up
his own axe and crushed his skull. "Remember Soissons!" he
shouted as he struck.

That, then, was the warrior who was also considered to
be the founder of the House of Bartenbruch, who was sup-
posed to have possessed the sword which Clara Cellé now
had carried in her arms. It was still in relatively quite good
condition, and certainly one of the best-preserved pieces of
this sort: a slashing weapon, with the hilt some ninety centi-

meters long. The pommel bore no parrying-shaft, or rather, pommel and parrying-shaft were the same; that is, there was on it no such cross-hilt as could be seen on the swords of the succeeding Carolingian epoch, and then on those of the entire middle ages, somewhat like that hilt on Charlemagne's sword in the Paris Louvre; this last-mentioned also had a sharp point, or *Ort* (the old Germanic word for the tip of a weapon). The Bartenbruch sword, as an exclusively slashing weapon, had a round *Ort*. The blade had perhaps a breadth—up by the pommel—of about six centimeters and narrowed evenly. It was a type of weapon something of the sort that we would recognize in the sword of the Prince of Flonheim, that dates from the time of the mass migrations. It is preserved in the museum in Worms.

Considering the character of the piece, it is quite unlikely that an ordinary Frankish warrior would have brandished this weapon (and some members of the aristocratic house defended, for this reason, the view that the origin of the family was a much higher one[*]). Quite more likely to be imagined on the belt of such a man is the *Sax*, a cut-and-thrust weapon about sixty-two centimeters long and up to five centimeters broad, sharpened on one side and with a thick parrying side (while the proper sword had two cutting edges), and with a twelve-centimeter-long knife hilt. It was sharpened around the point and then a few centimeters up the parrying side.

---

[*] We are also of such an opinion, and not only because of the sword, but also by looking at the way this family behaved. We consider the descent of the Bartenbruchs from the Merovingian kings a fact. The Merovingians of the 20th century were all descended from Childerich XXXIV (whom we have yet to meet). He begat more children than the President of Venezuela, Juan Gomez (see Chapter 6). The Merovinglans developed—after their dispossession (752) in the following 250 years (that is, until about the year 1000) in numerous side-branches of the family—an almost uncanny fertility and

Well, so it was not a *Sax*, but a Frankish sword.

To retrieve the time lost on such digressions into weapon history, there follows now a jump over half a year; and at the expiration of this time we find Childerich III long married to Clara, who in this way had become for the second time a Baroness von Bartenbruch and at the same time the wife of her grandchild.

This Merovingian was struck, however, by a dark paroxysm that exceeded his anyway already somewhat stormy interpretation of married life. That as the husband of his grandmother he had become his own grandfather stirred in him previously unsuspected possibilities. The twisted mustache that he henceforth let grow, inheriting from his grandfather not only marriage-wise, but also whiskers-wise, was but the first visual sign of a newly opened outlook and a mightily elevated self-assurance that now, like a high-swinging span of bridge, promised to carry him over the degrading memories of youth.

He steamed and perspired with energy in a completely new, bustling and (one could say) berserk way. Clara Cellé bore him child after child—the first son, the heir, Childerich IV, whom one then later used to call Schnippedilderich; he came into the world as a kind of giant baby of much over four kilos, was already at a tender age healthy as an ox, grew to an uncanny height and breadth, had stubborn red-blond hair, and at twelve fought like an old cab driver; also, he al-

produced a surplus of male descendants, even, of whom most were named Childerich. The old numeration continued until Childerich XXXIV. In the 19th century, his name emerged again among the Bartenbruchs, the single branch of the Merovingians not bastardized by commoners, which just then and for this reason began with a new numeration. Essentially they considered themselves a kingly—or at least a princely—house, and among themselves to use the epithet "high-born" seemed, therefore, almost an act of modesty.

ready straddled a horse like an uhlan riding master, and be-
sides this even as a boy beat up almost everyone without
regard for who it was, spoke excellent English, though at
the same time he never managed to pronounce French in a
manner worthy of a human being. When Childerich III once
showed him the Frankish sword—Schnippedilderich had just
turned fourteen—he swirled the weapon around in his right
fist a time or two, made some sortie or other, found the thing
much too light and, in the end, termed it an old toothpick.
One would think that the father would be pleased with such
a strong offspring; and certainly that was the case. But the
prodigious rate of growth and the resplendent energy and
health of the boy already touched on nearly uncanny dimen-
sions. One must really ask oneself from where this male came,
out of what period, from which ancient folk, and whether a
creature of that kind is not entirely unsuited in body and
soul to our conditions today. Thinking in the bathroom deeply
and with alarm of this, the little—by this time multi-
bearded—father examined with astonishment his frail loins,
between which hung a limp and trifling belly. Yes, such an
ancient family is like a mud-volcano, and suddenly something
or other comes to the surface from the depths—prehistoric
sticks or giant bones; this metaphor really fits Childerich IV.
He was a raw-boned boy and a true roughneck. At sixteen,
during training, he knocked his boxing teacher's lower jaw
out of joint, and that without the slightest mean intention.
Just the same, Childerich IV was in no way significantly be-
nign, not even good-natured. In the father some premoni-
tions began to germinate.

Two daughters followed the son, tender and sweet, in-
deed, of an insect-like transparency, Petronia and Wulfhilde.
There were a few years in which these girls together weighed
not nearly as much as the brother alone. He took no notice

of them. Had he wanted to beat them up, no one was in a position to stop him, his father least of all.

Clara Cellé gave up after five years: this time the Bartenbruch side won. Childerich's dark paroxysms had considerably increased, and those frenzies, which the lady born Knötelbrech had earlier learned of, had become the rule. !n the fifth year Clara Cellé was already drawn around in a little wagon. The face was almost completely shrunken into itself. However, the little death's head smiled happily. Still before the end of the fifth year of her second marriage she expired. Schnippedilderich already stamped through his nursery on sturdy columns of legs, threw a filled water bottle at the English governess of his older stepsister, and glowed with vigor and health.

It was not yet a half year after Clara Cellé had passed away that the baboon's son, Childerich III's widowered father (Cynocephalus tristis), became lustful. He began, as he expressed it, "at last to eat roast rabbit"; that is what he termed the matter of his love. The man was well along in his sixties. The younger sons pummeled him time and again (for that, one hurried hither from England); even Gerhild and Richenza took part in the beatings. But just as little as in the grandfather's case did anyone hit here upon the simplest and safest procedure: that is, to give Childerich II a psychiatric ad hoc pretreatment and in this way cause him to be interned. The whole recipe they seized upon was composed of beatings. They were perhaps too rustic. And Childerich III, who, indeed because of his terrible childhood, was not lacking in craftiness, restrained himself and secretly for his part now and again broke the almost complete boycott of the family against the father. Already he was moved by dark plans. This time, too, one and all were forthwith disinherited, down to the lowest legal amount: "the roast rabbit" became the sole heiress. The situation was now in a bad way, for she was quite a beautiful person, twenty-three years old and much more wealthy still than Clara Cellé had been. After one had already buried the remains of Childerich II, about a year after his wedding to "the roast rabbit," Childerich III immediately began a lively relationship with his stepmother, all the sooner because of his younger brothers, one or two of whom were inclined to do the same. But of course they had a much harder time than Childerich approaching their dear mother, whom they had shortly before boycotted, while she had regularly received diverse praises and friendlinesses from the older brother.

It has to be clear, if one sees in this whole thing Childerich III's first real planned action, that it ended then with his taking his father's bereaved second spouse to wife and thus, as the husband of his stepmother, becoming his own father, and in addition that of his brothers, who would soon come to feel it. The accumulation of family positions onto one and the same head, the totalization of the family, as it were, had here the really essentially conscious beginning. For in the case of the marriage that had made Childerich III into his own grandfather—that to Clara Cellé—everything had happened unexpectedly, had been as though the point was set onto an arrow already in flight, something that represented, to be sure, a very considerable feat as well. And here, when Childerich III hit upon the arrangement of growing the "Favoris," the short side-whiskers of the father, in addition to the grandfather's twisted mustache, it was like the placing of the period at the end of a well-considered sentence.

Now concerning the "roast rabbit," who had made possible such an enrichment of the beard design, it must be said that it was a tasty one, and the Merovingian appetite then increased soon to the improbable. She came from Cairo and was, strictly speaking, of princely origins, really a princess; a collision of the purest porcelain-white skin with the deepest ebony-black hair, both deliciously arranged in a vessel of incredible gentleness, with a passivity and purposelessness that approached the enigmatic. Everything about her was round, and even her soul seemed to be of a number of curves that curved into themselves, from which there was nowhere to be obtained a direction, a resoluteness, a will. For all that, she clung with tenacity to one point, in an almost authoritative, even imperative way: she wanted to live in Franconia; she loved this, for her, completely strange landscape with an almost determined fervor, as though she had discovered in it an up to now unknown part of her own self. Especially, she always wanted to see again the area of Selb, very near the Oberpfalz region, the openings of hilly fields penetrated by stripes of woodland, the gently ascending paths, the commingling of leaf and needle trees. To this area Childerich III made trips by automobile with his young wife (he looked pitiful next to her), and finally he built for her a comfortable country house on a spot she especially loved. All half-heartedly, for she should have lived entirely in the south. But even for a couple of weeks in January or February she was hard to hold down in her parents' splendid house in Cairo, in the north of the city, where the gardens began, although Childerich III gladly sojourned with his parents-in-law; and they themselves knew only too well that danger threatened their child in every rougher climate. The daughter—she was the only child—could have lived to an old age, in spite of her weak lungs, if she had remained in the south, and Childerich III had already resolved, much to the joy of his parents-in-law, to establish himself in Cairo in a manner suitable to his station, (and, truly, some things would have happened differently then!). But his wife continually pressed toward

Franconia. What was for her physically a poison, was for her spiritually a nourishment; and she declined at home and blossomed—even though at the same time with a cold and a cough—in Franconia. During a trip to Germany she had become acquainted with the widowered Childerich II, and it is quite possible that she married the countryside rather than the old man. But with that was her foreshortened fate decided, and she went from the father to the son. Who knows what ancient imagination was working in the young woman and perhaps even in her parents. At any rate, here was one of those cases of a second homeland, where something that was already mirrored in childhood dreams is discovered somewhere in the outside world; something that may, then, be really irresistible. The very old family of the Egyptian princess even admits the somewhat audacious conjecture that she had had, perhaps, some crusading Frankish gentleman or other as an ancestor, back in the remoteness of time, and for this reason the old homeland was beheld by her, already at her first sojourn in Germany, as one seen long before. After she had lived as the spouse of Childerich III for four years, she died in the villa that had been built for her not far from Selb in Franconia and left two daughters, Anneliese and Geraldine, of whom the first had fully inherited the beauty of her mother, but who was, however, completely lacking in her aimless and stubborn gentleness—when she was grown, she was a being of milk and ebony, but of the sharpness and watchfulness of a falcon. The second, Geraldine, was also a very pretty child. Later, in blossoming, she exhibited in the most strange manner nearly that same insect-like fragility and transparency that was characteristic of Petronia and Wulfhilde, the daughters of Clara Cellé and sisters of Schnippedilderich. Yet her sharp shrill voice little suited her appearance, a voice that sounded like the filing of an overdimensional cicada. From the death of the Egyptian princess on, Childerich III's younger brothers Dankwart, Rollo (Rolf) and Eberhard began to call the master of the estate nothing but "Bluebeard," unfairly and from envy, for they had envied him the beautiful, wealthy third wife. Those brothers had become officers—with the exception of the youngest, Ekkehard, all abroad, namely in the Royal British Army—lived altogether in extravagant wastefulness, and faced with certainty a dependence on the ever richer Childerich III.

In the meantime, as has already been described, the Kulmbach judge, Bein, died, leaving behind with numerous children his as ever exceptionally beautiful wife, Barbara—daughter of the brewer, Paust, and his wife, born von Knötelbrech—with her well-preserved Paustian inheritance. Here, then, began the really best example of Childerich III's strategies, with which he acquired in one stroke not only a beautiful woman and her indeed considerable inheritance, but also two new family positions and with them (also here one could say according to plan) two additional whisker designs. Then, because with Barbara Bein he married his own stepdaughter, entirely without a doubt he had managed to become his own father-in-law and at the same time his own son-in-law, and that meant a further step in the direction of the totalization of the family and the one-man principle (something like: *la famille, c'est moi!*). Straightway he adapted the whiskers of the assumed positions. The thick sailor's curls (throat whiskers), that the brewer Paust wore throughout his life, found room enough for their development on the under chin and connected well with the father's "Favoris," or side whiskers. Childerich III's flabby little face now looked out like from a kind of fur collar and nearly acquired force thereby, which also well-suited the pop-eyes. But to signify how the acquired positions or family ranks clearly differed one from the other, he allowed the whiskers to grow not at all rankly together, but separated Favoris and sailor's curls with a kind of carefully shaven-out canal, in this case a (one might say) no man's land between the sovereign territory of the father and that of the father-in-law. It was more difficult, however, to reconcile the grandfather's twisted mustache with the judge's prodigious "Schnauzer," due to the lack of space on the upper lip; so Childerich let this Schnauzer hang over like a bush in the middle and annexed the twists to the right and left, also here separating the territories of grandfather and son-in-law with carefully shaven-out little canals. Now, the Judge had worn, besides the Schnauzer, a very thick so-called "imperial beard" on his chin, actually a kind of goat's beard, due to its size; with this also Childerich's chin was no longer naked, although it did represent the relatively most scantily occupied part of his face; indeed, there was even a limited possibility for further arrangements. All of these designs flourished luxuriantly, dense and as ever blue-black. The barber who often came to the house in the morning spent a good hour with them every time. In spite of that there was a certain vagueness in Childerich's multi-whiskered countenance that was with the best of care hardly to compensate for or avoid; and just that is what it was that later made the wife of Soflitsch the caretaker ill at ease, every time, in a subtly annoying way, as she found occasion to ascend aloft in the elevator with the friendly gentleman von Bartenbruch to the offices of Professor Horn.

As for the name "Bluebeard" that the ill-intending brothers stuck onto the master of the estate and head of the family, this characterization was at first directly justified only through the blue-black color of Childerich III's whisker ter rain and beard; all the same, however, it later received a semblance of its real significance through the development and

end of Childerich's marriage to Barbara Bein. That was
Childerich's longest marriage. It lasted seven years. The
beautiful woman bore her husband three girls: Widhalma,
Karla and Sonka, healthy children, who then later grew up
to have a thoroughly bourgeois prettiness, aloof from all such
monstrosities and peculiarities as those that existed in the
insect-like, glass-fragile beings, Petronia and Wulfhilde, the
daughters of Clara Cellé (whom, strangely enough,
Geraldine, the Egyptian's younger daughter, somehow took
after, at least in regard to the collective habitudes.) But here,
on Barbara's children from her second marriage, a healthy
and banal stratum seemed to have been laid over the pits of
Merovingian precipitousness, that closed them over so that
neither baboon nor monster from the time of the mass mi-
grations could emerge. Childerich was pleased with the three
girls (as far as it was possible with the psychical natures that
later emerged in them), but was at the same time pleased
that he had no sons of this sort. For such, it of course seemed
to him that Clara Cellé's progenitors were far more appro-
priate. Among Barbara's children from her second marriage,
Sonka developed in a certain way a peculiarity, inasmuch as
it often so appeared, if only at moments, as though she some-
how looked like the first husband of her mother, that is, like
Judge Bein. Still, it was hard to put a finger on, and not to
ascertain in any single expression. It just seemed so some-
times.

After the three girls had been born, Childerich III, who
had now acquired forty-six years, became enthusiastic about
hikes in the high mountains. Incessantly he felt pulled to
upper Bavaria. Barbara kept up with him. She did not want
to appear unyouthful or to become too fat. Childerich marched
rapidly up mountains. The wind tore at his whiskers.
Childerich climbed as rapidly as ever. Beautiful Barbara was

somewhat plump. Often she perspired heavily (one already suspects everything and one suspects correctly). Also she went, following her spouse on difficult paths, in the end on the path of her first husband (whose Schnauzer was worn by her second); that is, she never arose from a bout with pneumonia.

*

Born in 1896 in Vienna, Heimito von Doderer participated in World War I as a lieutenant in the Dragoons, and was captured by the Russians. He spent four years as a prisoner of war in Siberia, experiences that helped to form the substance of later novels such as Das Geheimmis des Richs and Roman No. 7. Upon his return to Vienna in 1920, he took up the study of history and psychology at the University, and took his Ph.D. in 1925.

In those early years he wrote poetry and short novels, and from 1928 to 1931 he contributed many articles on literary and historical topics to newspapers. In 1929 he met the great Austrian writer and painter Albert-Paris Gütersloh (after whose Sonne und Mond Sun & Moon Press is named) and in 1930 wrote the significant monograph on Gütersloh. This, the turning point of von Doderer's career, restimulated him to write fiction, and over the next several decades he produced such masterworks as Every Man a Murderer (published by Sun & Moon Press in 1994) and The Waterfalls of Slunj. In 1956 he completed The Demons (published by Sun & Moon Press in 1993), begun in 1931. Von Doderer was awarded the Great Austrian State Prize in 1958.

Marianne Hauser

from *Certain Mysteries Concerning Father*

MINUTES BEFORE CLOSING TIME my old man appears at
the gallery. Now that he is technically blind, he condescends
to see my show. With measured steps he enters on the arm
of his lady companion or seeing eye, his custom made tweeds
too loose on his aged frame, his shoulders stooped. But his
commanding presence remains undiminished. An air of power
and money shields him like an armor. Old power. Old money.
You can smell it miles away.

His eyes are hidden behind shades. Yet I could swear he
has them trained on me. Abruptly he's pulling free from his
fur-swathed companion's arm. Well then, shall we take a shot
at it, Mrs. Q? His voice is raspy. He turns his head this way
and that as if to appraise the market value of the gallery
space. Then he snaps his fingers twice. Shall we have a look
at my son's…er…objets d'art? But first we must greet the
artist. Where would he be hiding?

*

Hiding. I wish I could. Again he's got me by the balls, the
old bastard. Now that he sees no more than an occasional
flash of light, he'll have a look at what he maliciously refers
to as his son's objets d'art. Mind you, not objets trouvés.
Not even junk. That would lend distinction as cult art to my

small sculptures. And the la-di-da lilt he affects as he pronounces the French…It's a studied provocation for which I ought to be prepared and never am. Each time I'm stung anew. Each time he wins.

*

And yet…The mere fact that he took the trouble to come to the opening…I'm grateful, damn it. I'm moved. For years I've mailed him an invitation. He never responded. Still, I continued the charade—why? Surely not because I'm after his money. Mother has left me plenty. No, those announcements I sent him (with a rather groveling note attached) had become a ritual, as our whole relationship is in fact ritualistic, managed from a safe distance. When he needs to get in touch, he will dictate a letter to his secretary. "Dear son" etcetera. A typed communication, with "Father" penned in thick strokes across the "sincerely yours." Not a hint of affection. Since mother's death the formality has somewhat lessened. But there's no warmth. None.

You may rightly ask why I don't just ignore the bastard. But ah! that is impossible. Nobody can ignore him, least of all I. He is unique, a genius not only in corporate business deals, but as a collector of ancient armor. The subterranean armory in our old family house glares, rattles and threatens with steely warriors who in my childhood scared me half to death. What former friend suggested I was working with metal to build my own miniature armory?

No matter. Father has come to my opening. His acknowledgment that I exist at all as an artist, albeit one without name or fame, flatters the pants off me. You'd be amazed how low a character like me can sink. A few hasty swigs from the flask, and I rush forth to kiss his ass.

Thank you for coming, father!

*

Gummed eyes searching the shadow walls of my loft. Jittery
hand searching blindly for the bottle. And all at once I real-
ize that I'm still in the clothes I wore at the gallery. Must
have passed out on my bed, too far gone to shed the formal
suit. Was it for mother's funeral that I last wore it?

The coat sits on my chest like an armor; and struggling
out of it, I hear the crash or clash not of steel but of glass as
the bottle topples and breaks on the floor. There goes the
rest of the vodka. And today is the day of the lord and every
liquor store in the city is closed and shuttered.

I morosely stare at the bottle shards in a smell of spilled
booze—the nostalgic smell of old saloons, I think, trying to
stop the hangover shakes as I set about to clean up the mess.

*

So what keeps him from running downstairs to the nearest
saloon? you'll ask. But I don't dare to, not since last night
after the cursed opening when I got so smashed at the neigh-
borhood bar I lost all judgment; buying round after round
for the cheering gang; proclaiming a wizened wino my buddy
for life; and finally, with drunk aplomb, smacking a wad of
large bills on the bar top: Help yourself, gentlemen! (The
saloon did not welcome ladies.)

From here on memory turns mute, up to the sudden night-
mare when I came to in a patrol car, squeezed in between a
pair of burly cops. Fortunately I am white. And I had my
credentials on me. Not that my cheap downtown address
would have cleared me of I still have no idea what crime. It
was my almighty father who came to my rescue by proxy.
When the cops had laboriously spelled out his residence from
an engraved card in my depleted wallet, they all but saluted.

They apologized profusely, and blamed a crackdealer on pa-
role for giving them the bum steer. They drove me home,
helped me up the stairs and kissed me good night. The latter
may be read symbolically.

*

Thank god they didn't contact my old man! I'd rather not
imagine the scene, had he got wind of my drunkenly squan-
dering the sacred dollar I hadn't earned. Such shameless dis-
posal of inherited wealth among the rabble would surely con-
stitute the ultimate crime, one he neither could nor would
allow himself to forgive, I ponder as I flop down again on the
bed; the telephone close at hand while I watch the first snow
of the season drive past the windows.

*

But this is becoming a winter habit, my slumping down on
the bed, waiting—for what? A phone call from Mrs. Q? *Your
daddy passed painlessly in his slumber.* Or a call from the great
man himself? *Come over right away, my son. I am old and I need
your love.*

The last scenario seems the most remote. I try in vain to
picture it. Reality cuts me short. The tape whirs back to the
gallery and freezes on father's eyes, then unrolls in slow motion.

His eyes behind smoked window glass are trained on me,
converging into a gun barrel. I'd like to have a closer look,
Mrs. Q. Why don't you show me one of his things.

This time around it's things. She happens to pick my lat-
est, a copper assemblage of seven triangles; spherical arcs
which are mounted on a cut of black rock. What will be the
verdict? I wait.

His shades reflect a toy-sized gallery as he motions toward the piece she is lifting up for him to touch. But his hands stay locked behind his back.

I manage to open my mouth. She is showing you my favorite work, father. I finished it this past summer. On Clone Island.

Clone Island, North Carolina? Off the coast of the Outer Banks? Good fishing and hunting.

His hands have flown up from behind him and into the light. Finely shaped, sensitive hands. Who'd guess they would beat up on a five year old for sobbing over a dead moose. The boy knee high in dry leaves and needles, bawling his lungs out: you killed him! You shot him dead! And the hands tearing the boy's leather belt off and administering twelve strokes, precisely and fiercely, on the naked buttocks.

*

But at the gallery I didn't think of that episode in the northern woods, even though it is a reoccurring nightmare as if he had whipped me routinely when he never laid a hand on me again. At the gallery my attention was caught up in the remarkable agility of his fingers as they sketched an invisible map into midair. Fish shaped Roanoke Island…the skinny branch of Hatteras stretching south between sound and sea…

…and here, my boy…(voice rising sharply, thumb plunging into the sea)…here you have your Clone. Correct?

Correct, father.

Indeed, he had with fair accuracy placed an obscure island and outlined a region I doubt he'd bother to visit. Our sort pass their summers down-east.

Or has he visited the island? Did he crouch behind a dune, watching me through a tremulant curtain of sea oats? Don't rule out anything with him. The man is a plethora of surprises.

*

An odd choice to be spending your summers—since you don't fish. Or shoot!

I'd be violating the law if I did. Clone is a wildlife refuge.

I can't help grinning while he snaps at me that the entire nation would be a wildlife refuge if I and my muddle-headed comrades were running the show.

What comrades? The birds and the beasts? But I'd best shut up. Maybe it was a mistake to tell him about my yearly escape to Clone. Down there where sand and sea and sky melt into undefinable space in the heat, I'm out from under his shadow and free to assemble my dreams. Does he sense it, however vaguely?

I think he does, for now he starts to downgrade my poor little island. No decent accommodations. Black, biting flies and nasty climate. And those unexpected, savage storms that whip the sea into mountainous waves and hurl the ships landward to smash on the beaches!

For five long centuries the narrow passage south around the shoals has been the dread of every sailor, my old man states sonorously. *A Graveyard of the Atlantic.* Isn't that what they call your region?

*

His voice echoed through the gallery—another graveyard. It was past closing time. The last stragglers had left. My dealer stood at an awed distance, hoping against hope she'd make a sale.

Spanish galleons, packed with gold from Mexico, wrecked on their passage home...wrecks scattered far and wide across the sand...

He paused, lost in the sixteenth century. Then he murmured absently: A boy on a treasure hunt.

He was that boy. His eyes behind the shades were looking inward. He was talking to himself and I was quick to pick up on cue, oh yes, the fury of the storms, they still blow in some treasures, when the worst is over I rush from my cabin and comb the beaches, I comb through huge tangles of seaweed and tar-stiffened rope, I crawl inside barnacled hulls to find my kind of treasure, the kind of copper I need for my assemblages, my work, father.

My work. At last he reaches out and touches it. And as his fingertips begin to explore, carefully stroking each surface, curve, edge and angle, I ask myself in a surge of affection or sadness: would he make a better father if he were born blind?

*

My ears still ring with the sudden click of his fingernails against thin metal. It's copper all right, he said. And lowering his head, he asked in the confidential tone of the versed collector to name him a price.

He was about to buy me! To own me! I was too moved to speak. I could only gape like an idiot while he repeated his question in the same secretive tone.

The price? Why, nothing! For you it's nothing, father! burst out. Please do accept it as a gift. (Would joyfully throw in the rest of the show. Would love to throw my arms around him if I dared. The man does have a heart!)

Come again? He bent an ear. A gift, you said? That's mighty generous, but you misheard. I've no intention to acquire or otherwise add to the excessive clutter of my home, unless (one eye seeming to wink at me through the dark lens) unless it so happens I chance across a rare find for my collection. In which case I'd be adding nothing new, of course, but something extremely ancient.

He chuckled and I felt the old hate rise from my guts though I knew at once that under no circumstances must I give him the satisfaction to notice. Calm down. Act cool, I warned myself.

Too late, I'd lost control.

No need to explain, sir. I never presumed you'd waste your oh so precious money on my objets d'art. And adding that he'd obviously just been enjoying a joke at my expense, I had, to mix two relevant metaphors, signed my own death warrant at the flip of a coin.

A joke! Won't you ever grow up? The rejected gift was back in Mrs. Q's plump hands. I'd better get it into my thick skull that money was indeed a precious commodity. His asking for the price did by no means imply that he wished to buy and collect me as my mother had, the poor dear. No! He was simply curious how a present downward trend in the art market reflected in my sales figures.

I'm still curious—well? How much? Or am I supposed to contact your dealer?

My dealer who charges me for the gallery space! I felt like laughing in his face. But I couldn't even force a sneer or a snub. I could only reply that my stuff, if it sold at all, sold cheap regardless of the ups and downs of a market which was a deep dark mystery to me in any case.

Bully for you, my boy. Few artists can afford such deep dark mysteries. I trust you can.

And with that ominous putdown or caveat my case was dismissed. He donned his overcoat, pulled the collar up to his nose, and on the arm of Mrs. Q strode off into the deepfreeze night to his hearse. At least that's how I saw his big black car at this black moment.

Let's get cracking. I need my sleep. Can we give you a lift?

Thank you, sir, but no. I'll walk.

And so we split.

*

Marianne Hauser was born and raised in Strasbourg, Alsace-Lorraine, a frontier province west of the Rhine, and a proverbial political football between Germany and France. The first World War started when she was barely 4. Still, its impact has left a lasting mark and translated into much of her writing.

She spent her final high school year in Berlin and briefly attended its University as the Fascists were coming to power. She left in time, while the Nazis were burning the Reichstag, and decided to stay in Paris. There, fluent in French and German, she earned her living at 22, writing interviews, fashion reports and journalistic pieces in both languages.

Through an assignment from the Swiss paper, Basler National Zeitung, *Hauser began a regular column on her impressions of Egypt, India, Malaya, Cambodia, Siam, Manchuria and Japan, and other places to which she traveled. During her prolonged stay in China, she started her first serious novel,* Shadow Play in India (Indisches Gaukelspiel, *1937).*

That novel was completed in Hawaii. And boarding a Japanese freighter at Honolulu, she sailed to San Francisco. She remembers her initial reaction to America as one of utter confusion, as a place more strange, perhaps, than any of the other places she had visited.

After a vacation in Switzerland and France, however, she returned to the United States to report for the Basle paper. Renting a small furnished room in uptown New York, she soon cut her ties to Europe, and resolved to write only in English. At this time she began her first American novel, Dark Dominion *(1947).*

In the early 1940s she married the noted pianist Frederick Kirchberger, and moved with him to various locations in North Carolina, Florida, and Kirksville, Missouri. A new novel, The Choir Invisible *(1958), was located in a small Missouri town, not unlike Kirksville.*

In 1963 she published her acclaimed novel, Prince Ishmael, *which Sun & Moon reissued into its Classics series in 1989. A collection of stories,* A Lesson in Music, *appeared in 1964. Another novel,* The Talking Room, *was published in 1976. In 1986 Sun & Moon published her novel,* Memoirs of the Late Mr. Ashley: An American Comedy, *which brought her again to international attention; Gore Vidal described the book as a "work of genius—witty, sad, in the American grain."* Me & My Mom, *based on an idea that came to her years ago in Missouri, was published by Sun & Moon in 1993.*

André du Bouchet

To the Lees

AND

Heat Face

Translated from French by David Mus

To the Lees

Today's wine overcomes me
already halfway through

midst red whirled
high noon

with a road at the bottom
whose metal belonging
to me wheels in vain

the whole earthen
crock keels over
caves in

comes to a stone house

stepped on

and I stop
each time sun strikes
pitted stones blind.

Heat Face

Halting,
           until air itself, lighting up, find me
out here, I stumble on this heat rising flush with
stones' brow.

           Before sky, drying, dry, will have
come into its own.

Akin to the air this clear air cleaves, in murky
depths of heat.

*

*Born in 1924, André du Bouchet traveled to the United States at
the age of seventeen, where he remained for seven years, completing
his B.A. degree at Amherst College and M.A. at Harvard, where
he was Teaching Fellow in English and Comparative Literature.
He has written a meditation on the work of Alberto Giacometti
and numerous essays on poetry and painting, as well as publishing
several books of poetry. Among his contributions to poetry are* dans
la chaleur vacante, ou le soleil, qui n'est pas tourné vers nous,
ici en deux, *and, most recently,* axiales. *Sun & Moon Press will
be publishing the major books of du Bouchet over the next few years.*

Luigi Ballerini

"III"

from *Track and Road Racing*

for Fausto Coppi, in memoriam

what's nice about an amphidrome is that
even stones do not leave it unturned and odorless
laws rub it in the folds of its luminous body,
in the downcast angles of an art that decrees thirst,
the irascible density of pursuit, of becoming
glove and breach and, through flattery,
a naked prosthesis, one that stared at, curls up
in the palm and portions out the cycle of travesties.
Impure law and yet a law that swims at last
and sets foot on shore, a sponge that shines,
that breaks through not unworthy, not without
arcane and indemnifiable slope.
Precarious signs used for disbanding
those who remain in the saddle or rejoice
at the neatness of the incision, of the whistle,
for linking repose to the ruminant notion of the lead.
A desperate harbor wanders in the fog
of disdain, an auto-da-fe taking hold
of your temples, to get them out of the den,
to reveal their price, the imprint, the cadence
of an adjacent race.

*

*Born in Milan in 1940, Ballerini was the Director of the program
in Italian Studies of New York University from 1975-1990. For
the last several years, he has been Chair of the Italian Department
of the University of California, Los Angeles.*

*Ballerini has translated numerous American writers into Ital-
ian, including works by William Carlos Williams, Henry James,
and Gertrude Stein. His poetry, essays, and translations have ap-
peared in periodicals such as* New Directions Annual, il verri,
Almanacco dello Specchio, TamTam, *and* Opera Aperta. *He
edited an anthology of contemporary Italian poetry titled* The
Waters of Casablanca *for a special issue of* Chelsea *magazine in
1979 and a larger volume,* Shearsmen of Sorts: Italian Poetry
1975–1993, *as a supplement to* A Journal of Italian Studies *in
1992. With Paolo Balera and Paul Vangelisti, he is currently
working on an anthology of Italian poetry for Sun & Moon Press.*

Among his several volumes of poetry are eccetera. E *(1972),*
La piramide capovolta *(1975),* The Book of the Last of the
Mohegans *(1975),* Logical Space *(1975, with James Reineking),*
Che figurato muore *(1988),* La torre dei filosofi *(1989),* The
Coaxings of Our End *(1991), and* Che oror l'orient *(1991).
With Paul Vangelisti he edits a series of poetry books, Blue Guitar
Books, as part of Sun & Moon Press's Classics Series.*

Raymond Queneau

from *Children of Claye*

Translated from French by Madeleine Velguth

BOOK ONE

I

"Just think, monsieur," she said, "just think, its area is almost ten centimeters. Not as impressive as a tongue, but still more important than in Bourges, I think."

After Ceyreste, came the forest.

"People used to hold lilies in their hands, but the custom's died out. Although there still are lilies."

They were gradually making their way to Cuges, wheels grinding the dust.

"Madame Gramigni stayed at the shop," said Gramigni. "I'm going up for myself. When it's for yourself, you better go up yourself, right?"

"Of course."

In Cuges everybody gets off, then climbs toward the chapel half-way up the hill, with the very old village right at the top, deserted: in ten centuries and a bit it's flattened out. They get there for vespers and the panegyric and the adoration of the Blessed Sacrament and the veneration of the relic. Gramigni invokes Saint Anthony of Padua.

If you seek miracles
in the sole name of Saint Anthony
death error calamities
demons and leprosy flee
the sick are healed
the sea obeys
chains are loosed
health returns.

"I'll give you five francs, a hundred sous, right here five francs of my money that I earned with my fruit and my vegetables, Saint Anthony of Padua, if this year the Paris people come back as usual, with their cars and their girls and their friends, 'specially with their girls, 'specially with the tall blonde, and that they come back to my place to buy my fruits and olives to have with the aperitif they have at my neighbor Bossu's cafe. Let them come back, let them come back, please great Saint Anthony. Their maid is next to me, maybe she's praying they won't come back. Great Saint Anthony, make my prayer stronger than hers. If she's asking for that, it's because her intentions are bad. But I don't have bad intentions. It's not even because of what I make on the fruit they buy from me that I want so much for them to come. It's like this: I want you to make them come back on account of it's a pleasure to see them 'cause they're rich and beautiful, the girls naturally. And I'm not saying that either 'cause of the girls, since I'm married, you know that great Saint Anthony, since I'm married and even if my wife isn't very nice to me."

And he added like a true Cugian:

"Dear God, pray to Saint Anthony of Padua for me."

And he finished:

"And besides, great Saint Anthony, I know you can't forget a fellow Paduan. We're from the same city, you and me; I'm sure that for you too that counts for something. Mussolini

had my two brothers killed; I crossed the border to sell veg-
etables, fruit and groceries, married to a fat bag from across
the Loire River that I went and picked up, I sure wish I hadn't,
in a real sewer, and my brothers died in Regina Coeli or in
San Stefano, I'm not sure which. That's the life God gave
me, great Saint Anthony, you see, it would put a little butter
on my pasta if you'd let a little sunshine into my heart, by
making the people I'm talking to you about come back, their
cars and their friends, and their girls too of course."

And now all he can do is wait for the results. Gramigni
takes the same ramshackle bus back to La Ciotat.

"You've got to be a real sucker," he hears as soon as he
gets home, "you've got to be missing some marbles to be-
lieve in stuff like that."

He puts his hat on a little shelf under the cash register.

"Did you at least see the relic?"

"No."

"Why bother going? So you didn't even look at the tibia?"

"It's not a tibia: it's a piece of the saint's skull."

"You damn fool."

He doesn't answer.

"Your brothers would be ashamed of you."

"You leave my brothers out of this."

"They didn't suck up to priests like you, they were real
men."

He smacks her across the mouth and kicks her butt out
the door.

A housewife comes in. She wants coarse salt, well-rip-
ened bananas, a can of Portuguese sardines, a box of sulfur-
ized matches and that's all for today. Right, she was going to
forget the tomatoes.

He wasn't all that religious, his childhood faith had, at

least apparently, quite worn off, and besides, he'd heard his
brothers explain to him often enough what it was all about.
But he feared that the flow of months wouldn't bring back
the girl he thought was so beautiful. The fruits and veg-
etables each came in their season and after their kind, but
the luck—he believed in it—of life might make her not re-
turn. So he went up to Cuges with his fruitseller's faith and,
one day in July, the car came and parked in front of his neigh-
bor Bossu's cafe.

Bossu's falling all over himself in welcome. Once again
there's something to read, for these were customers who
bought newspapers and magazines. They'd pick up their sup-
ply at Mlle. Chabrat's stationery shop and, after their drinks,
leave them behind. In the evening when the last belote play-
ers had gone, when the chairs were sleeping belly-up on the
tables, by the light of the single small lamp, Bossu would
treat himself and devour printed matter and rotogravure until
two in the morning. He learned the strangest things, his
brain buzzed with the complication and variety of it all. He'd
go to sleep his head in a whirl. The next morning, nothing
was left. He remained as dumb, dull and doltish as before.

Thus these ladies and gentlemen installed themselves as
was customary facing the port pleased and happy; ice and
siphon were surrounded by glasses sparkling with the mul-
tiple aperitif colors; a little fishing boat went round in circles;
a low sun, cool shade, and these ladies and gentlemen thought
that this was the life.

It was a splendid time not only because of exceptional
atmospheric conditions causing fine weather undreamed of
by former generations, but also because money was easy to
come by: all you had to do was put your hand in your pocket
to find lettuce, even if you'd imagined there was nothing there.
This singular and marvelous phenomenon naturally affected

only a certain class of the population, precisely that to which belonged the visitors so awaited by Gramigni and Bossu.

It was a splendid time not only because peace reigned disturbingly from Spain to China, but as well because money was liquid, fluid, volatile even, thus combining the very different qualities of mercury and ammonia.

It was a splendid time when money shone in the sun like crushed glass, watering in abundance this beautiful old dry Provence, where the weather's good all four seasons of the year, where harmony resounds from the violet indigo blue sky to the green, yellow, orangey, red earth.

II

She was near-sighted to the point of blindness but not at all deaf, and misshapen to the point of infirmity but not at all ugly. When her employers weren't living there, ten months of the year, during the long evenings of wind and rain, in the absence of Baron Hachamoth and his wife, their daughters, relatives and friends, this maid played the violin.

III

Damp and naked, Master Chambernac, principal of the high school in Mourmèche, heard a knock at the door of his bathroom where he was giving himself his second good scrubbing of the day, practicing ablutions in considerable number because of the intense sebaceousness of his dermis, an oleaginousness which he attributed to the excessive concentration of his cervical humors, nonvolatile but fixed and pearlifying absolutely everywhere on the surface of his body as a result of research and special studies which were difficult, singular and rare.

Damp and naked, Master Chambernac, principal of the high school in Mourmèche, was, then, stepping out of one of his daily baths, when he perceived through the drops of soapy water that were burbling in his ears, a knock.

"Don't come in," he yelled not sure that he hadn't closed his door.

"Would you be so kind as to repeat the last two words of the sentence you've just uttered?" said the knocker on the other side (he'll soon be on this one).

"What?"

"I was asking you to repeat."

"Who are you, dammit? the plumber?"

"No."

"Then leave me alone."

"What's that? I can't hear you very well."

"I'm telling you not to come in."

"'Come in', you *did* say: 'come in'?"

And in he came.

Flowing out the little hole at the bottom, the gray water, before disappearing, left on the sides of the tub a thin layer of mud.

The newcomer closed the door behind him and sized up his man, damp and naked, with a look uncontaminated by any subjective valuation, neither romantically disgusted by the nudity of a paunchy, flabby sexagenarian, nor homosexually appreciative of a novel anatomy.

"Well," went the stranger amiably, "your tummy certainly doesn't have any folds."

The principal, meanwhile, was slipping into the mazes of fright and the labyrinths of indignation. One was beginning slowly to relax his visceral activity, the other to reduce his pulmonary capacity.

"I," continued the stranger less amiably, "cannot understand that one tells people to come into his bathroom when one is naked as a jaybird."

"Quack?" stutstammered Chambernac.

"Well, it's simple," went the other, furious, "you tell me to come in and you're totally naked. Must be a pervert. I find that kind of morals completely revolting."

His victim was wiping his face, now humid not from healthy bathwater but from the sweat of dread.

"Do you think I enjoy looking at your pudenda? Certainly not! I prefer not to look."

And he turned his back; but in the mirror attached to the door, he was able to keep an eye on the behavior of his guinea-pig: for it was the first time he was indulging in this sport and he was not yet too sure of his technique.

The principal, taking advantage of this discretion, was starting to put his clothes back on; so he slips on his undershirt, he slips on his shirt, he slips on his shorts, what won't he slip on? his pants: they're in the next room. He explains the matter to the invader.

"All right, let's go next door."

He opens the door and shows the way.

"All the same," went the stranger dreamily, "what Mourmèchian father would ever think that the high school principal indulges in nudistic displays in front of—I stress: in front of men."

Suddenly abandoning his impressive calm, he started to strut back and forth shaking a handkerchief and uttering interjections considered faggy by people who know such things only through caricaturists and cabaret singers. The poorincipal, sitting on his bed, watched in dismay.

"Well," went his persecutor, "have you nothing to say?"

"Get out!" caterwauled the persecutee.

"Come in, get out, that's all you know how to say."

"But I never told you to come in! You're the one who simply came in. And besides, how on earth did you get into my apartment? I'm going to call the police."

"I dare you."

"We'll see."

"When you told me to come in, you probably thought it was one of your students."

"Dastardly slander," exclaimed the principal. "I'm going to put on my pants."

"That won't restore your worthiness."

"Ah, ah, ah, ah, do you think that worthiness is lost so easily?"

"I don't think it, I know it."

Chambernac puts the top of his body into a jacket, the bottom into a pair of pants.

"Now that I'm properly dressed, you will do me the favor of clearing out."

The other bats not an eye.

"Consider yourself fortunate that I'm not calling the police to cure you of playing jokes of more than doubtful taste."

"Oho, you've changed your mind from just now. Just now, you wanted to call the police. I see you've thought about it. That's wise. Now we can get down to serious talk."

"It would have been nice if you'd gotten to that a bit sooner."

"So let's sum up what's happened: one: I come in; two: you do dirty things."

"Oh!"

"And three, you owe me reparation."

The intrudee breathed easier. So that was all: with a bit of money he'd see the farce play out. The intruder read his mind:

"Really, what do you expect me to do with a forty-sou piece? Forty sous!"

Scornfully he spat (for real) on the carpet.

"I," he went, "am not asking for charity. I," he went, "don't live on alms. I," he went, "don't beg. I," he went, "am not a neurotic. What I want is work."

"Work?" repeated the principal, "you're saying: work?"

"I said: work, and I want work. Do you understand me, you nasty sex maniac?"

"And what can you do?" groaned the victim.

"It's not a question of what I can do, but of what I want to do."

"And what do you want to do?" roared the victim.

"I want to be a teacher."

"Rrrrrrraaaaaahhhhhh," roared the victim.

"Pull yourself together."

"A physical education teacher?" jeered the victim who found sufficient strength to emit several hiccups tinged with somber joy.

"Don't make fun of me."

"So, just like that, you want to be a teacher?"

"Yes, it's a vocation. The only thing I don't have are degrees. But what's so important about degrees?"

"Yes. What's so important about degrees," repeated Chambernac, his voice muddy.

"I'm not spiteful, I'll take whatever class you think best."

"God, what a mess, there *is* the senior humanities class. Bouvard just died unexpectedly."

"I like humanities," said Purpulan.

"God, what a mess, what trouble this is going to make for me."

"Less than if you didn't want me."

IV

One day while going to Soilac
The principal de Chambernac
Saw a policeman on the train
Whose boots gave his soul quite a turn
He bode his time and waited till
The train was deep in a tunnel
To the policeman
Then spoke his passion
His reputation would be marred
Had not the merciful trooper
Who bore the glorious name Magloire
Said to the principal: «Now sir
I know the vices of mankind
I'm understanding as you see
But all that you must leave behind
—The first time it's happened to me!
—Well let it be the last, you hear
Or you'll get my boot in the rear.»
Journey over, filled with rue
Chambernac had realized
At his age 'twasn't the thing to do
This experience quite sufficed.

V

When Purpulan had arrived in Mourmèche, he certainly
didn't know this detail of the private secret past life of the
principal. For a long time he'd hesitated. On whom would he
try out the precepts that, in the course of lessons, which had
moreover cost him a pretty penny, had been taught him by a

dwarf, an expert in the art of parasitism who had even created an entirely new technique in this area? He had naturally eliminated the poor, all the poor, whose kind hearts he felt it would be too easy to exploit: and it was not to the kind heart that, according to his master, one should address oneself, but to fear, funk and superstition. Though he was neither dwarf, nor bearded, Purpulan nevertheless possessed certain qualities of this nature which permitted him to hope for some success in this branch of so vilized contemporary human activity.

He was handsome, and he had fetid breath, rather more like hydrogen sulfide than sulfur, thus realizing in concrete fashion the terrifying and murky image of a fallen angel.

VI

"I'm going to go buy olives at Gramigni's," said Daniel without moving.

"You can take the car if you're tired," said Naomi.

"Who's Gramigni?" asked Pouldu.

"The grocer next door," said Agnes.

"His olives are fantastic," said Daniel. "I've never tasted better. Gramigni makes them himself; he's got his own recipe."

"You always manage to ferret out the good places," said Pouldu.

"Bah," said Daniel.

He gets up.

Gramigni proudly shows him his merchandise. He fishes for the little green drupes. He's happy. It's happened: the girls have come back. He owes Saint Anthony one hundred sous.

They're purebreds; he's never seen anything like them
from Padua to Marseille, including his bitch of a wife. They're
two sisters who are really beautiful, really tall, really curvy,
and what really bowled Gramigni over, so clean they're daz-
zling, and besides also really rich, really luxurious and re-
ally muscled, like their car. And then finally really athletic,
really noble and really polite. Young Bossu says if he wanted
to he'd make it with them and Lardi says all those people,
the summer people, are potbellied, bleary-eyed layabouts. All
the same, they don't have fleas, or lice, or bedbugs, or crab
lice; you can't imagine these young ladies with fleas, lice,
bedbugs or crab lice; it's true they'd catch some if they let
the Bossu boy mount them. Gramigni sighs. Beauty moves
Gramigni.

They live in a brand new villa beyond the Golf Hotel:
near Saint-Jean. The Claye family used to own a respectable
house built in the days of Alphonse Karr. Then Baron
Hachamoth had this one built in the modern style of Paris.
All the Ciotat dwellers went to see it, except Gramigni, both
because of his business which takes all of a man's time and
also because of something like timidity. But young Bossu told
him what it's like; he worked on it; he's the one who put in
the electricity, with his boss and a another guy who helped
him a little. Get this, there's glass on all sides and everything's
painted white. Next to each bedroom, there's a bathroom
(and to think they spend all their time in the ocean) and per-
sonal toilets (that's where you can see luxury turn to vice).
All the furniture is square and made of strange materials;
there are mirror tables, cork armchairs and rope chairs: lots
of people didn't want to believe young Bossu when he said
that, and when he added that there are paintings you can
hang any side up, people thought his frequent contact with
high society was discombobulating his brain.

Gramigni has a hard time picturing all these things; it kind of chokes him up; there's no doubt about it, beauty really moves him. Here they are right now, Agnes and Naomi passing, even more marvelous than last year. They're going to talk to the captain of their boat. Gramigni admires the way they walk and what gorgeous figures they have. He's interrupted by the sudden contact of his occiput with a can of peas, thrown with dexterity by Mme Gramigni.

"You dirty bum, there you are jerking off again watching those tarts. That's what you think about, poor moron, instead of paying attention to your wife and children."

They haven't got any children but it was a formula of her mother's; all she'd ever had were miscarriages, because of her illnesses.

Gramigni turned around and charged at the bitch. Before he could reach her, she sent the jar of olives flying; it broke and the olives rolled wildly under the crates.

"See what I'm doing to your special olives, you mucky butt cream, you. Your olives that you make 'specially for those sluts, see what I'm doing to them."

Gramigni, pursuing his course, slipped on some olives as if they were casters and cartwheeled to the floor. Taking advantage of this, his spouse dumped a whole assortment of canned goods on him. Her triumph didn't last long; the Paduan trapped her near the cookies and flattened her with two strong punches in the mug. Then he started to stomp on her in a businesslike way.

She vociferated with indignation.

Meanwhile, kids collected to see the wop clobber his wife. Various people, more or less idle, joined the group. It was quite a spectacle. The circle thickened. Scallywags stole wares. Finally, generous souls intervened; they pulled Mme Gramigni out from under Gramigni's feet. She was in no mood for ribbing. She was foaming at the mouth. He, sweat-ing.

"It was the grocer, putting his wife in her place," said Bossu. "She pissed, if you'll pardon the expression, in his special ol-ives."

"The lout," said Daniel.

One by one, he'd eaten them all up.

VII

Saint Anthony they're here I saw them
Saint Anthony Saint Anthony so you're as powerful as that
It's true they come back every year
All the same you never know: one year
                                  suddenly
                                  it can change
Saint Anthony I owe you one hundred sous
You can count on it
One day I'll go up to Cuges just to give them to you
Saint Anthony you're the Saint of my childhood
I learned to pray to you when I was little
You're right not to drop me
You can see that I'm always faithful to you
and yet I know very well that religion is the opium of the people
and that priests and money are like bees and honey
and seems it's the capitalists that invented God
But you great Saint Anthony of Padua nobody invented you
On the contrary you invented lost and found
and you go to the moon to look there for everything people lost
and you put each thing back in its place
and each year the pretty girls in their house
I thank you great Saint of my Home Town

If I forget that I owe you one hundred sous
Make me think about it again toward the end of the week
But I'd really be surprised if I forgot
Amen.

VIII

When Purpulan arrived unknown in Mourmèche, unknown
to Mourmèche and not knowing Mourmèche, he had no rea-
son to choose one person rather than another. Why the sub-
prefect rather than the jailer, the bailiff rather than the no-
tary, the banker rather than curator of the museum of pale-
ontology; or else, the grocer rather than the butcher, the
mason than the mechanic; or why a person of independent
means; or why a cabinetmaker? The fact that he was making
his career debut left the matter all the more open.

In the evening, he wandered about Mourmèche, looking
at the lighted windows, unable to decide on this or that fam-
ily. Some appeared to be so solid, calm and peaceful that he
would only have met with failure had he wanted to insinuate
himself into them; others seemed to reveal an anxious un-
certainty that would be favorable to his plans: but there again,
how should he choose? None of them, after all, appeared to
offer an appreciable probability of success. Then the lights
went out and he fell back into the night.

In this provincial obscurity he eventually discovered a
brothel. Suddenly he knew that the first respectable man over
fifty years of age to come out would be his man. A few mo-
ments later, Chambernac slipped out. All that Purpulan had
to do was follow him to the high school where he lived.

IX

"What trouble this is going to make for me."

"Less than if you didn't want me."

"That needs thinking about."

"It's all thought about. Either you put me in the class-room or I'll put you in jail."

"You think, perhaps, that my worthiness wouldn't stand up to the testimony of a suspicious character like you? What are you, after all: a thief caught in the act."

Purpulan smiled:

"How dense you are."

Then he began to moan and draw loud gasping breaths:

"No…don't do that…no…I didn't think that was what you wanted me to do…leave me alone…let me go…it's awful…to fall into the hands of such a dirty bastard…"

"For Chrissakes," muttered Chambernac, "will you be quiet."

"Do I start teaching tomorrow?"

"Tomorrow."

"Now tell me, don't you think that my hair is a little long and dirty, that I need a shave, that my shirt is hardly clean and it's the only one I've got, that my shoes are terribly worn, that my nails are dirty and need a manicure—I know there aren't any manicurists in Mourmèche, but a woman I know at the brothel does nails—to cut a long story short, boss, that I need to look more dignified, and my wallet's empty."

"I'll be right back."

He had just gotten a nasty idea. Before Purpulan could collect his thoughts, Chambernac had rushed into the next room and was already hurrying back with five one hundred-franc bills in his hand, bills whose numbers the crafty devil had recorded in a notebook, his private little notebook, the one where he jotted down memorable dates, like the day he'd met the policeman on the train and the one, rather recent since it was the last entry, on which he had, for the first time, gone to the brothel of Mourmèche.

Purpulan took them; Chambernac was triumphant. Once his adversary had gone, all he'd have to do was report the theft and give the numbers of the bills. What scandal would there be then? None at all.

Chambernac felt sorry for such ineptness.

"Go deck yourself out now," he said cordially. "Your class is at eight tomorrow morning. We'll see then what you can do."

"No," went Purpulan, "no, that's not how things are going to be," went Purpulan, suddenly inspired by the fiendish powers fermenting within him, "no, take back your twenty-five *louis*", he went softly, "I've changed my mind, I'll stay for dinner and spend the night here. I can't leave without getting to know you better."

Stunned by such inhuman insight, Chambernac bowed before the singular spirit who had taken up residence in his house for dark reasons of his own.

x

Mme. de Chambernac was quivering with impatience to see the face, and the body, of the new humanities teacher. The current one, the deceased rather, was bearded and Kantian. Would the new one be Bergsonian and clean-shaven? Mme. de Chambernac remembered her ardor when, at eighteen, she sat on the benches of the College de France afire with the passion of creative evolution.

The newcomer was in fact clean-shaven, but Bergsonian? She immediately spotted his worn shoes, his long hair, and what was more worrisome, one of her husband's shirts on the back of the new arrival. Chambernac sat down wearily after the introductions. Invited in turn to take a seat, Purpulan did it with the assurance of a man who's already scored and isn't afraid of losing his advantage.

While, in the uncomfortable silence that followed, Mme. de Chambernac, an educated person who was interested in etymology, was setting up the equation Purpur + purulent = Purpulan, the latter was exhaling in all directions, smiling blissfully, the colorless but odoriferous clouds of his fetid breath. Giving his hierarchical superior a penny for his thoughts, he said:

"Cur videris tristis?"

"Huh?" went Chambernac with a start.

"Quin respondes? Num obsurdescis?"

Chambernac said to himself: it's another one of his tricks to get under my skin and make me suffer.

"Dinner is served," said the maid opportunely.

Thus Purpulan finds himself seated between Madame and Monsieur and before an adequately laden table. So it wasn't any harder than that. As far as being able to teach humanities was concerned, that didn't worry him in the least. His two hosts seemed to be eating with difficulty. To frighten them, he acted even more gluttonous, sponging up sauces, crunching bones, swallowing husks, devouring soles. The others seem to be less and less hungry.

After dinner, Purpulan drinks a cup of coffee and a little glass of brandy while smoking a cigar. No one speaks. The silence is awkward. He examines the male once more: a large, skinny, potbellied body and a spacious skull where ideas are undoubtedly simmering; the female: thickset with a pinhead where ambitions are undoubtedly flowering to scale. They might not be all that easy to manipulate.

"How many students will I have?"

"There were three."

"Three suits me fine. It won't wear me out. And what are the names of these young prodigies?"

"Alexander, Caesar and Napoleon," answers the principal with a snicker.

"My predecessor was undoubtedly Aristotle?"

"M. Purpulan is quick at repartee," said the lady.

"But he has not yet caught all the flavor of my jokes."

"Indeed," said Purpulan impassively and he gulped his brandy liqueur.

"You should know," said Mme. de Chambernac, "that those weren't actually the names of the three students; but they *were* their surnames."

"It was a strange coincidence," said Chambernac.

"Indeed," went Purpulan, whom this bit of news didn't seem to faze. "By the way, why did you say: it was a strange coincidence? It's not one any more?"

"No."

"Why not?"

"Now they're separated."

"Why are they separated?"

"Because the school year's over."

Mme. de Chambernac's laugh rang out like a little drill.

"Monsieur Purpulan, you didn't stop to think that it's July 13th and that the school year is over," she sputtered through her hilarity.

Purpulan's face took on the pretty tinge of cyclamen leaves. It was the color Chambernac was waiting for; he whistled for his courage, crouched down behind his prudence, and sent it to nip the intruder's ankles.

First: a superior snicker, next:

"You see, my poor fellow, you aren't as crafty as you

thought. I must admit that you avoided the first trap I set you, but you fell into this one with lamentable facility. Imagine demanding a teaching job, when the school year is finished! How ridiculous! You're not too bright, young man. The best thing you can do is clear out and return to the obscurity that you should never have left."

First Purpulan didn't answer, then he began to sob:

"I'm only a poor devil."

"Poor excuse."

"I was just starting out."

"Bad start."

"You're not going to throw me out, are you?"

"Out and even further."

Purpulan fell to his knees before Mme. de Chambernac.

"Madame, have pity on a poor devil, who made a bad start."

"You certainly have strong breath, my dear fellow," said Madame, drawing back.

"Madame, I have a terrible heredity," he sniveled.

Chambernac's voice boomed:

"Enough mawkishness, young man, my heart is closed to pity."

The young man slumped to the floor, stopped weeping and started to moan like a whipped dog. The principal gave his wife a triumphant look. She brought her hands together in silent applause. Chambernac went to Purpulan and said to him:

"I don't mind your staying. I need a secretary. But you won't be paid. You'll have food and shelter. I don't mind your staying if you sign a pact with me in blood."

Purpulan signed.

XI

The car stopped near Cuges, at the spot where Daniel had noticed a little path on the Geological Survey map. The five of them got out.

"Wait for us in Aubagne," said Daniel to Florent. "We'll come back from the Sainte-Baume Ridge by bus."

The car turned back to dust. Worried, Pouldu looked at the hill.

"We're climbing up there?"

"How about going to see that little chapel," suggested Coltet.

"The chapel of Saint Anthony of Padua? Not the least bit interesting," said Daniel.

They started to walk on level ground, through a village of three houses with an amusing «Town Hall Square.»

"What charming people," said Agnes, then they climbed following a path painted in arrows on rocks by a chamber of commerce. The sisters and Daniel set a brisk, athletic pace, Coltet was lagging a bit, Pouldu, willfully bringing up the rear, was grumbling. When the marked rock wasn't too heavy, he'd modify the itinerary behind him.

"That's stupid," said Coltet. "What if somebody else had done it before us, where would we be going?"

"We'd get lost," answered Pouldu.

"It would be delightful," said Agnes. "Let's get lost."

*

Born in 1903, Raymond Queneau early became an advocate of Surrealism, particularly in the middle and late 1920s. He is best known, however, for his manipulations of style and language and his introduction of street slang into his literary works. Today

Queneau is recognized as one of the major voices of twentieth-century literature.

Queneau's publications include fourteen novels, shorter works of fiction, fifteen volumes of poetry, and four collections of essays, as well as numerous critical and theoretical articles. Queneau worked for Gallimard Publishing for nearly forty years, first as English reader, then as editor of, among other works, the Encyclopédie de la Pléiade.

Among his better known works are Exercices de style *(1947),* Le Chiendent *(1933;* The Bark Tree, *1968);* Un Rude Hiver *(1940;* A Hard Winter, *1948);* Pierrot, mon ami *(1943),* Le Dimanche de la vie *(1952); and* Zazie dans le Métro *(1959;* Zazie, *1960). His* Selected Poems *were translated into English in 1970. In 1995 Sun & Moon Press will publish his novel,* Les Enfants du Limon *as* The Children of Claye.

Paul Celan

from *Breathturn*

Translated from German by Pierre Joris

IN THE SERPENTCOACH, past
the white cypress,
through the flood
they drove you.

But in you, from
birth,
foamed the other spring,
up the black
ray memory
you climbed to the day.

*

SLICKENSIDES, fold-axes,
rechanneling-
points:
your terrain.

On both poles
of the cleftrose, legible:
your outlawed word.
Northtrue. Southbright.

WORDACCRETION, volcanic,
drowned out by searoar.

Above,
the flooding mob
of the contra-creatures: it
flew a flag—portrait and replica
cruise vainly timeward.

Till you hurl forth the word-
moon, out of which
the wonder ebb occurs
and the heart-
shaped crater
testifies naked for the beginnings,
the kings-
births.

(I KNOW YOU, you are the deeply bowed,
I, the transperced, am subject to you.
Where flames a word, would testify for us both?
You—all, all real. I—all delusion.)

*

*In the twenty-four years since his death, Paul Celan's reputation,
though already firmly established while he was alive, has grown
steadily. He is now clearly perceived as one of the two or three
greatest German-language poets of the century—today only Rilke
can conceivably match his fame and impact on both German and
world-poetry. As the critic George Steiner put it: "Celan is almost*

certainly the major European poet of the period after 1945." As Hölderlin functioned for the late Heidegger, so does Celan today function for thinkers and writers such as Otto Pogeler, Maurice Blanchot, Jacques Derrida, and Hans-Georg Gadamer, each of whom has devoted at least one book to Celan's work.

Born in Czernowitz, the capital of the Bukovina in 1920, Celan was raised in a Jewish family that insisted both on young Paul receiving the best secular education, with the mother inculcating her love of the German langauge and culture, and on his Jewish roots: both his parents came from solid orthodox and, on one side, hassidic family backgrounds. In the summer of 1939, Celan, returning to Czernowitz after his first year as a medical student at the University of Tours, where he had come in contact with contemporary French literature, started to write poetry and decided to study Romance literature. The next year Soviet troops occupied his home town, only to be replaced by Romanian and German Nazi troops in 1941. Celan had to work in forced labor camps, where, in the fall of 1942 he learned that his father, physically broken by the slave labor he was subjected to, had been killed by the SS. Later that winter the news that his mother too had been shot by the Nazis reached him. These killings, especially that of his mother, were to remain the core experience of his life. He was released a year later and remained for one more year at the now Sovietized University of Czernowitz. He left his home for good in April 1945, staying in Bucharest until December 1947, then clandestinely crossing over to Vienna, which he left in 1948 to settle in Paris, the city that was to be his home until his death by drowning in the Seine in late April 1970.

Celan's first major volume of poems, Mohn und Gedächtis, *published in 1952, brought him instant recognition and a measure of fame. A new volume of poems followed roughly every three years until his death. In the early 1960s, midway through his writing career, a poetic change or "Wende" took place, inscribed in the title of the 1967 volume* Atemwende *and lasting to the posthumous volumes. His poems, which had always been highly complex but rather lush in a near-surrealistic way, were pared down, the syntax grew tighter and more spiny, his trademark neologisms and telescoping of words increased, while the overall composition of the work became more serial in nature.*

Sun & Moon Press will publish Atemwende, *translated by Pierre Joris, in 1995.*

Kier Peters

A Dog Tries to Kiss the Sky

        Two men against the sky.

ALBERT: Hear him?

BOB: What?

ALBERT: Hear?

BOB: Who?

ALBERT: [*Cocking his head.*] He's barking.

BOB: [*Cocking his head.*] No. I don't hear him.

ALBERT: Hear him now?

BOB: No, I don't.

ALBERT: Far in the distance.

BOB: I'm supposed to have good ears.

ALBERT: Who says?

BOB: I say. My wife.

ALBERT: [*Cocking his head.*] Then you hear him?

BOB: [*Cocking his head.*] Nope.

ALBERT: Then you don't.

BOB: I can hear a train.

ALBERT: No train.

BOB: In the distance—there—the whistle.

ALBERT: No train in this part of the state.

BOB: Sounds like a train.

ALBERT: No. It sounds like a dog.

BOB: I mean the whistle.

ALBERT: It's a bark.

BOB: What you hear is—evidently. But I'm hearing a
        whistle—like the whistle of an engine—of a train.

ALBERT: No train.

BOB: Doesn't sound like a siren.

ALBERT: Ah—that's his howl.

BOB: Doesn't sound like a howl.

ALBERT: But that's what it is.

BOB: You've heard this all before?

ALBERT: Every day.

BOB: In the distance?

ALBERT: Far away.

BOB: And it never comes closer?

ALBERT: Not much.

BOB: And you never move closer to it—to him?

ALBERT: Why should I want?

BOB: To find out if it really is a dog.

ALBERT: Oh it's a dog all right.

BOB: Or why he barks or why he howls.

ALBERT: Don't want to know.

BOB: Maybe it would help.

ALBERT: Help what?

BOB: The dog. Maybe it's lonely.

ALBERT: Probably been beat.

BOB: Maybe he's hurt. You could help him.

ALBERT: I don't like dogs.

BOB: I do.

ALBERT: Then I wish you'd hear him too. You could go out
        and save him or shut him up.

BOB: I don't hear anything.

ALBERT: [*Shouting.*] You could go and shut him up.

BOB: Stop shouting!

ALBERT: Do you read lips?

BOB. [*Confused.*] No.

ALBERT: How do you know what I'm saying then?

BOB: I'm not deaf.

ALBERT: Then you shouldn't say so.

BOB: I didn't. It was just a figure of speech.

ALBERT: Well do you hear him or don't you?

BOB: I don't hear him, but I hear you.

ALBERT: Well, you're one of the few people who do.

BOB: Do what?

ALBERT: Hear me. Most people turn away.

BOB: Away?

ALBERT: From me.

BOB: Why should they do that?

ALBERT: Because they can't hear.

BOB: You mean the dog?

ALBERT: The dog. And then me, when they turn away.

BOB: They're just confused.

ALBERT: No. They just doubt.

BOB: Well, I have to say….

ALBERT: I know, you doubt me too.

BOB: It's natural. I mean, when one's hearing is perfectly normal—if not exceptional, which is what most people think perfectly normal is all about—and you hear something someone can't it's natural to doubt that you're really hearing this exceptional thing each and every day.

ALBERT: No, they don't doubt me. They doubt the dog.

BOB: Well they may say they doubt the dog, but it's you—your hearing it that is—that's really behind what they say.

ALBERT: Well hell, I'm here. They got eyes.

BOB: They don't doubt your existence, just your ability to hear.

ALBERT: Well, I do.

BOB: What?

ALBERT: Doubt my existence, after they all turn away. It's like I never existed. Just like the dog. And they certainly no longer hear—if they formerly did—what I have to say about anything—the dog, the weather, the time of day. So after all I go off and stay in a little corner of town where no one ever goes much. And I think to myself.

BOB: What is it you think?

ALBERT: I told you, I think he's being beat.

BOB: I mean, what is it you think to yourself?

ALBERT: Oh, like whether or not he's being beat. Or if he deserved it. Or if he's going to stop. Or if I should take a gun and go over to wherever it is he's howling from.

BOB: You don't like dogs.

ALBERT: That's what I said.

BOB: Why don't you like dogs?

ALBERT: [*Pondering it for a moment.*] They bark. And howl.

BOB: Well I know some who don't. Most don't howl. And some don't bark much.

ALBERT: Only takes one.

BOB: Do you hear other dogs?

ALBERT: Of course! All around town.

BOB: Now?

ALBERT: You hear 'em?

BOB: No.

ALBERT: Then why do you expect me to. I'm no better than you up close. When they bark most everyone hears. And that's why they get shut up! But this—he's different. No one hears him—so it appears—but me. So no one—except maybe the man who beats him—cares whether he howls or not.

BOB: Does he ever stop?

ALBERT: [*Looking with disbelief.*] Of course! He's gotta sleep. He's gotta eat. I live my life around those few hours. When he sleeps, I sleep. When he eats, I take a quick bite. And once in a while, for a whole day, he sulks. And I perk up and behave—according to the folks hereabouts—like a normal human being. I live in fear of those days. Get all on edge. It's almost a relief when he goes into his yaps again.

BOB: Have you seen a doctor?

ALBERT: [*Pointing in the direction of the hotel.*] He's right over there.

BOB: No I mean, have you gone to one?

ALBERT: He's the only one.

BOB: Have you gone to him then?

ALBERT: What for?

BOB: Well, perhaps he could give you something.

ALBERT: Nope. I tried cotton. I tried muffs.

BOB: I mean for your nerves.

ALBERT: My nerves? I'm not nervous. It's you who's nervous. It's the other folks. Nervous about me and about the dog who they can't hear.

BOB: You mean, you don't mind it?

ALBERT: What do you think I've been telling you? Of course I mind it! I detest it! I want to kill the mangy hound. But that has nothing to do with nerves at all.

BOB: It'd sure make me nervous.

ALBERT: What's there to be nervous about? He won't come any closer.

BOB: I mean the constant noise.

ALBERT: There's always lots of noise. There are clouds and the corn, and naturally the people.

BOB: Well, the people yes! But the corn? You mean the wind in the corn.

ALBERT: No, I mean the corn itself. I mean the clouds on a
    still night.

BOB: I don't think most people hear that either.

ALBERT: Some do. I met a man once who said he could tell
    you just from careful listening whether it was June
    or July in a field of corn. In June the corn just squeals,
    while in July it crackles like a blanket on a dry hot
    night. Someone once explained to me the difference
    between a cumulus and a stratus cloud. A cumulus
    got a high-pitched little effeminate voice that stut-
    ters to the stars, while a stratus got a flat uninflected
    pitch like a Midway carney Kansasan crying "Come
    on come on come on in." But no one hears this dog.

BOB: I don't know what else to suggest. Have you ever
    thought of moving away?

ALBERT: This is where I live.

BOB: I know. But there are lots of other wonderful places to
    live in. Without dogs in the distance.

ALBERT: I don't think so!

BOB: Just a vacation?

ALBERT: Besides, it might be worse. Another dog might
    growl or drool or hiss. And I'd miss him.

BOB: Who?

ALBERT: The one who barks. The one who howls.

BOB: I think you've got a problem!

ALBERT: That's what I've been telling you.

BOB: [*Turning away.*] What was that?

ALBERT: I know, it's time for you to go. They all eventually
    turn away.

BOB: I mean that noise?

ALBERT: [*Cocking his head.*] That's him!

BOB: He sounds so sad.

ALBERT: Doesn't he?

BOB: Actually he sounds sort of happy.

ALBERT: You think so?

BOB: Sort of silly. Like he's lolling on the lawn with tongue hanging out.

ALBERT: Could be.

BOB: Whining. No whinnying actually.

ALBERT: It's possible.

BOB: Sort of gurgling low in his throat. Growling now. Hear him?

ALBERT: [*Cocking his head.*] Not my dog.

BOB: No?

ALBERT: Nope. Mine barks. Mine howls.

BOB: [*Listening closely.*] Mine has gotten very quiet.

ALBERT: Mine hasn't let up.

BOB: Mine has put his head down beside his bowl to drowse.

ALBERT: My dog—the way he howls sounds almost as if he was the trying the kiss the sky. Like he was in love with that old cumulus queer.

BOB: I think you've got a great imagination.

ALBERT: You were the one just making it up!

BOB: Yes. But I was trying to show you what you say seems like to others.

ALBERT: That's the problem. They don't got good ears.

> *In the distance a dog barks, howls.*
> BOB *shakes his head.*

*

Born in 1947 in Iowa, Kier Peters is the author of eight plays, including The Confirmation, Past Present and Future Tense, Intentional Coincidence, A Dog Tries to Kiss the Sky, Two Women on a Terrace, Family, *and the musical* Flying Down to Cairo.

The Confirmation *recently premiered in the* T.W.E.E.D. *Festival at New York's Vineyard Theatre. The* Village Voice *wrote of this play, "Mollie O'Mara's confident and pellucid direction untangles...Kier Peter's arresting* The Confirmation, *a mystery play about family secrets. 'Families don't have to make sense,' one of Peters' characters cleverly points out. 'They just talk and talk.'"*

His Past Present and Future Tense *premiered at Next Stage in San Francisco this fall; and the same play is being performed as an opera, with music by Michael Kowalski, in New York later this year.*

Severo Sarduy

The Tibetan Book of the Dead

Translated from Spanish by Suzanne Jill Levine

YEARS AGO, in Tibet—or in the symbolic region that stretches from those overlapping patches of ochre earth north of India to the first excessive statues of Mao—I bought a vast book that I covered with silky and garish gilded paper, inscribed by a draftsman with an intricate purple and orange iconography whose ultimate referent, I suppose, is Buddhism. The pages—and this is a less frequent detail in those miniature Himalayan realms—are marked with the letters of our alphabet.

Remembering the sayings of a friend who deplored the confiscation of his address book more than his taciturn days spent in prison, I decided to compose in the thick volume a directory of names and addresses that would be as meticulous and up-to-date as was required by my phobia, my lack of close ties: the phantom that haunts every exile.

Sometime later—I had a taste then for the sudden mirrorings between East and West—the writer Hector Murena called me at my hotel in Buenos Aires to announce, amid "vamos, che" and other idiomatic devices to soften his harsh news, the death of Calvert Casey.

Some hours later, at the house of María Rosa Oliver who had known and admired him since Havana days, we roused ourselves from an embarrassing funereal silence by doing something that, deep down, shocked me because we Cubans adhere so strictly to our mournful rituals: "Let's drink to Calvert's memory."

From the Tibetan book I never dared to erase his name.

Striking out the address of a friend earned by that absence we insist upon thinking is temporary, substituting another for him, marking him with a sign that indicates the definitive uselessness of his address—a cross would be the most brutal and grotesque—erasing to leave an empty line, the ostensible indication of a lack between the aligned and identical letters, would be like eradicating him all over again, as if I were an accomplice of the void, subjecting him to another death within death, excluding him from the ink's blue day, from the sketchiest and most denotative writing: true disappearance for one who has lived by disseminating words.

Many others, so many that with them death has only confirmed the pulse of its repetition, have come, letter by letter, to indicate their fictitious presence, the empty simulacrum of their identity in what is already another *Tibetan Book of the Dead.*

The initial letters of the alphabet, through my Latin affiliations or the Reaper's dark anagrammatic manias, are the most solicited. One of the most luxuriant—several addresses, rural or secret telephone numbers—B, was decimated with one blow: Barthes.

Intact each year and increasingly ineffectual by definition, the Book has been gradually approaching another genre, both unexpected and generous: the novel, or biographical fiction. Its reading invents for the disappeared an anecdotal life on paper—freer or more apocryphal the more time passes: error or oblivion, scenes or chapters which they perhaps never lived, become accentuated and, thanks to my archival perseverance, sustain them in another life of myths and characters. Meticulously parallel to each day I consume this life, barely less deceptive than supposed reality, by using, writing or phoning the addresses and numbers that are still valid.

Thus I see Calvert, as I don't know if he was, sitting at the bar in the Tencén—phonetic adaptation of Ten Cent from the populous empire to the north—in Havana, with Lezama (the liaison is improbable) or with Virgilio (the coincidence is a sure bet) shredding to pieces layers of bakelite, crystal, aluminum and copper, all the solids and liquids of the establishment, to return them to their geological births in the remote formation of the island, in a hyperbolic and flagrant flashback. Virgilio, as usual, confronts a lethargic waitress with one of his metaphysical aporias, a Cuban *koen*, by demanding a papaya milkshake, but, because of his deficient liver, one made without first sugar, then milk, any kind of malt, crushed ice, and above all—to top off his vesicular phobia—papaya.

Calvert appears again—this reference is precise—in my house at Sceaux. We are on the balcony, a grayish and brief summer in the suburbs. He speaks to me of India. I know that he's one of the first to do so with the identifiable passion I now know so well and share, which contradicts the precedence of the Tibetan book and also—but here I shuffle the dates—that of a postcard from India I receive from Rome, torn out of carelessness, stuck together again, and accompanied by an explanatory letter: "The unconscious is well aware of these faux pas."

Another memory of the same day, and of his—always laborious—manner of speaking: he evokes the recent death of his mother and adds, with repeated though involuntary and, as I realized later, revealing vacillations: "we were so different…."

He liked the place where I live, with its calm atmosphere of a park in the provinces, and the nearby Romanesque-looking church where *fin de siècle* busts of troubadours form an enthusiastic and dark-green *ronde* around their instructor in prosody, Frederic Mistral.

News from Rome: in a letter he contradicts or reproaches me—as Lezama did when I suggested a similarity between *Paradiso* and Gadda's work—for the influence of Virgilio Piñera I perceive in his recent narratives: keys of a piano which don't jump back when pushed down by the fingers, signs of soggy abandonment, misery or ennui. An aura at once dense and icy, orthogonal and mechanical gestures, the ferocious and Kafkaesque profile of simulators from Piñera's version of Gombrowicz, take over the decrepit sets, the sullen stained rooms.

Latest news from Rome: a mutual friend in common withdraws his remains from the vault to place them in the family shrine. Upon leaving the cemetery—she writes me—she's caught by a tree branch that detains her affectionately, gratefully.

Final note: the names cited in these pages, almost randomly, belong to those I have not erased from the *Tibetan Book of the Dead.* I remember them today with a dedication written by one of them: "Le soir, en automne, je pense à mes amis"*: Calvert Casey, Hector Murena, María Rosa Oliver, Roland Barthes, José Lezama Lima, Virgilio Piñera, Witold Gombrowicz.

Addenda, June 1986, to the final note:

Italo Calvino, Emir Rodríguez Monegal, José Bianco.

*

* On an autumn evening, I think of my friends.

Severo Sarduy, born in 1937, is one of the most noted Cuban writers of his generation. He studied at the University of Havana, and, with Guillermo Cabrera Infante, was one of the few writers involved in the fight against Batista. At an early age Sarduy contributed to the Lunes de Revolución, *the official organ of the 26th of July Movement. In 1960 he left for Paris.*

In Paris Sarduy became the editor of the Latin American collection of Editions du Seuil, and became involved with the Tel Quel group. Among the books he introduced to the French were Gabriel García Márquez's One Hundred Years of Solitude *and Lezama Lima's* Paradiso. *Sarduy himself, meanwhile, published several works including* De donde son los cantantes (From Cuba with a Song, *published by Sun & Moon Press in 1994),* Escrito sobre un cuerpo (Written on a Body), Maitreyea, Colibri, La simulación, Overdose, *and* Daiquiri, *a book of poems that uses Baroque prosody to describe gay sex in explicit terms.*

Olivier Cadiot

"bla-bla-bla"
from *L'Art poetic*

Translated from French by Cole Swensen

The passengers have boarded/the boat has been boarded by the
passengers
The sky darkened/The clouds darkened the sky

(1) The patient is lost
(2) The bag was lost by my daughter
(3) The sea is rough

Peter, finding
        or Finding what he'd searched for, Peter is happy

The eyes^1 were turned toward him, the eyes^2 were turned toward
him…the eyes^n were turned towards him → The eyes
were turned towards him

I will do something to someone

        The paper is yellow

        But the following

The sun makes the paper yellow

becomes

The sun yellows the paper

That Peter is sick, that's what's disrupting
my plans → Peter sick, that's what's disrupting
my plans

(The one that causes worries is himself a worrier)
The $child^1$ is sick, the $child^2$ is sick,...the $child^n$ is
sick

The paper is yellowed

follows from:

The sun yellows the paper

(I want) silence – silence!

We've got to live here!

The wood can't float
This plan can't survive
These insects can hurt us
This idea can't jive
with mine

I want silence

[krwa]
[krwa]

When he comes, I will tell him

Hide behind these rocks   → See these rocks, hide
                                                    behind

Peter, finding what he'd been looking for, is happy
Peter, in finding what he'd been looking for, is happy

                                An illness is curable
                                A patient is incurable

Peter, as he has found what he was looking for, is happy
Peter, as he has found what he was looking for, is happy

                    sole → solitude; anxious → anxiety

This morning it is cool/The morning is cool
The following day it was hot/The day was hot

                            The little children play in the courtyard
                            Some little children play in the courtyard

This carpet doesn't go here: this carpet is red

                        Me, I'd live here! → I'll live here!

I live in a very small house

The door is closed,

                            (1) The door is closed and the window
                            is too
                            (2) Paul is sick and Peter is
                            too

fear of John's danger

Peter kills himself {by Peter, by accident}

> This carpet is red; this carpet doesn't
> really go with the room

I say:
To live here! it's impossible

This much is done. (2) The house is built

> the one (who is sick) is this boy

We did it so that the house could be built

My friends
had a house built at the seashore

Peter kills himself

(1) Peter kills himself by himself
(2) Peter kills himself in an accident

Paul is reading a text that is no longer being read by Peter (which is
no longer read):
garden/gardenette; pincers/pincerettes
louse/lousy; gnat/gnatty
sheet/sheeting; wing/winging
stair/stairway; float/flotilla

the one (who is sick) is this boy
it is this boy (who is sick)
it's this boy who is sick

Thus: This red carpet doesn't really go with the room
follows from:
This carpet, which is red, doesn't really go with the room

I'm sad that I had to see it so demolished → I'm so sad
to see it demolished

The carpet is red

This carpet, due to the fact that it's red, doesn't really go with the room
This carpet doesn't go here because it's red

Knowing the world, this is enriching

All the same
        To live here! I'll never get used to it

                *You, to be here!

Peter, who forgets his promises
Peter, who will come tomorrow

This idiot of a son   [poltc]—[poltrcn]
                                   [polisc]—[poliscn]

Peter isn't sick

I am building a house by the sea

could mean:
(1) I am building the house myself
or
(2) I am having the house built

To know the world is an enriching thing

1) The architect is building this building
2) It's slowed down

Only one person understood this question
(one and not the others)

[égra]—[égra]
[pyà]—[pyàt]

    These flowers enhance the garden,
is considered to follow from:
    These flowers make the garden become beautiful
such that:
    It is enhanced
corresponds to:
    It has become beautiful
which follows from:
    It makes itself become beautiful
  Thus
    This leaf is white,
white implies a   (this leaf)

            Only one person didn't understand the question
            (one and not the others)

we others (you others) we don't (you don't)
agree with them

            This question wasn't understood by a single
            person

We planted a pear tree in the garden

> The love of children of parents?

> The fear of danger to John?

to do something to someone

> The thought that he won't come?

My fear that he'll perceive it

> The doors are closed
> The trees are felled
> The rocks are fused

(1) I want him to leave
(2) I want to leave

I should inform, you should inform, someone should inform
Paul

He lies a lot, often → To lie a lot, often
What one waits too long for one ends up tired with → To
wait too long is to end up tired

> Paul overwhelms Peter
> worries overwhelm Peter

I wish a book would be for me → I wish a book would be
mine

It's madness to resist

It's enough to wait, it's good to hold your tongue, it's ok to act
like this

>We've got to go, it has to be said

Peter could be warned

It's madness that to resist

>>Me. I'd live here!

I wonder who listens

>I want to leave/I want you to leave

I have come to look for Peter → I have come looking for Peter

>>When he's on his

⌈way, I'll tell him

Peter is not Peter who is right

The quarry, the forest

>>things with their own dignity

spring—springlike

The enemy attacks our troops which attacked the
>>enemy

The front can't last

The wounded man who is grave and anxious → the grave and anxious
   [wounded man

He's next to me
He's next
The opposite of what's been said I believe
The opposite I believe
Stand by the fire
Stand by

*

*Olivier Cadiot lives in Paris, where he has published several books,
including* Roue, Vert et Noir *(1989)—translated by Charles
Bernstein and the author in 1990—*Romeo & Juliette *(1989)—
which was the basis of his opera in nine acts, with music by Pascal
Dusapin—*L'Art poetic *(1988) and* Futu, ancien, fugitif *(1993).*

   *Sun & Moon Press will publish Cole Swensen's translation of
the last two books in upcoming seasons.*

Credits and Copyrights

SELECTED SUN & MOON CLASSICS